THE SWORD
AND THE WELL

THE SWORD

AND THE WELL

ANN CHAMBERLIN

EPIGRAPH BOOKS
RHINEBECK, NY

Excerpts from *Desert Tracings* ©1989 by Michael Sells on pages 151 and 265. Reprinted by permission of Wesleyan University Press.

Images for Genealogy chart, pages viii–ix:
Mutammin: Goodall, Frederick. *The Blind Arab and His Guide*. I Am A Child: Children in Art History.
al-Harith: Tissot, James Jacques Joseph Tissot. *The Good Shepherd*. 1886-94. The Bridgeman Art Library.
Khalid: *Returning Peace*. <www.returningpeace.com>.
Zura: © Standard Publishing/Licensed from GoodSalt.com
Umm Taghlib the Witch: Wikimedia Commons.
Sejah (Sitt Sameh): Wass, Betty. *Dress of Bedouin Woman from Sinai, Circa 1950*. 1983. University of Wisconsin-Madison Libraries, Africa Focus Collection.
Musaylimah the Prophet: Rembrandt. *Jeremiah Lamenting the Destruction of Jerusalem*. 1630. Art Renewal Center.
Rayah: Goodall, Frederick. *An Egyptian Flower Girl*. I Am A Child: Children in Art History.

Printed in the United States of America.
Book and cover design by Sherry Williams.

Hardcover: ISBN 978-1-936940-61-5
Softcover: ISBN 978-1-936940-62-2

Library of Congress Control Number: 2013949069

Epigraph Books
22 East Market Street, Suite 304
Rhinebeck, New York 12572
www.epigraphps.com
USA 845-876-4861

For Francesca
and the dappled days we knew
once upon a time
in Damascus

MAIN CHARACTERS
THE SWORD AND THE WELL

In order of appearance; * indicates a real historical character.

Rayah . . . . Twelve-year-old focus of the story in Tadmor.

Adilah . . . . Rayah's "aunt," the woman who raised her.

*Sitt Sameh . . . . Rayah's mother, a strange woman of the desert who hides on the third floor of the turpentine sellers' in Tadmor. In this volume we learn her real name: Sejah bint al-Harith.

Ghusoon . . . . Rayah's friend, recently married according to her own wishes with Rayah's help.

Sitt Umm Ali . . . . Rayah's neighbor and instructor in religion.

*Khalid ibn al-Walīd (or al-Wahid) abu Sulayman (died ca. 644 AD)
    Called "the Conqueror," the main male focus of the story. Muhammad the Prophet's most famous general, conqueror of both Iraq and Syria, famous for never having lost a battle, fighting either against Muhammad or for him.

*Abd Allah . . . . The Prophet's father, who died before Muhammad was born. A relative of Khalid ibn al-Walīd. Also, in this book, the name of Khalid's fictitious eunuch scribe.

*Abd ar-Rahman ibn Khalid ibn al-Walīd
    Son of Khalid the Conqueror.

*Muhammad . . . . The Prophet.

*Malik ibn Nuwaira . . . . . . The younger of Khalid's milk brothers, sharif of the Banu Tamim.

*Musaylimah ibn Habib . . . . Called "the Liar" in Islamic tradition, a native of the oasis of Yamamah, near present-day Riyadh, a wonder-worker, poet and prophet who opposed Muhammad.

*Saffiyah bint Huyyay . . . . . One of the wives of Muhammad the Prophet, born a Jewess in the oasis of what became al-Medinah.

*Omar ibn al-Khattab . . . . . Second successor (khalifah) to the Prophet and a distant cousin to Khalid.

*Zaynab . . . . Arabic name of the Queen of Tadmor (Latin: Palmyra) who rebelled against Rome

*Mutammim ibn Nuwaira	The older of Khalid's milk brothers, a famous poet, blind from childhood.
Kefa	A boy "cousin" of Rayah's who lives in the house of the turpentine sellers.
*Layla bint al-Minhal	Wife of Malik ibn al-Nuwaira, later of Khalid the Conqueror.
*Khalid ibn Abd ar-Rahman ibn Khalid	Son of Abd ar-Rahman and grandson of the Conqueror, the cousin Rayah is destined to marry.
*Firuz	Also known in Islamic history as Pirouz Nahavandi Abu Lu'lu'ah, in this book a Persian slave to Abd-ar-Rahman.
	*A second character in this volume named Firuz is the hero of the story of the false Yemeni prophet called the Black One.
*Umm Mutammim	Khalid's milk mother, birth mother to his milk brothers Mutammim and Malik of the Tamimi tribe.
*Ayesha bint Abi Bakr	Muhammad the Prophet's favorite wife, daughter of the first khalifah.

Terms used in Arabic Names

Abd, feminine Amat	"Servant, slave." Used frequently in pre-Islamic times in front of the name of any divinity to whom a child might be dedicated; used in Islam in front of any of the ninety-nine names of God as popular masculine given names.
Abu/Abi	"Father of."
Al	"The." In front of certain consonants, the "l" changes to that consonant (as in az-Zibrikan).
Banu	"Sons of." Used to indicate desert tribes by reference to their distant ancestor.
Bint	"Daughter of."
Ibn	"Son of." Used to form patronymic last names to this day. Actually pronounced "bin" when in the middle of a name, I've kept this spelling to cut down on confusion.
Umm	"Mother of."
Ummi	"My mother."

Genealogies in the Woman at the Well

Tribal Affiliation — Tamim — Qur

Shaykh an-Nuwaira m. Umm Mutammim

Mutammim

Malik, the shaykh m. Layla bint al-Minhal

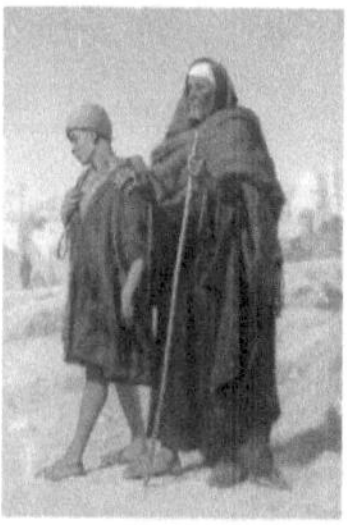

Adam and Eve

Many generations includ
Ibrahim and Isma'il

Morra

Many generations

Abd Allah

Muhammed the Prophet
blessings on him

Many generations

al-Mughira

Hisham

Khantamah

al-Khattab

Omar

al-Walid

Khalid

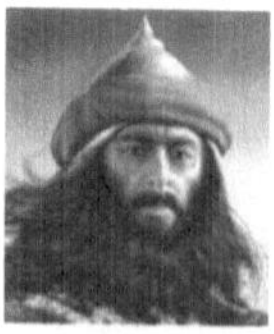

Many legitimate wives a
children including

Sulayman

Abd ar-Rahman

forty sons sa
to have died
the plague

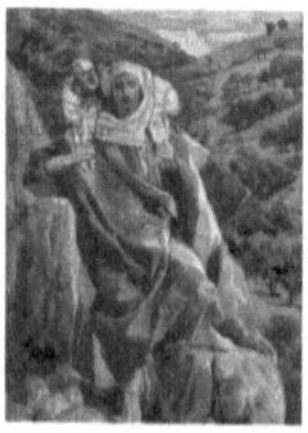

al-Harith,
their herdsman's son
said to be Sejah's father

Taghlib

Zura   *m.*   Umm Taghlib
                    the Witch

Bint Zura

an illicite
(and fictitious)
relationship

Sejah the Prophetess   *m.*   Musaylimah the Prophet
known as Sitt Sameh

Rayah

Roman
Empire

Mediterranean
Sea

Caspian Sea

Homs

Syria Tadmor
Damascus
Iraq
Ctesiphon

Persian
Empire

Yarmuk

Dhu Qar
al-Hira

Arabia

Egypt

Persian Gulf

Nafud

Tamim

Bahrain

Gulf of Oman

Hejaz

Yathrib
(Medinah)

Yamamah

Nakhlah

Mecca

at-Taif

The Empty
Quarter

Red Sea

N

Yemen

Arabian Sea

THE MIDDLE EAST
IN THE TIME OF MUHAMMAD

AUTHOR'S NOTE

Can I be assured that my faults will not devolve upon the scores of teachers, family members, friends, librarians and publishing people who have allowed my consuming passion to become theirs, if only for an hour? Hoping this is the case, and that my need to acknowledge them outweighs other considerations, here is a list of the most outstanding: Linda Cook, Jeri Smith, Francesca Koomen; all the women of the Wasatch Mountain Fiction Writers—some of whom had to struggle with this for a thousand pages before it began to grow on them; Teddi Kachi, Solmaz Kamuran, Karen Porcher, Curt Setzer, Ernö Steinmetz, Ralph and Ute Chamberlin, my mother, my sons; Drs. Leonard Chiarelli, Laurence Loeb and Peter von Sievers; Ann Wright, Marian Florence, Rod Daynes, Giles Florence, John Keahey, Connie Disney and members of Xenobia writers' group. Natalia Aponte, Linn Prentis, Christine Cohen, Vaughne Hansen, Virginia Kidd of blessed memory. Paul Cohen, Anastasia McGhee and Lori White of Epigraph Books. Miguel and Don Juan. All of the wonderful people I met in Syria. And of course, as always, Umm Khalil whose face veiled behind coins and shells in the Sinai desert first set me on this journey.

Those people I may have overlooked know who they are and know that I couldn't have done it without them. Thanks to one and all.

This is a historical novel. I have invented things, lots of things, the biggest one being Khalid's relationship to the prophetess Sejah bint al-Harith. No, I know of no tradition that says he was her father. But he did exist, fighting both for and against Muhammad at the dawn of Islam in the seventh century AD. And so, by God, did she.

On the other hand, I did do my best to research accurately. This novel is the product of a burning desire to answer, for myself, "What were the people in the time of the Prophet, blessed be he, thinking, doing, feeling?" So many things, even most things, are supported by one hadith, tradition or another. This is not to say that the traditions don't contradict themselves; they do. This is not even to say I actually believe the tradition I have chosen to follow is, in every case, the most accurate one. It was the one that best suited the story.

One final note: The land between the Tigris and Euphrates has always been called "Iraq" in the Arabic language, since before Muhammad. It means "the fertile or deep-rooted land." This is not an anachronism.

1

We created man from an extract of clay. Then We
made him as a drop... Then we made the drop
into a blood clot, a leech, then we made the clot
into a chewed substance.
        —The Holy Quran, Surah 23:12–14

Tadmor (Palmyra), Syria, twenty-fourth year of the Hijra,
644 of the Christian era

"**W**hat a selfish bitch, only ever thinking of yourself."

Something was certainly wrong with Auntie Adilah in recent days, ever since that night after Ghusoon's wedding. Such words had never come out of her mouth before.

Thirteen-year-old Rayah came to a panting halt at the top of the third-floor stairs, a basket of wet laundry on her hip, glad the attack wasn't aimed at her this time. She still couldn't see them—the woman who had raised her and the woman who was, in fact, her mother—the two who must be arguing. The curtains of worsted around Sitt Sameh's little room here on the roof were rolled down, the fabric of the door slapping on the threshold as it blew in the breeze. Or from the force of Auntie Adilah's wrath.

Rayah's mother—the girl still preferred the formal name Sitt Sameh—said nothing in defense. That didn't mean she wasn't in her room. She rarely left her room. Sitt Sameh's silence in the face of accusation was nothing new, nor was Adilah's presence in the third-floor room when she came to pick up the balls of yarn Sitt Sameh had spun to sell in the market. But such rancor was rare in the turpentine sellers' harem, even among the most vibrant personalities. No one was so unhappy. Or so Rayah had thought, as a child.

"Not once since we took you in," Auntie Adilah went on, "have you stirred outside these walls to help a woman in her time of need."

"I birthed Bushra, who came buttocks first and would have died and taken her mother with her had I not intervened." Sitt Sameh could indeed speak, low, her voice dusty with her foreign, desert accent. "I birthed all the rest in this house, too, by the help of heaven, even those long labors of very young brides who should not have been made mothers yet. Just because you, *ya* Adilah, for the sake of your brother, never married. It has made you as hard and bitter as colocynth."

Now it was Adilah's turn to seethe in silence. What a hard, hard thing to say to the woman who had raised your child for you. Rayah was ashamed of her mother, wanted to make peace between the two older women. She wanted to make up for her mother's shortcomings—and thought, perhaps she could.

Rayah knew she had a healing gift, inborn. More powerful than her mother's learned skills.

But Rayah was still a girl. A girl who'd already put herself too much in the public eye. When should she use her gifts and when should she hold them back, lest she bring shame to everyone?

"Stir outside the walls," Auntie Adilah had insisted. Leave these walls to attend a difficult birthing.

Rayah considered who the birthing woman might be. Earlier that afternoon, she had come into the courtyard just in time to see Auntie Adilah with a woman Rayah didn't recognize. Rage and anxiety flooded through the stranger's shroud of billowing black as Auntie Adilah accompanied her as far as the gate.

Rayah realized now that the scurry of injured self-righteousness belonged to her Quranic teacher Sitt Umm Ali, no one else. Sitt Umm Ali must have borrowed a stranger's veil to hide her notorious head of wild hennaed hair.

Sitt Umm Ali had come to beg desperately for aid from Sitt Sameh's healing hands secluded on the third floor. Sitt Umm Ali had come trying to hide her identity—and after that sacrifice of pride, she had been turned away. And Auntie Adilah had not wanted to be the one to deny the town's most powerful woman.

Rayah didn't stay on the roof to hear what Auntie Adilah's thin lips, working with fury, and clenched fists might produce next against Sitt Sameh, who had forced her to such rudeness. Rayah left the heavy basket right on the stair where she stood. She hoped Auntie Adilah would hang up the clothes. Of course, Auntie Adilah might be so angry when she came out of Sitt Sameh's room that she would trip over the basket. The clean clothes would tumble down a flight and a half of dusty stairs, and Adilah would utter some more words Rayah had never heard her use before. She would blame Rayah for being the worthless brat of a worthless mother.

Rayah certainly would never mean such a careless accident to happen. But if her mother, Sitt Sameh, would not leave her room—

Rayah fumbled for one of her mother's graven images, the one the girl had kept with her since it had helped her to ease the drought. The one with her great-grandmother's teeth marks pitting the wood.

Then Rayah threw on her own veil in such haste that it still fluttered loose as she arrived in the other women's courtyard. There sat Sitt Umm Ali panting and fanning herself from her own recent exertions.

Rayah knew only one woman with child from Sitt Umm Ali's household: her friend Ghusoon.

And it hadn't been three months since the wedding.

Almond and plane-tree wands peeled to their green-white insides, arugula (Ayesha's plant) and hair of a fox's tail for him, licorice and sesame for her. Rayah had learned these means to fertility from her mother's tale and had offered each of them to her friend just before the wedding.

For Rayah had seen the groom Jaffar after his circumcision, the rite preparing him for manhood and marriage. She knew how close he'd come to dying from the festering wound. She had heard her mother worrying that though she had saved the young man's life, he might never be able to sire a child of his own. He might be like al-Harith, the desert herdsman who had lovingly raised Sitt Sameh, although she was, in fact, another man's daughter.

Barrenness—whether the young bride's fault or her husband's—would certainly intensify the tensions between the old sharif and Jaffar's family. Worse, it would call jinn to infest Ghusoon's mind once more. So at the wedding, Rayah had done what she could to see that her friend did not live with such a burden.

When, less than a month ago, Ghusoon had embraced her friend and told her the happy news, worry had sloughed from Rayah's mind. Her mother's worst fears for Jaffar proved unfounded. All would be well with her friend now, no matter what Rayah chose to do about her own marriage. The option to follow fate away from Tadmor could not be ruled out, at least not for concern about her friend.

Now this.

No doubt about it, Rayah saw at once when she arrived and was shown blood clots saved in an earthenware bowl. Testimony to the Quran's surah on human creation—and its death. Ghusoon had miscarried in spite of all the family's efforts that had taken over after Rayah's aids to conception.

"We didn't deny her a thing," Sitt Umm Ali maintained. "Not one mouthful, which, ungranted, would leave a birthmark the size of the morsel on the baby's skin. I myself made her an amulet of a verse from the Holy Quran. We didn't leave her alone at sunset and, if she did go out, we gave her a knife to carry so the iron would keep away the jinn."

The evidence, as the Surah of the Clot of Blood described it, coagulated in an earthenware bowl, spattered heart-red up the sides. And with a twist of fear in her throat, Rayah saw the shadow of a madness-inducing jinni already hovering over the ashen-faced young woman who lay in the midst of her husband's female relatives.

"Oh, be off," one of the women told Rayah. "Sitt Sameh can't be bothered to come, and she sends one who's never known a man to tend such women's hurts."

Rayah realized her own lack of knowledge. Even her own moon blood had not come upon her yet. It didn't help her confidence when Sitt Umm Ali agreed with her kinswoman. The reciter of the Quran tucked tendrils of her hennaed hair up, erasing the effects of her borrowed outer veil. She broke her constant recitation of the words of God to say, "I said I made an amulet, *ya* Rayah. If the revelation of God, which I labored so hard to teach you, can do nothing, it must be God's will. We want no demons here."

Rayah turned from the room. They were right. She was too young, too presumptuous against the plain and simple will of God. Besides, what could she do at this point? Lay her hands on Ghusoon and suck the dead fetus back into a tomb to rise on the third day, as Christians declared?

"Touch her belly."

The voice of the jinni came so distinctly, so demanding into that room of death that Rayah felt compelled to answer him aloud. "No, I can't." The idol hidden in her bosom burned.

"Now *that* one with the demon eyes is possessed, too," said Sitt Umm Ali.

Rayah felt the steel blue of her own eyes as if they were knives in her skull. She wanted to pull them out.

Sitt Umm Ali muttered prayers. "Our new bride will catch it from her, God forbid."

Rayah knew Ghusoon had demons enough of her own, some of them merely sleeping like desert animals in the heat of the day, others who sat shaking their heads on the cushions around her.

And hasn't my mother only recently used her power to rid a woman of the life within her? the girl thought. I was wrong and lifted up with pride. The power I've inherited is not for mercy after all. I must work to crush it.

"Her belly," the smoky voice repeated. "Let it not be said among the Beings of this Place that I have chosen a fool for my leman."

Rayah elbowed her way to Ghusoon's side as if shoved from behind. The goddess image wrapped in a concealing cloth within Rayah's fist drew her down. She knelt, ignoring the women's restraining hands upon her.

"Do you still have cramping, my friend?" she asked.

She spoke to cover a growing fear. Although she had set the figurine on the suffering girl's breast, no lightning spark of healing shifted the still maiden-taut skin beneath her touch. No power would come this time?

"I am indeed a fool for listening to mischievous spirits," Rayah muttered under her breath to scold the demon away.

Catching up the figurine, she shifted her balance to rise and flee human censure. Then something twitched beneath her fingers. The power came not from her hands, however, but from what she expected to be just her friend's hollow, empty womb. Instead, she felt a heartbeat.

Setting aside the figurine, Rayah stretched her left hand to Ghusoon's throat. Her friend's pulse, against the young wife's will, beat slow and listless. The rhythm under Rayah's right hand jumped with hope, a life as yet untainted by any disappointment or sorrow.

And when she brought her left hand back to Ghusoon's belly, Rayah knew she didn't have hands enough to touch all the teeming life at once.

"Fenugreek in a strengthening meat soup," she prescribed. "'Do not skimp on the mothers of your sons by feeding them only beans,' as the Prophet, blessed be he, said."

Had Muhammad really said that? When had Sitt Umm Ali recited this hadith to her class of girls? Rayah couldn't remember. But she was certain that any prophet must have said something like this, so it must be a true tradition.

"Chamomile," she added with more certainty, "sage and cinnamon if, God forbid, she should begin to cramp again."

But Rayah knew her patient—her patients—were safe now. Her jinn-sensitive hands distinguished three sources of life in one body.

One of Ghusoon's in-laws had now lost patience and dragged Rayah away from the circle even as she prescribed.

At its edge, Rayah cried out, "Rejoice, my friend, and praise the merciful God who creates life from a clot of blood."

"Hush, blasphemous child," snapped Sitt Umm Ali.

But Rayah persisted to finish her announcement to her friend. "One child, the weakest, the ill-formed, may have died according to God's will, but two more continue to keep time in your womb. And this is due to your strength, my friend, and to Almighty God, nothing to me. Be of good cheer for the two who are saved to you because their weaker brother died."

The panic pumped by Rayah's own heart when she left ceased being for her friend and turned to herself. So must her grandmother Bint Zura have felt when al-Harith's herds doubled and tripled under her hands.

This power is so great, I must be careful, Rayah told herself. If it can make triplets where before was only prospect of death, I must be careful. Too much life as well as too little may kill all three. Dear God, help me to control this power according to Your will, lest it control me.

2

"Almighty God, Khalid is one of Your own swords on earth, so guide him and help him, my Lord."
—Prayer of the Prophet during the battle of Mu'ta

In the garden of Khalid the Conqueror in Homs, Syria, during the twentieth year of the Hijra, 642 of the Christian era

My son Abd ar-Rahman, governor of this town of Homs— supplanting me since my disgrace—came again this afternoon. Hoping to see my health worse today than it was yesterday. Hoping to inherit my sword, my glory, without lifting a finger.

God grant me the strength to thwart that calamity, at least.

Islam tells us who may inherit and what. But I had decided that some few things, at least, I must give to the daughter I never acknowledged in life, she whom I haven't seen for ten years or more.

In order to give, I had to find her.

Abd ar-Rahman grilled me again today, getting too close for comfort. "That time recently when you went to Tadmor? Why Tadmor? Whom do you know in such a distant oasis?"

What jinni told him that? I had been so cautious. For her sake. A rumor from the market of Damascus had led me to surmise she might be living in seclusion in the house of a turpentine seller in Tadmor. That recluse refused to see me. Her refusal convinced me further.

And broke my heart.

"A woman?" my son said. "Once a girl? *That* girl? That herdsman's daughter you made me play with when we were little? I do remember her name. She lives quietly in a harem now, I suppose?"

I grow sick. She lives in fear for her life.

"Under an assumed name?"

No one in the world Muhammad forged must speak her real name again.

Abd ar-Rahman lectures me. "Does not the Holy Quran tell us in the voice of God, may He be praised, 'Truth has come and falsehood has vanished'?"

My son's cunning ambition convinces me she must inherit something, for all she has been through. For all the fear.

My sword, forged the same night she was. My red turban—once the underdress her mother used to let me down from a tower with her kinsmen hot on my heels. The bits of a woman's camel litter I picked up from the wreckage of the Battle of Yamamah. And these written pages, which must tell the truth in a world that now censors me and my life, a truth she must understand. These things I hope to leave out of the court my son controls. Inshallah, if God wills, they will go to her.

My scribe and I, inshallah, must press on to the end of my tale. So truth may come and falsehood vanish, as the Holy Book says. If God wills.

And thus, in the sixth year after he escaped as a fugitive to the city that now bears his name, Medinat an-Nebi, the City of the Prophet, I followed the Messenger of God north and submitted myself and my heavenly sword to him.

In the Name of God, the Merciful, the Compassionate. . .

No man ever does anything for a single reason. If he says so, he lies. And most of the time, most of the reasons are hidden, even from his own soul.

I pause for a moment to wonder about the reasons my scribe has to do anything, to sit with me all these days in this dappled green garden with the emerald winking in his ear. The money I pay him—he's not storing it up to pass on to anyone. He is a eunuch. He has no family, nor any hope of one. Yet he has endured my blasphemies day in and day out. He used to protest piously—not so much recently—and still he comes back for more.

Well, by God, this is my story, not his, and his bears not thinking of.

My reasons for converting to the One God were as manifold as the Gods who had populated the Ka'ba in my hometown of Mecca before Muhammad's rise. Reasons of power play, honor, family. Conviction that Islam was, in fact, the way of the future, yes, that too was there, and, by God, I had no desire to lose. I still have none. If that is not God's will, then I know not what is.

And of course, the singular reason of the daughter I dared not claim led the rest. Gotten on a mother now dead, gotten beside the holy wells of Nakhlah the same night my sword was created. The daughter I had not seen for years. Islam blocked the desert road for me as a pagan, trapping me in Mecca. If I succumbed to Islam, the freedom of the desert would be mine again, to trade, to visit. To conquer.

Muhammad the Seal of the Prophets, peace be upon him, perhaps only he never did a thing save for the glory of the One God he preached. And is Muhammad the man upon whom we wish peace?

I knew no peace, neither before nor—and I sought it—after.

And no peace now, though the hoopoe splashes his feathered crest in my fountain that covers the sounds of public unrest in the city. No peace from my son's ambition, from my overweening cousin Omar's khalifate. The cushions are soft, the sherbet sweet, though the one gives my backside no comfort and the other gives my stomach indigestion. I eat anise seeds.

"Peace be upon the Messenger of God," murmurs my scribe like the fountain, and we press on.

Muhammad, blessed be he, consolidated my alliance with him by adding a young widowed aunt of mine, Maimunah, to his harem. Nevertheless, I let him know that I would always be my own man. I refused to join him in abstaining from lizard flesh, for instance. He was the Prophet of the Arabs. What else did he expect a true Arab to live on during the lean summer months if not lizard? Were Muslims to be as superstitious and picky as the Jews? I asked.

Muhammad did not appreciate my argument, and that and other such acts on my part did nothing to dissuade his mistrust of me. He was a man of deep spirit, may God bless him. He could read the intents of the heart very well. I never fooled him. He was wary of his great and sudden success, and knew that people were turning to him now for different reasons than they had at first. These reasons were wrong—wrong, at least, to his mind. To him, expedience was not to be trusted in the place of true belief.

To my mind, as I've said, every man does things for his own reasons, and they have to suffice for him.

In any case, Muhammad accepted my friends Amr, Uthman and me and hoped that time and service in the community would make us more stalwart. And, as I've said, I accepted him. I realized my faith would have to undergo a severe scrutiny. I was willing to put up with that.

I also accepted the fact that on my first expedition under the banner of Islam, I would march as any common soldier. Islam provided more than enough fighting to be done, but obviously I could not be given the post of commander right away. Not when we were attempting such a daredevil thing as the Battle of Mu'ta.

Mu'ta was the Prophet's first ordered confrontation with the forces of imperial Rome. Mu'ta presented us with everything that fighting for faith will make a man do but sound reason would prohibit. It was prideful, ill-advised and honor-seeking, where honor is of childish and extravagant proportions.

I went along, nonetheless. I would prove myself to Muhammad in the ranks.

After all three of his chosen and faithful commanders got themselves killed, I saw my chance. I took it. I picked up the command where it had fallen, shattered on the field of Mu'ta. I led the Muslims to use all their zeal, always their most effective weapon, to the best result.

For myself, I made a name by breaking nine swords against Roman armor, and none in vain. The tenth sword I picked up was the only one I had left—my divine one. I heard the whisper of jinn as I swung it, the twitch of their power in my right arm for which I had once bargained with them.

In the quiet of my yard with my scribe's pen scratching away, I hear the jinn whisper in the mere presence of the sword.

"In the Name of God. . ."

What can men do against the Beings of Smokeless Fire, whom the Almighty created before he created us of clay?

The heaven-forged steel did not break at Mu'ta, even after God-knows-how-many lives it cut asunder.

For all my swords, we did not win at Mu'ta. And yet, no one can say that we lost. In any case, not after I took command. Against all Rome, at least all Rome on the desert's edge, numbering ourselves but three thousand men, that was as good as a win. I, for one, do not think the vow I'd made as a mere boy never to lose was broken. We lost only twelve men ourselves. We learned the Romans' tricks and stable defenses for future reference. And we let them know that the Arabs of the desert were no longer a thing at which to laugh. For what greater victory could one ask?

But these were matters of war, not of faith. In matters of faith, I was still an infant (as the Prophet, blessings on him, reminded me again and again). The three commanders who had fought and died before me, they had been men of faith. No, Muhammad did not seem to feel as certain as I that the Sword of God was ready for a large command. Had I been a man of true faith, I would have led the entire three thousand to their deaths as martyrs. I would not have made a "tactical retreat." Islam knows no retreat.

I was given a small command when we marched against Mecca for the final victory against our own kinsmen. Muhammad and the other commanders easily found fault with what I did there. Mine was the only column that met with any resistance. All the rest of the Muslims marched in as a grand and joyful homecoming, embraced relatives, kissed the sacred Stone. Then they sat down in the households of their childhoods to catch up on what they had missed while they'd been gone.

"In the Name of God, the Compassionate. . ."

Meanwhile, at the Pass of Khandama, I had to deal with an ambush laid by Ikrama and Sufwan. By God, they were my oldest and dearest friends! Sufwan was my own sister's husband. Do you think I charged at them lightly, for no reason? As God is my witness, Ikrama and Sufwan chose my column to attack. They thought I might be more easily persuaded to rejoin them and then take on the other Muslims.

I beat them, but then let them escape to become fugitives. Muhammad's decree chased them from any haven throughout Arabia until they, too, came and laid their swords at the Prophet's feet. For this I am blamed as well.

My actions, my swift and powerful denial of any such hopes on the infidels' part, should have proved my faithfulness. But again Muhammad was displeased. He had wanted a peaceful entry into Mecca. By God, one moment he wanted blood, the next, any drop was too much! "It is a matter of faith and your faith is still weak, my brother." By God and by my life, how was one to prove such a faith at all?

Still, I continued to try. What else could I do? Mecca had been taken now. Even Abu Sufyan had lowered his proud old head, declaring Muhammad God's Messenger—and his own son-in-law with the gift of his daughter Umm Habibah. No place remained to which I could return even if I'd wanted to. The whole Hejaz—all of western Arabia from Yemen in the south to the very borders of the Jordan River in the north—sought Muhammad's smallest notion of what faith might entail.

So I continued to surpass my own demands upon myself. In order to win the Prophet's trust, I sought to succeed now in the only direction success was to be found. God willing, I might be trusted with enough freedom to move as something akin to my own man, as I had once been.

But Muhammad, blessings on him, knew my soul better than I did myself. At length he devised a test of my obedience, both final and supreme.

On a certain day, Muhammad called me to him and presented the terms of his test to me.

"Sword of God," he said, the name no credit of my own, but because of the sword fate and a night in the desert had given me. "There is a valley halfway between Mecca and at-Ta'if. Do you know the place?"

I could not conceal a blush. "Do you mean Nakhlah, O Messenger?"

"I do indeed. Where idolaters are still worshipping their false divinities, where foolish women still commit their superstitious blasphemies."

I swear by God and by the look with which His Messenger pierced me that Muhammad remembered what had caused the Satanic Verses to enter his mind. My little daughter, sitting on his knee. He also knew in some dark way just what both Nakhlah and those verses meant to me. My daughter, her conception at one place and her power manifest at the other. How could he? And yet it seemed he had knowledge of the night the stars fell into my sword. The secrets of my love—

By God, he was asking me, as closely as he could, to sacrifice my daughter for his religion. Just such a sacrifice God asked of Ibrahim, in asking for the life of his son Isma'il.

I was no Prophet, to be proven thus. I had no desire to be.

Still I nodded as calmly as I could. "Yes, I know the place."

"Good," the Messenger said. "Then this task should be easy for you. I want you to destroy that shrine. Utterly."

He was mocking me. The Prophet of God was mocking me! I could see it in the superior gleam of his blue eyes.

By what infernal jinn did he know?

Had Muhammad been seated there alone, I might have risked all future advancement and hope of command to refuse him. I would have risked my life. I would have pleaded, by his One God, for mercy.

But next to him sat Omar and on the other side Abu Bakr. These two men shared every secret with Muhammad. Between them, they controlled the world. To deny the orders of those three altogether was to deny the way everything is obliged to move, to seek to fall up instead of down.

I hesitated as best I could and tried to bargain their price down. "Which men shall I have as my command to fulfill this task?"

"Oh, no men," the answer came. "What, to overturn one old shrine you need an army?"

"One or two men I thought. . . ." Anyone at all who would relieve me of the horrible task.

"One old caretaker, a few straggly trees, a hut no bigger than this room here. Surely the Sword of God does not need seconds for such a task? No, you shall go alone. And if you take so much as a slave along with you, I shall call you faithless and a coward."

Such was the word of an All-Knowing God.

3

**When tongues begin to be busy with a woman's name,
then they who have wings should fly.
—An Arab saying**

Rayah felt she was becoming a stranger in the house where she'd been born. Her doubting had begun with the arrival of Abd Allah the eunuch at the turpentine sellers' gate with the sheaf of parchments under his arm so many months before. She could never wish that deed undone; she loved the scribe, loved learning the stories he had brought with him about Khalid the Conqueror, who had somehow become her grandfather. She loved the way these stories and the eunuch tempted her mother to speak that which she never had before.

Rayah wished with all her heart that Abd Allah's coming had not caused him to be imprisoned and tortured, so devoted had he been to keeping her mother's secrets. But Rayah had set his broken leg, mended the ear that would never bear another glinting emerald. And the man stayed, reading his parchments and standing beside her mother as she kept Abd ar-Rahman ibn Khalid at bay.

For the Conqueror's son, attempting to make good on his claim as half-brother to Sitt Sameh and therefore uncle to Rayah herself, had followed the eunuch to the desert oasis. He had been responsible, through his Persian slave Firuz, for the eunuch's torture, by which means he had caused Rayah to betray her mother's whereabouts. The relationship—accepted now by everyone in Tadmor, not least by the turpentine sellers—gave this powerful stranger from Homs the right to arrange Rayah's marriage.

He had freed her from the distasteful marriage to Ghusoon's former suitor, the unpleasant Sharif Diya'l Din. But in that man's place, Abd ar-Rahman offered his first-born son, Rayah's own cousin in al-Medinah, far from any friend or anything she had known. And further, as bride-price, he demanded the Conqueror's heaven-forged sword. Few in Tadmor had a word to say against the match. Many, in fact, spat with violent jealousy.

Rayah didn't wish this fate for herself. Her mother definitely didn't want this. In order to save her daughter from this fate, Sitt Sameh was willing to give herself up as hostage to this Abd ar-Rahman, possibly to death by stoning for a witch. To whatever fate she had buried herself away from in a Tadmor harem for thirteen years.

"Inshallah. All will be as God wills."

This Rayah murmured to herself as she learned from the doorkeeper that Abd ar-Rahman was once again spending the day with the turpentine sellers, watching for her to return. She said it again as she pulled her veil closer, pursued by the town's rumors that she had once again healed and given fertility to her friend Ghusoon.

"Inshallah" again, a prayer as she passed her own doorway by and let herself into the house of the two old sisters next door. From there, she easily climbed over the wall their yards shared and entered the safety of her own harem.

Rumors of her healing had preceded her. "You expose yourself too much with these healings against the will of God," scolded Auntie Adilah, who only earlier that same day had scolded Sitt Sameh for not using her gifts. "No man wants such a bride, least of all the son of such a great one as the governor of Homs."

Uncomfortable in her own home.

"Inshallah," Rayah said as she took the stairs to the rooftop and her mother's room two at a time.

All Rayah's desperate debates with herself had found only one possible escape from her situation in this household. Sooner or later she had to marry. Which marriage would permit the best use of her healing gift? Ah, hard to say. Which was worse? Ghusoon's, birthing child after child until she was gray and worn at thirty in a house not two doors down from where she'd been born? Rayah's local option was not even a pleasant Jafar. Or what of the choice Abd ar-Rahman offered Rayah, that of a daughter-in-law, hardly better than a slave, to a powerful man who hated any inkling of her own power?

Bursting in through the tenting that covered her mother's rooftop room, interrupting whatever her mother and the eunuch were discussing, Rayah flopped down on the rugs and demanded, "Did a *shaytan* once beg your hand in marriage, Lady?" She dreaded to hear her mother's answer to the question it had taken her prayer time after prayer time to form. Yet she had to know.

Because a boy with dark eyes and a dark tumble of curls had come to Rayah on a twist of desert sand. He had rescued her when helping the eunuch had become too dangerous. He had kissed her. He had asked for her hand. He had priority over any governor's son.

He was a jinni.

Sitt Sameh and the eunuch exchanged a glance. Rayah ignored it and stared at her mother, demanding.

"Of course, *shayatan* found me attractive," Sitt Sameh said with a fierce twist of her spinning. "It is the fate of all women of our blood."

If her mother had taken a jinni to her bed, what did that make her, Rayah, her daughter? Was this flesh and blood she'd always taken for granted, then, half insubstantial smoke and fire?

"Then am I—?"

"Hush."

Rayah took a breath—to still her anger as much as to recover from her rush up the stairs. She reframed her question. "Is it possible, then?"

"I think I've already told you. In the eastern desert is a clan who claims *jinniyah* as their foremothers. Ghuls, Allat shield us, have been known to trap unsuspecting men in the form of pretty women and then suck the life from them."

Abd Allah murmured a prayer of protection.

Rayah echoed him, then said, "The Prophet, blessed be he, told us that of the ten parts of creation, the Most Merciful made one part human and nine parts for the jinn."

"I have no knowledge of such things," Abd Allah admitted. "I must defer to those who do. But I have noticed that whenever the two letters *jim* and *nun* occur together in the Arabic language, they convey the meaning of the hidden or unseen."

"I know nothing of letters, nor do I want to know," Sitt Sameh said.

"And yet you cannot speak your native language without understanding how word roots work to parse meaning," Abd Allah told her.

"Anyone who has lived in the desert knows the cities of the jinn that shimmer in the heat on the horizon and then vanish or move as you approach. They told me that such was Tadmor, that Solomon, who commanded the Smoke Spirits by a twist of the ring on his finger, had commanded them to build this place. That, in part, was why I chose to come here. I thought, perhaps, the jinn, who had made me hated among men, would take me in—"

The side curtains on the little room were rolled up for the air, and each of the three looked out over the rooftops of Tadmor with his own thoughts.

"I learned when I arrived, of course, that this is very much a city of men's hands, of clay and the stone of ancient empires—although, of course it is slowly whittling back into the desert sand. Close enough to mirage. For a few years anyway." Sitt Sameh reached out a finger to touch the crumbling clay base of her walls, then gave a twist to her thread. "There was supposed to be an enchanted well here, too. One that shrank down to nothing as the thirsty traveler approached, but that teased him by growing again as he turned to go. Just as jinn wells sometimes do in the desert."

"'A woman at the well.'" Abd Allah repeated the words of his master's tale.

"Of course, there is none," Sitt Sameh declared, angry. "All has been taken from us."

"Not all." Abd Allah's gaze rested on Rayah a moment. He gave her a smile. "Such a well is pretty useless," he went on, "unless the spell be broken. I think I found such, here in the hidden jinn city of Tadmor. I think my master did as well, although it shrank from him."

His gaze was back on Sitt Sameh now, and intense, demanding. She concentrated on her spindle.

"Will it always shrink?" Abd Allah asked. "Will the spell never be broken, the jinn open their power to good?"

Rayah wished the pair of them would stop talking in myths and words that, like the stories' well, seemed to vanish as she approached.

Abd Allah's musings had returned him to his words, to his letters of *jim* and *nun*. "Paradise is *jannah*," he said. "The fetus in the womb is *janin*."

And the womb is the same root as mercy as in "God the Most Merciful," Rayah thought.

She could feel again Ghusoon's belly beneath her hands, feel the little lives pumping away in there, how these hidden things had been revealed to her. She knew this was a gift; to deny it would be like taking a burning stick to her own eyes.

She thought, too, of the surah of the Quran entitled "The All-Merciful," *ar-Rahman*. Sitt Umm Ali used it to teach her students the Arabic use of the dual, because two beings are addressed within it, humans and the jinn. *"Ath-thaqalayn"* the Holy Book addressed these beings, "the two weighty, honorable communities." So God did not wholly condemn the Beings of Smokeless Fire.

"The expression *ajannahu al-layl* means 'the night covered him,'" the eunuch continued in his delight.

"Hidden doesn't mean nonexistent," her mother said. "Far from it."

"And *majnun* means crazy. *Majnunah*," Rayah added the feminine form, as if for herself. For her mother, who had always remained hidden in the harem. "Possessed by the jinn." Must they always hide the truth with words, words and more words?

"'Making what is hidden manifest,' perhaps." Sitt Sameh then dropped what Rayah had found to be an irresistible new image, fascinating and horrible as the sight of death, and concluded, "But my jinni only ever gave me poetry."

"'Only' poetry is too dangerous. I don't want this, Mother."

"Allat and Manat shield you, of course you don't. But it is the only life I could give you. A life the world needs now, beginning with your pregnant friend, but many, many more need you in the harems of this new world."

Rayah shifted uneasily. So her mother knew what she had done for Ghusoon, without a word spoken. Prophecy went with poetry and with the jinn, that much was clear. But her mother had not always kept such gifts secret.

"A jinni has asked for your hand in marriage, daughter? So be it. But remember this: The Ones of This Place are creatures of smokeless fire. Don't always believe what you have seen; they play tricks."

Others play tricks, Rayah thought. To prove it, she suddenly demanded, "What's your name?"

Beneath the desert tattoos, her mother paled.

"Tell me the true given name of my mother," Rayah demanded.

Her mother worked her lips, but they made no sound.

Rayah stared, angry blue eye to blue eye. Her mother was crazy, *majnunah.* So her name had something to do with the *jim* and the *nun*, too?

But God in the Quran is called the Outward and the Inward, two of His beautiful names. "Praises to Him," Sitt Umm Ali had said, "God unveils himself through infinite creations, yet veils Himself in absolute secrecy in His Oneness."

How did her mother get away with this, keeping one name hidden while God gave away ninety-nine?

Something–something was in the air. Something pressed upon Rayah, upon her belly, at her very core. Something was about to happen. Why could it not be this, that her mother would finally tell her name?

Rayah knew she didn't belong to the people below, the world that smelled day in and day out of turpentine, even though she had lived there all her life. Now her only refuge, her mother's tent upon solid clay, had grown too uncomfortable as well. With a defiant leap, Rayah got to her feet. She flew from the worsted walls and sprang up on the low brick wall that circled the roof. She walked there, balancing, as only daredevil boys did. These things inside her, possessing her, making her *majnunah*—

She spread her arms as if she could fly, escape.

All around beneath her ankle bangles lay the miraculous green of the oasis of Tadmor, new washed by the rain. Rain Rayah had wept to heaven for—and caused with an ancient rite to the Mother of Rains. Again she lifted her face, remembering the mixture of rain and tears muddying her drought-stained face, knowing her power to move, to act with the storm-roiling jinn for good in the world.

Beyond her feet rolled the desert to which the fortunate daughters of the wilderness had returned, now that their wells were full again and green dusted the swelling cinnamon sand blow. And here Rayah remained trapped, she who had given them their freedom back.

Her mother tossed the spindle against the rooftop ridge and caught her daughter's shoulders. The touch was awkward, unaccustomed. For a moment, Rayah almost lost her footing. Mother and daughter struggled there, the one about to take flight, the other binding her to the ground.

Did Sitt Sameh—whatever her real name was—fear Rayah might have been preparing to jump from the rooftop? That retreat occurred to many a woman who found her life unbearable. Most disturbing was Rayah's thought that perhaps she had indeed been planning to do that thing, depending on the answer her mother gave to the question of her name. Would she have jumped if her mother persisted in her silence? Or if she didn't? Perhaps both. And what worse answer could Rayah have been expecting?

Or rather, was death what her jinni had in mind for her? If so, one removal from the edge would not stop another occasion. As long as she felt this pressure within, as if she would burst, she would not let another occasion pass.

"Later," her mother whispered. "I will tell you, I promise. Meanwhile, it is normal, in a woman, sometimes to feel thus."

To feel so much she wanted to die? To want to feel the snap of her neck on the pounded dirt below just to know she had once been alive? Rayah felt the tremble of true fear in that voice down the full length of the body of the woman clinging to her. Never had her mother held her thus, even as an infant.

"Later," her mother crooned in a voice that knew the God-defying gift of poetry. "When you know—know more."

Rayah did not take flight. She let her mother win. Their bodies moved awkwardly apart.

"First listen to the tale," her mother said, hustling her into the little room and sitting her down once again on the rugs with the eunuch in attendance. "This part of the tale begins with Malik ibn an-Nuwaira."

"The Conqueror's milk brother?" Rayah asked, since it seemed something was expected of her.

Sitt Sameh exchanged a glance with the eunuch, then nodded so the coins and shells on her headdress jangled. "He became sharif of the Banu Tamim when his elder brother was blinded by the jinn and their father died, yes. Musaylimah, the prophet of the Hanifa who'd bought me from slavery, he had taken me back to them, to the pastures where I was born. You will recall this; Musaylimah was going to wait until I grew into a woman before making me his bride. . . ."

4

And We gave David bounty from Us:
"O you mountains, echo God's praises
with him. . .!" And We softened
for him iron: "Fashion wide coats of mail,
and measure well the links. . . ."
And to Solomon the wind; its morning course
was a month's journey, and its evening course
was a month's journey. And We made
the Fount of Molten Brass to flow for him.
And of the jinn, some worked before him
by the leave of his Lord. . .
fashioning for him whatsoever he would—
"Labor, O House of David, in thankfulness;
few indeed are those who are thankful among My
servants."

—The Holy Quran, Surah 34

And this is how Sitt Sameh continued her tale to Rayah and the scribe on the third floor of the turpentine sellers':

The year I became a young woman, grown ready to marry, Sharif Malik brought our houses of hair down off the plateau as our native pastures on the Najd uplands began to dry with the end of the rains. The spring caravans had never run so frequently nor been so numerous, north and south from Syria to al-Medinah and beyond. In the hot season, such was the lifeblood of our desert tribe. So the day came when Sharif Malik was patrolling the wells and routes of his people, and he came upon the caravan of a man of the Jewish tribe Banu 'n-Nadir, Huyyay ibn Akhtab.

"Take your passage fee and let us be on our way," the man said. "We are in some haste."

"Indeed I will," Malik said, pacing in front of the goods, unpacked from their camels' panniers and laid out on the sand for his inspection.

From the height of my camel, between the howdah curtains parted but a finger's breadth, I, too, wondered at the scene. Maces, armor, swords, spears and spearheads, arrows, quivers and bows: weapons for an army.

"This fine sword, O sharif," suggested Huyyay. "Take this sword of Bahraini make. Easily worth a tenth of all my goods."

Malik studied the sword. "Rudaini?" he asked. He must have remembered his milk brother Khalid's boasts about the sword he had had made of sky stones.

"No," the son of an-Nadir admitted with unusual haste. Of course, the Jew knew he would pass that way again and that his host would have means to find out the truth of his claims. This was a relationship he needed to foster with honesty. "But there are many sword makers in Bahrain with skills nearing or equaling those of the old kahinah whose eyes, we must admit, are not what once they were."

Malik snorted skeptically but had other doubts on his mind. "What is this?" he asked, gesturing. "This pile of beams, these wheels and pegs? The desert sands swallow any wheel; it must prove useless where you are going. These ropes?"

"That's a catapult."

Malik didn't know the word; I didn't either. I made my camel kneel and slipped out the back way.

The son of an-Nadir unrolled a parchment that showed how the machine was to be rebuilt on site from this heap of timber. He showed how it would then throw great crushing stones—easy enough to find in the desert—at defiant walls. Malik was used to fighting a highly mobile enemy who could vanish into the desert at a moment's notice. Once a man—or a crew, for the maneuver required a crew, something also foreign to the desert—had aimed the contraption, the foe would certainly not be in the same place by the time the great stone flew.

Malik, getting little satisfaction for his questions, changed the subject again from this alien, and as far as he could see, useless object. "So everything, even what I took to be beams imported for house construction, turns out to be a weapon as well," he said. "These are all weapons. What, son of an-Nadir, has become of your silks and spices, lapis, gems, gold, all the other things you and your kind usually spill from your packs? What, by all my fathers' Gods, has become of them? It seems to me that every weapon in the world is being funneled now away from Rome and Persia, the old adversaries, toward Mecca and al-Medinah, where once was only desert and peaceful trade. What is the meaning of this?"

As much of the men's conversation as I stayed to overhear ended. The son of an-Nadir had a daughter named Saffiyah, five years or so older than I was. I found her of more interest, and when I had opened the curtains to her howdah and invited her to drink our camels' milk, I had questions of my own for her. "How is it that your father brings you along with him on his trading journeys?"

Hand in hand we went to the women's section of the tent to have our talk.

Four days' camel ride north of the Prophet's city of al-Medinah, Saffiyah told me, the eight towers of the Jewish fortress named Khaybar marched up the mountainside. Each contained homes, stables and storehouses. Using the skills the Yemenis perfected with the waterworks at Ma'rib and their own religious rules of purity, the Jewish tribes brought water from the mountains behind them. They canalled it to their kitchens, their ritual baths and to their palm trees, counted in the tens of thousands.

Khaybar is where the Jews who could no longer live under Muhammad in al-Medinah had fled, among them Saffiyah and her family. Khaybar is where Huyyay ibn Akhtab led his caravan of weapons, his daughter and me.

Rayah's pulse raced as she heard Sitt Sameh's words. "You were at Khaybar?"

The woman sat now alive in front of her; that she had been at that scene of Muslim revenge and triumph—on the losing side—was hard to credit.

"Worse straits are yet to relate, my daughter. Khaybar is not the worst. Yet bad enough."

"But how did you come there?"

"With my friend Saffiyah, of course, Huyyay's daughter."

"Surely Malik ibn Nuwaira of the Tamim would not let you leave his protection. Not when he'd had the Jews' weapons laid out before him on the sand. Not when—"

"Not when he had given his oath to safeguard me until Musaylimah could claim me as his bride, no."

"Exactly," Rayah said. "Or there was Khalid—your father's—claim that you be safe."

"Not that he was very active in pursuing that aim."

"So how did you come to Khaybar?"

A half smile played in the creases beside Sitt Sameh's thin mouth. "Are we not women who ride in the *qubbah*? Saffiyah's camel rose with more protest than ever. Its feet sank deeper than usual in the desert dust. Two of us rode in her closed howdah, after her father had given the Bahraini sword as safe-passage fee. By the time Sharif Malik understood what had happened, even a fast-riding camel could not have caught up with us. We had reached the fortress of Khaybar."

"Besieged by Muhammad." It took Rayah a moment to remember to add, "Precious blessings on him."

"Yes. Besieged by Muhammad and his Muslims."

"Every rebel in the Hejaz was finding refuge in Khaybar," Rayah recited the justification Sitt Umm Ali had always given for the Muslims' action. "He couldn't let it stand."

"No. He couldn't let it stand," Sitt Sameh repeated.

"But why would you go?" Rayah insisted. "You had a *shaytan* who gave you poetry, who could also prophesy future events."

"Indeed, I did."

The tone in her mother's voice sent a chill down Rayah's spine. "I still do," seemed an echo behind what Sitt Sameh actually said. Rayah couldn't believe such courage of a woman who never left the third floor.

Or such stupidity, that's what it must have been. The jinn's dishonesty.

"There is no God but God, and Muhammad is His Prophet," Rayah recited. "Surely this confession of faith shows that all other prophecies are false."

As rebuttal, her mother poured forth these words:

"Heave the breast bones of your camels
Up off the sand and leave, daughter
of my mother. I lean to a tribe
other than you.

"What must be is at hand.
The moon is full,
mounts and saddle frames secured
for distant crossings."

The words her mother recited ran like an elixir through Rayah's veins, hot and strong. "This is a poem your *shaytan* gave you?"

"At that particular time, yes, telling me I must go. Saffiyah had told me her story, how her first husband, the love of her youth, had died fighting Muhammad when they fled al-Medinah. Her father had just promised her to an older man named Kinana ibn ar-Rabi'a, guardian of the treasure of Khaybar, and the marriage would be solemnized as soon as they reached home."

The Quran was God's own revealed truth. Rayah had thought its fiber the very marrow of her bones. But she had also heard her own jinni speak and couldn't deny that, either. The smoke-haired boy who came to her—his words weren't even in poetry, but she understood why her mother had obeyed the words she had been given. Bones and marrow made up a woman, but she embodied flesh and blood—lots of blood—besides.

Indeed, at the sound of her mother's poem, Rayah felt her belly cramp. She pressed it against the pain, and blood curled from her.

Her first blood. Like a boy's hunting.

Her mother saw, and helped the eunuch to his feet. "Time to strengthen the leg," she told him.

Emotions of fear then pride then power shifted through Rayah like jinn until her mother returned—alone. They had been expecting this—and yet, it was nothing like what Rayah expected, the lack of control, the total consumption. And where she might have been ready to dismiss all the women in her life, suddenly they became flesh of her own flesh.

"Good against leprosy, a woman's first flow," her mother said, showing Rayah how to catch the drops by squatting over an earthenware bowl when she didn't need to be moving. So much like the miscarriage of her friend Ghusoon. "Much better than Quranic verses written on a stone, the stone soaked in water, and the water drunk down."

> "In the Name of God, the Beneficent, the Merciful.
> Say: 'I seek refuge in the Lord of the dawn
> From the evil of that which He has created—'"

Rayah recited in her discomfort, as Sitt Umm Ali told her she must, when her courses—when no man could touch her, not even a good, believing husband—should come upon her.

"But it isn't evil," she heard herself say instead. "It's life." And she knew she couldn't reject anything that came from herself, or from her own *shaytan*, just because some man declared it unclean.

This new event had to be dealt with before the story of Khaybar could continue. Sitt Sameh even enlisted Auntie Adilah in the matter. Auntie Adilah boiled sweet halwah for the arrival of a new woman. The rest of the harem trilled, a sound as natural and as intense as that of a swarm of mating locusts. They drummed and danced and gave Rayah little gifts; most of them cycled together.

Little Bushra, years from attaining the power herself, was the only one innocent enough to point out the undeniable evil in the midst of rejoicing. "Now you have no excuse to refuse the governor Abd ar-Rahman's son any longer, *ya* Rayah."

That hushed the trilling for a moment, every woman conscious that they might betray themselves to the *majlis* and the will of God waiting them there. Rayah knew it was true.

When this time came to her in the future—Sitt Umm Ali had always sternly pressed upon the girls—if it were the month of fasting, they would eat as normal during the day, alone, away from the rest of the faithful, the men. As if the All-Compassionate who had Rahman ("womb") as part of His name, did not want her unclean sacrifice at this time.

Except that Rayah knew that in this house, most of the women would break the fast with her. They would pause and snack together from their preparations of the evening's lavish meal, the spread the hungry men would only later enjoy. As if God the Merciful gave women reprieve for these few days a month to be themselves as He created them, strong enough to bleed and not die; to create, like Him, from a clot of blood.

The flow continued the natural course of days after the first celebration. While Rayah waited to go to the baths with the rest of the women, she went to her mother.

Abd Allah was there again, his leg causing pain from too early use. Rayah met his eyes and saw acceptance. So she touched the leg and, even in her condition, she saw the pain ease. The eunuch thanked her with a smile. He then had a different sort of smile for her mother.

"Please, Sitt Sameh," Rayah said into the silence of the woman who—earlier, wonder of wonders—had come downstairs and lent her own desert trill to the rest. "Hurry on with your story."

"Muhammad's *shaytan*—" Sitt Sameh settled back on her own cushions once more.

"The Angel Jabra'il," Rayah adjusted the earthenware pot beneath her as she corrected her mother.

The spindle jabbed the air with anger, celebration forgotten. "Is this going to be your story or mine, new woman?"

Rayah cursed her tongue, the discomfort that made her brash just when she should be quiet. With such a beginning, she knew better than to ask her mother to give her real name again as part of today's story. So even becoming a woman did not allow this secret. Yet.

But these events did put more urgency in the tale, that much was clear: becoming a woman and suitors in the *majlis*. Rayah didn't insist as her mother pressed on.

"Muhammad's *shaytan* taught him to dam the canals bringing water into the fortresses of Khaybar."

"You must have suffered."

"We did, rationed to a cup a day from the great water jugs, and the Jews denied their washing rites. But at that point, the Muslims suffered more. Positing a God above the flow of nature, as both faiths did, can have that effect. The backed-up water made swamps around the Muslim camp."

"Did people catch swamp fever?" Rayah asked her mother.

"The people of Khaybar had always avoided the fever by setting their homes and fortresses above the swampy plain, by diverting the water and, they believed, by keeping the rules of purity their God had given His people on Sinai. They had also assembled the catapult my friend Saffiyah's father Huyyay had brought down from Rum, and thus they kept the Muslims and their disease confined to the swamps. So Muhammad caught the fever."

"Blessings on him," Rayah said.

"He caught the fever and handed command over to Abu Bakr."

"The first khalifah, God rest him."

"Yes. But Abu Bakr caught the fever, too."

"Did Abu Bakr then hand command over to Omar, may God lead him and all Muslims rightly, as history has done?"

"Omar never left al-Medinah for Khaybar," Abd Allah added his first part to the story that day.

"As was common, he pleaded the leg broken in childhood—" added Sitt Sameh.

"Broken by my master Khalid ibn al-Walīd." Abd Allah shifted his own leg in sympathy.

"As he related in his parchments, yes." Sitt Sameh adjusted the eunuch's cushions and laid the parchments once more at his elbow.

"Are you saying Omar did not press on with jihad?" Rayah asked. "But today under him, the Muslims are spreading farther in the world than ever before."

"Each person has his own jihad, his own quest under God's hand," Abd Allah said from his bed.

"Omar counsels Muslims to 'Hang your whip where your wife can see it.'" Sitt Sameh countered. "That is how he makes jihad, using his religion to make things comfortable for himself, uncomfortable for everyone else."

Rayah shifted on her seat at the thought of the oppressive family Abd ar-Rahman, son of the Conqueror, intended to make her join.

"The commander after Abu Bakr at Khaybar," Sitt Sameh went on, "was not Omar but Ali ibn Abi Talib, Muhammad's son-in-law. Ali was very young, but that is probably why, even though Ali caught the fever, he remained strong and convinced his God meant victory for the Muslims, to teach the stubborn Jews the power of a new prophet." Sitt Sameh sighed and picked up her spinning. "So Ali, young and on fire, picked up his double-bladed sword and took command of the Muslim army at Khaybar."

5

The Apostle of God once mentioned al-Uzza, saying, "I have offered a white sheep to al-Uzza while I was a follower of the religion of my people."
— *The Book of Idols* of Hisham ibn al-Kalbi

"Peace to you, O Sword of God. You have returned from the Valley of Nakhlah."

"Peace to you, O God's Apostle. I have."

"Is the deed done?"

"It is done, O Messenger."

"What did you do?"

"I chased old Dubayya from the shrine and threw a torch up into the palm-frond roof."

"Old Dubayya will return and rebuild the roof. Go back and destroy it permanently."

"I have returned, O God's Apostle."

"What did you do this time?"

"I cut down two of the trees."

"And what did you see?"

"The trees. Trees and sand."

"Go back and destroy until you see more."

"But green is such a precious thing here in the desert. And a well. . ."

"It is a pagan grove. Go back and root out the evil completely. Or shall I let Omar the Firebrand know that you are no longer to be counted among the Faithful?"

"By God, I shall satisfy you, O Holy Messenger, or forever live dishonored."

"Well, Sword of God. Returned at last. You seem a little worse for wear."

"Forgive me, O Apostle of God. I have neither eaten food nor drunk water these five days."

"A fast is always a good thing when a man is struggling with his soul. Is the deed done?"

"It is done, O Messenger."

"Tell me what you saw and what you did."

"Forgive me, O Messenger. I hardly dare to speak of it."

"I will send Omar away."

"Thank you, O Prophet."

As soon as my cousin left the room, I could hold back my tears no longer. The wonder is that I had any moisture left inside to shed any tears at all. Muhammad was patient; he sat cleaning his teeth with a pick while I wept. He had gold incisors now in place of the ones he had lost at Uhud, and he was fond of them.

At last, when I was too weak to weep more, I began to tell the tale.

"As I approached the final tree, she—al-Uzza, the goddess herself—appeared in flames to defend it. She was black as night and wild-eyed, fearsome. I called on God, upon the single God, for strength, and then approached her reciting this spell:

> *"'O al-Uzza! May you be blasphemed, not exalted!*
> *Verily I see that God has abased you.'*

"With one blow I struck her down. She gave an unearthly scream, and both she and the tree behind her crumbled to a pile of ashes. Then I killed old Dubayya. Then I broke and buried the stone, her stone, the stone with breasts where the women were wont to. . ."

"And then?" Muhammad asked quietly.

"And then. . .and then I filled in the holy well with sand and stones. By God, I was mad. Only a madman would fill in a well in the middle of the desert."

"Hush, O Sword of God. No, you were not mad. Here, break your fast with this cool water."

I drank the water greedily, but its coldness made my sun-baked head ache.

"You are not mad, O Sword of God," the Prophet continued. "You have done well. You have proven yourself. You have won yourself a place in paradise. Do you not know this revelation?

> *"'God truly will not forgive the joining of other gods to Himself.*
> *Other sins He will forgive to whom He will: but he who*
> *joins gods with God has erred with far-gone error.*
> *They call, besides Him, upon mere goddesses.*

They invoke a rebel shaytan.
On them is the malediction of God. . .'"

But I was not listening to the Prophet's revelations. I was thinking of what I could never tell him. Things I could never betray to a soul pounded in my mind until I could think of nothing else. Clearer than Muhammad's neatly trimmed beard, I saw before me the Valley of Nakhlah.

The Valley of Nakhlah, she haunts me. Fresh rain had just passed on towards at-Ta'if when I arrived. Her boundary of rain-splashed mountain heads was thrown back and pillowed against the passing clouds, like dark goat-hair cushions in both color and texture. As the sun came out, it lightened the crags and valleys to the blushing pink-brown of woman's flesh upon which I was an unsightly stain.

It was not old Dubayya, as is today commonly reported, but rather I, Khalid ibn al-Walid, who sang this plea as I rode down to do my deed:

"O al-Uzza! Remove your veil and tuck up your sleeves.
Summon up your strength and deal this presumptuous
Khalid an unmistakable blow.
For unless you kill him this very day,
You will be doomed to ignominy and shame."

Death would have been sweeter for me than victory in this and many later battles. Yet my vow and Fate, my stubborn pride and my foolish clinging to life drove me on to it.

O you, Believer in a single God. Do not doubt that al-Uzza defended herself. True, she did not pick up the sword Dubayya had left hanging between her breasts for her to swing. You might believe she did not swing because a mere block of lifeless stone could not. But by all that is sacred, I saw her life force, a dark and smoke-like shadow with the power to scream at its destruction.

Scream, my God! I would shut that sound out of my mind, but it will not go. It leapt at me and entered me—how, I do not know, for I am not a woman, used to being entered. Like serpent venom through my very flesh in pinpricks, it seemed to go. Even so, they say, did Adam, father of us all, fall prey to a serpent's beguilement and spawn all the race of jinn while the world was as yet but new.

She took possession of my mind, feeding there upon my fear and ancient love and emotion, and I haven't known a moment's peace since then. She engendered a guilt and self-loathing within me so black that for three days after I had done the deed, I was as separated from my own wits as poor Ummarah, my dead brother, under the Abyssinians' spell.

I came to myself in some degree only by crawling to sleep in the very hollow in the ground where once I'd slept and worked magic before. This hollow of sacred earth endured. All my new-found faith could not efface it. And under this influence, I could at last find my camel to ride back home.

As I rode out of the Valley, it—she—appeared uniform and gray under a warmth-stealing winter sky. No trees would now refresh a traveler's sun-strained eyes that had rested upon not so much as a clump of grass since Mecca and could expect no more relief until at-Ta'if. That place apart had faded and become like any other desert valley.

Just so may a woman, when she is wronged, pulls down her veil and fades into the shadows at the back of a tent. Her husband may curse and shout or even beat her for her sulkiness. In the cheese he will taste the tears she is too proud to show him, and it will do his stomach no good. And though she will continue to live with him, to tend his flocks, make his clothes and cook his food, until the wrong is in some way mended, she will never lift that veil for him. The man may tear the veil from her, force himself upon her, within her, time and time again. To be master of her veiling is, no doubt, his right. But women have a veil not of human making and this, under no circumstances, can be torn from her. The man must know that for all the brutishness of his strength—with which he may even in anger or in wounded pride snap the life from her—he may never again enter the softness of her heart. And only in that place is his true satisfaction. Never, unless he makes himself worthy of her mercy.

Just so, I thought, did the Valley seem that day, closed behind the iron-gray and death-cold blank and as-if-drugged stare of an offended woman's eye.

I stayed to my bed with a fever for close to a week after my return from Nakhlah. Had I not had the disease once as a child already, I would have sworn I had caught the smallpox, only this time I had no chance of recovery.

But then Muhammad sent for me again, and I got up and found that, for all my dizziness and moments of total darkness, I could still answer his summons.

"O Sword of God, I have a commission it is God's will that you fulfill. I will give you your own command of some three hundred fifty horsemen. Yet, if you feel you are too ill, I will call another—"

"No, don't call another. I will fulfill your wish—if God has mercy on me."

I led the expedition to call the tribe of the Banu Jadhima to submission. They counted our numbers, saw that I headed the band with my miraculous sword, then threw down their arms and called themselves Muslims without a fight.

I knew full well it was the Prophet's practice to make peace with all who said so and then promised to pay the alms tax to his coffers in al-Medinah. But I had my men take the sons of Jadhima captive anyway and bind them hand and foot.

Then I ordered them executed, every last one.

In the cool of my garden with the singing birds in the pomegranate tree, I stop and stare at the tendrils of ink my scribe has just finished. I cannot imagine that someday they may evoke as much reality to men unborn as this peaceful surrounding does for me now. Or as much reality as there had been for me on that day in the meadows of the Banu Jadhima when the wind whipped the skirts of my robe about me, my back to my appalled men.

I could obey orders. Could they?

I turned from the shock on their faces and combed the sweat off my mare with a bit of dry calligonum. I smelled the combination of horse and herb and thought I had done well.

All felt so real and right—

More real than scratches on parchment can be: That animal is dead; the one in my memory was alive and blowing warm beside me. The pain was better than feeling nothing. I felt alive, finally, once more.

I bury my face in my hands, as soon my whole body will be buried.

I felt alive, the first time since Nakhlah's shrine had destroyed me—

"Master?" the eunuch says, pen raised.

Could his writing be used to create a reality to condemn me? More than I condemn myself? Now, when that pasture and that horse are no more?

Why should the Banu Jadhima find salvation as martyrs when I cannot?

Or did I mean to save the Prophet, blessed be he, from followers as divided as myself? Such an excuse will sit well with those whose souls are undivided. Yes, let us stick with that—

Or did I mean to blacken Muhammad's name as black as that ink on that stark white page? As black as my soul felt after Nakhlah?

Once a man has submitted, once you've asked him to give up honor and love, the tokens of his heart, for victory, for what—mere *belief*? A wisp of jinni flight through the mind?

Can I say a demon made me do it, everything?

"Master?"

I see the scribe does not condemn me. Less than he has for other things, anyway.

I groan. I tear at my hair. What jinni was in my head, my arm?

"Master?" The scribe is on his feet, spilling a whole lot of black.

I try to rise and cannot.

"Master, shall I burn what I have written this day?"

I breathe deeply once, twice.

I order my eunuch, as once I ordered Muslim men-at-arms: "Let it stand. Mop up the ink. Make more. Then write."

People will excuse me as I excused myself later to Muhammad—I did not be-

lieve the tribe's profession was in earnest. By God, their conversion was at least as true as mine had been. Let history remember those early days for what they really were.

Praise God, less than half of all my men obeyed the order. The rest were better followers of Muhammad and obeyed him over me, so you may still find a son or two of Jadhima yet alive in your wanderings through the world. But enough blood, enough lavish and flagrant use of force and power of my own, eased the burning of my fever.

And then Muhammad ordered me to join with him at the siege of the Jewish fortress of Khaybar.

6

**O Prophet, We have made lawful for you
your wives to whom you have given their wages
and what your right hand owns, spoils of war
that God has given you.
—The Holy Quran 33:48**

Rayah's mother took up her spinning and her memories of the same period in early Islam as Abd Allah had just read. Rayah sat in her new womanhood and saw the smudge of spilled ink on the parchment. Somebody had cleaned it up, but he hadn't burned it.

Rayah thought of the lowly position to which her body confined her. With dismay, she thought of the newly converted Banu Jadhima. With more dismay, she realized that any Muslim soldier might disobey his general on the battlefield, save a Believer's life and enter paradise. No woman could ever do the same, would ever be allowed the same strong, hard choices.

And yet—

And yet, her mother told of conversations among the Muslim commanders that she, in the fortress of Khaybar with the Jews, never could have witnessed—

Even under the double-bladed sword of Ali ibn Abi Talib, the Muslims did not get the upper hand at Khaybar. Summer's heat was approaching, and both Muhammad and Abu Bakr suffered with the swamp fever. The army of Believers was about to turn and trudge back the four days to al-Medinah, when one of those Believers in the lower ranks stepped forward.

This soldier had seen lights burning late in the fortresses and heard the festive songs.

"Why is this night different from all other nights of our siege?" Ali ibn Abi Talib wondered.

And memories arose in the lowly soldier's mind.

"I was put to milk with a Jewess when I was young in al-Medinah," he said.

"Yes, much as I was to the Banu Tamim." Khalid ibn al-Walid sat with the commanders before Khaybar and tried to dismiss this voice from the lower men. The future Conqueror champed at the bit like his horses with the constraints of a siege. He wanted to charge, yet was held back while graybeards and then youths were given command.

The lowly soldier stalwartly persisted. "I remember some of their customs." He would hold the line well when battle actually came.

Perhaps Khalid wasn't listening, but Ali ibn Abi Talib was. "Enough to betray your milk mother for God?" Ali asked.

Abd Allah shifted his leg and said, "And at some point, my master must have asked himself if he would make the same betrayal."

Sitt Sameh exchanged a meaningful glance with her patient when he interrupted her tale with these words. "He cannot deny it," she murmured as she rose to readjust the eunuch's leg, itching with healing.

"He will come to that in his parchments," Abd Allah told questioning Rayah. "But he does not mention his presence at Khaybar."

"He did know I was there," Sitt Sameh said. "You'll see. That part comes soon." To the eunuch she added, "He will not have had you write every engagement in which he participated, I suppose."

"His age was also catching up with him. He felt he didn't have much time. And his mind could not always remember what he had had me write and what he'd only rehearsed over and over in his mind."

The eunuch stretched and added, "Yes, that's much better, Sitt, thank you. I think I might try to walk again—with a stick—as far as the edge of the roof. A man, even one who can't do other things, does like to make water without help."

Rayah and her mother bent their heads together to share a smothered giggle, full of relief that their patient was doing so well, full of the sharing of women. Then Rayah had a moment to think of the grandfather she had never known and what of him was in her: her submission to Islam, conflicted by the presence of this woman from another time. How could she be stronger than the Conqueror, to resist this woman when he never had?

Was that even something she wanted?

Then Abd Allah returned, strong enough to take his part of their amusement, and her mother's story went on.

The lowly Muslim soldier stood straight at attention before the commanders. "I know enough," he promised them. "I know that every springtime of the year they celebrate their deliverance in times long ago. To do so, they leave every door open on these nights to welcome in the stranger, the guest as well as the ancient prophet, who, they believe, might one day return to feast with them."

"They leave the doors open?" Khalid said in disbelief.

"Even fortress doors?" asked Ali ibn Abi Talib.

"If they are particularly faithful, yes. They are also commanded, at this same festival, to make merry with wine."

"And they will be faithful, will they not?" Ali was on his feet in spite of the fever. He saw the way.

"Particularly so since they seek new deliverance from our siege as heaven delivered them from Egypt in days of old." Tones of ancient, half-remembered liturgy rang in the soldier's voice, but he stood unflinching in new belief.

"This year, they will indeed make a prophet—a new one, the Seal of the Prophets—welcome at their feast," Ali declared with fervor.

Khalid considered and asked, "But will your milk mother welcome you?"

"Hearing I was among this force, she sent me a basket of dates, pickles and unleavened bread over the fortress walls, in memory of the festival." The soldier studied his campaign-dirty nails as, for one moment, two honors battled inside him.

"She did it to curry favor," Ali dismissed the inner battle as nothing.

"She makes me remember I took life from her when I was young and helpless. Now, if God wills, I should have similar compassion on her and her people."

"No, now I truly do make up the tale." Sitt Sameh finished winding another ball of yarn, then took up carded wool to begin a new one. "I doubt the soldier said such things aloud to his commander."

Then she took up the tale again.

The soldier may not have spoken his doubts aloud, but they must have conflicted him.

"God wills it," said the new Prophet, feverish in his tent but without conflict when they took the plan to him for his blessing.

As if a straight line of the verse of Muhammad's revelation could do away with the helplessness of infancy from which we all come and the helplessness of old age toward which we all curve back.

And so that night, the first of Khaybar's fortresses fell. Its commander, Abu Rafi, died stabbed in his bed when new religion overrode and exploited old rites and the even older connection of blood and milk. And so the lowly soldier also died, a martyr at the hands of his milk family, and faded from history.

Though the Jews fought hard, one by one Khaybar's fortresses fell. Their young men fell. My friend Saffiyah's new husband fell captive without them ever having consummated the marriage for the lack of water to make the necessary purifications. Muslims can clean in sand and so are better suited to that place.

As the fortresses submitted one by one throughout two weeks in the late spring of that year, Muhammad allowed some survivors to depart and head north to return to Rum-held Jerusalem. They could take whatever their camels could carry—as long as all the weapons, including the catapult, went to the Muslims and as long as nothing was concealed.

Kinana ibn ar-Rabi'a, Saffiyah's new husband, had had custody of the treasure of the Banu 'n-Nadir: gold, gems kept in a casket. Before his capture, he buried it. Once captured, he denied its existence.

Muhammad declared prophetic sight and righteous indignation at the man's dishonesty. "Put fire on his breast," came the Messenger's order.

I held a collapsing Saffiyah while her husband was lashed to the ground and a stick, twisted with a bowstring, started a fire on his chest. It burned among the dark curling hairs, then flesh, until he died. His screams were hers as I held her. He did not reveal his secret.

The terms of conquest left those of us women remaining alive without male protectors as part of the spoils. My friend and I stood clinging to one another, although Saffiyah seemed to have lost all sense of the world. Besides her husband, her father and brothers had also been slain. Muhammad, leaning on his son-in-law for strength, the henna worn out of his beard so that every gray hair of his almost sixty years stood out, walked down the line we were forced to form for his choosing. My friend wouldn't look up from my shoulder.

I, too, had to wonder. "Heave the breast bones of your camels up off the sand"? What had my *shaytan* meant when he gave me these words, when I joined Saffiyah in her curtained howdah? Was I driven to the place only to fall into the fate I had barely escaped earlier, to become a slave again? My mother had suffered the same thing after Dhu Qar, so I knew the jinn did not always spare our blood as they worked their purposes. I did not think a Muslim, however, any Muslim could be the same sort of captive holder as my kind father, al-Harith, may the rain fall gently upon his grave. And I was, like many of the girls in the line, not yet a woman.

Still, I knew I had not misinterpreted the verses I had been given and that my *shaytan* never told lies for my best care. I had some purpose, perhaps, to help these women among whom I found myself.

I met Muhammad's gaze, blue eye to blue eye.

He remembered the Satanic Verses. I knew he remembered them. So did I.

He left the support of Ali's arm. I saw his struggle against pronouncing any further Satanic Verses under my jinni's inspiration. If I were Muhammad's slave instead of a small, free child, he could certainly crush any such future blasphemies. I saw those very thoughts cross his face, and my *shaytan* remained silent.

I recognized one other in the trooping, leering army: Khalid ibn al-Walīd, milk brother to Sharif Malik. He had become a Muslim? Treachery! How I wished I'd ignored my *shaytan* and stayed in my native tribe with Sharif Malik and his blind poet brother Mutammim! Here again was the son of al-Walīd, victor, and once more taking an interest in me that made me uncomfortable. He had planted himself at his prophet's elbow in place of Ali. Was he going to claim me as his plunder? Take me to his bed? I had always received feelings from him that made my flesh creep.

Khalid ibn al-Walīd and his prophet were having a rather heated discussion of which I, among the weeping captured women, heard only a portion.

"Yes, I claim her," I heard Khalid insist. So he did want me for his wife? The notion appalled me. But no— "And you, may the One grant you long days, have honored many of your other commanders by taking their daughters or sisters to wife."

Was Khalid offering me to the Muslims' prophet? By what right?

"So their sharp tongues may plead for their relatives day and night." Muhammad sighed with amusement over wives, daughters and sisters in general.

After taking a moment to wish the older man health enough to deal with such, Khalid ibn al-Walīd pressed on. "Does not the generous Quran which you, O Messenger of God, revealed to us, say that women taken as spoil are lawful to the Muslim conqueror?"

"Indeed, Jabra'il gave me those verses, in the Surah of The Women. Yet he adds that we should not take them directly on the battlefield, but give them time."

"Time to accept us and Islam?"

"Time to cleanse themselves, so we may be certain they do not carry the seed of previous, conquered husbands. God does not condone the confusion of blood."

Ibn al-Walīd nodded his red turban, then called to the army as a whole. "Do you hear that, O Believers? No captive woman is to be forced upon the battlefield."

I didn't hear what was said next between the Messenger and his commander because one of the Believers, having failed to hear the commander's voice—or perhaps having heard it—had taken a sudden deep interest in Saffiyah, an inert heap of rags and shock leaning against me.

I tried to concentrate on what Khalid ibn al-Walīd was saying about me. "I have never given permission for this one to be married yet, O Apostle of God," I heard.

He continued with a groan of emotion: "You know the secrets of our hearts, the secrets of Nakhlah, O Messenger. You must also know that her Tamimi foster father could never—"

Was this Khalid truly trying to claim me as his daughter? Why would such an exalted man want this? In order to solidify his sudden and treacherous relationship to Muhammad? Surely Khalid ibn al-Walīd had many daughters from legitimate wives to give. And the whole world knew I was Bint al-Harith, the daughter of al-Harith, the Tamimi's simple and murdered herdsman, anyway. It all compounded the man's treachery.

But the other soldier had begun to drag Saffiyah off. I tried to fend him off with my sandal; I was no match for him in his mail. He pushed me into the dust and took Saffiyah away.

At this juncture, God's Messenger pointed me out, hurt and tumbled into the dust.

"Very well, O son of al-Walīd and destroyer of the demon of Nakhlah." God's Messenger smiled at me with his prophetic blue eyes before turning to announce, "This one. I'll take this one as my share of the spoils. God willing, she may be the source of sons He's never given me."

"God willing," echoed Khalid the Conqueror.

Rayah's heart raced for her mother in the story, about her same age. But she thought of the present negotiations for her own hand, too. And what would she have wished for herself if God had allowed that the Prophet, blessed be he, had pointed her out of a line? Was this cousin in al-Medinah, the Conqueror's grandson, as close as she could come to such a marriage in this day and age of lesser men?

7

**The entire woman is an evil, and what is
worse is that she is a necessary evil.
Men, never, ever obey your women. Never let
them advise you on any matter concerning
your daily life.**

**If you let them advise you, they will
squander all your possessions and disobey
all your orders and desires. It is easy to
get pleasure from them, but they give you
big headaches, too. . . They complain of being
oppressed when in fact it is they who
oppress. . .**

**Let us implore God's help to escape their
sorcery.**

> **—Ali ibn Abi Talib, the Prophet's son-in-law,
> on women**

The next time she went to the toilet, using the cleansing water liberally to deal with her blooming womanhood, Rayah overheard the men talking in the *majlis.*

"It is said the girl has her first blood." The turpentine sellers took care not to mention who had told them: their own women. But they felt no such qualms in laying her most private affairs open before strangers.

"Then it is time to get her married," said the stranger known as the governor of Homs and the son of the Conqueror. "My offer stands, good men. My eldest son waits to take her hand in al-Medinah where he has gone to improve his education. All we ask is that the sword come with her as her dowry, for which you must find my generous offer of bride-price more than recompense."

Among the turpentine sellers' murmurs Rayah heard not one declining voice.

Above the *majlis*, in the little room on the third floor, Sitt Sameh picked up her spinning and her tale once more.

One of Khaybar's older women, Zaynab, whose father had been named the same as mine—al-Harith—had also lost her entire male kin at the fall of the fortress. Her fame as a cook, once this became known to the Muslims, had them contending for her services. She did not seem as affected as the rest of us slaves, as Saffiyah, for example, who lay in her Muslim captor's tent and couldn't move or even recognize my presence when I went to her.

I had gone as plunder to the Muslims' prophet. Although Quranic verses put off the consummation of this match, I felt trapped. The feeling made me pace the limits of the encampment like a wild animal caged. The rich voice of Bilal, the black slave calling the Muslims to prayers, drove the rhythm of Muhammad's *shaytan* into every corner where I sought refuge, however. And devout Believers guarded the perimeter beyond which I could not go.

That was how I came to Zaynab bint al-Harith. Zaynab had offered to cook a congratulatory meal for the victors. No other women among the captives had the heart to do so, but I was glad to find occupation for my hands in helping her. I had to understand what mistake had happened in my *shaytan's* message to bring me to this pass. Was this command to travel to Khaybar my own satanic verse, come in a false form first to try the prophet's faith? If so, when would my reworked, my true, meaning be revealed?

Zaynab squatted beside a stone thrown by her people's catapult that had, in the end, accomplished nothing. On that stone, she sharpened a knife.

"Do you know the tales of my namesake, Queen Zaynab?" she asked me as *swish, swish* she sharpened the blade.

I suggested I might sharpen the blade for her.

"I'll do it myself," she replied. "I want it done right."

I was relieved. I worried I might not be able to control myself with something sharp in my hand that might be turned on the Messenger. Or upon myself. My heart twirled in such a turmoil of fear and confusion of betrayal and loathing against Khalid ibn al-Walid and all his Muslims, against my faithless *shaytan*, against myself if I had misunderstood him and betrayed my own life in this manner.

"Tell me the stories of Queen Zaynab," I asked her then, although every puff of desert wind knew the tales.

Curiosity, too, made me anxious to hear the Jewess's words since her namesake, Queen Zaynab, was not a figure from her own people's past such as Esther or Deborah.

All the Arabs claimed Zaynab as an ancestress.

"She had, you know, blue eyes, just like yours." Zaynab went on in rhythm to her sharpening—which was not the rhythm of the black muezzin Bilal.

Now that she was a woman, Rayah knew her hands should always be busy, either with a pestle or a spindle. She had picked up spinning of her own as she sat and listened to her mother tell the story.

"Spin tighter," Sitt Sameh instructed her daughter's inexpert hands before going on. "And the ancient queen of the Arabs dwelt in Tadmor, this very town at the edge of the desert where you and I now sit, *ya* Rayah mine."

Sitt Sameh added thoughtfully before returning to the tale, "Which is why, when I had to find haven, I came here."

Zaynab bint al-Harith, the Jewish cook, stood up, her sharpening done. With firm steps that would have set her bangles jangling—if any such jewelry had been left to her as a captive—she strode to Ali ibn Abi Talib, the young commander, Muhammad's cousin and son-in-law.

His hand went to the double-bladed sword at his side. The Muslims with him, just finished with their thanksgiving prayers, squared their shoulders and stepped between this commander and the approaching kitchen knife.

"O Father of al-Hassan," she said with all politeness and with a sudden smile that made the men relax. "I hope you will kill a sheep or a goat for me from those you have taken as plunder from my people, the best of the flock for your honored master. You will kill it according to your rules of sacrifice. All the men who sacrificed for my people are dead."

"Of course, *ya ammi*." Ali ibn Abi Talib smiled, safe in his victory. He reached for the knife, its edge brighter than the rest of the blade with keen sharpening.

"And tell me, too," Zaynab stopped the young man, half turned to carry out the task, "what part of the animal does your father-in-law and master prefer, that I may take extra care with that portion?"

"The forelegs," Ali ibn Abi Talib said, and went to find the flocks.

Zaynab nodded, as pleased as if she'd heard news of her delivery, and went back to the cooking.

I helped Zaynab bint al-Harith pound the onions, garlic, salt and herbs to coat the skinned flesh, slipping slivers of garlic under the veil-like fell with the point of the knife. While we worked, she came around to tell me something of her namesake, Queen Zaynab.

"Zaynab—Queen Zaynab—was the daughter of the king of Tadmor."

Sitt Sameh spun and told her tale.

The confusion of names, the layering of name upon name, may have been with the old captive Jewish cook as it was with Sitt Sameh now, the listening girl thought.

Sitt Sameh seemed to be doing it on purpose, poetically, for she admitted, "The same sort of rhythm with which she had sharpened the butchering knife now worked the woman's pestle in its mortar."

Just so the older woman had told it before, just so Sitt Sameh retold it now. The palms of Tadmor waved in the night wind below them, rustling.

Rayah shivered, and it was not the wind. She had heard the stories of Queen Zaynab before, as she had heard the rustle. What child had not? Never had it come to her this powerfully, however. Jinn were in that wind along with the smell of water in the canals and spirits of those who had gone before.

Rayah had been born and lived all her thirteen years in Tadmor. She had played among the fallen pillars of Queen Zaynab's palace; she had seen the lifelike carvings from those ancient times used as bench slabs in the baths. The ancient queen herself had probably bathed in those same tanks, seen the ancestors of these same plantations, the same naked mountains beyond.

The royal woman of ancient times—like Rayah, like her mother—had had blue eyes. And thus must have shared her royal blood with them. Under Islam, blood no longer meant what once it had, but the eyes meant the same. Queen Zaynab must have made her own deals with the jinn and their power, too.

Like layers of an onion, pounded in the Jewess Zaynab's mortar in the ruins of her defeated fortress, the story, its telling and retelling, wrapped Rayah's core over and over.

Pounded onions gave excuse for the tears to run unheeded down both our cheeks, mine and Zaynab the Jewess's, there beneath the ruins of Khaybar.

"Jadhima king of al-Hira killed Zaynab's father, the king of Tadmor," said Zaynab the Jewess. "So Zaynab the queen plotted her revenge. She offered her hand to the king of al-Hira. 'To unite and strengthen both our realms,' read the message she sent him.

"King Jadhima came, crossing the desert at her bidding, and welcomed the warm bath the queen had prepared for him. Zaynab's most trusted maidservant waited upon him there. The maidservant gave him mulled wine in his bath and then, with the knife she used to pare his figs, she opened his veins while the drug in the wine lulled him gently in the warm water.

"Queen Zaynab, for all she was a woman, had her revenge!"

The spinning stopped. The story stopped.

"Isn't there more?" Rayah asked. "Did not Zaynab then become a victim of revenge herself from Jadhima's heirs? Didn't they betray her to the Romans and—and a bitter end in chains rather than bracelets?"

"That is where Zaynab the Jewess ended her story. That is where I will end it now," Sitt Sameh said. "For the onions were well pounded then with the herbs."

"Now is the time to rub the goat before we thread it on the spit." That was Zaynab the Jewess's excuse to end the tale there. "Let us not keep our conquerors waiting. You do it, child. Take a handful, rub it well into the fat, into the creases."

I did as she bade me, onion juice stinging the raw cracks in my fingers from the deprivations of life under siege.

"But not the forelegs," she said.

"Muhammad's favorite portion?" I asked. "Should that not be the most flavorful?"

"I will attend to that myself."

From her skirts, she produced a fine alabaster jar. When she pulled out the stopper, I saw that it was filled with cinnabar, that powdered mineral the color of burnt brick such as a woman might dust on her face to give it life. I was surprised. How had some one of our conquerors not found that treasure and added it to his own pile of booty to take back to al-Medinah for his wives or daughters? Stranger still, why would this woman, her menfolk only just buried, think to paint her face? But why would she make a fine meal for the murderers of her family in the first place? I hadn't puzzled that question out, either.

When Zaynab the Jewess shook out as much cinnabar as might well beautify a dozen faces into the last little bit of pounded onion I'd left her, curiosity loosed my tongue. "But Auntie." My eyes widened as she spread her mixture on the goat's forelegs. "Isn't that cinnabar you pounded in last of all?"

"Indeed it is."

"Cinnabar? A poison? Women are always warned not to let vanity injure their health."

"Ah, and so you have proven yourself a prophetess, my little Blue Eyes," said the Jewess of Khaybar. "Now we must see if this Muhammad of Mecca has the same gift." And she laid a finger to her lips to encourage my silence.

The goat was roasted to perfection, the flesh melting off the bones and running with flavorful juices, and presented to the conquerors. "*Bismillah,*" they called God's blessing down upon the meal.

Then all the men put forth their hands and ate, including a Muslim named Bishr ibn al-Bara who had a place of honor at Muhammad's side and who ate quickly with great hunger. More slowly, Muhammad put a morsel of the foreleg in his mouth, then immediately spat it out.

"Take your hands away from this food," he announced. "Jabra'il has revealed to me that it is poisoned."

Muhammad's vomiting kept Khalid ibn al-Walīd from giving me away as a bride that night.

They brought Zaynab bint al-Harith the Jewess before Muhammad on his rugs and cushions and asked if they should kill her, stone her as a witch.

"Why did you do it, woman?" he asked with surprising gentleness.

Why? Why, when her husband, father and sons lay newly dead? Zaynab the Jewess had more reason than her namesake the Queen of Tadmor to seek blood price.

Zaynab did not cringe but looked the ailing man straight in the eye. "To see if you were indeed a prophet."

"Let the Jewess live," said the compassionate Messenger of God. "Her faith has saved her."

Bishr ibn al-Bara died that night; he is known for no more than this, and that God's Messenger survived.

8

When what you want doesn't happen,
learn to want what does.
—An Arab proverb

Rayah thought of her friend Ghusoon as her mother's story went on to the next scene. Ghusoon had all but stopped breathing with horror when she thought her future was the bed of Sharif Diya'l-Din, and she saw no way out of it.

My mother and I are made of sterner stuff, Rayah thought. At least—she was when she was young, as her story tells. And I have gone from the sharif to an even more threatening marriage proposal: one far from home and with Abd ar-Rahman's son. What should I do instead of inaction? I am desperate to learn what my mother did.

And yet, after the events of this tale she spun, Sitt Sameh had chosen to come to this live burial on the third floor of the turpentine sellers' house.

I cannot live a life like hers. I will not. Rayah twisted her mind as tight as she twisted the thread of her spinning.

But what did her coiled thoughts mean? Which part of her mother's life was unacceptable? Would Rayah ever attack the prophet or his followers with poison so? God forbid! But was denying her gifts and hiding from life in a third-floor tent for a dozen years the only other way to live?

Sitt Sameh spun and Rayah spun. And Sitt Sameh told the story and Rayah listened, uninterrupted.

The first of three nights on the journey from Khaybar to al-Medinah, once Muhammad had recovered enough from the cinnabar poisoning to travel, the Muslims halted at the wells of Thamad. Here stood a few wind-twisted palms at the tawny edge of the massive lava field that pockmarked the earth with crater-topped mountains like bubbles in cooking halwah turned to stone.

The red leather tent they pitched for Muhammad there, once the pavilion of the great God Hubal, was named my marriage tent. How many brides have felt as constrained by family and duty as I was in fact? A slave's leather thongs bound me to the center pole. I had, after all, been implicated in the poisoning of the victors' meat, although not so much as to make Muhammad change his mind that I was the prize of Khaybar he wanted for himself. Still, trussed like a sheep in the market, I awaited Islam's prophet to finish his business and come to claim me as a conqueror's right.

That Khalid ibn al Walīd had been the one with the nerve to tie the thongs, telling me his madness: "I will see my daughter safe and in the Prophet's harem."

I had pulled away from the touch of such a man—he couldn't be my father—but to no avail. His departure—flushed and sorrowful yet determined he was doing his best for me, leaving me alone—was my only cause to rejoice.

"Is the poetess-kahinah to be his bride, join his other wives as the ninth Mother of the Believers? Or will she merely be his slave and concubine, as is his right by conquering this rebellious and unbelieving people?" One man-at-arms speculated to another in almost the same words as my thoughts while the pair of them passed within my hearing outside the leather wall.

"If he has her wear the hijab, veiled from view like his other wives, that will tell us," his companion replied. "If her face is open to view, we'll know she's to be a slave like any other."

I could have stilled the man's curiosity. Although I hadn't known there were options, Muhammad had had a length of cloth brought for me to put on. It was more like the anonymous veils of Christians than the coin- and shell-heavy emblems of honor and pride grown women wore in the desert to show off, guardians of their families' wealth and honor.

I hadn't put it on yet. I wanted to do nothing my captor had in store for me. At that moment, from my point of view, "slave" sounded better than "wife." A wife is supposed to have her husband's interests at heart; no such demands are made upon a slave, who might at least hope to earn her freedom. The time where choice was left to me, however, could hardly be longer than one round of Muslim prayer.

Something scratched at the back of the tent. I jumped, pulling the thongs binding my wrists until blood came. An animal? Or was it Muhammad? Why would God's Messenger come at a bride like that?

Saffiyah unfolded herself from beneath the tent flap.

"Oh, my friend!" Trying to run to her, I yanked my restraints again.

Saffiyah put a finger to her lips, urging me to silence. In two strides, she was beside me, plucking at the knots of my bonds. Her own skin and blood still clogged her nails from how she'd scratched her beautiful face and chest in her grief.

When I was free, I stood dumbfounded, rubbing my wrists. "Muhammad will find you here," I warned.

"Yes. But not you."

Back at the rear wall, she lifted the flap to give me the idea.

On my knees, ready to crawl out into the night, I said, "You will come with me, of course."

She shook her head.

"We'll have to steal only one camel, I think. One can carry us both."

She shook her head again. How quiet these captive women were! When I'd first known Saffiyah, the slightest movement of her head would have set her necklaces and earrings jangling. Now, the gesture was soundless, her throat and earlobes empty, and her finger once more to her lips, begging silence.

"Muhammad chose me, not you," I insisted. "He wants to control my poetry, whether the body it comes from has grown to womanhood yet or not. And that monster Khalid— One look at you will betray us both and cut down on my time to escape."

Saffiyah gave yet another sign for silence then picked up the wife's veil I had neglected. Once she'd put it on, in the darkened tent, Muhammad would not notice the slight differences in our height and maturity until the marriage was consummated. Then it would be too late for him to save face. As Zaynab had suggested with her ruse, making Muhammad prove himself a prophet who was able to see through the devices of men—and particularly women—was necessary for God's Messenger.

"But I cannot leave you to this fate, my good friend." I made one last attempt to sway her.

"What is ever a woman's fate?" Saffiyah asked. "We must marry someone, and all the men of my people are gone. Besides—"

From her skirts she pulled an alabaster jar I recognized. I had seen it pulled from other skirts just recently.

"Friends prepare a woman for her marriage," she said, and I knew she thought of Zaynab. She dipped a feather into the powder and brushed it upon her cheeks herself. "And as Muhammad's wife, I will take my turn with the others preparing his meals, won't I?"

"Indeed you will."

Scrambling back, I gave her one more embrace before escaping out into the night.

On silent feet, I passed the place where black Bilal, a sideline to his duties as muezzin, was laying out the Prophet's wedding feast on a bare camel skin upon the desert floor. Here were dates and dried yogurt and butter. Khalid ibn al-Walīd was there, overseeing and complaining that he would not marry off a daughter without meat. "Too poor a wedding for my honor, let alone the Prophet's!" But it would be a while yet until Muhammad attempted meat again. I felt my *shaytan* with me, concealing me from the men's eyes in the dark.

Once I'd stolen the camel from the many herds taken from the Jews at Khaybar,

I turned its nose toward the lava fields. That would be harder going, but our prints would not show.

9

And say, "O Lord, these are people who do not
believe." Bear with them and wish them "Peace." In the
end they shall know their folly.
   —The Holy Quran 43:88–89

When you meet the unbelievers, strike off their heads;
then when you have made wide slaughter among them,
carefully tie up the remaining captives.
   —The Holy Quran 47:4

"**M**aster," *I said to God's Messenger where he sat in the mosque in al-Medinah, "will you not take my daughter to wife? Other men have sealed their submission to you in this fashion."*

It went without saying. Even with everything Islam was doing to undermine traditional clan and tribe, a man's daughter in another, powerful man's bed continued to be the time-honored way to catch and keep his ear. Abu Bakr had given Muhammad his Ayesha and my fawning cousin Omar his Hafsa. I had succumbed to the new belief later than these men, so I must not miss a single opportunity to catch up with their influence.

The Prophet smiled a patient little smile, whisking flies away with a palm frond. "We tried that once already, Abu Sulayman, did we not?" At least he still awarded me with my honorific name. "With the girl with the blue eyes. Yes, together we might have made a dynasty of blue-eyed prophets, I might at least have had one son who lived—but it will be as God wills. Instead, she connived her escape, exchanging herself for that sullen Jewess by ruses I, as the Messenger of God, should not have had to cover."

Muhammad wouldn't have said this had any other man been present. He meant it as a reflection on me, on my lack of faith. My lack of faith in him, I suppose it was. My faith in another had been justified, although not in myself.

"To save face, I've got to keep the Jewess now, God give me strength." Muhammad rubbed the henna covering the gray in his beard, thicker now than ever. "That girl you said was yours, although nobody else seems convinced she was anything more than an orphaned captive. Why would you want to claim her? Are you mad, jinn possessed?" Here the Prophet threw a spear of words with deadly accuracy, straight at my heart. "A captive with a tongue and an evil spirit, both of which would need sharp curbing, like a willful camel with the reins threaded through his nose."

The Prophet of God sighed. "Inshallah. It will be as God, not I, wills."

The thought of that girl turned my stomach. I fought the reaction. Was it misbelief on my part? The Prophet was right, of course. What other way were women to be handled?

"I have other daughters," I suggested.

But we both knew, between us, I had only one daughter. God's Messenger even said it, "That is the only daughter of Khalid ibn al-Walīd I want," with a flick of his frond. A daughter who had given the Prophet of God the slip and forced him to accept a woman as a political match even though all of her menfolk were conquered and dead. That event went a long way, I knew, to undoing all the proofs of faithfulness I'd managed when I'd destroyed the shrine at Nakhlah.

"Well, that Jewess is a good cook after all," he mused in a divinely forgiving mood.

"With your permission, O Apostle of God, I will go and find the one with blue eyes. I will bring her back to you, reforge our deal. I'm certain I know where she's fled."

Where else would she have gone alone—for the jinn would not let their own perish in the desert—but back to my milk brothers and the tribe of her misbegotten birth?

"I should hope a man knows where to find his daughter," the Prophet suggested, blessings on him. "As the Angel Jabra'il revealed to me, 'Men. . .spend out of their wealth' to support women, so we are responsible for their care."

The reproach stung, even if he had not meant it so. How could a man claim a daughter if he had not cared for her? No doubt she would lose her wild ways and quiet her rebellious jinni if she had caretakers she could trust. In this I had failed. And I blamed my milk brothers. They had failed.

"I mean to amend this, as conversion makes me amend all behavior from my time of ignorance," I assured the Prophet. "I beg you, give me leave to go to the Tamim now, where I have milk kin, and find her."

"Your milk kin have not yet converted to God's revealed word."

"True, O Apostle of God. Perhaps, with God's help, I may preach something *while I am there to convert them."*

Muhammad sniffed skeptically. "If God should will it." He again stroked his hennaed beard. "Between us and the dirah of your milk kin lie the tribes of Hawazin and Thakif, also stiff necked."

"Our caravans have always had safe passage at their wells. I do not fear to pass them."

"There is commerce, and there is God's community. Those tribes have not submitted. They do not pay God's tax."

I swallowed and nodded. The truth could come from the Prophet's mouth in short, simple sentences. The road to the Tamim lay through these tribes' conversion. "How many faithful Muslim men-at-arms will you lend me for this excursion, O Mouthpiece of God?"

"Fear not. I myself will come with you."

I swallowed again. I was very afraid.

"Afraid? Of what?" My scribe stops his scratching in puzzlement.

How can I stop to explain my fear? Deep in my soul, I understood that the presence of God's Messenger would hinder any negotiation between his firm-set lines of revelation and the blowing dust of the tribes. I could have done it on my own. I had once licked a white-hot blade and brought about reconciliation in the traditional manner. But these were new, uncompromising ways, and his presence would hold them stiff against the tribal necks.

While he himself followed with ten thousand faithful Muslims, Muhammad, blessings on him, gave me the charge of leading the advance guard. I had about two thousand men, most of them newly submitted but hardly converted Meccans. The lesson we were meant to learn, I suspect, was that inspiration and foresight moved with God's Messenger. Riding from the ruins of Nakhlah, which gave me sunstroke to look at, we entered the Way of Nakhlah. The opening to this gorge was about a quarter day's ride in width, but after a while it narrowed to only twenty paces or so.

There, I was stupid enough to ride into an ambush. The tribes we had set out to conquer had gained swift-blowing wind of our coming.

As my forces bunched together in faithless chaos, I received a wound in the thigh—a long groove now—transfixed to my horse's side by a Hawazin arrow shot from the rocks above. My horse squealed and rolled down on top of me.

As the enemy horses and camels pounded over my head, I heard the Thakif battle cry: "Revenge and glory for the Queen of Nakhlah!" At the sound of that name, my new-Muslim men deserted me, for they knew whose hand had destroyed that shrine they still held sacred. Myself, I felt the creeping black void of my madness come over me. This time I welcomed it as a relief from the pain; I slept in its warm arms as if my milk mother had given me the breast again.

I would have been content to lose that battle at Hunain. Granted, because of my vow on the Day of Dhu Qar—I would win every battle or die in the attempt— that would have meant my death. I could have accepted it then. I welcomed the blackness, as I have said, like a mother's arms.

But Muhammad and the Muslims came and found me lying there. He had his companions drag away my horse and extract the arrow. Then he himself blew upon my wounds with that same healing breath that brought forth the Holy Quran. The darkness faded and became a glaring, painful light. God is great, and I blinked and grew used to the garishness of my life. I rose to lead, fight and win again that very day.

I nursed that wound throughout the siege of at-Ta'if to which shelter we drove the enemy tribes. There, the cold and damp leaked through the broken skin and made my very bone ache like cold water on a rotten tooth. I continued to wear dressings and to lose blood from time to time throughout the months that followed. And, obeying the Prophet's orders, I forgot that my first goal in coming this way had been to reach my milk family, Mutammim and Malik and the girl they sheltered.

Islam was growing as a flash flood does, carrying everything with it, and it left me no time to be invalid. We marched north and subdued Ayla, Jarba, Azruh and Makna. Then came Dumat al-Jandal, then south to Najran and to the Yemen. My days formed one long, continuous march, relieved only by the battles and the plunder-taking, and then by the treatying and the collection of tribute. It was a driving, exciting time to be alive, and I had no desire (for I let my mind sink no deeper) than to be a Muslim at war and to tell the tales of war about the campfire.

Now, in my old age, I find such soldiers' tales a waste of what precious little breath is left to me. Then, when I was younger, I took my time going to my milk brothers again. And that was what, I had told myself, I'd converted for: to be free to come and go in the desert as once before.

Except for the brief excursion south to Najran and the Yemen, my conquests were taking me in the general direction of the Tamim. I was conquering the self-same people who had been my hosts on many a cross-desert drive. Conquering takes a little more time than passing through with a caravan; that fact did not make me anxious. Fighting for Islam kept me fully occupied in body and, if it did not quite satisfy my spirit, well, I didn't have time for that.

I never stopped to think what it meant, that the day would come when the borders of a swelling Islam would brush against those of my milk family. Nor did I consider that the violence on which I thrived would be no respecter of my personal milk relationships.

Then, suddenly, it happened. No time remained for me to pay the Tamim a friendly call, to warn them gently of the possible danger ahead, nor to try to justify my position to them.

Our first blow against the Tamim did not fall upon my milk brothers' clan. We attacked the sons of al-Anbar who depended upon Malik for their protection; in that way, they were almost my brothers.

The Banu 'l-Anbar had been camping at the Lake of al-Ashtat with certain clans of the Khuzala tribe. The Khuzala had submitted to Islam (as they had earlier submitted to Qurayshi control of the Ka'ba) and promised to pay the tax. When Muhammad's agent came to collect a tenth of all their goods, he tried to collect from the members of the Tamimi tribe as well.

But they refused, rattling their arms and saying, "Who is this Muhammad that we should send him even so much as a sack of dung? By al-Uzza, we are free sons of Tamim and owe no man allegiance."

Muhammad heard the news with anger and sent a force to teach the Banu 'l-Anbar the fear of God, of His Messenger, and the insolence of such an answer. Before my milk brother Malik could send his clients aid, before I could get the news at Dumat al-Jandal where I was stationed, before I could try to turn this violent wave, the Khuzala had been attacked and beaten. Those who could had escaped into the desert. Eleven men, however, eleven women and thirty children were carried captive back to Mecca.

Such were the facts as I received them. But rumors, thick and heart-pounding, of what the Tamimi retaliation might be accompanied that news. I knew Malik would retaliate. He must, and for honor's sake win back his clansmen, their wives and their children. I did not know which side I ought to join, but I knew I must waste no more time before deciding.

This time I asked no leave of the Prophet. I left my men holding the pass near Dumat al-Jandal, our furthest penetration north, and rode alone along the desert coast eleven days to the Lake of al-Ashtat, where the Khuzala defeat had occurred.

10

"Did the poets leave no tune to sing of?"
—The qasidah of Antar ibn Shaddad

Toward evening, I rode down the wadi from Usfan, the place of the winter floods, to the lake. The first rains of the season were more than a month away, and al-Ashtat was not a lake as those here in Syria understand "lake" at all. The fertile imagination of one familiar with the desert was required to turn the mud pan into the sheet of shimmering water that earned this valley its name.

The water had retreated from the heat into one or two slight depressions, and here alone could a man tell how popular the place was for camping. The feet of flocks and herds made no impression on the lake bed. Only at the waterholes lay mud and not seeming stone. Here, animals looking for drink had sunk in up to their hocks and left the surroundings as pitted as the pox had left my face. A mass the color and texture of camel liver went by the name of "water" at that season.

And yet, by the numbers of tents and animals spreading like a thousand dainties over the platter that was the valley, al-Ashtat might have been an oasis. It might have been a small portion of Syria transplanted halfway down the Red Sea.

What was the reason for "the shores'" sudden great favor with the tribes? Cracks four fingers wide and a full span deep scarred the dried mud.

All Tamim was gathered there, letting the scene of the recent outrage serve as a goad to their revenge.

"What man are you?" a sentry stopped me as I approached. More security than such large numbers all of one kin would usually require, and while light still held.

"Kin to Malik ibn Nuwaira, as al-Uzza is my witness."

I carefully did not say "milk kin," but this was not a complete lie. I worked to keep more of the desert I had learned as a child in my speech than the citified accent I had affected since becoming a man. I also didn't lower the end of my turban I had passed across my nose and mouth, but the dust of such a crowd of men and beasts explained that. The young fellow took me at my goddess-bolstered word, *never thinking what perjury one God could devise.*

Any number of other men were pleased to show the new arrival the exact hillock where this or that great hero had made his last stand and fallen to Muslim treachery. My guides paused a moment before the spot where the tent of such and such virtuous woman had been surrounded and violated, the woman and her children carried into slavery. The deeds and losses were already taking the form of poetry, for the Tamim have always been known for their great poets.

Speech takes this form when emotions grow too heavy for the plodding tongue of prose to bear. Such was the power of our Arabian poetry in those days, a magic that fertilized and made the dust of the desert bloom like roses in a carefully tended Persian garden.

I was uncomfortable enough at these testimonies to my factions' dishonor to invent justifications—"Well, they would do the same to us"—although I didn't express them aloud.

I saw no sign of Malik's clan, but I did not hesitate to ride on in and couch my camel. This, even though I was a Qurayshi and a Muslim, and my people were responsible for the seething anger in the encampment. The Sons of Tamim were not converted. They would still follow the ancient laws of hospitality. And an armed man alone could only have come to help their numbers. I pulled the corner of my turban tighter across my face as a precaution anyway.

The great sharif's tent, seven broad strips of cloth wide, sideless so the walls would not set any limits on who could be present, was already full. I managed to wedge my body between two others in the shade only because the sun was setting and shadows reached from one end of the lake bed to the other.

"Praise the Gods," I said cautiously to my nearest neighbor. If Muhammad had been near, I would have died for my apostasy. "The sons of Tamim are like the stars. Muhammad should only see this war council."

"Not a war council," my neighbor replied. "We will not waste our arrows on the Muslims. We will challenge and beat Muhammad with his own weapon: the slinging darts of great inspired poetry."

"The Tamim were afraid!" my scribe interrupts triumphantly. "The great cowards. Too afraid to engage the armies of Muhammad, blessings on him, on the battlefield."

"Not at all."

"Then that Tamimi heaping scorn was no more than the passing of gas."

"This, too, is not so, my friend. You do not understand what poetry was for us in those days. In those days before the Quran came to be the words no one can defeat or even aspire to, a contest between poets was the field of the greatest, most divine honor. The Tamim sought to engage al-Medinah in a battle that would win them more glory than a thousand Muslim heads. They sought an eternity that outlasts any corroding wood and metal. Challenging Muhammad to such a duel dispensed with all the useless preliminaries. Everyone knew that the power to curse the other side and praise one's own with inspired words was the victory of any battle anyway, arm the two sides as you would."

"Deluded time of ignorance," the boy—and that is all he is—says.

I sigh and press on with my tale.

Suffice it to say, my desert heart began to throb like the beat of heat waves at the prospect. I gave no one my name and hoped none would recognize me.

"I don't see the Banu Yarbu clan of the Tamim," I said to my neighbor after another little while, for to sit and say nothing would be questioned. Also, the lack of my milk brothers made me more anxious than I cared to reveal. On the one hand, their absence gave me relief: A mere turban across my nose would not disguise me from them. They knew me since childhood even by my footprints alone. On the other hand, I might need to claim their protection in any moment.

"They have a great poet in the person of Mutammim ibn Nuwaira, brother of the sharif Malik," I tried to explain to the look the man gave me, keener than I thought necessary. "I have had the honor to hear him myself."

"There is no sign of the Banu Yarbu, no. They may not be able to send a delegation. Their pastures are so far removed from the lake at this season. We may have to choose our champion without Ibn Nuwaira."

Yes, that made sense, but gave me little comfort.

Within the cool of that tent's shadow, my wits revived from the stupefying heat of the day. Within that sanctuary, from the sharifs and great ones sitting on their cushions in the center to the common herdsmen among whom I sat, the men spoke not of Islam. The pressing search for water, the pursuing specter of hunger, the demands of their blood feuds, these, too, they ignored. The men spoke, when they spoke, of nothing but poetry. Anticipation and reverence weighted their tongues, stung the corners of their eyes. It made them strain to listen rather than to talk so they would not miss the very first verse when it flew.

I supposed things were much the same among the women gathered in shadows around us, for, if one heard them at all, it was to hush their children. They'd banished the usual shrill and rowdy gossip. All waited for the evening to begin, for the poets to open their mouths. The competition that would last far into the night would end with the greatest singled out to march into al-Medinah to defend the tribal honor with his words.

The competition began from the audience itself, as naturally as had it been a fever, without introduction or ceremony. One man turned to his neighbor and recited. His neighbor replied in kind. Slowly, as the better and better voices began to recite, conversation in other parts of the tent receded. Attention, of its own free will and without pomposity, riveted to the one who spoke.

Great were the deeds the sons of Tamim could boast of, and great were the tongues that did the boasting.

While a broad base of competition still held sway, I considered reciting something myself. I have a passing voice and I had strained since early childhood to catch something of the intonation and the sort of whir affected in their throats by the best of poets.

"And you, master, had heard Muhammad recite," says my scribe. "Muhammad, blessed be he, the Seal of all prophets and poets. You could have recited some of the Holy Quran and silenced them all."

"I could have, but I did not."

I knew a poetical introduction by heart. I had adapted it during the quiet of my long desert rides from one of az-Zibrikan's that spoke of "my love's deserted encampment by the brink of al-Kaid." That would capture interest and fellow feeling as only songs of lost love can. After that, I could have given quite an honorable piece, at least as good as those that were passing now. Meter and rhyme come naturally to one who has swung for any amount of time upon the back of a camel.

But there, sitting among the sharifs, was the great poet himself, az-Zibrikan ibn Badr of the Banu Said clan of Tamim. He was a reverend gentleman of the desert whom age had not yet hunched. He received honor for a fine, strong body as well as for his white hair and sparse, pointed beard. Few people give others so many reasons to honor them, and az-Zibrikan knew it. From time to time he would fold his arms across his chest with great pomp. I had the impression that this solemn ritual constituted the man's gesture of prayer. But it soon became obvious that he was merely reaching up to pull his cloak back upon his shoulders when it slipped off.

Many of the first poets to speak thought nothing of padding their own doggerel with the old man's lines right there in his presence. Az-Zibrikan did not mind, but took the imitation as compliment. He smiled and nodded at the applause to take his due. For my part, I did not feel like giving my clan such secondhand compliment.

Besides, I had to remind myself that in this strange new world, I had to keep my presence and identity unknown. Malik still hadn't arrived and, without his pledge of kinship, I might very well be taken for a spy under these circumstances.

But what else was I, really? I meant to warn my milk brothers of the danger they were in. But if I learned something here of danger to Islam, would I tell Muhammad?

I hate to lose. I hate to die.

I hate being dishonorable.

I remained silent.

Finally, when it had grown dark enough for the leap of fire to stand in contrast to the shades of deepening gray all around, my milk brothers entered the circle of firelight. They took the places their status had reserved for them, far from me. Relief to see them did not make me rise to greet them at once. I could only guess the forced speed of their march from the pinch of their faces and the dust upon their clothes.

My neighbor sighed with contentment. So did others. They did not interrupt the poetry to mention it, but they were almost as relieved as I to see the new arrivals. I would have a chance to see and speak with my milk brothers, to claim their protection even though I was a Muslim. The rest of the tent rejoiced because blind Mutammim would give us poems that would do them credit.

I did not make my presence known to Malik and Mutammim at once because that would mean shoving in there among all the sharifs where I would have to prove that I belonged. Even with the protection of the sons of Nuwaira, I might have trouble proving I was neither traitor nor spy to the tribe in general. The last few poems had all dealt with the recent attack, inflaming the spirits of many.

Malik was bursting with a new poem his long ride had helped him to compose. He insisted on being allowed to speak it at once. Mutammim had always been a better poet than his brother the sharif; well, he had given the jinn his eyes as a child. No one, however, gainsaid Malik.

The Fire Spirits had given him a humorous piece of the sort mediocre poets often produce. I would have chuckled once in my beard along with the rest and then forgotten the little ditty as if it had never been spoken. Except that the tale he told in such a ribald fashion was the tale of how they had happened to make the journey to al-Ashtat in spite of the distance.

What reality I caught between joke lines suggested that Malik had decided the whole clan could not travel so far across uncertain lands with uncertain wells. Leaving women and children and flocks unguarded at that raiding time of the year was also out of the question. Except that one of his dependents had insisted.

He didn't say so directly; what man would? But by metaphors—"From behind," "Whispers from an enclosed garden," "The voice of moonlight on the sand"—I knew he meant the insistence had come from the harem. The final line of the poem was in the form of a riddle: "Tell me now, what greater fool is there than a sharif who listens to his women?"

Though Malik left the riddle unanswered, the poem satisfied the hearers. It did not, however, satisfy me. Puzzled and wondering, I hardly heard the next poem at all, my other milk brother, Mutammim, making a very somber eulogy on the death of their father Nuwaira. It could rouse the men of Tamim to fight even after all these years. Tears in the eyes of my neighbor who had never even known the great old sharif of the Banu Yarbu announced that it far outranked Malik's ditty. I am sorry I missed it. Nuwaira had been like a father to me, and I should have liked to shed a tear or two for him. But hidden meanings behind Malik's verses kept my mind consumed elsewhere.

I knew who that "voice of moonlight on sand" must be: the daughter I had neglected, like her mother I had lost. And the daughter, my *daughter, must now be here on the dry lake bed of al-Ashtat.*

11

Let him give to the females before the males, for whoever brings joy to a female is like crying out for fear of God, and he who cries out for fear of God will be safeguarded by God from the Fire.

—A hadith of the Prophet related by Anas

One evening a week or so after Rayah's first women's blood ceased, her protective cousin Kefa came into the harem with the other boys to carry the dinner trays out to the *majlis*. Abd ar-Rahman, the son of Khalid the Conqueror, still lingered there with his Persian servant, requiring the meat due a guest in guest-sized portions. The honey jar would need to be scraped to make pastries and the baskets of dates emptied.

"So now there will be no more discussion, I hope," Kefa said, as hard as stone. "Rayah will give this governor the bloody sword, go with him to al-Medinah and marry his son, finally. We will have the powerful connection to sell our turpentine. It will heal wounds and cancers as far away as Mecca and al-Medinah, for I'm sure even in the holy cities people suffer from such ailments."

"*Ya* Kefa, hush," urged Auntie Adilah. "It will be as God wills, even for you. And even for a Conqueror's son who makes himself a guest for months on end."

"Yes, and what will you do if Rayah does not go with the guest?" young Bushra teased her older cousin Kefa.

"Well, I'm not going to marry her," the boy insisted. "She's not my real cousin, after all."

Bushra might have held her tongue, but since her injury and miraculous recovery, everyone in the household indulged her. "And why would she want you? She must listen first to the Fire Spirits."

Rayah herself took Bushra's hand and squeezed it hard to try to stem her. The saucy girl only squeezed back, harder. And Kefa, as he hefted yet another tray of shingled bread to his shoulder, called back. "Well, then I give her to the jinn. See if that suits her."

Even as he said it, the wick in the lamp at the turn of the stairs slipped into its oil. It went out with an angry hiss and a twist of stinking smoke.

Instead of chuckling off the words as a jest, all the women sucked in breath. The brash boy hadn't even said "God willing." Adilah made Kefa kiss the amulet around his neck, but then he swaggered off to the safety of his *majlis*.

That night, sleeping on the rugs in her mother's room, Rayah saw the full moon come through the tenting carelessly left furled. To be touched, sleeping, by moonlight was a sure way, as everyone knew, to be possessed by the jinn.

Rayah saw the danger. She wasn't sure, but she thought she was awake. How else could she have seen the danger? And yet she did not rise quickly to pull the thongs and let the curtain down.

Moonlight slicked with silver the still-exposed blade of the Sword of God where it lay beside her on the patterned wool. The moon-drenched soul of the desert breathed hot and heavy upon her. It sucked her breath, filled her mouth with molten sand. It mounded her tiny breasts firm and hard.

The space between her legs misted like a distant mirage. Her hips rocked camel-like over dunes with desire she'd never known before. Then, then a spring burst forth, dry rock struck by a magician's staff. The compulsion to spread her legs she could refuse no more than the driver can turn the camel, two weeks without water, that gets the wind of an oasis in its long nostrils.

And the sword, forged by her grandfather's love to her blue-eyed, jinn-possessed grandmother, rose off the rug. By whose hand, she couldn't say. Only that the jinn were creatures of smokeless fire and could do anything—or nothing.

The hilt entered her, hard and cold, and brought searing pain until the moonlight on its blade shattered into a million stars that filled her womb, expanding like the entire universe.

She'd never been happier.

She'd never been more afraid.

A dream. She told herself that's all it was when she woke with no pain, gasping, with only jinni laughter coursing through the hollow of her ear, laughter like the sound of water where none flowed. Still, Kefa's words echoed there, too. A man of the household had said aloud that he gave her to the jinn.

In the morning, blood stained the sheet. Her mother found it. "Untimely blood?" she asked first.

But her mother knew Fire Spirits, and realization came instantly after. "My daughter, married? The jinni?" She stared at Rayah with a grin so rare, it seemed out of place.

The sheet over one arm, Sitt Sameh stood to fly it from the space in the tenting where the moonlight had entered, fly it for all the town of Tadmor to see. She cupped her other hand before her mouth, preparing to give the high, shrill zaghareet of joy and triumph used when they wanted the world to know, as women did at weddings.

Rayah jumped after her, knocked away the hand and covered her mother's lips.

"Mother, how dare you?" she hissed, trembling at every joint. "You who only wanted to be hidden?"

"But now my daughter is married to One of This Place, and I want the world to know she came to that clan a virgin."

Was ever there a mother who didn't want the world to know, on her daughter's wedding day, what a good job she had done raising the child? Daughters, even, were proud to uphold the honor of their clans.

Rayah, who had let her mother's mouth free to speak those words, slapped her hand over the lips again. She wanted to let the hand fall farther and wring the amulet-encircled neck. "Mother, it was a jinni. He's a jinni. Do you want the world to know that? The world where your half-brother, the son of Khalid, holds sway?"

When Rayah removed her hand, her mother's mouth was set in a line like the silence of a distant desert horizon. "I want Abd ar-Rahman to know he does not control you," she said.

"And that will be less dangerous for you? For me?"

Then Sitt Sameh saw blood also on the naked sword's hilt. Her lips went together in their straight line. She folded the sheet and set it up among the rest of her few sacred belongings, the broken litter, the faded red turban. She insisted on applying salve.

But Rayah kept it in her mind as a dream.

The next afternoon, the turpentine sellers carried the ruins of a young life home, all the way from the rendering camp in the desert. They carried him within the protection of Fatima's silver hand and the lapis lazuli eye, through the harem up to the little tented room on the third floor.

All the while, Rayah clung to the post behind the jasmine vine and wished she could become part of the plant. This horror wasn't happening. Her next thought: No, this wasn't her fault. It couldn't be. She had done nothing.

Between two burly uncles, Kefa lay moaning on a stretcher made of a ladder and a pair of old cloaks.

At least, they told Rayah and her mother it was Kefa. The young man himself was burned beyond recognition. The smell was like fires cooking for the Eid sacrifice mingled with the ever-present fumes of terebinth sap.

The eunuch gathered up his papers and hobbled from the room on his healing leg. Sitt Sameh had put the Conqueror's sword—Rayah's blood still on it—up on her carpet-covered heap of belongings, but she hadn't resheathed it.

"Kefa was stirring the scrape as we rendered it," Uncle Aharon said in a low whisper. "His tunic got soaked with turpentine. We told him to step away, to stay away until he had changed. But a sudden, unnatural wind blew live sparks from the fire. He went up like—"

"He went up like a resin-soaked torch," Uncle Elias concluded.

Rayah saw the event as clearly as if she'd been there herself.

"Did you make the proper offering to the trees?" Auntie Adilah wanted to know. Tears streaming and hands wringing, she had followed the stretcher upstairs. "And was he wearing his amulet?"

Rayah didn't hear the answers to these questions. Nor did she join her mother in reaching for poppy juice and burn salve. A vision of the smoke-haired jinni boy had flickered before Rayah's mind when Uncle Aharon described the shower of sparks. The hair prickled on her arm as the inhuman boy twirled away, burning Kefa, laughing. She remembered how the jinni had laughed the night before. Overhead, the tenting snapped with his mirth once more.

The uncles took their chance to escape the horror, but Adilah did not. She squatted beside her dying nephew. She wanted to take his hand, but any touch there made him whimper with pain. One ankle only did not weep pus coated with dust from the long trudge from the terebinth camp. Auntie Adilah held that. The wonder was that the blackened chest still rose and fell, shuddering with agony.

"Why do you not touch him, Rayah, ungrateful child?" Adilah wept. "Touch him as you did your other cousin Bushra when she slipped and hit her head."

"He will be happy in paradise, Auntie," Rayah murmured. "He was a good Muslim and protected his women. He protected me." Gave me to the jinn, she thought. Taunted them who will not be taunted, no not even by those who say "God willing." "God willing, I will pray for him."

Rayah felt her mother's eyes on her, but she couldn't meet them.

"Paradise? Prayer? What is the girl talking about?" Adilah demanded of the other woman.

How could Adilah deny what was clearly God's will in this matter? Again this gentle, quiet "aunt" of hers was more agitated than Rayah was used to. The woman had been more of a mother to her than Sitt Sameh. Was Adilah crazy, jinn-touched?

Kefa was indeed dying. The whole household would soon beat their breasts and tear their hair in grief. But the demon, not content with the life of this boy, almost seemed to have possessed the woman as well.

"Rayah." Kefa choked her name as if still breathing smoke.

Auntie Adilah quieted for that. "What is it, my pet, my heart?"

"Bracelet."

"A bracelet, my jewel?"

Kefa's voice grew suddenly strong and vibrant. Jinn laden. At the same time, the tenting overhead popped in the wind. "In the niche above my bed. I meant it for my own bride. Take it and give it to Rayah—for her dowry."

"Rayah?" Adilah furrowed her grief-stricken brows in Rayah's direction.

"Cold," came Kefa's own voice as the Fire Spirit left him.

Rayah stretched her hand toward the unrecognizable face on which had once sprouted the beginnings of a beard and now would grow no more. Sitt Sameh's salve swirled there mixed with pus and grit.

"Oh, now you will touch him?" Adilah snapped. "He has bought your duty with a trinket?"

Rayah did not hesitate after that, but laid her hand on the bloodshot and lashless eyes to close them. She felt the life pass from the boy with a shudder. Overhead, the tenting gave a sigh and then popped again.

"Where did dear Kefa get such a thing?" Adilah wanted to know.

Rayah fingered the bracelet—silver, tarnished, but heavy and valuable. She didn't yet care to put it on her wrist with the few cheap bangles a fatherless girl like her had managed to collect in her short life. She knew Kefa was not responsible for this jewelry; he'd probably died thinking nothing of bracelets at all, only pain of which she'd been blessed to relieve him.

The jinni boy. This was his doing. This is what it meant to marry into the clan of the jinn. And this bracelet was meant as his bridal gift to her, the price of the blood that had slaked the thirst of the drawn Sword of God. If she put it on, last night's encounter would become real, no longer just a dream. They would be man—or Fire Spirit, rather—and wife. Demon bride.

But what girl ever got to marry according to her own choice? None. From the talk of the women in the harem, Rayah knew only too well there was something wrong with every man.

None married according to her own wishes but Ghusoon. And that match, too, was the jinn's doing.

"And after she kills him," Adilah went on, "she gets the jewelry?"

"Hush, Auntie," Cousin Falak said, pressing Adilah firmly to her breast. "You know Rayah is just a child. She was nowhere near the rendering fire."

And Rayah dreaded her own strength. How could she learn to control such things? She must.

The turpentine sellers' harem mourned while men alone saw the charred corpse to the clan's tower tomb out in the desert. Sitting in a circle in the main courtyard, their veils drawn close, the women received the condolences of all their neighbors. The best singers improvised praises for the dead boy. Adilah couldn't put her words into poetry, but she would have her say.

Several women laid calming hands on her between the verses, but her grief could not be stemmed.

"My brother was the best of brothers," she intoned.

One death blurred into another in Adilah's grief. All deaths were that of her long-lost brother, but mourning allowed that: one grief to fortify another.

All this while she'd been learning the stories of the Conqueror and of her mother, Rayah realized the world was full of other stories she'd been neglecting. As one woman broke silence, so did another. Adilah told more about Sitt Sameh's arrival than Rayah had ever heard anyone confess before. Sitt Sameh had come as a stranger to this house that had always smelled of turpentine and now smelled of these other spirits, spirits of smokeless fire. And Rayah wasn't sure that her mother, making herself the heroine of her own story, could ever tell this side.

For years, until just recently in fact, Rayah had thought she was the daughter of this dead Yaqub, son of the house, Adilah's brother and Kefa's uncle. All the turpentine sellers' household suggested this was the case. Her mother's tale had begun to suggest to her that she was not, and now Adilah confirmed it.

"Kefa was but a toddler. His parents had died in the plague, as had my husband. I had returned here to my father's house to care for my nephew, my sweet, strong nephew.

"Soldiers of Rum came through Tadmor, throughout all al-Jazirah in fact, looking for men to fight the barbarian invader on the side of the Roman emperor Heraclius. My brother Yaqub— Isa and His Mother Maryam bless him—refused. Innocently blind to what such a call meant, he thought he would take our kegs of turpentine to sell in Aleppo and Damascus as usual."

This was also new, that Adilah, who had kissed Rayah off to her Quran lesson every day, should invoke Christian belief in Isa and Maryam. She even stopped briefly now to cross herself in the Christian manner.

"He was gone longer than usual. This little lad who now lies dead, he missed his uncle. Every day, I prayed for my brother's return. When word came to us that the Muslim barbarians held him captive in the fortress of Shayzar, I prayed harder. When at last he returned safe, with this pregnant woman he called Sameh who now infests our rooftop, I thought my prayers were answered. Little did I know, my brother would immediately turn around and leave her. And she would give birth the very next day to that one I cared for as my own, that one with the accursed eyes."

Rayah flinched.

"He left her at last to take up arms, although he had no experience with any weapon but a terebinth scraper.

"'Take care of them until, Christ willing, I return,' Yaqub made me swear as he packed to leave by early-morning lamplight.

"'Of course I will care for your nephew, your brother's son. I always have. He is like my own.'

"'And the others, too. The woman and her child. Swear to me you will.'

"I swore, but then asked, 'The baby is your daughter then? Do we give her a Christian name?'

"'She is not my daughter. Let the woman name her what she will. But it's for them I fight. I fight for them as if the woman rode before Heraclius's troops upon a sacred white camel.'

"And he was gone, never to return. He fell with so many others at the battle of Yarmuk, may Isa accept his martyred soul into paradise. He left this one who lies here dead an orphan. And now—now see? The cuckoo's chick has kicked the other from the warbler's nest, this demon chick from the Ones of Smoke. Kicked him from life altogether and left him lying dead beneath the nest. I did not have to marry as long as there was his nephew to care for, but now there is nothing left of my beloved brother at all.

"This one—" A trembling finger pointed directly at Rayah's heart. "This one and her mother, I am through with them."

The other women took Adilah into their arms to console her, murmuring that only grief made her say such things, but Rayah scrambled to her feet. She knew she couldn't mourn Kefa with the rest of the household for one more moment.

But she slipped the bracelet on as she went. To remember Kefa? Or her jinni husband?

12

Verily, time is rich in strangeness.
It leaves us a stump and cuts off our head.
It leaves our warriors in obscurity and hits us in our
    heroes: there they are, cold cadavers in their
    shrouds.
Behold, the night and the day in their perpetual
    succession
Keep their youth. Corruption doesn't touch them, but it covers
    the sons of man.
           —Verses of the pre-Islamic poetess al-Khansa

It was like ants crawling in a place I could not scratch, like watching another man's beautiful wife dance, like fasting for Ramadhan with Christians' bread baking in the next court. Just so madly tantalizing of my milk brother Malik to have given us his few verses about a female having brought his clan to the poets' contest at al-Ashtat. I wanted to know all the details. Surely, surely, somewhere here was news of my daughter. Yet the competition went on, other poems demanding that my emotions follow them here and there, to that height and then this.

Now the common voices grew silent. One by one the best poets arose to meet the challenge. And great ones spoke there that night, sitting like a glorious crown upon the forehead of the slovenly and undeserving Lake of al-Ashtat.

Zaid ibn Adi was there. Upon his father's treacherous death, Zaid had taken proper revenge. But for this, he had been forced to flee al-Hira and now lived by his poems in the desert. That night he recited a beautiful piece in praise of his father.

From a long line of poets came Ka'b ibn Zuhair ibn Abi Salma. The Tamim welcomed Ka'b beneath the tent in spite of the fact that he was no son of the tribe at all but of the people of Muzaina. His younger brother Budjair, however, also gifted with poetry, had converted to Islam some two years previously, causing a great and bitter rift within the family. Now, wherever word of poetry being recited against the Prophet arose, there you would find Ka'b ibn Zuhair, venting his spleen with *the best. "O God, spare me from Muhammad's poet-stifling jinn," was his song, for which he received much praise.*

But in the end, az-Zibrikan reverently folded his arms across his chest, hitched up his cloak, and recited the best of all. He had a powerful jinni with whom he discoursed most familiarly on many a lonely desert night. A jinni is a more powerful force for poetry than either anger such as Ka'b's or sorrow such as Zaid's. Az-Zibrikan praised the sons of Tamim and fired their hearts with the following words:

> *We are the nobles, no tribe can equal us.*
> *How many tribes have we plundered?*
> *In time of dearth we feed our meat to the hungry.*
> *When no rain cloud can be seen,*
> *You can see sharifs coming to us from every land,*
> *And we feed them lavishly.*
> *We slaughter fat-humped young camels as a matter of course.*

At the end of every couplet, as the rhymes came unerringly, the tent full of men and the shadowy veils beyond exclaimed together. The exclamations rose, accompanying the poem to its crest like the great swells of sand in the Empty Quarter, commanding equal awe.

"Az-Zibrikan," the men, with one voice, proclaimed when he had finished. "Az-Zibrikan is the natural man to lead the delegation to Mecca. He will turn Muhammad's verses on their heads."

And so it seemed settled. Men at the edges of the assembly had even begun to dissolve back to their own tents, like water from the edges of Lake al-Ashtat. Now is the time, I thought, to meet my milk brothers. I will see them alone for a few words tonight, just to get my presence accepted. There would be plenty of time to ask about my daughter in the morning.

Then Malik spoke above all those private little conversations splintering the sharif's tent. "Brothers. O my brothers, wait. Here comes yet another to challenge az-Zibrikan."

"Another?" murmured the men. "Who?" And even "Challenge az-Zibrikan? Who dares?"

Craning my neck over the rest of the heads, all I saw in the firelight by the side of my two milk brothers was a heap of robe and veil.

"That's not a poet," someone smirked. "It's a woman."

"But women may be poets as well as men," others remarked.

"Indeed, most women are jinn-possessed, are they not?"

"But these will not be jingles for the entertainment of women as they weave. These will have to be mighty poems to take down Muhammad himself."

"In bygone days the Tamim produced one of the greatest of female versifiers, Dahtanus bint Lekit al-Tamimi. She often followed her father and husband into battle to put black spells upon the enemy with her words."

"Yes, I remember hearing Bint Lekit recite when I was a child in my milk mother's harem," I told my nameless neighbor. *"It was a lament for the one time when she had not gone out to battle with her kinsmen, and they had fallen fighting against the great hero Antar."*

Years and frosted hair had not cooled her sorrow. I remembered how she had sung:

> *"Dawn brought the sinister messenger. 'He is dead!' he cried,*
> *'The sharif, the glory of Hindif, whom no strapping*
> *youth, no ancient sage could equal.'*

Ka'b the son of Muzaina, too, said, "I boast as much over my two poetess aunts, Salma and al-Khansa, as I do over my father. The latter of these two sisters was called al-Khansa, 'the Gazelle,' for the fleetness and grace of her tongue rather than for doe-like eyes or long limbs such as win other girls that name."

"Al-Khansa yet lives, doesn't she?"

"Yes, and turns the hardest hearts to wells of water with her words:

> *"'Verily, time is rich in strangeness.*
> *It leaves us a stump and cuts off our head.'"*

"'Time is rich in strangeness,' indeed."

I recited the old poetess's words under my own breath. For I recognized the woman who'd slipped beneath the rolled-up tent wall to stand veiled among the men to speak. She was Malik's wife, Layla bint al-Minhal.

I looked at her, and I found her looking with equal keenness back at me. As a matter of fact, I had the impression that she had spotted me long before from her place among the women in the darkness, like a leopard crouches to watch its prey. This watching was what drove her to find the courage to enter the men's tent and the competition.

Malik was surprised to see his wife there. Her own presumption seemed to embarrass her as well. She took a seat between her husband and her nearly grown son Tamim as if for protection.

"Before you recite," Malik said, *"we must see your face."*

With a clink of coin, Layla pulled aside her husband's wealth, worn jangling before her cheekbones.

Time had been kinder to Layla than it is to most women who are beautiful as girls—and to them it is no kinder than it was to al-Khansa's heroes. Usually such beauty is almost one with their virginity, gone in an instant to the rigors of married life, the envious sun, hard work, cares and childbearing. Age comes to plainer girls with dignity and not the devastation of the pretty turned ugly overnight.

When a man is forced to flee into exile, when he can trust no one either where he is coming from or where he is going, he may bury his treasure hoping someday his fortune may change. Even so was it with Layla, her exile among the Tamim and her single treasure, her beauty. Time had given her looks the tarnish of disuse, not the nicks and sagging thinness that were the result of constant, everyday employ. Were fate ever to turn in her favor, she would brush off the sand, polish up the metal, and find her beauty as serviceable again as if she'd never left it.

Even then, as she appeared in the midst of all the men, many might have found some well-used line of poetry to describe her. But now she proposed to make the poem. The still-taut skin curving from cheek to closely veiled chin, surprising in a woman who had a son old enough to bear arms, ceased being important compared to poetry.

I had known Layla as a girl in her father's tent; a wit for poetry was the last thing on earth with which I would have credited her. I could not help but wonder what had happened to the insides of that beautiful body to fill them, to make them capable of the art. Sorrow, they said, was one sure way to make a poet.

Like a woman in grief, she averted her eyes from the assembly.

Returning the veil gratefully to her face renewed her courage. And as she began to recite, it became clear that in reality, she feared nothing, or at least, that she had no need to fear.

> "I dreamed while my companions slept
>   that my clothes were on fire.
> When a shooting star falls, I contemplate the eternal
>   stars that do not set. . ."

I was the one who shivered. I was the one whose throat went dry and whose face washed white with fear, not hers. The poem brought everything unknowable and terrifying about the powerful night at Nakhlah back to my mind so vividly that I felt I was breathing the same air again. I thought I should perish at the thought. By God and by my life, Bint Zura must have told Layla about. . .about it all.

I'd been able to pass unknown among the Banu Tamim, but here, with mere words, my every secret lay discovered.

When Layla finished her recitation, I was not the only one who sat in total and waxy silence. Once or twice az-Zibrikan cleared his throat to begin an answer to her mighty challenge. But he knew nothing of poetry if he did not know when his jinni had been beaten. The great poet himself withdrew into his thoughts; the *silence of admiration reigned.*

"Let us hear the poem again, Umm Tamim," Malik said after a while. He spoke quietly as a man speaks to his wife when they lie together at night. "It seems you are unchallenged."

Layla hung her head to regroup her senses before beginning again and, as she did, I noticed a smile, jarring in its lack of poetry, come to her lips. *Something is not quite right here,* I said to myself. Because of this thought, I was not startled when, after she was only two stanzas into the poem, she was interrupted. Confusion, a break in the circle, and yet another new figure stood among the men.

"Layla Umm Tamim, before all this company and as al-Uzza is my witness, I call you a liar and a thief."

Such words of insult could only cause a commotion no matter who the speaker was. In this case, the identity of the speaker made an even greater stir.

The figure was a female at that indefinite age between girl and woman, perhaps eleven or twelve years old. A heavily embroidered veil completely covered her face: Her family was in the process of finding a husband for her.

Her family. Not *I*, her father.

If a man thinks of this veil at all, it is not as a person, but as a thing, an *it*, emotionless, feelingless, thoughtless and, most importantly, sexless. No, that cannot be, for nothing is more fraught with sex than a female in such a state. She is like a chilled vessel set directly in a fire the instant before it shatters, when it sits there smoking and beaded with sweat. Perhaps that is why we avoid thinking of them. They are too explosive, too dangerous, too unpredictable, too powerful. So full of sex are they, we dare accord them no other consciousness. To grant reason to such irrational power, to grant it a mind, thought, would be to put it in a class with gods: He of the landslide, She of the flood.

I had never heard a creature in such a veil speak more than a single word at a time. Even my own milk sister had turned her face to the tent wall whenever I came in once she had reached that age. And Malik made no request that this one unveil, although he had done so for his own wife. He had neither the courage nor the authority.

This one spoke, her tones with the pierce of a flute. "Layla Umm Tamim, you know that's not your poem."

She also used the language of women, the feminine forms of the verbs, the feminine inflections that are the only way, the unique way, for women to express themselves. Every soul in the great tent took such usage, coming from behind a veil, as revelation.

But they were more than a revelation to me. I knew the identity of the person behind that veil, hiding her power that might otherwise kill our common, everyday *souls.*

Mutammim jumped up. Fumbling blindly, he caught the figure by its—her—muffled hand. He whispered some charmed word that had a calming effect and sat her down by his side.

"O Layla, mother of my son, it seems you have found a challenger," Malik said, smoothing his beard in consideration, a smile behind it.

The veil, as if frightened by the sound of her own raised voice when she'd called Layla a liar, caught my milk brother's sleeve and whispered to him. The blind man must have taken a special interest in the young, parentless girl. Mutammim whispered to Malik, and the sharif was finally a personage respected enough to make the whisper known to the general company.

"It seems," Malik said, "that my dead herdsman's daughter thinks you claim her poem as your own, O mother of my son." Rather than scolding his wife, it seemed the whole situation amused him. Happy couple, when even a fray amuses!

More rapid whispering. Malik's translation: "I am corrected. Not her poem. The poem given her by her shaytan.*"*

A buzz arose in the tent, speculation as to who this girl might be. No other poet that night had made such a claim to inspiration. Even seers, who read men's lives and dreams in pebbles and feathers, never claimed that. Az-Zibrikan himself had but hashed his poem out in the company of spirits; they had not given it to him whole from the very center of their burning fire. Muhammad made such claims, although he called his shaytan *an angel. Muhammad—and now this girl.*

Layla Umm Tamim made no counterclaim, now that she was challenged. She sat quietly toying with the tassel of the cushion she shared with her son, a satisfied smile playing about her lips.

For a good long time, the veil filled Mutammim's ear while the tent checked in anticipation. In the silence, I could hear beyond the fires. I knew that, in the background, the women were watching with equal silence and hope. The eternal emptiness of the desert and the smallness of man within it—in spite of all his kin—made its presence felt deep in my soul.

Finally, Mutammim began to laugh and broke the transcendent moment. "Enough! Enough!" he cried. "I will not act as your reciter, child, and tell the whole poem for you."

"That you must do yourself, veil or no," Malik agreed. "That is, if you do not wish to withdraw your challenge. Do you wish to withdraw?"

The veil shook "no" with a jingle of ornaments for emphasis.

Whispering.

"Layla Umm Tamim," Malik said. I have rarely seen him in such a good humor, sailing like a rain cloud before the wind for the very thrill of the contest. "It

seems you misquoted from the first stanza. You used the word 'sana' to mean the passage of time from pilgrimage to pilgrimage, rather than 'hijja.' 'Sana' is such a common, unpoetical word—so common, indeed, that I did not notice the mistake." Laughter rang at the sharif's interjection.

Mutammim spoke now to continue the transmission of my daughter's whispered words, which was rapidly becoming a greater task than two men could manage. *"Besides,"* he said, *"it throws the meter off. I can't remember half of what else I was to tell you of your poetical misjudgments, O my brother's wife. Oh, yes, there was this—I quote our tribe's young daughter—'The camel that made the journey was a she, not a he. Not only do the sounds in "he" and "his" jar with the sounds of the other words in the passage, but you know, Father, as well as I, that my Mriza is a she. Didn't I help you when she birthed last spring?'"*

The tent laughed and shook off some of its awe. It could not have maintained that much longer without breaking into prayer. If such things were capable of it, the veil would have blushed.

"So, Layla. You will give us your poem again, as you started to," Malik said. *"And then we will hear from—"*

I pronounce the Poetess's name without thinking. My scribe's pen snaps on the parchment with a splatter of ink. The name that has rung in my head like a bellwether for all these years comes at him like a murderous bolt.

"You did not say the name I think you said, Master."

"You heard me well enough."

"I hoped I did not."

"Well, which woman known as the daughter of al-Harith—although you see now that she was not really such—did you think I meant all these months of dictation? Al-Harith is a common enough name among the Arabs, although not the girl's name, I suppose. But sooner or later it must be told, sooner or later you must write it. Take up another reed and sharpen it."

He will not write it.

"Does this mean you quit? That I must head out into the market tomorrow on my bad leg and hunt for another?"

He says yes. He packs up his pens and ground gall. The eunuch looks around my garden one last time just as the call to prayer comes.

"I shall pray on it," he says.

"You do that."

13

We are still in need of you.
We were sparing you for the hardships.
We used to voice our grievances to you,
O young lion crouching in your den.
It is a shame, O our foremost defender,
That the sword drops from your right arm.
If you were redeemable with our souls,
We would redeem you, O chief of the youth.
Masud, O fledgling hawk,
It is a shame for you to go into the earth
Instead of soaring,
And for your arm to tire out in battle,
And for your sword to return to its sheath.
> —Funeral lament for a young man from
> Lebanon

Up on the third floor, Sitt Sameh was reciting improvised verses for the dead boy.

"Kefa, O fledgling hawk,
It is a shame for you to go into the earth
Instead of soaring."

Rayah knew they were better verses than any being created in the yard below. Her mother had a *shaytan*, the gift of poetry. But was this heartfelt? Or only demonic?

Because reciting was not the only thing Sitt Sameh was doing. She was pulling the large wooden pins out of her roof, undoing the tackle. A panel of tenting dropped to the rooftop with a sigh.

"Mother?" Rayah asked.

Sitt Sameh stopped her chant, but she did not stop her work with the woolen panels. "I cannot stay within this house another moment," she said. "I have stayed too long already. Many years too long. I only waited until you were grown. And now a boy has died."

"I don't want to go."

"Very well, stay here then. Abd Allah will come with me, the two of us, clanless, tribeless, friendless. Thank Allat, his leg is well enough to travel."

"I don't want to stay here without you. The both of you." Rayah found herself more concerned about this than about her mother's evocation of the demon goddess. Or the disturbing notion that Abd Allah didn't seem to find this travel to an unknown future an unpleasant prospect. Sheepishly she said as explanation, "You haven't told me the end of the story yet."

"Well, this is as much as you need to know," her mother replied, "to live this life in this house. Or in the son of Abd ar-Rahman ibn Khalid's house. Whichever. It's nothing I can help you with. I've done the best I could."

What sort of mother was this? Rayah thought. What sort of mother had this woman ever been, especially compared to Adilah?

Still, Rayah went and stood in the way of the next peg to unpin. Sitt Sameh tried to step around her. Rayah stepped in her way again. "Mother, please—"

Like flint on steel, blue eye flashed to blue eye. Sitt Sameh looked away first. She bustled instead to her heap of simple belongings, exposed now to the sun.

"I will need a litter, ya Abd Allah, to go with the two camels you will purchase. Here is gold. And the remnants of my grandmother's litter. See if the saddle maker will incorporate them."

Leaning on his cane, the eunuch took the proffered gold and the wreck of a litter he had brought to Tadmor from Homs those many months ago. He did not meet Rayah's eyes as he moved to the stairs, but he did say, "My master sent me to her."

Next Sitt Sameh found her trio of pagan idols, the full-breasted wooden figures of women that had been her grandmother's and her mother's before her. The figures made Rayah's flesh creep. They wouldn't have that effect if they didn't have power. Her power. Her mother kissed them and began to wrap each one carefully in linen.

"You certainly won't need these, my little Muslimah," her mother snapped.

But Rayah had just used the one to aid Ghusoon—

The sword, however, still lay unsheathed on top of the heap. "The Sword of God—" Rayah snatched it up.

Sitt Sameh stopped halfway through the bundling of the goddess Manat. Again, blue eyes met. Then Sitt Sameh looked away with a jerk of her head that might have been a nod. "Take it."

"You have not resheathed it," Rayah pointed out.

"The heavenly metal possesses an otherworldly thirst. It cannot be resheathed until it has slaked its thirst in blood."

"And so it has. It took my virgin blood." It didn't matter what she believed.

Sitt Sameh gave another jerking nod. She fumbled for and found the sheath. "Here." She shoved the jeweled case at her daughter. "I stayed in this house only until my daughter should become a woman. Now she has."

Rayah spat on the blade, then rubbed the hilt with the hem of her gown to remove her blood. She slipped it into the case. A glint of swirling starlight caught the metal edge. She quickly withdrew it before the hilt quite reached the lip of the sheath. The blade seemed to chuckle with the voice of the curly-haired jinni.

"But now I withdraw it anew."

Sitt Sameh sank to her knees. Rayah had never seen this woman afraid before, not of things on earth nor in the realms of smoke-and-fire mirage.

"Daughter, don't."

"If you leave this rooftop, so must I." Rayah didn't resheathe the sword.

"It isn't necessary to leave. Not for you. Just for me and Abd Allah."

"Indeed it is necessary. I cannot stay in this house where I have never really belonged. They would have me married and off their hands, the jinn as far away as they can ever be shoved. I must take the best match I can."

"You have a match. You have the jinni."

"I have the jinni." Rayah rubbed her hands over the sword as she agreed. "But a jinni cannot give me a blue-eyed daughter. To continue your story. There is the world of smoke, but I must also live in the world of flesh and blood, where men like Uncle Abd ar-Rahman live and rule. I cannot hide from that."

Rayah felt the terror of the unknown, but took bravery from those who had known more terror before her. She added, "Still, Mother, I would like you to come with me. At least for a while. At least until— Say you will come."

Sitt Sameh looked off over the rooftops to the desert. Under her breath, she murmured something. A prayer? Verses?

"Daughter, yes," she finally spoke aloud. "I will come."

Without a pause, Rayah left the dismantled room at the top of the stairs, carrying the Sword of God flat before her. She took the steps to the house below, feeling the yank on her silver bracelet as she passed the turn where the jinn dwelt. The huddled, mourning women of the family did not stop her, although they called her name and tried. Nor did leaving the protection of the silver hand with the lapis eye in its center, although here she felt another tug at her braceleted wrist.

Without Kefa's guardian eye, she stepped into the men's *majlis*. Here uncles and cousins lately returned from the cemetery were receiving the condolences of their neighbors parallel to the women in the other room. Here sat the Conqueror's son, Abd ar-Rahman.

Strangely, although she hadn't given a thought to him being present in the *majlis*, the Persian Firuz caught her attention for a moment. Slave that he was, he stood behind the arc of important men on their cushions, his powerful arms quietly folded, waiting command. The man capable of breaking Abd Allah's leg. The thought made Rayah's stomach lurch, whittled her confidence in her ability to do what she must do.

But Firuz was beneath the other men, even beneath her, as a free Muslim woman. She owed him no heed at all in this play for power.

Rayah did not look down as she always had before, as was only proper for an unmarried woman before strange men. She met Abd ar-Rahman, the Conqueror's son, face to face. How much did this full-bearded, sharp-nosed man resemble her grandfather? Could she imagine this face beneath the famous red turban? How handsome would be the son he wanted her to marry with such a heritage?

"Peace upon you, O son of Khalid son of al-Walīd." The drawn blade in her hand belied that wish of "peace."

Abd ar-Rahman was on his feet, as were most of the other men. His eye was not on her, but on the blade in her hand.

"So this is the bride-price," he said in silken tones. "*Sayf* Allah, the Sword of God." He took a step in her direction as if he would claim it that instant.

Rayah pulled the sword back. "I will not give it to you. Only to your son. When we are married."

"But my son is in al-Medinah, serving the Khalifah Omar."

Rayah nodded. "I will go on pilgrimage to the two holy cities. I will meet your son there, if it is God's will. Then I will marry him, if it is God's will, and the sword shall pass to our sons. If it is God's will."

For several quick heartbeats, Abd ar-Rahman ibn Khalid hesitated. The glint of the hilt and its heavenly blade moved through his eyes. Clearly, he wanted to lay claim to his father's sword then and there. But how could he? Rayah knew she had presented the shadow into the mix, the mirage. If a woman expressed a pious desire to make the pilgrimage, he couldn't very well force her sword from her in front of all these men who stood as her kinsfolk, could he?

"And my mother wishes to accompany me. My mother will come with me to Mecca. With our eunuch guardian." She spoke for herself, presenting as many claims as she could. She knew that not many more chances would come, and after her passage through this volatile time, upon her marriage, perhaps none at all.

Then Rayah heard the whisper of bare feet behind her and knew her mother had also entered the men's room. Instead of stepping closer now, the Conqueror's son sank back onto his cushions in the place of honor. He seemed completely comfortable in victory.

Rayah knew her chance to direct her life had ended. The governor stared only at Sitt Sameh.

"So once again you honor us with your presence, Sitt Sameh as they call you. Witch, poetess, prophetess." His words dripped venom. "This time I hope we can come to some arrangement, O my half-sister. My father sought you all his life. I have succeeded as Khalid the Conqueror did not. No, even the whole Muslim army could not find you as I have done. I bring you out of your harem, and I call you by your true name. Sejah bint al-Harith, bastard daughter of Khalid ibn al-Walīd."

An intake of breath swept the room. The turpentine sellers were such good, honest men, still suffering the death of their youngest member. They kept silent beyond their first gasp in the same hurt and confusion that made Rayah's head spun.

"No, my mother's name is Sitt Sameh. No, you have it wrong." The girl wanted to speak this way. But the sudden halt of the bare feet behind her stilled her tongue.

Why didn't Sitt Sameh deny this? Why didn't she open her mouth and sing out the poetry that would disprove his words?

Because her mother's powerful poetry would only support the terrible truth, wouldn't it?

Of course Rayah had heard the name before. In Quran class. Even uneducated Muslim women hushed their fussy children with the warning: "If you don't keep quiet, the evil witch Sejah will come and get you. She opposed our Messenger, blessings on him, blacken her name. I will hand you over to Sejah and her *shaytan*."

Rayah's mother and the Conqueror's parchment had told her of their relationship; they had told her all the history of father, mother, grandmother. Still they hadn't spoken this name, "Sejah." And no one had told the events that made this name so infamous.

The entire Muslim army would willingly receive martyrdom to say at last that they had captured and killed Sejah bint al-Harith for the sake of the One God and the glory of Islam.

14

My poetry is so powerful that even blind men can read it,
My words so meaningful that even the deaf can hear.
—Al-Mutanabbi, a tenth-century Arabic poet

Wonder of wonders and *mashallah*. My scribe is here on time in the morning, scraping out the splatter of the evening before with his penknife.

"So? Did you pray on it?" I demand, hauling myself out to my cushions on my cane and the shoulder of a little black slave. "My daughter's name."

"I did," the eunuch replies softly.

"And? God speaks to you as well as to the Messenger?"

"The truth must be written," is all he says.

To ease him into the task, for a while I avoid pronouncing the name he dreaded to write at first.

Malik spoke now, countering the girl-poet's fears with these words: "When a poet is born, he no longer belongs to mother or father, but to the Gods, and to all the people. A clan may own a well, but the rain is for all."

His proverb made her realize that she would be as wrong to keep the gift from others as she would have been to keep the knowledge of a last pool of water in the dry season from thirsty kinsmen. The veil arranged itself, hung its head in humility, and began. After the first stanza, no more hesitation wavered in her voice; every guest in the tent joined her tale with a full heart. Her voice was strong, rich, mellowed by its passage through the layers of fabric—and it was beautiful. Layla's poem had limped along, a mere outsider to the night in Nakhlah; this one soared— the very goddess herself.

> *Oh, yes! Al-Uzza left me the perfume of virtue*
> *That penetrates the most intimate fibers of my*
>   *heart.*

When the veil fell silent, not a soul within hearing remained unconvinced of who had actually made that journey to Nakhlah, at least through shaytan's *eyes.*

Grown men were weeping, wiping their eyes on their sleeves, worshipping with their faces in the dust.

Layla's poem had made me blush to remember my night. The veil's version made me shake to live it all again with rejoicing. I had fancied the breath of my lungs, the words of my tongue, the very thoughts of my mind to be private and safe from the world. The poem took these from me, polished and strung them out like pearls on a thread for all the tribe to see and covet. The great she-voice of Nakhlah had spoken—the voice I thought I'd killed and silenced—and everyone knew it. But I knew it most of all.

Malik lowered his eyes. He let a long pause pass, then he cleared his throat. Not for hereditary reasons alone did dwellers in stone and tents alike from all over the peninsula refer to him for righteous judgment.

"Thank you both. We have now heard the poems. A poet," he continued, "must know the history of our people. He must recite it perfectly, so our sons may have a careful story of our ancestors and the deeds that have made them great. Not one name must be forgotten lest a curse come to us. Therefore, my women, if you will each favor us with the epic of the sons of Tamim, we may better judge between you. Layla, first. The other afterwards."

It was not such a remarkable thing to know all the history. Every son of Tamim knew a good number of verses. I myself remembered three or four stanzas from my childhood. This one could be consulted if a question arose about the wars between Tamim and Bakr, who had led the attack on which day and who had fallen by whose hand. This one knew perfectly all the stanzas boasting of how the sons of Tamim had carried out their sacred duties as judges and peacekeepers in the markets of Ukaz and al-Hira:

> *People know our excellence*
> *When they rally attending the markets. . .*

This one knew of the favors shown their forefathers by the kings of al-Hira. This one knew the genealogy of blood feud, this one all the details of Suwaid ibn Rabi'a's rebellion against tyranny. . . .

The careful precision of Layla's version reminded everyone that her art was studied by one whose ancestors had had different stories to tell. The veil she had replaced, on the other hand, gave all those past souls new life. Her rich voice filtered through it, capable of striking chords, the authority of unseen spirits unlike the single string of any other mortal.

> *"Father Tarif wore out his body, as the blade of an*
> *Indian sword destroys an inferior scabbard*

And he was called to his God and his fathers—
May the rains make smooth the mound of his grave."

Az-Zibrikan repeated this part of the saga thoughtfully when the veil had finished. Usually men recite history among men. After having become used to women's
voices in the past hour or so, this male voice sounded clumsy and harsh as it tried
to describe the softness of rain. Yet he knew whereof he spoke. As he himself said, "I
learned the tales of our Arabs from my father and he from my father's father. And I
do not feel there is a man here who would hesitate to have his sons learn the history
from my lips."

A murmur through the tent indicated that indeed, no one would hesitate.

"I could not have brought the words out any better than Umm Tamim," he
continued, thus gratified. "But. . .but none, I feel, will argue with me here: The
herdsman's daughter went on after those verses I just recited and added others. I
cannot remember them all, but they began with something like this:

"'Like the daughters of Pharaoh watching processions
under sunshades on a sunbaked day. . .'

"I can't go on. Such lines were never in the poem as I learned it. You will back
me, I'm sure, O sons of Tamim. The herdsman's daughter told us all about Umm
Taghlib, who might well be her grandmother, as she suggests, but she was a woman
foreign to us, a stranger, a refugee in our land. Can such a one have any place in
our illustrious history?"

"None," came the general response.

Malik agreed, his ploy to draw both sides out when he oversaw an argument. "It is good
that you, O az-Zibrikan, have called this to our attention. For greater evil than to forget a
name is to add to our history as one might invent a romance to entertain lazy womenfolk
who have nothing better to do. By what right do you, Bint al-Harith, add these verses?"

"The tales of all my father's ancestors I learned carefully from the mouths of the
poets among our women," the veil explained. "But I could find none to tell me of
my mothers to my satisfaction, and I dared not approach the honored az-Zibrikan
to rid me of my ignorance."

"So you invented verses?" accused the poet. He, like any Arab, reacted to the
implied dishonor of being inaccessible to the poor and helpless.

"My. . .my shaytan told me what I should say," responded the girl, not unsure
of herself, only unsure of how her words might be received.

The crowd murmured with discontent, dangerously close to the tone in which
one speaks of stoning an adulteress. They did not like the notion that some spirit
had had access behind that veil before one of their young men. Shayatan were too

commonly known as licentious beings.

I fingered the dagger at my side. I could not hope to win single-handedly against the entire tribe of Tamim. But I was willing to try in this girl's defense, vow or no vow.

"I do not make it a practice to enter into a competition, nor to give evidence in a trial of any sort," said Malik. "This time, however, I cannot keep silent, lest judgment be perverted through a lack of facts. I will say only this. I knew Umm Taghlib as, I'm sure, did many others here. When I was a small boy, my mother took me to see her. We went to ask the whereabouts of another small boy—al-Harith, the father of this girl here. Without the old kahinah's second sight, the hyenas would have found him before my father did. This tale found a place in this child's recitation, though how many of you caught it in the words about a landslide of rocks and a seer stone? How many of you even knew of this event so you could have passed it on to your children?

"I remember my mother telling me that had Umm Taghlib not interceded with the spirits during her times of birthing, to warm her insides and help them to expand, either my elder brother Mutammim or I should have been the death of her; neither one of us should have ever known life. Is this not as great a deed as that done by any man who ever saved the life of his companion on the field of battle? Go you, ask my mother back there among the women if this is not true, if she does not agree that this is so. She will not be able to tell you these things in poetry, for she is not gifted with an ear for rhyme or meter. Go back, ask any of your women. I had forgotten until now, until—"

And now in my garden I, the Conqueror, remember so clearly the voice of my milk brother Malik saying her name. "Sejah" flows through my head like a drink of cool water.

But I look at the turban bent over his parchments and inks and think to spare my scribe a little while longer. I amend the memory.

"—Until she, the young poetess, brought it back with her words. The past is brought to the surface of my mind as a divining stick can bring forth a well.

"Consider, O my father's sons, that Umm Taghlib died before this girl was born. Unless it be by some greater power, by the will of heaven, how should she know of these things? Even her own mother died when she was born, so who but a shaytan could have given her these words? As the Gods of our fathers are my witnesses, her verses ring true to my heart. We must think twice lest, remembering the spears and shields that have preserved our people, we forget the wombs that bore us to bear those arms. Now I dare say there are other men here who owe that same debt to that same strange woman—or other debts greater than mine. And I swear by al-Uzza I shall never taste spring milk again if I let her be forgotten."

Other men began to nod, slowly at first, then gathering momentum. If they did not admit that they, too, owed a son's debt to old Umm Taghlib buried deep in their hearts, such a powerful member of the spirit world would cause them a serious haunting. And no one could deny that they had heard that spirit, singing through that young girl's words.

In short, the tribe accepted the new lines of history. They called upon the poetess to repeat her new lines until others had committed them to memory so there would be no chance of their ever becoming lost.

"Do you remember the lines, Master?" my scribe asks.

How long have I been silent, while he waits patiently, pen poised? I haven't been here, stifled by green in the late afternoon garden. I've been breathing the clear air in a desert night, floating with the fire jinn on a *shaytan's* words.

"You learned them with the rest, I suppose?"

"I did," I reply. "But then I lost them again. Other demands, foolish though they seem now, came to take their place. Still, a description of the desert pastures of Tamim as given by the mouth of the Poetess I've never forgotten. Every day, to the one on which I die, something in my surroundings, even here in staid old Homs, will recall the words to me:

> "Now are her sons and daughters scattered over all the
>   land, just as gold coins are scattered over a bride,
> Over all the land from the Valley of Nakhlah in the
>   West to al-Hira where the sun rises.
> This goodly land, where the snowy whites of acacia
>   on their stems are like pearls mounted on the
>   foreshafts of lances
> And the jasmine, delicate and pure, is as the secret
>   thoughts of the gentle lone stroller
> And the cypress in her ample robes displays her leg
>   like a pretty girl
> And the slender-statured palm tree is turbaned and
>   adorns himself with belts and sashes
> And you may behold heaven's plain like a wall of
>   marble set in order with marvelous tablets.
> The clouds therein like fat ostriches kneeling and
>   others circling on wing
> And the sun brighter than a bride, veiled on the day
>   of the wedding procession in a veil of shining
>   gold."

The acacias and jasmine in my garden are dull by comparison.

"So, mother of my son," Malik said to Layla. "Do you still sit here facing your challenger? Very well. Let the contest continue. I will now ask both of you to prove yourselves with extemporaneous verses. To make sure you do not use something composed beforehand, the topic must be this evening and this Lake of al-Ashtat. Umm Tamim?"

Layla cleared her throat, huskily, as a man might, and then said, in prose: "O sons of Tamim. I am not a poetess. And yes, the daughter of our lamented herdsman, she did repeat her poem to me until I could recite it. She trusted me to be her rawi, her understudy, to hold the words for her while she played with them and waited for her shaytan to speak more to her and set them right. As a piece of parchment is to the scribe, so was I to her, to be torn up and scratched out at her will.

"Do not judge my betrayal of this trust harshly. Here among us, I knew, was a heaven-inspired Poetess, the daughter of my dead friend Bint Zura. But I also knew she feared to let her gift be known. Perhaps the people would think her mad, she thought. Perhaps they would condemn her as an adulteress for consorting with a shaytan. Earlier, Bint Zura's mother was sent away by her own people, followers of Isa ibn Maryam as we know, for showing forth this same power. But should the Arabs perish for want of a voice? Should the sons of Tamim be defeated in their contest with the followers of Muhammad because they did not use the power of cursing the enemy sent into their midst by al-Uzza? Should they forget the name and deeds of their great ancestress? All this because the Poetess was young and of humble parentage and afraid? No, that should not be. Heaven turn my son to stone if I would stand by and let this happen.

"So I contrived this way to make her known, without her bringing shame upon herself. Now, I say, let it be secret no longer. Let fires be built on the hilltops, let every traveler tell it in the tents where he finds rest. Let our enemies grow as pale as sand when they hear the word. The daughter of Tamim has heard the voice of the spirits. They reside in her, break their meat with her and enliven her tongue. Let our sons and all those who are our friends rejoice with us."

Thus Layla withdrew her challenge. Couching it in such terms, she saved face and indeed won the praise of the tribe.

"Is it possible?" my scribe asks. "She must have had some doubts, this—this girl. She must have thought that her shaytan was indeed a Satan. Else why would she have hesitated to make her poems known?"

"My good fellow, recall how Muhammad, blessed be he, shrank from taking up the mantle of his calling. It is said he even thought of leaping to his death from the mountain height rather than to face it. How much more might a girl of ten or twelve fear the burden of such a demand? And, remember, she already had some knowledge of the Messenger of God. She had already felt his wrath, at the death of the poetess Asama, at the siege of Khaybar."

And the memory of the tiny girl sitting on Muhammad's lap, speaking to him of heavenly cranes, satanic verses, makes this old man's gruel sour in my stomach. I knew why she had hesitated to come forward. And as her father, by God, I wanted her safe in her harem.

A man, for pride, will give more camels than blood money demands. Layla left her husband's side and went back to the women in the darkness outside the tent. I noticed no regret in her as she left. Why should a woman have regrets at leaving public life?

But the Poetess remained and was given the place of highest honor. Malik had his new herdsman go through all the flocks, refusing those first brought to him, until he had found ten without blemish. These were sacrificed, their throats cut, their blood spilled on the earth and, the coals stirred alive, set on the fires to roast. We feasted throughout the night.

I ate, but kept myself hidden, like a woman, in the dark.

Children, if they had fallen asleep, were awakened and told that they must never forget this night of revelation, this birth of a Poetess. They must tell it to their children and their children's children. Like the day of battle, this day would be used to mark time. People would say for years to come, "It was the summer the Poetess was discovered," or "He was born three or four months after Bint al-Harith, may glory be hers, was made known."

But all fell silent this night every time the veil stirred, every time she was encouraged to recite, which was as often and as frequently as her voice could endure. Date wine was brought forth and she was encouraged to take it to give her voice strength. But she refused. "If I fill my head with wine," she said, "there will be no space left there for my shaytan."

So others drank it to heighten their enjoyment.

And—

Here I steal another glance at the bent turban of my scribe. Well, it cannot be put off any longer.

I pronounce the name, trembling with love. "Sejah."

My scribe takes a breath, dips his pen, poised to write—

And Sejah, Sejah, whet her tongue with water from the sacred wells of her ancestors instead and spoke her poetry all night long.

Sejah bint al-Harith. No, not the daughter of that emasculated herdsman. Bint Khalid ibn al Walid. My daughter. Singing of the night of her own begetting, so only magic could have given her the words. Singing of that night when my own Sword of God was forged in Nakhlah, now destroyed by my own hands.

Sejah, Poetess and Prophetess, standing in opposition to the very Messenger of God. I, the strongest of warriors, had succumbed to him. How could she stand?

15

It is narrated that the Prophet (the peace and
blessings of God be upon him) said: "No [message from
the dead in the form of an] owl and no [superstitions of
the month of] Safar."

Muslim and others add the words, "No [control of the rains by
the] stars and no ghoul."

—A hadith of the Prophet, related by ash-
Shaheehayn

*The Poetess's words fell like rain: Everything they touched revitalized, stiff with
new life. Even so lifeless a thing as the red silk of my headdress seemed fifteen
years younger. It was new and crisp beneath my fingers as I unwrapped my
face to reveal myself to my milk brothers on this happy occasion. I made my way
through the tent to embrace them—and to accept the seat they would give me, closer
to the Poetess. But as I did, a row of tall men, arms folded across their chests, belts
studded with blades, stood and stopped me in my tracks.*

*The sons of al-Anbar, whose wives and children languished now as slaves in
Mecca, rose like startled serpents from the gathering.*

"Khalid ibn al-Walīd?" they echoed.

"A man of Mecca, a Qurayshi and a Muslim?"

"Revenge for the death of our brothers and fathers!"

"Revenge for the captivity of our women and children!"

"Revenge for the destruction of Nakhlah!"

"Why are we gathered here at al-Ashtat if not for this? Upon his head!"

*Hands as hard as manacles clamped on my right arm, then on the other, a
painful twist of blood fury in each.*

*I looked desperately to Malik. But Malik, who had at first risen to greet me,
now turned from his irate kinsmen and sat back down in his place. His gaze refused
to meet mine. At some point, the demands of one sort of honor had to give way*

before another.

"You should not have come," his actions said clearly to me. "Did you come to spy or to mock our solemnities? Do not bother to answer a defense. These men are my brothers, my flesh and blood. Only woman's milk attaches you to me, as partner in crass trade. And what honor is in trade? I will maintain honor with my tribe, even if the decision is to kill you. You know how such things are."

I knew indeed. Honor would force me to kill him, too, if ever the day arrived when our positions were reversed.

Malik, without speaking a word aloud, did manage to inject a bit of rational thought into the tent that bristled with the instinctual defenses of a striking serpent. He did it by his silence and his actions alone. That was not much, but enough for the sharif of al-Anbar to turn from me. He coughed to call the attention of his kinsmen to him.

With great dignity that made me feel a blasphemer for imposing my person on such an occasion, the sharif of al-Anbar said: "Let the Poetess judge this case."

The manacle hands shoved me towards her. I smiled with hope as she herself rose and came toward me. That was not the gesture of a judge. That was what a dog did, to smell out the intentions of another. And if I could be smelled— I quickly lost that smile before the blank impartiality the veil presented.

"Remember me, Sejah?" I coaxed in an undertone, hoping the angry tribesmen around us would not hear. "Khalid ibn al-Walid Abu Sulayman. You stayed at my home in Mecca when you were a little girl. I carried you on my shoulder and you played. . ."

Sejah herself was not without an undercurrent of fierceness as she replied: "I remember, O father of Sulayman. But I remember Khaybar, when you wanted to sell me as your daughter to that man you call a prophet."

"But you are. . ." I began to say then carefully stopped myself. It would not go well if I began to explain how I'd besmirched the honor of one of the Tamimi women.

Fortunately, Sejah covered for me—after a fashion. "I remember, too, the death of my father al-Harith and the poetess whose mantle I now wear, Asma bint Maysa. Not at your hand, perhaps, but at the bloody hands of those with whom you now consort. You say you were my friend and protector when I was a child, as a man should do for his milk kin. But we see that a man, like the landscape of the desert, may change over time, however permanent his character may seem at first passing."

I flinched. It wasn't pain in my pinioned arms this time. I flinched for no other reason than that she had raised a hand towards my head. What harm could a hand do, her small and open hand? Yet I, as she, sensed its power as she purposefully picked up the trailing edge of my headdress and fingered the red silk. Just that size and shape had her mother's hands been. The flesh of my back crawled, writhed beneath the star scars it bore as if the burns were but fresh. In that hand, my fate was sealed. I closed my eyes in fearful, yet tantalizing anticipation.

"Let him be a guest among you," her verdict came, tossed carelessly behind her as she dropped my headdress and turned away. "For the traditional three days. It is honorable. And we are more honorable than they."

From man to man grumbled the protests, gaining strength and precision as they passed around.

"He has beguiled her," they said.

"She is but an unwed girl, after all. A child such as could be bribed with sweets and bits of colored cloth."

"She is a female. Everyone knows that the greatest female weakness is compassion."

Some even went so far as to grumble, "Should such a one, no matter how inspired her poetry, be sent into the den of al-Medinah?"

Fatherly protection made me want to urge this last way of looking at things. But the word of a captive like me would lessen my chances of seeing her safe.

Sejah stood in the opening of the tent listening—to the men, to the night, one could not say. I began to doubt the resolve of her first decision.

The night lay old and feeble. The moon set behind the hills: a weight that would finally turn the scales one way or the other as it dropped. As if in reply, a flutter of wings stirred outside the tent, the low call of a night bird lost on its way home now that no light shone but the stars. Its talons scratched about on the roof. A sag in the woolen strips told us that the bird had taken a perch near the center pole. The men about me paused, and the Poetess grew motionless to listen.

"Let's go shoo it away," one man near me said to another.

Then they, too, grew still and decided it must be an omen:

"See how it settles directly over the Poetess's head."

"It would be bad luck to disturb it."

"It is the final great confirmation of her calling."

So in the end, no one moved. Breathing stifled like a fire in no wind.

At last Sejah called life back into the tent by stirring from her own reverie. When she did, a new poem sat distilled behind that veil, brought directly from heaven on the wings of a night bird. She recited it from where she stood and, as she did, the manacles of flesh melted from my arms.

> *"The man without mercy shall live in his day*
> *But the man with mercy shall live in the hearts of*
> *his children*

> And his enemies' children, generations without
>   end."

I don't suppose a soul in all Tamim was unmerciful toward so much as his goats for a full turning of the moon.

But what might the effect of such a poem be when the tribe came to face Muhammad?

For better or for worse, my captors dropped their grip and, wiping their hands on their robes as if they had just handled camel dung, went to sit with their clansmen again.

I tried another smile toward the Poetess. I meant it to convey thanks. Perhaps I displayed some triumph, though I tried to conceal it.

"Don't compliment yourself," Sejah advised me quietly but firmly as she passed to reclaim her seat of honor. "It's for my mother's sake that I spare you. She is dead, but she lives on in me. What is not in me is now in the body of a haunting night bird—as you see. She remembers the man who tried to save her when she rode in the sacred qubbah at Dhu Qar, who was kind to her daughter when she was an orphan. But you have changed since then. Like the face of the desert, you are suffering now from drought. This drought will be the death and hardship of many if you do not temper it with the dew of mercy. A truly noble man is gracious toward those he has in his power—remember?"

She interrupted my protest. "No, do not try to guess how I know all this and I will not try to guess what it is that has caused this change in you. But you have grown brittle, and your once-refreshing sources of water have run dry. I still hope for rain for you, for I did love you as a father when I was young. But I must also take care lest you cause the same thing to happen to me. That is a very real threat. By my shaytan, what has filled in your sweet wells? Be warned, O Abu Sulayman. I will do what I have to in order to preserve myself inviolate."

Her words of warning were so clear. How is it that I forgot them so soon? I did not even wait for dawn.

16

Sons build up a home, but daughters tear it down.
—Arab saying

"I am the most magnanimous of men."

Abd ar-Rahman sat back in perfect triumph on his cushions in the *majlis* of the turpentine sellers. He had let the woman he called his sister Sejah live.

"By rights, she should die here, Sejah bint al-Harith, in this very room, as you who know her true identity must confess. To keep her honor and the honor of my family name, she must also not be allowed her own head to return to the desert. All praises to God—"

The *majlis* of the turpentine sellers murmured their echoing piety, "Praise God."

And the sword lying across Rayah's palms dropped to one hand like a dead weight, swinging behind her skirts, a thing of shame.

"God alone knows," Abd ar-Rahman continued, "what further mischief she might stir up among the tribes who once supported her in the rebellion my father—her father—put down. But I will care for her under my roof, as a brother should, so no other has the responsibility for her. I cannot, however, grant her more than the name of slave for her actions against Islam."

The *majlis* murmured its agreement that the governor of Homs could not be more magnanimous.

And Rayah wished the floor beneath the rugs would open up and swallow her. Her and her faithless, wicked mother.

"Come, brothers—I may call you all such—come." Abd ar-Rahman rose to his feet and turned with a sweep of silk to face the south. "The muezzin has called. Let us pray together."

Rayah sat on bundled tenting, huddled against the cold night sky, on her last night in Tadmor. She wanted the arms of the women downstairs. None of them offered.

Rayah's mother made fitful attempts to pack, but what use was that? To pack thirteen years into no more than a camel could carry? Her mother had always been of that unnatural jinn-possessed breed of desert dwellers who lived on nothing, who cared for nothing. Nothing in the material world.

What need had a slave for chattel anyway? A slave *was* chattel. And that's what her mother was. Her stories had related how she'd fallen into bondage twice before, how she had escaped. There would be no escaping now, not in this new world. Slavery was indeed better than an enemy of truth deserved.

Only that morning, Rayah had thought the name of "wife" a hard thing. Now, daughter of a hated, blasphemous slave, she would be lucky if they let her marry.

Rayah's head ached from crying, from breathing the dust of her mother's accursed tenting, rolled up for moving. Forced moving now. Never to be at home again. There was no going back. Not after the reaction among the turpentine sellers to the revelation of her mother's name.

All had ended with the venerable old grandfather, head of the turpentine sellers' clan, saying, "Tomorrow at dawn. You will be on your way and never shadow this place again. You've abused our hospitality long enough, O devil's dam. And devil's spawn." Even the kind old man whose mind was mostly elsewhere had been adamant.

The loss of the harem's support hurt the most. With the grandfather's words, the turpentine sellers' women had finally let the world of men cross the barrier of blue eye and silver hand. They could have said, as they had for years, "Let it be as God wills," then retreated quietly behind the walls where even the Conqueror had failed to reach. But they had chosen not to. Auntie Adilah had opened the first tiny crack. Auntie Adilah occasionally let slip beliefs that suggested her submission to Islam was due more to devotion to her brother than to God and community. Her fear made her welcome the diversion of attention elsewhere.

Men's judgments could reach even in here, after all. The place that had always been Rayah's safety; Adilah's, too. The God Rayah worshipped—One above the selfish ambitions of men, even men speaking in His glorious Name—had toppled from the sky.

Rayah had hoped to claim some little power of choice for herself. She had offered the bargain of her marriage, the accursed sword thrown in. She saw now that her mother had ruined it all, rendered them both perfectly powerless. Just by being.

Everything about Sejah, the demon Poetess, gave Rayah a headache. Worse. It was a black madness: the plague-ridden words of that eunuch's parchments, the very sight of her mother, thin and dark and hard. Tattooed for the demon. As Rayah had let herself be marked with ash on a needle. She scrubbed at the place on her cheek as if she could rub it away. And managed only to raise more tears. She hated everything about her. . .her mother.

The only thing that could help might be more verses from the Quran. And Rayah tried, "In the Name of God. . ."

She never got to "the Compassionate." Abd ar-Rahman had claimed a similar qual-ity when he called himself magnanimous.

"Sejah, Poetess and Prophetess, standing in opposition to the very Messenger of God, peace be upon him. . . . How could she stand?"

By guttering lamplight, scarcely protected from the desert wind by the half dis-mantled tenting, the scribe Abd Allah was rereading the most recent portions of the Conqueror's record. The ragged edge of the eunuch's ear, where once the emerald had winked, matched the ragged gaps in the little room's walls.

The words seemed to calm him against the world crumbling about them. Did he think they calmed others? They did not. Had he had no qualms as he had written them down? Something about the sight of black ink balancing white parchment beneath his hands must bring stability when his life teetered.

But he was neither male nor female. Who could credit anything about him?

Those parchments proved that her mother had lived a lie all the years of Rayah's childhood. Sejah was the most demonic enemy Muhammad the Apostle of God—may peace be upon him—ever faced.

Peace be upon him. Peace, peace.

Nothing but blackness. Rayah groped for the Holy Quran's light.

As if none of this had happened, with studied dispassion, the eunuch read on. "Hands as hard as manacles clamped on my right arm, then on the other, a painful twist of blood fury in each."

Rayah's belly lurched with tension, but not for the fate of the Conqueror in that far-off time. Who cared? What did he know of manacles, he who'd only ever felt those of the men of an angry desert tribe, not those of a female body and its veil? Her stomach lurched for its female self. She wished the scribe would just be quiet.

She had said she would leave everything she had ever known, marry Abd ar-Rahman's son, her own cousin although she didn't know him. She herself had said it, taken action, now—

What she did know of her uncle and grandfather, and what she now learned of her mother, made her regret her decision as she would regret blasphemy. And when the full weight of both sides of the tale came upon her, she had cried to the *majlis* full of men, "No. I take that back. By God the Merciful, I forswear. I will not marry!" Then, pushing past her evil mother, she had run back under the safety of the silver hand and its center of the cool lapis eye.

She was still carrying the unsheathed sword.

Why had that monster of a Conqueror given it to them? He thought he was being generous. He'd sent them nothing but grief and blood and hellfire.

Abd Allah read more of his master's words. "I had their meat within my belly. That should preserve my life among any honorable people for at least three days."

The turpentine sellers had been giving the governor Abd ar-Rahman the best meat for more than a month now, better meat than they could afford to eat themselves. But the city-bred son, unlike his desert-bred father, accepted everything as his due. He was a Muslim, one of the conquerors. He could imagine no reciprocal duties; he sat with that food in his belly, talking and waiting for more to be given to him.

Rayah had wanted to ease the burden on the turpentine sellers. She had merely wanted the tension in the once-calm house to ease and knew that giving herself was the only thing she could do to make it happen.

They'd been giving her mother the same hospitality for even longer, all under false pretenses.

So Rayah had given him herself. Herself and the sword. The sword that meant more to Abd ar-Rahman ibn Khalid than her whole life.

And then she had forsworn. Did her confused swearing mean anything? No. Nothing she ever said or did would ever mean anything.

As if oblivious, the eunuch read on.

Rayah had given herself and the sword to this greedy stranger. Showing herself among the men had weakened her, she felt it. The act made her seem forward, even sluttish, a definite weakness in a woman. No wonder her mother had used the weapon of a harem in self-defense all these years.

By accepting her offer anyway, Abd ar-Rahman had shown himself generous but also willing to take everything thrown at him and more as his due.

Worse, her action had forced her mother to show herself, too. An identity Sitt Sameh had worked so hard to conceal for thirteen long years, all of Rayah's life. She did this for Rayah's sake, so Rayah could make her life without violent outside events crushing her.

Abd ar-Rahman accepted the submission of Sejah bint al-Harith as his due as well. He could afford to be magnanimous; he had not slain her on the spot. Slow torture was more his game. Look at Abd Allah's ear. Now, certain of Sejah's identity, having revealed it to everyone, he had complete control over both mother and daughter.

Rayah had forsworn, but it meant nothing.

Rayah and her mother had been allowed to retreat into the harem—with the sword as well—to finish packing and to sleep one more night under this roof before leaving it forever. But what consolation was that for a life about to end? Two lives.

And here was Abd Allah's attempt at consolation, to read more of the narrative to show how completely the Conqueror and his son after him had conquered. "With great dignity. . .the sharif of al-Anbar said: 'Let the Poetess judge this case.'"

This Sejah bint al-Harith—about to become homeless, a slave and a captive of war in the present—had once judged cases, cases against Khalid ibn al-Walīd himself!

Abd Allah's voice droned over the Conqueror's notes:

"'Remember me, Sejah?' I coaxed in an undertone, hoping the angry tribesmen around us would not hear. 'Khalid ibn al-Walid Abu Sulayman. You stayed at my home in Mecca when you were a little girl. I carried you on my shoulder and you played. . . .'"

But that was the whole crux of the danger, wasn't it? Rayah fretted on. Her mother was Sejah bint al-Harith, had admitted as much to the shocked turpentine sellers and to Abd ar-Rahman, who gloated with triumph. With the pilgrimage caravan, Abd ar-Rahman would carry a captive enemy of Islam, wanted for over a decade. Sejah bint al-Harith, perhaps the last fugitive in the world as empire after empire had fallen, turning into no more than huddle after huddle of refugee women and children. More than the triumph of a bride for his son, maybe even more than his father's divine sword, was the value of this victory.

With this prize, Abd ar-Rahman would ingratiate himself to the Khalifah Omar. Perhaps it would be enough to overcome his father's unhappy history with this relative. In a quieter, woman's way, Rayah might find Omar's approval, too, as a Believer, submitting to God. Why did that not satisfy her? The past would not let it satisfy.

Her proud mother, to be taken in chains to the center of power even as had their ancestress, Queen Zaynab, from this same Tadmor to Rome.

Rayah had done her duty. She had supported the community of Believers. Before them, before God's will, what was a lone, rebellious woman, a woman who had never been much of a mother, only an enemy of God and His Messenger?

And all the Conqueror's written pages did was to reveal Sitt Sameh's real identity and the real threat she was to truth in the world. Rub it like salt in a wound.

Going to a marriage with such a mother in tow would make Rayah more powerless than ever, more powerless even than to have left all the kin she had ever known so many days of hard travel behind her. More powerless than to have deserted the inspiration of a jinni lover.

Rayah shifted the bangle on her arm. It seemed to be made of fire.

Oblivious to her dilemma, the eunuch read on.

Rayah chose to be oblivious to him. For some reason, she began to think of Abd ar-Rahman's slave, the Persian named Firuz. Why did Rayah's mind keep running over that small, dark form? She did not find him attractive, God forbid, his nose slit so. A bridegroom she had yet to meet could not possibly send the shivers down her spine as did this man. And yet the bracelet on her wrist burned whenever the man was nearby. Did her curly-haired jinni want to leap to possess him? Or did the jinni merely want to say, "Look at that one. That is how men become slaves of Islam. Be you ware, my love"?

Was it because Firuz was the only person she knew who might be more powerless, have less to lose, than she?

Centuries of conflict between the eastern empire of Persia and the western empire of Rome meant that many Persians were slaves on the Syrian side of the desert. Firuz, however, was a new arrival to the country, part of the flotsam and jetsam of populations overturned by the Muslim conquest on both sides of the Believers' homeland. Because he had fought against Khalid ibn al-Walid and because he refused to convert—like Sejah bint al-Harith, in fact—rather than being left to his Farsi religion, slavery was his fate.

Firuz had been conscripted to fight with the Persian army under its Queen Puran-dokht.

"God will never prosper an army led by a woman," Omar the Khalifah had promised the Believers.

The khalifah spoke truth; he had spoken the same concerning Sejah bint al-Harith. What else could be expected of such a monstrosity of nature? And yet was hiding in a harem the only way to protect a self that could not deny the jinni in her in this new Muslim world?

"In the Name of God, the Compassionate. . ."

In compassion is power, the very power of God. Compassion such as Sejah the Poetess had shown her would-be father in the lands of the Tamim.

Again Rayah's bracelet drew her mind to the Persian slave.

Before his conscription, Firuz had been a carpenter. So torturing uncooperative eunuchs was not the only way he got his hands dirty. In some part, he repaid the turpentine sellers by doing odd jobs around the house while he waited for his master to get the spoils for which he'd come. Firuz built new vats for the rendering shed, new tables, new doors.

This work included repairing a grille between the harem and the *majlis*. That had been a week or so ago, before Kefa died. Rayah had overheard the slave speak to his master.

"No," Abd ar-Rahman had said. "It is forbidden for captives of war to enter Mecca and al-Medinah. Our Khalifah Omar—may he ever be right-guided—wants to keep the holy cities pure. He believes a slash of his whip can keep good separated from evil forever."

The sound of a planing blade taking off one sweet-smelling curl of blond wood after another in quick succession was the only response Firuz gave for a while: a slave's response to something he didn't like. Rayah could hear Abd ar-Rahman behind the laborer cracking melon seeds and trying to see if he could spit the shells through the gap Firuz's grille would soon fill. So much he cared for another man's harem.

Rayah busied herself sweeping those shells up from beneath the grille—in this house that no longer accepted her.

Prisoners of war could not go to the pair of holy cities in Arabia. Omar the Khali-fah preached purity, but perhaps he feared more for his life from these displaced people than he did for his soul.

Prisoners could not go, but a woman brought as a bride could.

Firuz had reached up to set the lattice in the hole. Rayah longed to have the lattice quietly in place so she could go back to using it as a means to spy as well as eavesdrop upon the men. She needed to learn further how their world would impinge upon her own.

As he *tap-tapped* the frame into the tight opening, Firuz said, as if only absent-mindedly to himself, "But there cannot be very many craftsmen in that world of goat-hair walls and cushions on the floor who know how to build all the permanent furnishings of civilization."

"Omar is an austere man." This time, with a spit of seeds that hit the grille, Abd ar-Rahman did not carefully bless the khalifah when he mentioned his name.

"Yes." Firuz still mused in his accented Arabic, not his native tongue. "He must want to make his new capitals surpass the glories of Syria and of my native Ctesiphon, now that his conquerors have seen such places and can afford their riches. Not every chair and table can be carried weeks across the desert for every suddenly wealthy warrior who wants such things."

Under the *tap-tap-tap*, Rayah found it hard to be certain. It seemed to her, however, as if Abd ar-Rahman's *crack-crack* of shells had stopped. Was he, too, considering what it might mean for his honor if he provided not just a bride but the carpenter who would make mosques and homes in Arabia to stand as wonders of the new world?

On the dark rooftop, the eunuch scribe looked up from his parchments, denying Rayah further echoes of this scene from her recent past. Abd Allah said, "I suppose you have your own version of what happened next, Lady, with my master's sword and all."

Sitt Sameh, no, Sejah—Rayah found she could not give such a woman the title of "Sitt"—replied, "I do. But first I must ask you—do you think your leg well enough?"

Abd Allah nodded and set the parchments aside as he got to his feet. Rayah gave him a hand.

"Take the ruins of this litter down," Rayah's mother said. "I asked you to go to the saddle maker before, and there wasn't time. Now I ask you to go to the Persian carpenter. Ask him to repair it worthy of us, so my daughter and I may ride in it on our pilgrimage, on her marriage procession. On my ride into slavery. I won't continue the tale until you return."

17

Test your husband before taking a step and before showing boldness toward him. Remove the edge of his spear; should he remain quiet, hack bones with his sword; and if he should still be quiet, then put the saddle on his back and ride him, for he is your donkey.

—Advice Arab women give their daughters

The shattered *qubbah* had been delivered into the hands of the Persian Firuz below. None of the three could sleep, so Sejah the Poetess, as promised, took up her tale.

"Who are you?" hooted my demanding, feathered *shaytan* on the taut stretch of tent over my veiled head. His voice had more reality to me than all the tribes meeting on the dried Lake of al-Ashtat. "You who have betrayed my existence to creatures made of common clay."

"How can you ask me to keep quiet about your gift that occupies me day and night?" I retorted to the owl. "And how can you ask me not to defend my tribe against Muhammad and the Muslims when more than swords and weapons are called for?"

"You and I wrestle in the dark to sharpen those word-weapons I give you. Wrestling with another will blunt their edge. Especially another whose contact before has seen you enslaved and almost married to that Muhammad."

"You mean this same Khalid ibn al-Walīd? The one who thinks he is my father? Is he my father, as the poem says he is? Do you never lie in your poems?"

But the night bird said only, "Who?" That was his answer.

What other choice had I that night in al-Ashtat but to deal with the man Khalid?

Sharif Malik called for music to celebrate my discovery, my betrayal. Then there was dancing.

The dance was appropriate to times of new beginning: circumcisions, the first winter rains, before a battle when success is looked for, whether it be a battle of swords or of words. It was the only dance men and women dance together—if it can be called together and not against one another. A girl in her veil of eligibility dances alone between the leaping flames of a fire and a line of all the young men. The young men are cheered if they dance close enough to the young woman to touch her, and eventually they drive her off, back to the women's tents. But victory need not come easily: The fire guards the young woman's back and she is given an unsheathed sword with which to defend herself.

From my place of honor, I watched the first two girls called forward one by one to play the part. The sword they were handed was old and nicked; they giggled a lot. They tripped about the dance floor weakly, conscious only of men's eyes on them. After a while, the men felt no scruples about turning to talk to their neighbors again instead of watching or dancing.

So I stopped letting my *shaytan* rule, urging caution. Urging me to consider that this was not my battle, al-Medinah was. Then he flew away in a fury. The third girl who rose to dance came not from the great black darkness beyond the fires where the women sat, but from the midst of the men.

I, Sejah, Poetess and Prophetess, rose and stood before the fire, leaping gold against the dark night, illuminating the young men's sweating faces. They shifted backwards before me. I arranged my veil so my eyes showed, nothing more.

By God, I read that son of al-Walīd's thoughts: "By that single God of my new creation, my new destruction, she has remarkable eyes. Just like her mother's."

No, not like my mother, who let you love her, if you are to be believed, then died of the pain.

"Her eyes—" Abd Allah found the place in the manuscript. "Her eyes were a deep blue such as one might expect to pass with her infancy. But it had not, and they remained like bits of sky, like wells. They seemed to be not all present as normal dark eyes are, and yet they seemed able to see beyond the horizon. They glowed, even with her back to the fire. They glowed off the reflection on the young men's faces."

Yes, I read the pockmarked face, which he, that Meccan and Muslim, dared to show among the sons and daughters of Tamim. Let him see the unnatural and powerful where he would. He saw it in Muhammad, did he not?

For the dance, I needed one more prop beyond veil and eyes. I bent to pick up the dull, nicked sword from which the last girl dancer had fled.

Instead, Khalid ibn al Walid held his out to me. I met his gaze. Hunting far off, the owl hooted encouragement to me. I twisted the hilt out of Khalid's hand.

His sword was heavy. I could not wield it like a man could. Indeed, this was probably the only time in my life I would ever be allowed to touch such a thing, lest the well of my femaleness leach all the virtue from it. Gritting my teeth, I did not stagger foolishly, however, nor did I require my whole body to heave its weight into the air as had the two girls who danced before me.

"This is the daughter of my love."

I heard Khalid's proud thoughts. But if he would not claim me aloud, I would resent every morsel of pride my deeds might give him.

"She will be the mother of. . ."

"Of sharifs" would have been the usual compliment among my people, but in this case I knew not how to finish. It was beyond my ability to prophecy what I might bring forth. My *shaytan* had abandoned me in this moment.

The blade poised in the air caught the firelight.

"The night of Nakhlah," came to my mind. I had only ever heard of the place from my *shaytan*.

The power of my poem leapt like lightning to its origins, then from there to my hand where it belonged. The melding of heaven and earth, of fire and wind.

The drums began, slowly and gently at first like the creak of a litter with the sway of its camel. The young men began to move in time to the music, to stamp their feet, to clap their hands, to sway backwards and forwards, to one side and the other. None of them had yet the voice of a man, so their singing seemed no more than the sound of sand wisped across bare stone. Their spirits were high. They chatted and squawked in all directions and at cross purposes like birds in a thicket.

They began to dance closer and closer to me and, the object of the game, to tag me with the palms of their hands.

"Watch out, watch out," was the chorus of their song.

From time to time one or another of them would improvise a line of poetry to be repeated by all the others in unison and with melody, in time to the clap of their hands.

Some will tell you the dance teaches the young men not to fear the flashing blade of a sword so they will not flinch in battle. It makes them quick.

Others say there is symbolism there. I, Sejah, the young, veiled, half-woman with a blade in my hands stood surrounded: the fire at my back sending me forward and all the young men in front driving me back again. I was meant to be veiled so the scene could represent, perhaps, Any Woman against All Men.

But no. Khalid ibn al-Walīd danced among them. He didn't really dance; he was too old for that role. He acted more like the guardian of a *qubbah*, thwarting the young men's movements.

Countering him, the young men let themselves become carried away by the movement of their own bodies and the challenge of the game. They forgot this was the

Poetess they faced. Any other woman I have ever seen perform this dance set down the sword and fled in giggles after the first dozen touches or so. I, Sejah, did not flee. If I were a symbol for anything, it was not shrinking modesty and defeat.

Khalid jostled the men and the men jostled me, backwards until the fire lapped at the ends of my braided hair where they appeared beneath the veil.

"Does al-Harith's daughter wish to join the sacrifices in the fire?" the men sitting in the tent asked one another. They laughed with excitement.

Suddenly the blade seemed to leap, pulling my hand after it. I heard the air protest; it had no time to move out of the way of my lash.

"A lucky stroke," one young man commented, but he was the last to speak so boldly.

The sword repeated the movement at an interval so close that it could not be called luck. The audience could respond only with an "ooh" and a hissing of teeth before it fell silent.

A dozen conversations had dropped to one: the chant of the young men, their rhythm driving harder, harder, being answered again and again by the sweep of the sword. It took a hawk's speed to avoid that flight.

Men recognized whence came the power behind the blade. Its familiarity stunned them. On a raid, when things grew desperate, this violence would carry them beyond themselves and make them invincible. Some say a jinni enters into a warrior at such a time.

Now one dancer wore the jinn like necklaces constantly about her. The clapping, the drums, the flash of the sword. Harsh, unexpected violence erupted from me, a mere girl. My words carried power. No one had ever considered that there could be such in my hand as well. Now they could no longer doubt.

"Watch out, watch out!" The young men's voices compacted now. Effort and—yes, fear—deepened their voices to the throaty, dry call of a leopard on the hunt in his oasis. Such a sound bounces off the walls of the wadi, honing itself.

The blade brought them together, the blade gave them their strength. The firelight struck eyes and sweat, making the dancers seem like live coals. Those torrents of sweat alone kept the dust from rising, from choking us as our feet rocked to and fro, to one side and the other.

My breath, growing ragged, matched the ragged *thunk-a-thunk, thunk-a-thunk* of the drum.

"Sejah, my love," I heard the Meccan who claimed to be my father. He prayed. To a partner God.

The sword fairly spilled through the air. The same fire forged the blade and my eyes as they flashed over the veil at that instant, neither iron nor flesh, but something in between. The sight enthralled me as well as my male opponents, the way the eyes of a viper can. No young man had scored a touch for a good sixty beats of the drum.

Enough time had passed for people to begin to wonder what would happen next. What would happen if I should win this contest as well as the poetry? Win? It was not a question of winning. At least, it had never been before.

Finally a boy, the son of Sharif Malik and his wife Layla named Tamim, called out, "O Khalid Abu Sulayman of the Meccans," and winked conspiratorially at the interloper. Tamim would not be out-maneuvered by a girl, even if she was a new-made Poetess. And the Meccan had forgotten my prophetic words: "Like the face of the desert, you suffer from drought."

"On his life," interrupted the scribe, who knew Khalid's mind better than any, "Khalid the Conqueror swears he meant nothing against you, Lady, when he joined his milk brother's son."

"So he says," said Sejah. Everything packed she could pack, she was spinning. As she would do, no doubt, all the way into slavery.

"He swears to it."

"By his God."

"By his life. The boy enticed him."

Sejah laughed bitterly.

"He meant only to play."

"He was the adult, the boys but children." Sejah the Prophetess did not accept this interpretation.

"It was play to him, as he had played with you when you were a toddler."

"But I had grown up, and now it was deadly serious. He was playing with God. I called out to him to tell him so."

"What did you say?"

"'The jinn. Remember what you owe the jinn.'"

A breeze breathed through the little room's open tenting. Rayah shivered.

The scribe cleared his throat nervously. "He must not have heard you."

"Then he purposely stopped his ears," said the Poetess and went on with her tale.

Dancing all the while, Tamim and the Meccan separated and began to attack from different directions. While the Meccan acted as distraction, young Tamim scored and scored again. Nobody cheered. Nobody said anything.

I, Sejah, still danced. I could hear my own breath tortured in the silence, but the rest was a trance of swinging blade and falling stars. Where my own weak self failed, my *shaytan* maintained.

"The jinn," I panted to the Meccan. "Remember what you owe the jinn."

Then Khalid feinted, scored—and screamed out in surprise and in pain. The crowd fell back. The drum beats choked and died.

Khalid stood in the firelight holding his right arm. In that strange light, the blood flowing down to the dust at his feet looked no more serious than a spill of water—it was that color in the reddish light.

I also saw a curl of black smoke rise, equal to the blood from the wound. Jinn.

I stood still with my back to the fire. The adversary, my own *shaytan*, left me, his price taken. I came to myself. I would not look at my victim. I lowered the veil back across my eyes. In my hands, the sword was no longer like something alive and winged. Only a strip of metal slowly dropped to my side, dragged down by its incredible weight. Was that blood there on the point? If so, then it must be my own, my own woman's blood. I'd stopped feeling anything; my arm seemed drained of all life.

The sword fell to the dust and I, Sejah, Poetess, turned and ran from the firelight, from what I had done, defeated at last by no one but myself. And by the first physical blow I had dealt Islam.

Nobody in camp moved or called after me. That's what she, the dancer, was supposed to do—run, overwhelmed by the light of the fire and the joy of the song. Except she was not supposed to draw blood before she escaped. Such a thing had never been known to happen. As soon as the camp came to itself, they took steps to prevent the evil that must accompany such a departure from the normal ritual.

In the dark of the desert, owls flew. Mice died. A clan of hyenas chuckled madly at human foolishness along the dry lake's edge. Away from the fire, sweat chilled on my skin under the veil. Against the distant, dying light, I watched the clan of Tamim see to their bleeding guest. Would there be blood price to pay?

"My master says he had known worse wounds, but never one that seemed so justified, so satisfying in its pain. Even his circumcision had not had as much ritual meaning for him. Perhaps women feel thus when a difficult birth rips them open—that the pain is worth it."

Sejah met Rayah's gaze but said nothing. Rayah looked away. She wanted to get up and leave but she found she could not.

"And the pain you felt when they made a eunuch of you?" Sejah turned her attention back to the scribe.

Abd Allah would not speak of it.

"Or when that pair of monsters downstairs broke your leg?"

Sejah sighed when she still received no answer and continued her tale.

They brought him to the women's tents, to his milk mother, the mother of Mutam-mim the poet and of Sharif Malik. Seeing this, and abandoned for the moment by my *shaytan*, I came out of the desert into which I'd run alone. I rejoined the community, the crust of the dry lake bed cracking invisibly beneath my bare feet.

I pushed aside Umm Mutammim's tent flap. I squatted in the circle of concerned women, one pressing the corner of her veil to staunch the blood, Umm Mutammim herself pounding the white stone alum with garlic as a paste. Applied to an open wound, the garlic would sting. Its powerful scent floated under the stretched wool overhead along with the stinging smoke from the dung fire by which they worked.

I pushed my way in among the women on the Meccan's right-hand side. Without the veil's pressure, the gash immediately welled with fresh blood. A fairly deep wound, but thin and clean, it would heal, Manat willing. I took off my own veil and pressed.

"Oh, you look like your mother," said the Meccan, befuddled with loss of blood. "When first I saw her by the well in al-Hira."

"Keep still," I ordered him, none too gently. I'd never known my mother. "She died," I said. "Abandoned me." Because of him?

I called among the women for a gazelle-bone needle, smoothed by much work on the family's garments, and plucked one sweat-moistened hair from my head. I pricked at one side of the gash. The Meccan hissed but was otherwise quiet. I pricked through the flesh on the other side and, with the hair-threaded needle, pulled the edges together. So I went, all the way up, while Umm Mutammim dabbed at the spilling blood.

But should I have let the wound bleed more, to let all the evil out? I knew I sewed jinn in. I felt them with my fingers as I pulled the skin together.

No. Much more blood would have killed him.

I left the needle stuck in his skin, spat upon it to help the healing, and applied the paste. I enjoyed how the Meccan drew in breath between his teeth again at the garlic sting and how the white paste turned pink as it mixed with blood. I bound his arm with a rag.

"By God the Merciful, your hands were skilled," the scribe told the Poetess in her third-floor room. "He showed me the scar."

"Manat is merciful," Sejah replied.

"And that was the scar I saw upon the Conqueror's right arm. I saw him finger it, up and under his sleeve.

"'Curious,' he told me. 'It is not like the others. It does not ache when rain is coming. It bothers me only when I am deeply troubled in my soul. Then it feels as if it would split open at that ancient seam.' He had been feeling it quite a lot lately."

"And what did you say?"

"Nothing. The Conqueror probably thought I was doodling on my parchments, paying his mutterings no mind."

A night of feasting and poetry had worn the encampment down. It drowsed in the warming dawn around me. In favor of sleep, the sons of Tamim put off debate about my future challenge of al-Medinah and about the future of the wounded stranger in our camp.

Perhaps Khalid the Muslim was the only one to hear the curious sound that came from the space where the camels of the sons of Tamim couched. He may have heard it only because he dozed off, fitfully nodding against the crook in his good arm, feeling the dull throb in the bad as if his heart had moved to that part of his body. Clearly amid the snorting and wheezing that comes all day, every day from a herd of camels, came the sound of a single animal being loosed from its hobble. The beast growled, struggled to its feet, grew suddenly swift and graceful beneath me.

"That is Sejah, my daughter," he might have said before sleep completely overcame him, "who has saddled a camel, who is now riding away to—"

Evil jinn possessed him and his right arm, the arm I had attacked, or my good jinn had. His evil jinn would seek revenge for bloodshed. I, a woman who bled monthly and never sought revenge for the loss, should seek asylum.

I'm going to Nakhlah, I could have answered his question. That place I'd never been and yet which haunted my poems, my dreams. Rumor told me that this Muslim had destroyed the shrine. He could not have done so completely. My *shaytan* still whispered the name in the night wind.

But I did not seek it for asylum alone, for I had seen my jinn attack his and triumph.

I had not wanted to win the poetry contest. I had no desire to be in the same half of the desert as Muhammad they called the Prophet, not since his one minion had killed my mentor Asma for her verse. But now his other minion Khalid had found me. And focused the name of the Valley into the blade of a dancing sword.

If the Gods had determined I must face Muhammad ibn Abd Allah, his words against mine, I must gain what strength I could where I could. In Nakhlah. Alone.

18

The morning she set out, camel-borne
through the tribe's acacia ground, I
wept as a man cracking a colocynth.
—The qasidah of Imru 'l-Qais

The sons of Tamim awoke that late afternoon in their encampment on the dry lake bed of al-Ashtat as if from a jinn-inspired dream. Some denied outright all that had seemed to happen during the long night—contest, revelation, dance. Most agreed that nothing like this had happened in all the days of their fathers. No precedent existed to guide their behavior. In the majlis, the debate grew as long and fierce as the heat of the day had been: What should be done now that the winner of the contest had fled? Not only that, but she had proven herself out of control in the most traditional of dances.

I remained recuperating and visiting with my milk mother in her tent while she tended to my arm. I could have no part in such discussion, though the topic vastly interested me, and I'd firmly resolved my opinion on every point. I forced myself to set behind me the temptation to enter and speak where I was not welcome.

Layla brought us the news.

"The men are mounting now," she reported. "They will ride on to al-Medinah during the cool of tonight's moon without her."

"Without whom?" I asked.

"Without Sejah, of course."

"But they can't."

"What other choice is there? The foolish girl is still not to be found since that business with the sword, the sword and your arm."

"Sejah is gone? But where?"

"That's what half the yelling has been about these last hours in the men's tent. Do you think they care so much about you, a Qurayshi that one of their women can dispatch? My master Malik feels they should wait and hunt for her a while longer, but the Banu 'l-Anbar are most anxious about their captive brothers, wives and children. Can you blame them?"

"Who will recite for them before Muhammad?" I asked. I knew Sejah was the only answer to my own question. Anyone else meant defeat for the Tamim.

"Why, az-Zibrikan, of course. Perhaps he was defeated last night, but he at least has the sense not to run off when the tribe needs him, and that is worth twenty such flighty jinn."

"But where, by God, has the child gone?"

I do not know what my face looked like at this news. My mind was so full of images from the past—those eyes, those words. Her creation in the Valley of Nakhlah. And even long before that. I remembered the child now called her father who had also run from camp and been all alone in the desert at night. Perhaps a closer relationship existed between Sejah and al-Harith than I suspected, than I liked to admit. My mind reeled with such things. What those present about me revealed, much less what I myself might say with a colorless face and staring eyes, hardly found a conscious place there.

Whatever I looked like, something pulsed there that made Layla stop. She was not quite the limitless, senseless talker she had been when I first knew her in her father's tent. Sand sifted before her eyes, those eyes that had been dulled in self-protection for so long.

"You love her, don't you, brother of my master?" She stated it rather than asked, though her voice was careful and quiet.

"Like a daughter, yes," I said, flustered, discovered. "Like my own daughter."

"Like your own daughter," Layla repeated and let the words sink into her mind. She had nothing else to tell me after that.

My milk mother and the rest of the camp protested when I threw my saddle on my camel (with but one hand) and myself on after it. They assumed I meant to follow at the tail end of the delegation riding towards al-Medinah. Indeed, I assumed as much myself—at first. If he could, who in all the western deserts would not try to be there in al-Medinah for this contest?

But, by God, I knew az-Zibrikan, and I knew Muhammad. I knew with prophet's vision of my own whose words would carry the day. Az-Zibrikan was good, the Prophet's equal, perhaps, in favorable circumstances. But what was favorable about the world of Islam that no longer accepted the power of poetry except Revelation?

Besides, the past night had taught az-Zibrikan that he was not the best. I had seen it the last couple of times the honored old poet had readjusted his slipping cloak—by hunching his shoulders with the brute necessity of any slave. He had lost a vital measure of confidence, and that doomed him.

Should I not go to al-Medinah anyway, to gloat over the Qurayshi victory and *be able to say to my milk brothers: "I told you so"? Few men would refuse the chance to take such a gratuitous victory. Or, once the proud Tamim had been forced to humble themselves and set their hands beneath the son of Abd Allah's, should I not be there to ease their pain? Should I not go to speak for the release of their women and children once they had sworn to pay the tax and to fight on the side of Islam?*

I should have gone to stop the flame in my arm. Muhammad might have spat on it, driven out the jinn.

But I thankfully left that post of spokesman on my brothers' behalf to another, to az-Zibrikan.

Az-Zibrikan lost the poetry combat in al-Medinah. With mercy, however, all the prisoners of the al-Anbar were eventually returned, save one girl who had caught the fancy of her captor. After payment of a suitable price, she was duly added to his harem. Had she been returned, her kin would have had to kill her for the dishonor, so it was just as well. The Tamim got better than they might have hoped for from the business. Their best hope, the young Poetess, remained behind them somewhere in the desert.

And I meant to find her.

I set my teeth on the dry grit between them, mopped the sweat of fever from my brow and rode on.

I had left al-Ashtat taking the way to al-Medinah. I followed that way, the dust and jumbled spoor of the Tamimi delegation, for some time. But I never got where they were going.

By the oppressive heat of midday I rested in the puddle of shade beside my camel, but otherwise I did not stop for a night, a day and a night. Near a rocky outcrop, I found other tracks to follow: a single camel with splay feet and small, irregular stool that told me she had eaten nothing since the thistle growing in the cracked mud at al-Ashtat. This beast had passed through that scrap of desert no more than half a day before the delegation. I might have been fooled into thinking that the camel was unmounted, her feet made such a light impression on the ground. But a camel will not leave a place with easy food and water unless she is driven.

My suspicions were confirmed when I found the spot, the smooth round ovals where the camel had knelt to rest, and there were the prints of other, human, feet. The driver was hardly more than a child. But the sweeping pattern of an edge of robe, the impression of a ring on one bare toe: These things told me that the rider was female. And alone. Such a thing was so uncommon in the wilds of the desert, I did not have to guess who the rider might be. I knew.

I had meant never to see Nakhlah again. I had meant even to avoid the journey from Mecca to at-Ta'if, but if that were not possible I had planned always to take the longer way around and to give any excuse necessary. I did not think I could bear to look upon the ravished and desolated landscape that was my handiwork.

But the good air, the pure air, the thin air entering my lungs made me rise along the track like a bubble. Something stirred within me, like a seed, cast by the wayside, favored after years and years by just the right rain and sun. I had not planted it there. It was something beyond the experience of my years. It came from my father, perhaps, or my father's father. Something that was strong enough to counteract the weight of the sword he had given me. Or perhaps it came from my mother, one of my mothers. For it felt distinctly feminine, as if some great Woman had impregnated me with Herself.

Did Adam feel so when Eve labored within his ribs to come out? Would that God might cause some great sleep to come over me, to miss the sweet pain of this birth of which I, a man, was physically incapable. And the evil and the fall to come. . . Might I be spared!

From the height of a mountain, I saw all the Valley, all Creation, all in one glance, all pure and golden, untarnished, untouched. The very horizon threw itself at my heart with a love incomparable, inescapable. I yearned, I ached, for everything and in the same instant, was satisfied, satisfied and yearning exquisitely at once together. I could not have stopped my climbing if death had lain in my way, as indeed it seemed to. And even death was part of the great attraction. It was intoxicating, compulsive and prurient.

I found that I was weeping, tears warmer, more profuse and more wonderful than any I'd shed even as a child. All impurities washed from my body, from my heart.

At last I reached the top of the pass—I knew it must be the top, for there was nowhere left to climb. I stood on a smooth open space, meeting the sky. Nothing stood higher than myself but the sky. The sky arced blue-gold and perfect.

Below me, the ground was alitter with chips of stone as if it had been the site of a celebration, strewn with bunting and streamers. Rose petals. When I could actually smell the roses, I knew I was slipping sideways into the realm of the jinn.

I made my camel kneel, dismounted, then began to lead her for reverence. I took off my sandals. My bare footfalls sent the rocks singing. When I kicked one stone against another, they rang like the peal of bells. I took air into my lungs and let it out again. The air was good, never before breathed by mortals. With each breath, I imbibed not just air but divinity.

I began my descent into the Valley. Then I stumbled on the path. I fell on my face and was conscious of nothing but the rich smell of heavenly burning without and within my soul.

19

She swore a solemn oath by the hair of Her
Who made the branches of the trees of Suqam
to be protected and interdicted.
— Abu Jundub al-Hudhali

I came to my senses and saw her, her qubbah *with its drifting curtains, she standing beside it. Perhaps both events were one and the same, my seeing, my revival. One, at least, caused the other, though I am not prepared to say which came first.*

She saw me, too, and would, I think, have hid, but that no place remained in the smooth, empty bowl of that Valley to hide, not even the shade of a child-size boulder. The fever raged; my arm felt very heavy. Fresh blood came through the fine stitches and the rag. I got to my feet in spite of that and continued my descent.

I considered Nakhlah's desolation as I descended. Some might say the combined delirium of a long desert ride and an infected wound allowed me to see it with eyes unclouded and not throbbing with guilt. Nakhlah was so changed! The jinn of the fever separated my conscience from consciousness, lulled it to rest so it no longer bothered me with the knowledge that my hand alone had changed the face of the earth.

The place might have seen a natural disaster. A great wall of mud carried by the winter rains had come, ripping ravines now raw, eroding the surrounding hills, blanketing the level Valley.

But as I drew nearer, I could see that nothing natural existed about the devastation. The stumps of the three sacred trees stood white, exposed beneath the sky, like eyelids hanging straight across the emptiness where once had been an eye. A flood may rip up trees by the roots, lightning shatter trunks to rags, but only man would be so thorough as to take all three at once. Only a man's ax could have honed them so unnaturally. Only his fire could have so systematically burned all that could be burned of the little shrine. Only his shovel could have silted up the sacred well so completely.

Her greeting brought my impartial study of my surroundings to a close. By any measure, it was a curious greeting. "Draw your sword, Uncle," the girl said, "and do not hesitate. I am prepared to die, and it is easier, so they say, if the hand with the sword does not hesitate."

"Whatever are you saying, child?" I asked.

"That you should kill me at once."

"Why, for the love of God, do you think I would want to do such a thing?"

"Blood for blood," she said simply. "For what other reason does a man follow another in such hot pursuit? So, Uncle, go ahead. Slay me for the drawing of your blood."

"You mean from the dance?"

"Of course from the dance."

"Oh, daughter, that was nothing. It was only a scratch."

"Uncle, you lie. I can see the wound now. Oh. I cannot bear to look at it. Uncle, how awful! It is not a scratch. Here. Cut off my hand for it at least." And she pulled up sleeve and bracelets to expose a delicately tattooed wrist and forearm. She turned her head away to avoid the sight but none of the pain of the expected blow.

"It is nothing, I tell you," I tried to reassure her. "I forgave it as soon as it happened. It was mostly my fault, anyway, playing so roughly and unfairly with you."

"The cutter dance is not a game," she said.

"No," I agreed. "You are so right, and it was disgraceful of me to treat it as such. But see now, the sons of Tamim have forgotten all about it. So let's have you forget it, too."

"Have they truly forgotten?" she asked, but strangely no hope enlivened her voice.

"No one seeks your life. They worry, rather, that you left them, alone and without a word. I swear it, by my life, by God, by this Valley all around us."

Though I tried to increase the holiness of my oath as I progressed, she seemed neither convinced nor impressed. Had I been told an attack of mine had made little effect for all my effort, I would have been disheartened, too. She was like her mother in that she pitied harm done. But she was very like me, too.

"I warned you," she said, sighing under her breath. "Didn't I warn you not to press me, Uncle?"

"You warned me," I agreed. "Uncle," never "father". I pressed on through my disappointment. "You were meant to defend the tribe in al-Medinah as the poet that you are. They will not have forgotten."

She pulled the sleeve down over her wrist but said nothing.

"Now the Tamim will have to be content with az-Zibrikan as their champion, and you and I both know the old man won't have the strength of words to stand up to Muhammad." I was working it out for myself as if I had a prophet's gifts. To counter that blasphemy, I said, "As God wills," before continuing, "az-Zibrikan will submit to Islam, and the world will forget his name." There are worse things than death.

"And if I had gone in his place? What if I go now? There is still time. And believe me, I would not convert."

"No!" was all I managed. Convert? Indeed, I knew she would not.

She looked at me keenly. "What do you prophesy then? Can I save my people?"

A wave of nausea washed over me, for I had been too afraid that whole ride of what this alternative might lead to. She might have become lost in the desert, she might have been captured by a hostile tribe, she might have perished of thirst and hunger, but none of these events seemed worse than had she gone to the contest instead. And submitted.

For she could not win. No matter what poem she recited, once words have a sword behind them, no other words can win.

"No." She repeated what I had said, then quietly put it into poetry: "Throats and windpipes cannot stand."

"I only want you safe. Believe me."

"The honor of a whole tribe is not worth me daring my safety? Because I know. What you really want is not honor, only to win."

Someone so young should not see through their elders so well. For what did I offer her, after all? Marriage to the Prophet of God, may peace be his. Not the freedom to use her words. Only the safety of a hearth, a home, a family. And the shadow of my ambition.

"I would go. I would not fear to go," she said, "even now. But for what I found here in this Valley."

A full turn that sent her veils swirling emphasized what she had found: nothing.

"I thought there would be a shrine here," she went on.

"You meant to seek asylum at its altar?"

"I need strength to stand against Muhammad. That is what I was led here to find. I see now that I was led astray. How could such a foolish one as I stand up to a Prophet such as yours in al-Medinah?"

Only then did I realize her sorrow, the sorrow I thought only men could know: not to have let the world see their prowess.

She laughed, whether she found it absurd or otherwise, I know not. "I see that the trickster jinn meant only to mock me by putting that feeling in my heart."

With another tactic, I suggested, "We are of the same blood, too close to demand compensation."

She considered this and then shook her head, refusing to accept. "I am but the daughter of Malik's herdsman," she said, "and you aren't Sharif Malik's true brother at all, only by nursing."

I pressed the bridge of my nose, remembering the pain of old taunts, taunts I myself had given. It would take something closer to satisfy her. She had that something in the words of her poem, yet she would not see it as anything apart from her. And I still could not bring myself to turn her young world upside down by explaining to her just how close we were, and what part the Valley of Nakhlah played in that closeness. I have always lacked that sort of courage, especially in the face of a veil trustingly turned to me.

"But you do not seem so desolate and strange to me now," she said in a tone that sought to lose its stiffness. So saying, she began to search for another way to closeness. Another reason for us finding each other here.

With more courage than it took to face the whole Persian army, I spoke. "Child, dear daughter. I am your father."

"Why do you keep telling people that lie?"

"It isn't a lie." Tears hot with fever streamed down into my beard. "By this holy ground where you were conceived as your own poem declares, I swear, and I swear it should be no dishonor to you or to your blessed mother whom I loved more than my life." I fell to my knees under the beating of the sun. "Let me. Let me care for you as a father should."

"Fathers bury their daughters at birth if they do not care to raise them."

"Muhammad, blessed be he, has outlawed the practice as from the Time of Ignorance. He has only daughters and understands their blessings." Weakly, I added, "Help me to understand."

"Has he indeed?" She considered, then rejected the thought. "But he has not outlawed the killing of daughters when they are grown and you do not care for the dishonor they bring once you—you—have raised them."

My turn to struggle. She was right. I remembered my first-born girl, never as dear to me as this one I had no power of life and death over. I had spared the other at birth, loved her as a child—and then had been forced to kill her for the dishonor she carried in her unmarried womb. "Yes," gurgled in my throat.

Again Sejah thrust her arm at me, her breast at me. "So you might as well go ahead and do it now in this place you have made the most desolate in all Arabia."

By what demon did she know? "I—I had my orders," I attempted.

"Orders!" She turned from me with scorn and a jangle of shells. More quietly, she added, "Well, my shaytan gives me orders of my own."

My head sank beneath the weight of its red turban. "Do not say that word, child."

"What word? Orders?"

"Shaytan."

"*You would keep me from speaking the truth?*"

"*I would keep you from what is dangerous, what could get you killed.*"

"*What?*"

"*Muhammad, blessed be he, has turned that word into Satan.*"

"*And so he is, my* shaytan. *An adversary. An adversary is that which makes you strong. To be more than you are by yourself.*"

The meaning made perfect sense. "*But Muhammad would kill every adversary, everyone.*"

"*Christians do. So do the Jews. He joins with them.*"

"*He does, as People of the Book.*"

"*As people of power, people of empire, people who create Satan as opposed to* shayatan *and cannot feel strong without him dead.*"

I saw that, with such a connotation, yes, I was indeed among those Believers. "*We Arabs are tired of being the poor man of the desert, a laughingstock of those holier-than-thou's.*"

"*Poor men, but free beneath the Gods of the desert sky and the jinn of the desert wells.*"

Oh, she should bite her tongue! For her own safety. I told her, "*You must let me take you to al-Medinah for the poetry contest, to protect you against what you may find there.*"

"*I need you to make me strong? You who would give me as a bride to Muhammad ibn Abd Allah for your own advancement?*"

That I had no answer to, for it was true. She must have seen it by a demon's prophecy.

A sigh rose from deep in her chest. "*I came to this Valley to find my* shaytan. *I cannot fight this fight without such strength. But I see he—or perhaps she—has been chased away.*"

"*Child, I would not be your adversary. Never.*" *But what I had already done sickened me.*

"*Yet you would have the right to kill me for dishonor. I cannot go with you to al-Medinah. Al-Uzza knows I would dishonor you in that town.*"

"*I mean protection.*"

"*But the fear is there, and where there is fear, for one such as you, you also find dishonor.*"

I would kill anyone who said I was afraid. But she was right.

It was a matter of honor.

"*I am your father,*" *I whimpered.* "*By this sword, by this holy, hollow place, I am your father.*"

"I could give you some of my milk," she said, laughing at the notion of herself as a mother, "and make you my son. Women often do such things to increase the circle of their kinsmen. Alas, I am not a mother yet."

I tried to join in her good humor over this. But she was so innocent, so in need of a father. I was embarrassed to laughter by all the implications of such a thing, at which she did not even guess.

"No?" With a sudden movement, she lunged for my sword and pulled it from its sheath, toying with it as she had toyed with the blade during the dance by firelight.

She had feared I might kill her. Now I knew she would kill me. "That sword, forged with heaven stones which fell in this very place, cannot be resheathed until it has drawn blood," I said.

"Then we shall have to mingle blood as men do," was her final decision. "So much blood you may by rights demand of me."

She did not even flinch as she made the necessary cut. Right arm to right arm, her short pale one against the tangled hair and puffy flesh of my burning. Her blood, it seemed, was the warmer of the two, though I was the one with the fever. It bore the curiously refreshing warmth—hot as one can stand it—of a cup of boiled water.

"Al-Uzza," she invoked the Goddess.

I pulled my arm away too soon, seeing that was what she wanted of me: The jinni that had invaded me when I destroyed the place.

But why did I want to keep such a thing?

"Never mind." She seemed to have read my thoughts. "Enough jinn remain in that arm of yours to satisfy their claims against you since you were a child."

How on earth did she know? Except that her grandmother had been there at my bartering with the Beings of Smokeless Fire.

"Still you look pale." Her laugh rang clear as desert air after a storm. "They are shayatan, *adversaries. They will make you strong."*

At last she sighed with relief that life was still hers for some time yet. She did not really long for death. She loved life and loved to see it—no, not prolonged in hopeless suffering but— reach possibility.

And because of that, she would not come with me to defend her tribe in al-Medinah.

20

You have purposely broken your jar
And its water has sweetened the earth.
My soul cries out to God—
Would that I were the dust of that earth.
                        —A traditional Syrian poem

We sat thus in Nakhlah afterwards, my sister-daughter and I, crouched upon the barren ground in the camels' shade where first we had met. No more hospitable place to seek shelter existed in that wasteland. Sejah continued to hold my sword, cradling it between her bent knees and studying the blade with more-than-girlish interest.

"I'd heard you had a rare sword, O my uncle—my brother," she said. Still not "father." But this would have to do. "I did not get to see it properly in the dark when we danced."

What I saw then were her blue eyes reflected on the hammered metal over the white shells of her veil. That was, I thought, as it should be. "I will leave it to you when I die, if you'd like," I suggested.

"Al-Uzza forbid," she said and laughed. She thought I was teasing her. "From heaven stones, is it really?"

"Yes," I said. "I found them here." As I found and forged her here.

"I could tell."

Of its origin no more than of her own could I bring myself to speak any further, for they were one and the same. I protected my own heart by seeking to uncover the mystery of hers.

"Why did you not go to Mecca?" I asked.

"Why should I want to go to Mecca? As opposed to al-Medinah, where others must defend the tribe, for I have not found my spirits here."

"Mecca is a place of sanctuary. You might have sought there. It is closer to al-Ashtat than this Valley of Nakhlah."

"Nakhlah," she repeated, loving the name. "So that is what this place is called?

Like in my shaytan's *poem."*

"Yes."

"Mecca is changed, I hear."

"Who told you that?"

"Oh, everyone. Isn't it, then? Isn't it changed since Muhammad took it?"

I nodded. "It is changed."

"If it is changed so much that only those who agree with Muhammad have asylum, what sort of asylum is that?"

I had no answer.

"You changed, too, my uncle. Only now you are my brother and not so different."

"Nakhlah is changed," I mused.

"Is it? Is it really?"

So some things she saw and some she did not.

"Greatly," I confessed.

"I thought so." The veil turned here and there to look about now as if it hung not on her head but on a clothesline, being tossed about by the wind. "Since Muhammad, too?"

"Yes, since Muhammad."

I did not offer her details of this happening, either, and she did not ask for them. This time, however, I had the distinct feeling that she already knew the whole story. Perhaps she knew all about the sword and our kinship as well, and was quiet on the matter to protect me as I was protecting her.

"This man Muhammad. I remember him, from when I was a child."

"Do you?" I asked.

"Yes," she replied and paused on the memory. But what or how it was that she remembered did not penetrate through the veil to me.

"He has the gifts of a prophet?" she asked.

"Yes. At least he says he does."

"Brother, if a man says he is a prophet, believe him. It is not something one says for a joke. It is too demanding a calling to be taken lightly. It is very possible to abuse what one has been given, that is true. But heaven does not allow such abuse for long."

She gave me time to nod at the wisdom of her words. "And if a woman says she is a prophetess?"

She ignored my question. "This man, Muhammad. He is a Qurayshi, isn't he? A member of your own tribe."

"Yes," I admitted.

"Then maybe you can tell me what he is doing. I do not understand it. Why is

he changing everything? What will the Arabs have to stand on when he has changed our basis?"

I shrugged and then said weakly, "He says he means to end the harm done by the wealthy and strong against the weak."

"Yet he would leave us weak ones without our ancient sanctuaries to run to when we are afraid for our lives? That I do not understand."

"I don't understand it, either," I agreed. "It is as God wills."

"Perhaps we should look for another prophet to come after him," she suggested.

"He says there will be no others after him."

"Does he, now? Then who shall temper this sword he has unsheathed when he is gone? Who will temper it with spirit?"

"I do not know."

She took her turn to stop and think more than she said. "Oh, well," she at last conceded. "Perhaps he is right. Heaven alone knows."

"Heaven alone knows," I agreed. A jab of pain ran through my right arm.

After this I suggested that perhaps we should start journeying back. "Both we and our animals have been without water for a good long while. There is none in Nakhlah, and we must ride at least another day before we come upon a sure and decent source."

"No," Sejah declared.

I thought then she must have gone mad. Leaving the sword unsheathed, she got to her feet and ran away like she had before, like a sulky child who will not listen to sense. I got to my feet, too, and watched her over the backs of the camels. At some distance, she began to walk slowly over the ground, looking as it were at each grain of sand individually for a moment, then sliding on to the next. After a moment's hesitation, I crossed to her over the ground made drier and harder still because it had been forced into barrenness.

"O Sejah and Poetess of the sons of Tamim, what is it?"

The dark veil looked up, startled. It took her several moments to bring her mind from where it had wandered to answer: "There is water here. I know there is. I thought it before you came."

I felt myself blush. It wasn't just fever. "But it has been buried and filled in."

"Water, unlike infant girls, does not die when buried. What kind of foolish, impious man would bury what gracious heaven has given him?"

I thought I could see a light playing upon the black embroidered veil, and I knew not what to answer but a halting: "I don't know what sort of man."

Sejah took the camel goad from my limp hand and murmured a short poem on the spot about the blessing of water and of al-Uzza. Then she bent down and used the good strong wood and her recently cut arm to dig in the dry sand. As I watched, clear, fresh water curled into the hole she made.

"Here," she said. "Dig here. There will be water enough for us and for all your tribe forever." From her belt she drew out a handful of grain and sprinkled it on the ground about the holy site. "This, this is why my shaytan *called me here, so much more than the public flaunting of the words he gives me."*

With my good left hand, I helped her to dig. As we dug, we uncovered a small wooden statue of the kind Muhammad specifically forbade, of one of the mothers of heaven. Sejah snatched it up with a nod and quickly slipped it into her bodice. We uncovered another, then another. She did the same with them, nodding, as if she'd known these would be here, too.

And then, lo, the water flowed from the hard stone.

"Blessed be your clan of Tamim," I said quietly, feeling the pallor of a faint about my mouth and eyes. "And blessed be al-Harith the son of Sufwan who fathered such a daughter."

At that miraculous instant I felt no right to claim her.

She saw then that exertion had made my wound bleed and my head swirl with the fever of infection. She cupped her hands and gave me water, the edges of her veil dripping like black rain clouds. Then she made me lie down and made sure I always had the shade of at least one animal while she watered the other. She removed my headdress, dipped it in the miraculous moisture, still cool even after its exposure to the glare of the day. She laid the silk, its red color brightened like new, on my forehead to let the delicious wetness trickle down into my hair and behind my ears. Then we sat to wait for more life to come with the cool of the evening.

The water did what only water, and no other thing on earth, can do. Somewhat revived, I turned on my good arm and looked where she rested her head upon her camel's bent knees. She had also brought a spindle and wool from beneath her veil. She was spinning, rolling the shaft over and over across her thigh and then letting the spindle drop to gain the necessary tautness.

I swear by God that women spin themselves to sleep as they wake the world with the butter churning. They fill any void with energy lest, if they were to stop, so would life on earth. If she has milked the camels, curdled the milk, gathered enough dry thistles and dung for two nights' fires, a woman takes to her spinning. Or she combs the foothills for tufts of wool shed by passing herds. Or she digs for roots and gathers dry seeds to add to the diet.

The thought that often overcomes me—that life is too miserable to be worth any effort—seems completely foreign to them, for they are always about some such effort to make it bearable. I am tempted to think that certain women, at least, can always act with hope because they are simple in the head. But I could not think that of what went on behind the red-and-yellow stitched veil hung with cowrie facing me now. Whatever it was, I could not pass it off as simplicity.

I did not know what was going on behind that curtain that made a harem sanctuary wherever it happened to be, tent or no tent. She would not remove it even to sleep with me present. But I decided to venture a question to probe its depths. "O little one, my sister," I asked. "Has my milk brother, your sharif, found a husband to take away that veil from before your face?" What else do women think about as they spin?

Sejah laughed not so much with embarrassment as with surprise; that was obviously not what she had been thinking about at all. "Yes, he has," she replied.

"And who might that be?" I asked, not without some twinge of jealousy. I could not tell whether I was jealous of the groom or of Malik who would always be able to do such things for her that I would not.

"Tamim the sharif's son, of course. He who was so determined to drive me from the dance ring. Yes, he is somewhat younger than I am, and I shall have to wait. But he has spoken for me, as is his right." No sorrow shadowed her voice at the lack of love here. Indeed, such things seemed of little concern to her. Marriage was marriage, and everyone did it. Rather like breathing.

"But I promised myself to someone else long before," she said, "and that is where I'm going now."

"Who is this someone else?" I sat up, startled.

"I won't say his name. He is old, but he is a prophet."

I flinched. "Child, do not say that."

"He was kind to me when I was a slave. He dwells in a place called Yamamah. I am headed to Yamamah now."

And without another word, she climbed into her litter and whistled her camel to its feet.

Leaving the sword naked in the sand for me to regather when my health returned.

21

The Messenger of God, blessings on him, said, "Whenever a woman hurts her husband in this world, his houri wife says: 'Do not harm him, may God reproach you! For he is a stranger in your house who will soon depart from you to join us.'"
—A hadith related by Mu'adh b. Jabal

"The Eid at the end of Ramadhan is over, the month of Shawwal already shows a fingernail of moon," announced Abd ar-Rahman ibn Khalid. "We must leave today or tomorrow—the Day of Congregation at the latest—in order to meet up with the hajj caravan in Damascus. We don't want to miss the pilgrimage. If we do, others will get their petitions before the khalifah ahead of us. Our piety will be questioned and our—"

He said nothing of his son, nothing of their marriage, but Rayah didn't hesitate to interrupt, to insert her own life into his. "Your servant the Persian has finished building our litter, Uncle. The turpentine sellers are through with us. My mother and I are ready to leave this moment."

She called Abd ar-Rahman "uncle" from politeness. She realized, however, she could claim the title in fact, for the woman she had to accept as her mother and this powerful lord before her shared a father.

The powerful lord, Abd ar-Rahman ibn Khalid ibn al-Walīd, stared at her from the best cushions in the turpentine sellers' house. He seemed to be hardening his face to mete out discipline to a recalcitrant female. But as he sat, he had what he wanted, hadn't he? They would leave as quickly as possible.

Abd ar-Rahman gave a quick nod, sensing yet another triumph denied him before the battle was engaged, and went to organize his far-from-ready party. Khalid the Conqueror, Rayah thought, must have sometimes looked like that.

Sejah, who once hid behind the name Sitt Sameh, stood on the rooftop looking eastward to the desert, *her* desert. The endless sky curved pale above her, the confining girdle of green oasis spread at her feet. Two or three days out of the year—no more than four—Rayah remembered the fragrance of the desert in spring bloom coming from that direction. This morning, as most days when her mother stood thus, she smelled only the dust of the herds and their keepers leaving the oasis for their daily graze.

The curtains that had surrounded Sejah's life for the last thirteen years were all dismantled and packed for travel. Before the next Muslim call to prayer, she and her daughter must leave in the direction of the sown, away from the desert.

Sejah turned and nodded to Rayah. Rayah could see a family resemblance of her mother to the governor from Homs, in that nod, the set of their eyes, what must have been the line of the Conqueror's mouth.

Mother and daughter each hoisted a final bag to her head. Sejah's, Rayah knew, contained the three wooden idols mothers without end had used to help with birthing, with barrenness, with all women's losses.

"I will not carry them within the precincts of Mecca," her mother had promised.

And Rayah had to be content with that. What else could a daughter do to control her mother's beliefs? And she had to have her mother with her. Undertake such a journey with Abd ar-Rahman alone? He was her uncle, so they said, but he was also that very threatening sort of man, a potential father-in-law.

Rayah's bundle contained the Conqueror's red turban. The sword, still unsheathed, had gone down with Abd Allah earlier, disguised with the tent poles.

"Don't forget the bride-price, the Sword of God," Abd ar-Rahman had said, following every bundle.

"Have no fear, O uncle," Rayah had assured him, keeping her own vigil on their possessions. "I know where it is and shall keep it safe against my marriage."

With her eye on him, even a governor did not attempt to breach a woman's privacy, especially not when he hoped her honor would soon be added to his.

Together, in silence, mother walked with daughter down the two flights of stairs. At the bend where the jinn lived, Sejah stopped to recite some poetry under her breath. Not knowing what else to do, Rayah copied with a verse of the Quran, the Surah where the Prophet, blessed be he, converted the Fire Ones with his preaching.

After that, seeing what awaited them below, Sejah pulled her veils tight, up to her eyes.

All the harem stood around the fountain to say good-bye. Something had happened that morning: old Roman plumbing finally rusting through, a blockage, no one knew yet; the fountain had ceased to run. Women had had to trudge to the well down the street again. The marble in the courtyard had already grown warm to the touch.

Each woman's embrace of Sejah was politely formal, a little fearful of what life without the blessing of the guest of the last thirteen years might mean. Their parting words were generous, but the generosity of rote.

But was that really the evil Poetess, tamed, standing in those veils? The one who had opposed the Prophet, blessings on him, the one whose name was cursed, whose eyes had once turned faithful Muslims to stone?

No one could tell through the layers of black cloth. Best not to look that way in any case. More and more attention showered upon the dear, familiar girl gave the necessary excuse.

Only when Rayah filled their arms again and again did the tears begin. The words grew clumsier, perhaps, but arose from the broken hearts that often filled a harem upon the marriage of a daughter.

Two things kept Rayah from balking and turning into one of those brides whose families have to drag them, kicking and screaming, to their future with a strange man. The first was her mother, standing alone but veiled, her farewells over, waiting. Rayah couldn't read her reaction.

The second was Rayah's discovery that Auntie Adilah's were not among the arms she fell into. The lack of this woman who had raised her left Rayah speechless with grief.

Only when Abd Allah came to say that the caravan and Abd ar-Rahman were waiting did they leave the turpentine sellers' women sobbing and waving beneath the silver hand centered with the lapis lazuli eye. Rayah felt the loss of *barakah*, of blessing, like the step from shadow into heat. Sobs bent her double, but she kept walking.

Out in the alleyway stood the two old widows from the house next door as well as other women from the neighborhood, including Sitt Umm Ali. The Quranic teacher said, "I always knew she was such a good student, she would win a husband, if God willed, among the highest in Islam."

Ghusoon kissed Sejah's hands in reverence. Her round belly was invisible under her gown and veils, but it bumped Rayah's with a firm ripeness in thanks as they embraced.

Many others offered more tears, more embraces, more "Ah, God, shall we never see you again, O light of our eyes?"

Still no Adilah, no Adilah. The ache gnawed.

When Rayah at last caught breath to look over hunched, aged shoulders, she saw her mother pacing: a little space of two steps in one direction, then back. Rayah realized that this was the first time Sejah had been out of the confines of a house in thirteen years. An alleyway draped with vines did not, however, offer much more spaciousness.

With one final embrace all around, Rayah wiped her eyes, then led her mother into the wider street beyond the alley's portal with its own wooden doors opened wide.

Abd ar-Rahman and the beasts of the caravan waited outside. The governor would not want his state of religious purity tainted by contact with more women than necessary. He especially wanted as little contact with the evil Poetess who nonetheless he had to take on pilgrimage.

But another reason for his willingness to wait out in the sun became clear as Rayah and her mother stepped from the shadow of walls and vines to the glare of the old Roman flagstones: The great wings of the restored *qubbah* could never have fit through the narrow passageway. Such conveyances needed the wide spaces of the open desert. Already, wind from the west tugged at the curtains, trying to catch them off to emptiness.

Abd ar-Rahman's servant, the Persian carpenter Firuz, stood dressed in pilgrimage garb beside his creation on the kneeling camel. The eunuch scribe, dressed likewise, stood on the other side.

Rayah saw her mother's gaze meet each man's in turn with equal satisfaction. Rayah wasn't sure how the Persian understood what Sejah's gaze meant; he knew the woman so little, had received the ruins of the litter and the orders for its reconstruction only through the eunuch.

Something in that brief, wordless exchange, however, made the man leave, beaming, and go to see to the comfort of his master. Persians had skills learned in the fallen empire to offer the new one. Were such craftsmanship to come sailing through the Hejaz on pilgrimage— Such hope had burned in the man's eyes just before he turned.

Rayah couldn't help but think that Sejah the Prophetess riding in that *qubbah* would not do the Persian's case any good. Then, again, Abd ar-Rahman, the governor of Homs and son of the Conqueror, rode at the caravan's head. That could alter Sejah's status to that of prisoner of war, a crowning triumph in the unstoppable spread of Islam.

Sejah paused to take a breath of sun-drenched air as they left the alleyway. She kicked at the Roman flagstones. These were still not the desert dust she could kick up into a dust demon, but the air— Then she paused again with what must have been a prayer of thanksgiving before leaving that light for the gauzy interior of the litter.

"Have you the sword? Have you remembered the sword?" Abd ar-Rahman stepped nearer to ask, and not for the first time.

"It is safe," "At the wedding," and "No, sir, I must insist that you respect the women. You may not search their baggage. The child is to be your daughter-in-law, after all. It is here. Patience, my lord," was all Abd Allah would tell him.

Rayah pulled the red turban from her bundle. Reaching over the camel's placidly chewing head, she tied it to the litter's center beam with a double knot, adding one final dust-cutting drape to protect the interior.

"Stop! What evil is this?" cried Abd ar-Rahman, braving women's pollution to run nearer still. "Would you women go on pilgrimage declaring yourselves whores? Loose women flew a red kerchief in pilgrimages before the purification of the One God."

"We Persians accept that a man traveling long distances may need to contract a *mutah* marriage." Firuz, too, stepped forward, trying to temper his master's righteous fury. "Does not the Holy Quran allow it, saying, 'Give those women you have enjoyed the agreed dower'?"

"You, a Persian and a servant, presume to dictate religion to me, an Arab, who saw the Prophet, blessed be he, with my own eyes when I was a child? No Muslim woman I travel with shall carry the sign of a worshipper of filthy idols."

And Abd ar-Rahman stepped forward to rip the silk from its post.

The camel, startled over its cud, made a lunge for the governor with its teeth.

"Damn jinn-infested beast," Abd ar-Rahman cursed, and raised his camel goad for a heavy blow.

The animal, knowing what that meant, tried to lurch to its feet. The rider in the litter must have received a jolt, but she gave no sound. Perhaps she had seen the event prophetically.

Rayah had a moment's frisson of blasphemy, to think any man might strike a *qubbah*'s camel. She stepped to take the blow herself. Abd ar-Rahman managed to halt most of the descent of his goad when he saw his future daughter-in-law beneath it. Most of his blow, but not all. Rayah gasped at the sting in her shoulder, but she did not back down.

"O Uncle," she cried. "Do not profane, not as we set forth on the pilgrimage. Don't you recognize the turban your father wore into all his battles? And look. Here, here is the lock of the Prophet's hair he always had with him, tied within its folds."

Abd ar-Rahman stared. Firuz stared. Both men, the master first, kissed the relic then stepped away.

"Can't we get this caravan on the road?" were the governor's first words after that. "The sun is already high in the sky. And a brutal bitch today."

Attention away from her, Rayah took a breath to calm her nerves from the thing she had dared. Then she steeled herself for her next daring act. She felt the weight of her own first entry into the sacred litter of her foremothers, as a woman of her blood. As if she were indeed a virgin.

Her great-grandmother had given birth in Mecca in the precursor of this conveyance; her grandmother had ridden in another at the Day of Dhu Qar. Her mother had used one to rise against the Prophet himself. . . .

Rayah felt the terrifying weight of this past in her mother's helping hand—for the litter would carry the two of them on a strong riding stallion camel's back.

Perhaps through similar curtains, Zaynab Queen of Tadmor, Zenobia Queen of Palmyra, had taken her last glimpses of these same streets as, in golden shackles, she had ridden off to the Romans' triumph. She had ridden through these same rows of marble columns—when this drum of stone had still stood upon that one. When the facade of this building had still stood intact and had not been mined for the houses of Rayah's childhood neighbors.

The neighbors—the farmer with the hoe on his shoulder, the woman with a basket of dates on her head—waved and cheered the departing caravan. But Rayah knew they cheered Uncle Abd ar-Rahman the governor, not her, not her mother. Or they cheered the pilgrimage, as if they thought their cheering would one day let them leave the circle of their lives and undertake the duty, too.

Rayah felt only the absence of Auntie Adilah's applause.

Distant Rome, but a rumor now, had been the capital in Queen Zaynab's day. Mecca and al-Medinah of the Prophet had replaced it.

Do I ride a prisoner now, as she did then? Rayah asked herself. Or is this triumph to be my own? Only I can make it so.

22

O men. If anyone here worships Muhammad, know that
Muhammad is dead. If anyone here worships God, know that
God is alive and immortal.
>   —The words of Abu Bakr, the first right-
>   guided khalifah, upon the death of Muham-
>   mad, may God bless them both

Muhammad, the son of Abd Allah, sat on his low bench made of tamarisk
wood in the court before the houses of his women in the city named for
him, al-Medinah. His ever-present friend and father-in-law, Abu Bakr,
supported him. He they call the Prophet of God began to be old, over sixty, and the
fever that shook him made him seem older still, gray and palsied. A white cloth,
soaked in well water in an attempt to bring the fever down, swathed his head. It ran
rivers down his face, across the bridge of his nose, behind his ears and into his matted
beard, still more black than white in color, and orange with henna.

Prayers were over and the mid-morning sun had just crept over the courtyard
wall. I found myself still in the pleasant shade of a roof of palm fronds that served as
a shelter to homeless Muslims by night, to congregations of the great men of Islam by
day. But the sun did fall on the son of Abd Allah at an angle that made him blink,
magnified his fever and sent his hand involuntarily up to his face to shield his eyes.
Abu Bakr shifted his position the better to shade his master.

Noises from the women's half of the court distracted me from the sermon, what
proved to be the Prophet's last. Usually I had the skill to ignore them, but not today.
Children squirmed and fussed to win back their mothers' religion-stolen attention.
Some had been pushed off with a nursemaid or older sister into one of the Prophet's
women's huts lining the courtyard wall. They vigorously howled their protest. The
heavy rugs dropped before the doorways provided precious little muffling.

Besides the competition, Muhammad's own voice worked against communication. He had always been soft-spoken and sometimes when he addressed a very large
congregation, he needed to station criers at certain points to relay his words along to

the outer edges. Now ill health rasped at his throat. The hollowness of another world came up from his lungs along with the phlegm. I sensed the spirit of death hovering over him, stealing half his voice.

Still, I did hear some of the words, forced from him with a power that was not natural to his frail body. "O men, the fire is kindled and rebellions come like the darkness of the night. By God, you can lay nothing to my charge. I allow only what God allows and forbid only what God forbids." One might have heard those words outside the courtyard, they were so full of conviction.

"The fire is kindled and rebellions come like the darkness of night." I repeated his words to myself and shifted with anxiety as I did so. It did not take a prophet to see that there would be fighting enough ahead to satisfy any craving for blood. If, God forbid, our Messenger should die, what certainty existed that victory would always belong to Mecca and al-Medinah? To whom could we look for a leader, then? By God, I coveted the position myself, lest it fall into pious but incapable hands. Abu Bakr's, for instance. But I knew Omar would oppose me every step of the way. Beyond that, the factions made one's head ache to contemplate.

Doubtless, the Prophet's passing would leave a great and chaotic void.

The squabble of birds in the pomegranate tree over my head, the women in my kitchen, the bustle outside my garden walls tell me I cannot say the same for my own death: The void and chaos have already closed over my head and left me buried alive underneath it. The ignominy to which I am reduced tells me I was not the man to replace Muhammad at his death and that I was wise not to attempt it.

But plenty of others had ambition to spare. At the mere rumor of the Prophet's illness, they sprang from nothing like spring flowers from the barren desert at the first hint of rain. Indeed, some whispered "poison." Ambition does not wait for a void before it lays its plans.

Though Muhammad had told us he was the Seal of the Prophets, replacing one messenger with another was the most natural assumption one could make in those days. I remembered well Sejah bint al-Harith's saying that if a man called himself a prophet, one should believe him. I, like many others, had begun to look around and to wonder where next to throw my devotion and my sword.

The trouble was not a lack of prophets but a glut: The way one straw bends, as they say, so bends the entire field. Prophets, false prophets we call them now, were the bane of Muhammad's last days. All of us knew their audacity would grow in the first days we were left without him. God knows best, but the difficulty was to choose among them.

From the Banu Hanifa in Yamamah came the dispatch: "From Musaylimah, Messenger of God, to Muhammad, Messenger of God. Greeting. I have been given a share with you in this matter. Half the earth belongs to me and half to you."

Muhammad had sent him the reply: "From Muhammad, Messenger of God, to Musaylimah the Liar. Greetings to whomever follows the Guidance. Lo! The earth belongs to God. He gives to whomever he chooses from among his servants."

And I had to remember that my daughter had said she would give herself in marriage to someone in Yamamah—although I had forgotten the man's name and doubted she would get that far on her own.

Never in his life was Muhammad, blessed be he, in a position to do more to Musaylimah than that, to call him a liar and put it in God's hands. Yamamah was too far away and too powerful to make demands upon.

But then Muhammad stood on the verge of death—God favor him and us— and Musaylimah went on with his preaching, to which he added miracles such as Muhammad never did. I'd already heard how he could press an egg unbroken through the narrow neck of a bottle. Though I hadn't believed it at the time, that had been when I hadn't believed Muhammad could die. Perhaps, with Muhammad gone, Musaylimah could indeed take all the world to himself.

Sharif of the Banu Asad, Tulaiha ibn Khuwaylid, also called himself a prophet. He had joined the fight against Muhammad quite early—just after Uhud. I had fought beside him while I was yet a pagan, and I knew he was an able general, though as for his skill at divining, I knew nothing. Quite possibly, it was as he said: that the Angel Jabra'il visited him when he was not with Muhammad. Now, if Muhammad was taken from us, Tulaiha could have the angel—and the power—all to himself. Proof of his dealings with the jinn lay in his poetry. He even composed one verse about me:

> *My spear shall play havoc*
> *With the regiments of Khalid.*
> *And I trust thereafter*
> *It shall also crush Omar. . . .*

I did not know whether to be flattered, threatened or challenged. God had taken Muhammad. I didn't know whether to go and make the son of Khuwaylid swallow his fool verses before I slit his braggart throat—or invite him to adjust his revelation by joining my regiments to his.

Behind their own prophet, the Banu Asad stood as sporadic antagonists to the Muslims. Behind theirs, the Banu Hanifa in Yamamah were so powerful that all Muhammad had been able to do was send threatening letters and hope his messengers were not killed.

If these worries nagged, Yemen was one great dread. Yemen had nominally become Muslim, but even before Muhammad came down with his last fatal illness, the Yemenites were in full revolt behind their own prophet, known as the Black

*One, al-Aswad al-Ansi. Muslims now call him disparagingly the Drunkard, but in
those early days, one dared not say it too loudly lest it be heard all the way to Yemen.*

*Al-Aswad had driven out or murdered all the Muslim governors and tax collec-
tors from his land. Even as the Prophet, blessed be he, lay dying, this new prophet
in the south was living in the deserted governor's palace and enjoying, among other
luxuries, the Muslim governor's widow Azad.*

*The tale of al-Aswad recites like the old Persian tales of Rustam the Hero. By
God, do they still tell those tales in the market of al-Hira, or have the stark lines of
the Quran replaced that as well as poetry and family ties? How I used to love the
stories as a young man, and how the news, coming north from Yemen in my middle
age, made me feel the hope of youth once more by association.*

*Here we have in real life the beautiful princess, young Azad, who has been
forced to marry the loathsome Black One, murderer of both her husband and her
father. Here is the young and handsome Firuz, Azad's cousin, who pities her plight
along with the plight of his country. His pity turns to admiration, his admiration
to love for the beautiful Azad and that love has its opposite, a violent hatred of the
Black One. But the young hero's hated enemy lives in a great walled palace guarded
by men of perfect faith in their prophet. Only one possible entrance remains—to
swing over on a rope and climb up the wall as does a fly.*

*It is a superhuman task, but it has this benefit—the easiest place to scale will
land our hero at the bedchamber balcony of the beautiful Azad. Here is the rose-
wood lattice from which a sigh or a bunch of rue can be dropped down to the handsome young man below. Can you not hear the scene as a Persian story monger would
tell it? Here are the plush rugs like gardens of roses underfoot. Here are the crimson
cushions, the tassels of gold, in Azad's room. The moon comes out from behind a
cloud and discloses the shadow, like the smoke of heavy Yemeni frankincense, upon
the gauze of her curtains. Her cousin, her deliverer, the most handsome of men with
shoulders broad and firm as the stones he has just climbed. He is her love.*

*Feigning a sudden aroused affection for her captor and husband, Azad plies
him with drink until the old black soothsayer nods witlessly. Firuz can come out
of hiding and saw off that great black-bull head. Al-Aswad does manage to regain
consciousness and full sobriety in the midst of the attack. He bellows for aid, but
fair Azad stands at the door and raises a finger to the guards.*

"Hush," she whispers. "The Black One is receiving messages from God."

*Most things that are passed around lose matter: trays of sweets at a feast or a
sheep's-bladder ball that sooner or later loses air and puts an end to the children's
game. Unlike such things, this tale from Yemen gained details instead of losing
them after al-Medinah had bandied it about for a while. Azad and Firuz were
devout Muslims—that was added—and their hatred of al-Aswad stood on moral*

ground, helped by the right and might of God. This addition is a loss indeed, the reduction of their love to a simple statement of religion. It gives the tale the ring of blatant sermonizing—falsehood, in fact. On the other hand, however fabricated a story of death-defying and courageous love may be, the hearer always wishes it to be true, and that wishing, in a way, makes it so.

Muhammad won over the critics and, in the end, perverted popular taste to sermons. And yet, the party loses life and the guests are insulted when the sweets are gone. And sorry is the street corner when the ball has gone flat and none can repair it.

I can prove that Islam did not triumph in Yemen with that one blow to al-Aswad's neck as the khalifah's storyteller would have you believe. For, though the Black One met his doom at just about the same time as Muhammad, blessed be he, Muslim armies were more than a year subduing the region. Two more years passed before the coffers of al-Medinah ever saw a dinar in taxes of Yemen's great wealth that grows on their trees in the form of frankincense and myrrh.

"Yea, they shall be shut out from their Lord as by a veil," was Muhammad's verdict.

This verse reminds me of the fact that al-Aswad is also known as the "Veiled Prophet" because he would cover himself with a veil when (as he said) the Merciful One was with him. As the black and heartless villain of the romance, I can reject all his claims to prophethood with ease (rather would I follow young and handsome Firuz). But I was reminded of another one whose veil was not an affectation, but an integral part of her station in life. The vibrant life within her demanded a veil to preserve it from sacrilegious contact with the profane.

That was, I suppose, the whole cause of my quandary at the Prophet's death. For whatever other reasons people grieved or feared or felt uncertain, I myself suffered all of these things simply because no word came from the pastures of Tamim. My best deeds I knew would always be led from that source. If no leadership arose, I found it best to do nothing at all rather than to accept a baser substitute.

Cousin Omar, always a firebrand past the point of all sense, refused to believe that Muhammad could die and leave us so unguided. He stormed and fumed. They who brought him the news he called liars and hypocrites and, brandishing his sword, swore he would cut off the head of the man who dared to repeat that blasphemy in his hearing. But old, sober Abu Bakr, leaving the room of his daughter, in whose arms the Prophet had died, said in his quiet but determined voice, "O men. If anyone here worships Muhammad, know that Muhammad is dead. If anyone here worships God, know that God is alive and immortal."

Abu Bakr was wise beyond the usual wisdom of men. I cannot say the same of myself. I sat there, taking shelter from the sun with the others like dates beneath

their fronds. We heard the dreaded news. Wondering, praying in my helpless inde-
cision, my mind grasped one single thought as something true and to be believed,
namely Abu Bakr's words. But I'm afraid that what he called "God" was not the
same unknown power, granted from generation to generation, to which I gave that
name. Burn me in hellfire, but that is so.

23

To win the war against those Arabs, you have to do but one
thing: Kill that man they call Khalid.
——Harmaz, the Persian governor

*S*ince the death of the Prophet, blessings on him, I had heard no word from
the northeast, still nothing from the Tamim. Nothing. Let those in Mecca
and al-Medinah pick sides as they would, I must remain undecided until
that word came.

My cousin Omar brought me the word.

*Now Abu Bakr was solidly and generally confirmed as khalifah and com-
mander of the Believers. To his gentle, faithful spirit, Omar provided a strong right
hand. As the Prophet himself declared—according to my cousin's partisans only, of
course: "If a Prophet were to come after me, it would have to be Omar." I would
rather say Abu Bakr and Omar together made a successor for the Prophet, one to
drive forward and one to constrain with reason. But even so they were the Prophet
without prophecy. Prophecy, you understand, was declared to have ceased.*

Shrewd politics had taken its place.

*Omar led the prayers as strictly as you could please. The rank upon rank of men
in their disciplined prostrations could make even such an army as Rome's blush
with envy. Days, weeks, months passed when attendance had been poor, limited to
what would hardly make a decent raiding party. Immediately after Muhammad's
death, every man had gone back to sit under his own tent and wonder and watch
what would happen next.*

*But now they—we—folded and unfolded with such unified drive and—I shall
admit it—martial beauty, that the sight alone could overwhelm many an enemy.*

*When the worship was over, Omar beckoned to me, to Amr, and to several
other commanders present. We met with him in one corner of the mosque while all
the other men broke rank and went mingling off.*

*My cousin sat waiting to begin what he had to say. I watched him, studied how
he pulled the corner of his mustache down and into his mouth to suck on it. This*

constant habit of his, when he was on guard or angry, was as if he wanted to assure himself of his manhood for the confrontation to come by actually tasting it. I might have thought he wanted to console himself for the loss of hair on the top of his head had he not done that little trick ever since his lip could support a mustache at all. He was still as broad-shouldered as he had been in youth and tall, very tall. He sat on the mat, as straight and proud as if he had a wall behind him. I studied his leg and remembered how it had felt to break it during that wrestling match when we were boys. I remembered the sound—snap!—like breaking rag-wrapped kindling. I remembered. . . .

But now Omar was speaking, telling of the trials that lay before the Muslims. All the while winding his mustache as if it were the rope about a toy top he would soon let fly, Omar listed the tribes that had fallen into apostasy at Muhammad's death. "And they still refuse to pay the alms tax," he fumed.

"Amr." Omar turned to my friend beside me after this litany of general failures. "You are not having the success we would like up there on the Syrian front."

"It is slow," Amr admitted. "They are rebellious. It is God's will."

"It is God's will," Omar agreed. "But it is also God's will that you submit to Him and triumph, Amr ibn al-Asi.

"Word has just reached me of another sharif who has refused," my cousin Omar said then. "Can you think who that might be?"

He had turned directly to me. What had I to do with Syria? I was pushing toward Iraq. All I could think of was that Omar might have saved time and been more to the point if he had simply enumerated those who had paid the tax. That list would have been much shorter. I couldn't remember the vast hordes he had already listed. I certainly wasn't ready to make guesses. I shrugged.

"Malik ibn Nuwaira at-Tamimi," he said and suddenly stopped playing with his mustache as if he had produced a dagger with those words. That statement was proof enough of his manhood; he could put the facial hair aside.

"It seems," Omar continued, "that Malik collected all the dues from his tribe. However, on hearing of the death of Muhammad, may God reward the Apostle of God in paradise, Malik declared to his kinsmen that they were 'free of the settled man's yoke as Arabs have ever been.' Then he gave to every man his portion again. I have reports that he is emphasizing his rebellion by making raids along our borders.

"At first I thought we should give the command against Malik and the Tamim to Khalid ibn al-Walid Abu Sulayman, seeing that he has already had two fine victories in that same general direction."

I squirmed at the way he said my name but held my tongue to hear my cousin out.

"What would be more natural," Omar went on, "more in accordance with

God's will, than to see the Sword of God sweep across the desert to the very doors of Persia? And yet it was Abu Bakr, the khalifah, may God strengthen him—always ready to feel compassion for another man's weakness, too ready—who suggested that perhaps Khalid was not the man for this task. The sons of Nuwaira are his milk brothers, Abu Bakr reminded me. Perhaps we should move Amr from Syria and have him replace Khalid there against the Tamim. Perhaps Khalid will find his abilities and his faith stretched to the breaking as he attempts to deal justly with these apostates, all the time remembering that they shared the same breast as infants. Perhaps Khalid—"

"By God!" I cut him off, suddenly more devout than I'd been any time in the past five or six months. "Let me move against the Tamim. As God is my witness, I shall spare not one faggot from the fire of their punishment if it happens—and God knows best—that they remain unrepentant."

Though my words were fierce, they were spoken more with a thought to sparing my beloved brethren than might seem at first brush. I had looked over and seen Amr's face. It was true, as he said. Things were not going well on the Syrian front. The tribes there had the backing of Rome, who used them as a buffer to keep us out of their lush territories. To strive with no more than five thousand men against the might of all Rome was a task with little glory and many disappointments. Like some petty tribesmen, Amr and his troops raided for their supplies but got little else.

I could tell by my friend's face—once handsome and well-fleshed, now somehow gaunt—that he was feeling the pinch. He craved nothing more than the refreshing taste of a victory. He would stop at nothing to take it from Malik if the chance were given him. Things would go very ill for my milk brothers then.

And my daughter—

I had to speak up and swear to go. Our instructions for all campaigns were, after all, not necessarily bloody. When we made contact with the enemy, we were to give the call to prayer. If they responded, they were immediately forgiven, no questions asked. Only if they failed to respond were we to draw our swords and not resheathe them until every man of them was on his face, either in death or in earnest prayer.

I could speak to Malik. I must speak to Malik. Surely some compromise short of slaughter could be reached between us. I was the one to reach that compromise, not victory-hungry Amr.

Omar nodded. That was what he had wanted to hear. He remembered the lesson he had learned from Muhammad his master. He remembered how I had been sent to the Valley of Nakhlah and what a compliant change it had wrought in me.

Never mind, I told myself as I rode out of al-Medinah with fresh troops all ready to become martyrs for the Faith against anyone. Never mind that you are marching against those you wish most above all to save. That is only the appearance of things. You actually ride to save them, that is your purpose.

As soon as the bright star Suhayl rose on the southern horizon, promising that the worst of the summer heat was over, I led a force of Muslims against Tulaiha the Imposter. We defeated and captured him at the Battle of Buzakhta. I feel no regret for that. There is only so much taunting verse a man can take of anybody's tongue, prophet or no, and still have his honor intact.

> "My spear shall play havoc
> With the regiments of Khalid."

In a madman's dreams, and the madman is dead.

From there, I led my men east and a little south. Here those sons of Assad who escaped that first battle and were still rebellious made a second stand less than two days' march away at Ghamra. By the first rains, I had subdued more rebellious tribes at Naqra. The flotsam of these victories silted up against a ridge of mountains running in hard, dark basalt northwest to southeast, funneling a sea of reddish sand dunes toward the Empty Quarter.

Circles of standing stone and carvings of camels, gazelles and humans performing strange rites haunted the area. They spooked my mare more than the scent of battle up ahead did. Her dainty hooves skidded beneath me. I, too, got a dryness in my throat to think of the souls of these long-ago creatures strapped still living in the rock by the power of the Fire Spirits of this place. The same magic that conjured up mirages danced this life upon dead boulders. No wonder the Prophet, blessings on him, forbade Believers to practice the dark art of drawing and carving. When he chained the jinn into submission, he also chained in them this demonic force.

"Brother Khalid."

I nearly jumped out of my skin to hear this voice where had been only the murmurs of enchanted stone and a bustard scurrying out of harm's way through last year's dry scrub. The human voice belonged to my second in command, Dharar, strict in the Muslim forms of equality even when they disrupted military discipline. His appointment to the position at Omar's behest was for unbending religious prowess rather than fighting skill.

Nonetheless, I'd fitted him out with a dun-colored gelding only marginally less fine than my own. The result was that, despite the fact that this was his first horse and countermanding his appetite for equality, he cut a fine figure. A dust demon caught up the wings of his cloak behind and prepared me in some fashion for his words, once past the shock of his human presence with me among silent stones.

"*Brother Khalid, the enemy are forming their battle lines.*"

"*As God wills, Brother,*" *I replied.* "*Has the muezzin called them to prayer?*"

"*He has, Brother.*"

"*And?*"

"*And they are not repentant. God wills that we kill them.*"

"*Then let it be as God wills.*"

The spell of the surrounding stones broken, I urged my mount into the real world where soon men and horses would scream, and my divine sword would sing blood from men's veins.

"*There is one other thing you should know, Brother Khalid.*" *My second in command struggled to trot his mount level with mine so he could continue.*

"*I need know nothing before entering into this fray but that God is most great.*"

My second nodded his submission to that truth, but went on. "*Their leader—*"

"*No earthly leader is more than a shadow to our God, the Merciful.*"

Another nod, more submission. "*Their leader rides in a* qubbah, *a sacred litter.*"

"*What did you say?*" *I felt myself magicked into stone at the word, my very marrow gone as dry as my throat.*

"*Her name is Salma—*"

"*Salma? Are you sure? Not—?*" *Too close, too close to Sejah for my comfort.*

My second looked hard, confused, at my face. "*She's just from a minor tribe, the Ghatfan, but hereditary in her post, riding on a sacred camel that had belonged to her mother before her. Clearly idolaters.*"

I gave no reply; I couldn't.

Finding no discouragement, my second went on. "*This just shows how deep is their ignorance and apostasy, how easily God will deliver their condemned souls into our hands and into hell. In the Name of—*"

His mouth continued to move in Quranic quotation. I heard nothing but the wind twisting off the dunes in a roar. I was the demons' slave.

Without even stopping to form prayer-like ranks of men behind me, I snatched our green banner from the hand of its bearer as I galloped past and charged with a bloodletting scream.

Then everything went blank. I remembered nothing until the battle was over and waterfalls of unbelievers' blood cascaded red over the black basalt.

"*Who—who did this?*" *I asked, knowing all the while what the answer would be.*

Who had brought down the howdah at the center of the tribesmen? Who had left its curtains so heavy with blood that the wind could no longer lift them? Who had gutted the beast, leaving the gash for flies, which now flocked to the welcome moisture and wriggled their larvae on spilled and tangled guts? Who had wiped the blasphemy of a strange woman from a minor tribe presuming to take to herself the honor of my dead Bint Zura? Who had hamstrung the back of the woman's own knees as she had tried to pull a scarf over her bare breast and flee to the mountains on foot?

Her staring dead eyes found a reflection and an answer in the eyes of my men. "Mashallah, surely you, you are the Sword of God, O Khalid ibn al Walid."

But none of them wanted to sit too close to me when we broke bread in the cool after sundown. Our fires gave the figures carved into the rocks around us a new, leaping life, but not the lifeless corpses of the enemy, prostrate, who would not kneel in prayer. Hyenas now prowled among them.

Thus, I brought Salma of the Ghatfan down in her own gore along with one hundred of her tribesmen, suicidal in her defense. I am glad to see, at any rate, that folk have since given that mountain chain her name and not mine, though I was the victor there. She, the woman on a sacred camel, is a more permanent feature of the Arabian landscape than I ever was. The Salma Range teaches me the inadvisability, indeed, the futility, of hacking away at such things, even with the Sword of God.

Thus, I led Muslims in these battles that were in favor of the Muslim cause. But if you had asked me then, I would still have hesitated whether to call myself a Muslim or not. I hesitated as all sorts of tribesmen I challenged in the desert hesitated over the same question. If the first stranger one met would kill him for refusing to acknowledge Muhammad, every chance existed that the next would kill one if he did. So rife and confused was this new blood feud, no respecter of ancient blood lines nor of the sanctity of clientship.

But I failed to preface that purpose, as the Quran commands, with an "as God wills."

For as God willed it, my second in command, Dharar, a fierce fighter as I've said, took a virgin of the Bani Assad there on the field soaked with the blood of her father and brothers. When the blood jinni left him, Dharar came to me full of remorse, for hadn't the Prophet of God, blessings on him, revealed specifically that a captive woman could not be taken on the battlefield. And "as long as she is on her religion" (meaning still a pagan) "she is unlawful to a Believer."

I dismissed his concerns. I didn't want to lose such a great fighter over such a quibbling matter. But also, in the back of my mind, niggled this thought: Sooner or later, if our progress across Arabia continued, if Malik and Mutammim did not submit freely, we would fight the Tamim. Indeed, God would allow the event sooner rather than later, for the Bani Assad shared wells and pastures with the Tamim.

So reason said we would shortly fight the Tamim. We would fight them; we would beat them, now that the remnants of the Bani Assad, the Ghatfan and the rest added their camels' dust to our own march. Then my daughter might be in the same victim's position as Salma.

The thought, I suppose, was too horrible to form in my mind. Something must happen to prevent it. My milk brothers would not oppose us; they would quickly kneel and pray at our approach. Or they would beat us. Or, if worse came to worst, God would never allow that I could not protect my daughter once we arrived. I would make a pronouncement, "Save the daughter of al-Harith the herdsman for me."

In the meantime, "I, your commander, make it lawful to you," I told Dharar.

"I cannot rest easy until you write a message to Omar about the matter," Dharar said, the dust of remorse in his beard, the blood of the woman and her kin on him from the waist down.

"Stone Dharar," was Omar's quick reply, speaking for the old, pious Abu Bakr, who could no longer be bothered with the day-to-day discipline of the armies of God.

It came back to me, too, that Omar had pressed old Abu Bakr with my messenger still kneeling on the ground before him. "O khalifah of the faithful, may God always lead you aright. Khalid ibn al-Walīd has committed adultery. If he permits it to his seconds, he commits it himself. Stone him along with Dharar."

"But the blessed Quran recommends only flogging for that carnal sin." Abu Bakr looked up from his recitations to protest.

The whip twitched at Omar's side. "Flogging, yes. But the Jews' scriptures say it must be stoning. We are the perfecting of religion. How should we have less? Stone Khalid to death."

"I can't stone Khalid," said Abu Bakr.

"Then dismiss him as commander of the faithful."

Poetry misted Abu Bakr's speech. "I cannot put back in its sheath the sword God has pulled out against our opponents."

Fighting jihad always kept me from learning Quran. I never took much interest in such squabbles over mere words when a sword in my hand had the power to decide any matter once and for all.

And yet I cannot squabble with the saying, "God knows best."

24

A'ishah reported: "The Messenger of God (may peace be upon him) came to me, and I said to him: 'Messenger of God! Two old women from the old Jewesses of al-Medinah came to me and asserted that the people of the graves would be tormented therein.' He (the Prophet) said: 'They told the truth; they would be tormented so much that the animals will be able to hear it. . . .' Never did I see him (the Holy Prophet) afterwards but seeking refuge from the torment of the grave in prayer."
—Muslim, *Kitab al-Salat* (*The Book of Prayers*)

The small caravan of pilgrims did not take long to leave the oasis and enter the desert. They still hadn't reached the limit of where Rayah had been before in her life. She had been to the tamarisk groves. She had been to the tomb towers on days when the turpentine sellers remembered their dead.

But already, in the *qubbah* rather than on donkey back or on foot, she felt she had entered a different world. The camel's sway beneath her, well-padded with cushions and shaded with curtains, was comfortable enough. Once the green of the oasis vanished behind them, they could even open this curtain or that to snatch the slightest movement of air.

Rayah wondered if her jinni came with them, his thick curls caught up on a breeze.

Sejah had parted her veils but didn't speak; she did not pick up her tale. She had, however, taken up her spinning once more. She sat within the woven walls of her room in the third floor of the turpentine sellers' made suddenly mobile. The wind breathing through the curtains was the same—no, subtly different. Even though the camel behind them carried jars of turpentine to help fund their journey, for the first time in her life, Rayah's nose breathed free of the resin in one form or another.

Nonetheless, there, after less than an hour, the tomb towers appeared. They cast almost no shadows westward across the gravelly desert where only here and there a stone rose a few finger's height above the sun-baked level. Light glared. No foliage eased the eyes; the caravan was still too close to Tadmor, and every leaf had been gathered either for fodder or for fuel.

The camels stepped off the stones of the old Roman road wherever they still appeared through blown sand. The Romans had built for a different world, for animals whose feet were different from the camel's padded ones. The caravan of pilgrims would not travel by night at first, since here in Syria, the worst of the summer was already past.

To Uncle Abd ar-Rahman's ongoing loud annoyance, the farewells had taken such a long time that, particularly since they were on pilgrimage, they had to halt for noon prayers. They made their halt beside the towers—they meant nothing to Abd ar-Rahman as a place for the dead of the Time of Ignorance. Tadmor still hazed the eastern horizon with green.

Her mother did not descend from the litter—as a woman, that was her prerogative, even on pilgrimage. Rayah, alone, found her place to lay out her rug a little behind and to one side of the men. What before she had enjoyed now felt like a chore, the first chore of a new bride whose life would be filled with chores.

When she rose from her prayers, the wind kicked loose dust demons among whom she listened for her own jinni. She saw a figure instead. The figure stood in the doorway of the turpentine sellers' ancient family tomb, built in the days when trade had made them richer. The moment the figure took solid shape out of the desert's jinn-stirred dust, Rayah's heart jumped.

Bandits?

The next moment she saw it was Auntie Adilah.

Rayah ran to the woman who raised her. "I am so glad to see you. When you weren't among the others, I thought—I thought you were only too glad to see me go."

"No, by God, let's waste no more time in farewells," Uncle Abd ar-Rahman complained behind them.

Rayah ignored him. She had already said her prayers.

"I had to say good-bye to my brother." Adilah spoke in the undertone of women in men's company.

Rayah noticed that her aunt did not deny her gladness to see the back of either witch or daughter.

"I'm coming with you," Adilah added.

Rayah stared at the older woman. "You're coming?"

Adilah nodded. "On pilgrimage."

"But I thought you weren't—" Rayah stopped herself from blurting out more. If she had learned anything from the storytelling of the past months, it was never to label another person or their religion, particularly those older than she or strangers whose stories she had not yet earned.

"Of course," she said instead, and took up the small bundle of possessions Adilah had by her side.

"I should bid him farewell, too," Rayah said upon the next shove of wind at her back.

"No more farewells." Abd ar-Rahman might almost have been wailing the death of some of his own.

Still Rayah ignored him. And, because they were women, what could he do about it but curse the emotional lives of all females everywhere?

"Your brother, though he died before my birth, was as close to a father as I shall ever know." Rayah took her auntie's arm. "A man who gave me his life with his."

Adilah nodded gratefully. Together, they stepped into the cool of the tower, the darkness chilling the glare-strained eyes like the blessedness of tears.

Rayah easily found the empty tomb of Adilah's brother Yaqub among all the other generations of sleeping matrons and stern-faced patriarchs. A lamp still flickered before it. Incense curled, saffron crocus wilted in funereal purple.

Rayah saw that, since her last visit, some zealous Muslim had gouged out the somber young man's sandstone eyes. "These were Muslims. I'm sorry," Rayah wanted to say. She was certain Adilah must have noticed the desecration, too, certain that this was the cause of more than half the tears drying in salt streaks across her cheeks.

Adilah recited something, something from the Christians' scripture:

> "Now upon the first day of the week, very early in the morning, they came unto the sepulcher, bringing the spices which they had prepared. . .
> "And they found the stone rolled away from the sepulcher.
> "And they entered in, and found not the body of the Lord Jesus. . .
> "O death, where is thy sting? O grave, where is thy victory?"

Then the two stood before the echoing space in silence.

"*Ya* Rayah!"

Together, the women ignored the shouts from outside. Abd ar-Rahman did not come in for them, nor did he send his servants.

Rayah let Adilah be the first to turn. Picking up the older woman's bundle once more, Rayah followed her back into the desert's glare toward the kneeling camels.

Sejah, spinning, made no comment either as she invited Adilah to ride beside her in the sacred litter. The curtains closed over them, and Abd Allah urged the camel to its feet, urged it to take its place in the center of the train that lurched ahead in fits and starts.

Rayah fell into step beside the eunuch. And though her sandals quickly filled with stones and then raised blisters, she tried to keep up without complaining. The eunuch had his dead master's tale to tell.

25

I have an old camel that needs no excuses.
A coward cannot govern her.
Forbidden to her is the settlement,
The gate and the rustling of palms.
She rejoices when I gallop to her
And signal to her with the hem of my light mantle.
　　　　　　　—A song of the Rwala Bedouin

T*he khalifah's orders to all Muslim armies are and were clear: If the apostates answered the call to prayer and paid their alms taxes, they were to be forgiven and admitted back into the community of the Believers. Only if they remained rebellious on both counts were they to be attacked and, God willing, slaughtered.*

I sent a messenger forward to meet Malik and to warn him.

"Milk brother, don't be a fool," I prayed. "I know your numbers and their strengths like my own. For the sake of the milk we shared, submit. For the love of God, submit."

God answers prayers. Shortly, I found myself drawing a deep breath of relief, filling my lungs with the choking dust raised by the hooves of a large herd of camels and goats. My milk brothers were forwarding their negligent taxes. We could accept the sons of Tamim under our protection.

I laid my hand on the neck of a camel, fingered the cauterized scar. They were from Malik and Mutammim's herds, all right. The tough brand lay like a bare rope upon the strong, hair-covered muscles.

With a pang, I remembered participating in the branding of just this mark. In two quick movements, clouds of seared flesh, and bellowing beasts, their Christian cross appeared like magic with the pass of one iron. The dot beneath the left arm of the cross was done with a second, single iron point.

I'd been too young, of course, to do much of this work, but I had loved learning what it meant to be a man from Sharif Nuwaira and al-Harith's father: the camaraderie, the skill, the daring to fetch the young calves from their kicking, biting dams, the strength to hold them down. The smell of the fire, the dung, the burning camel flesh, both from the branding iron and from the young roasted calf. The branding songs:

> *"You who beat the camels and my mother*
> *Had better look out for me."*

Or:

> *"I have an old camel that needs no excuses.*
> *A coward cannot govern her.*
> *Forbidden to her is the settlement,*
> *The gate and the rustling of palms.*
> *She rejoices when I gallop to her*
> *And signal to her with the hem of my light mantle."*

The mark on the tax camel's neck— My milk mother wore the same in miniature on the back of each calloused thumb to show that she, too, enjoyed the protection of such men. She belonged proudly to the Tamim. Had my love Bint Zura taken the needle to prick such a sign with wood ash after her capture? I didn't remember her skin being marked so, only the crawl of heavenly fire branding my own back. It crawled again as the tax men counted.

Had Layla taken the vanity of the tattoo, so much more resigned to her fate as a captive wife? Did my daughter, born into the tribe, wear the indelible mark of the Tamim? They were my foster kin, but nonetheless—my daughter, that perfect flesh of my loins—

Neither Malik nor Mutammim came himself with the taxes to parlay. That made me uneasy, even as I distributed the beasts among my men after having sent the customary one-fifth back to Omar's new-built storehouses in al-Medinah. My milk brothers had forgiven me the death of their young kinsman Hala. But might more recent acts diminish their tribal honor in ways they could not forgive with a saved face? Had I crossed that line? Did submission to Islam make me blind to such a line?

Questions unanswered, we marched on. Every small clan of the Tamim, fanned out over the countryside in their customary dirahs, responded to the call to prayer as we came upon them. They might have been camels who know no other way to lower themselves but to their knees. The approach to the pastures of my childhood was peaceful and, to me, very relieving, although not so much to some of my seconds.

And I still had yet to meet my milk brothers face-to-face.

Rain had recently blessed the Tamimi pastures at Butah. I rode into them at the head of the Muslim army, seven hundred strong, the setting sun at my back and my camel's shadow stretching long before me. Butah is high, rocky ground, tucked in around a spar of the great stretch of sand called ad-Dahna.

Its vegetation is sparse enough, but the rains had enlivened it all to brilliant color: The prickly hamat was silver beneath new blue flowers. Yellow as straw was the smooth nasi grass, a favorite of camels if we let them pause, in spite of the sand clinging to it. The arta shrub, nearly leafless even in the best of times, is the color of ash. The small ader was dark green, almost black, and the raza tree with its long, flexible boughs and needle leaves, was bright white, its new young sprouts yellow with a greenish tinge. All these stood stark in the clearing light against the reddish ground.

A herd of stately oryx with their long, straight horns moved away from us over the dunes, and some of the men rode off to hunt them. Herds here would not go hungry, and neither would men, but as soon as the sun set, it would be fiercely cold in Butah. Water would freeze.

I led the men around a sand bluff. Its crest, blown into shape and catching a blade of light like a crescent moon, towered far over our heads. The rain had carved its sides with shallow cracks that had dried again but not reclosed. Around the bluff, just where my scouts had said they would be, we came upon the tents of Malik's Banu Yarbu clan of the Tamimi tribe, twenty hearths at most. In other times, happier times, I had always spurred my mount to a trot at the familiar sight, my milk mother's handiwork stretched between tent poles. I rejoiced at last to see my childhood fire, longed, after so many empty miles, for that original embrace.

Now, instead, I felt a weight of dread. The Tamim had sent camels, but now I must call the men themselves to Islam. If they refused, I must draw my sword against them. My heaven-welded sword. No other option existed for the apostate.

I raised my hand for the column behind me to spread out, then halt. In serried ranks, my men made their camels kneel, then dismounted and stood beside them, their robes pulled back to show sword hilts in their baldrics, at the ready. I called old black Bilal forward. He stood beside me, waiting. No one came out of the tents to greet us; I sent no one in.

Then, behind me, the sun set. I gave Bilal a nod. His deep, rich voice began the call that shivered over the rocky ground like heat waves. "God is great, God is great. . . ."

Until we should reach the wells guarded by the Tamimi tents, we had no water to spare for cleansing. But water was not what we came for. We came for the hearts and souls of men. Each Muslim squatted where he stood and scooped up sand to perform his ablutions. Still nothing moved around the tents before us.

Then each man stepped away from his beast and formed up in neat rows be-

tween our animals and the tents.

For God's sake, Malik, Mutammim, I thought, answer the call. And Sejah. I must see Sejah. Her only safety, and yours, O brothers, is with me. If you do not, I must do what I must do. If it were up to me, I would let you be as you ever were. But no place remains in the world for someone who does not answer the call.

As one body, the army turned to the last of the light, blood and straw and an emperor's purple streaking the sky.

"There is no God but God."

Bilal's final phrase died away on the air that had already perceptibly cooled. And into that awe-filled silence behind me, from the tents, I heard a shuffle, a murmur, a scrape.

"Thank God," went into my prayer with the first prostration. "Thank God," more heartfelt than ever before. The Tamim had answered the call. They had joined us, folding in prayer at our backs. I would not have to kill my own milk brothers for apostasy. All might be forgiven. All might yet be as it was.

As it was? No, not quite.

After prayers were over, I followed the footprints of Tamim back to their tents. They had returned to their tents as quickly, as silently as they had come out. Unopposed, I made my way to the central tent. Malik and Mutammim received me here in the men's section. Their greeting held a stiffness, perhaps, but the forms of hospitality were conformed to neatly enough. I had imagined I'd have the honor of being received in my milk mother's harem as ever before, have her come and greet me, at least. I was milk kin here, after all.

But other men entered with me, soldiers. That explained the fact that I received no such invitation. And who knew what other women were with her? Sejah, perhaps? I hoped it might be so.

Therefore, once Malik assured me, over sips of warm root tea against the bitter evening, that all behind him was well, I sat comfortably against the padding of a camel saddle. We talked, all the forms of politeness. Everything, I was convinced, would reveal itself in God's own time.

It grew colder. I gestured to one of the two men with me who had not yet crawled off to bed after the long day's ride. This was Dharar ibn al-Azwar al-Asadi, my second in command, whom Omar had ordered I should stone for his rape of a woman of the Bani Assad on the field of battle. I had defied my cousin and ignored his command. Dharar's big square teeth snapped over the tea like a camel's. He still had a new convert's hot blood, something that frightened even me on occasion. Nonetheless, he was a good lieutenant.

I gestured to him to add fuel to the fire. The flames leaped in the stone-encircled pit at the point where the tent's side curtains were drawn close to make but the nar-

rowest of openings for the smoke to escape.

Dharar didn't move, and at first I assumed he hadn't seen me, or that he'd misunderstood. "Build up the fire," I told him.

Dharar rose, and Bilal, the one other man who had stayed with me as something of a guard, did as well. "I don't need a guard," was going to be my next statement. "Go off to bed."

But Dharar did nothing to the fire. What he said was: "There is no fuel."

I thought this very strange. I had never in my life known Umm Mutammim to let a fuel pile dwindle. Something in my face must have told Dharar that I took this as a personal affront to the woman who had suckled me, for he explained: "I had the men take all the Tamimi fuel for the Muslims' own fires," he said.

I struggled for an iron control. "The Tamim answered the call to prayer," I said. "They are Muslims."

"We will see how they pay the tax," Dharar said.

"They paid the tax," I reminded him.

"How will they pay it from now on?" Dharar's gaze raked over my milk brothers. "They can begin with fuel."

"You let me worry about the tax," I said sharply. "Just see that this fire is built up."

Dharar and Bilal bowed and disappeared into the night. That, I hoped, would be the end of that.

26

> Once a man asked the Prophet, peace and blessings be upon
> him, "Who is first worthy of my kind treatment?"
> "Your mother," the Prophet answered.
> "And who is next?" the man asked.
> "Your mother," the Prophet replied.
> "And who is next?" the man repeated.
> "Your mother," the Prophet said again.
> "And who is next?" the man asked.
> "Your father," answered the Prophet.
>   —A hadith of the Prophet

"And this is the place where the Conqueror dictated all his story to you."

Rayah knew it before she said it, her voice lowering in reverence. She had watched Abd Allah enter the courtyard and go directly to one spot beneath the pomegranate tree as if he expected to find his favorite cushion there. She had seen him stop suddenly, look around, realize he'd been dreaming, remember what else had happened and feel his heart break.

But she also recognized it as if she'd been there before, in some childhood dream, perhaps. Here babbled the fountain, here flickered the dappled green under the pomegranate tree that still caught the color of the emerald the eunuch scribe would never wear again in his scarred ear. He'd had the jewel made into a ring.

What rest to the eyes after days walking over the desert, even if sometimes in the comfort of a curtained *qubbah*! The hoopoe bird himself had contrived to sing his pulsing song upon their arrival. Here and there, however, a clump of grass growing through the stones, a corner full of rotting leaves or the broken slats in a shutter showed just how long the house had been neglected. Since the death of its master. The Conqueror's son lived in a palace elsewhere.

Without fail, every twenty-eight miles beside their roads throughout the desert, the Romans had built a well—no matter how deep they had to dig—coped it, and set some sort of shelter nearby. At the end of the third of these, instead of a well, the hajj caravan from Tadmor had approached Homs instead.

Homs stood as the egg in a nest of trade routes. The city naveled a broad valley greening with winter wheat, studded with apricot trees, their leaves turning. Twenty olive presses oiled the expanse, although some had recently fallen into disuse. The locals had served as horse breeders for the Roman Empire; with Khalid ibn al-Walīd's support, this tradition continued for Islam.

The locals called the valley's river the Rebel. It flowed north to south rather than the other way around, the way all other rivers of their knowledge flowed. Coming from Tadmor in the desert, this was Rayah's first, only river, a promiscuity of water that frightened but delighted her. Would any river be different?

The Rebel was notoriously difficult to tame with either canals or levies. Any time the rains fell heavily—at least once a year and without warning—he would leap his margins, destroying roads, fields, homes. When his tantrum was past, he would take up a new bed in the valley he made fertile one moment, destroyed in a jealous fury the next. Homs's permanent buildings were built so far from the banks as to make the river useless for daily water needs, yet even so they could not be certain of safety.

The Roman invaders, in their arrogance, had built a dam across the stream. The Rebel had long since torn stone from stone, leaving things worse than before in the valley that had betrayed him to conquerors. The lake behind the dam had turned into a swamp that bred noisome vapors and fever in the inhabitants of the town, trapped like mosquito larvae in the bottom of a shallow tray, wriggling helplessly. Only a few ever managed to fly elsewhere.

The Sword of God, this latest victor, the hero of Abd Allah's record, may have forged more permanence over the land than the Romans. Rayah found it difficult to imagine the Conqueror in this Syria. The garden may have provided him some comfort—but not much as long as he could never enter the desert again. She knew how he must have felt in his last days, trapped, with only the wasteland of empty parchment to escape to. Who was the Conqueror then?

Rayah had not heard from her husband the jinni since noon, when the green of the Rebel's valley had heaved out of mirage and into reality. She already missed the boy. His absence made her nervous, so she paced within the Conqueror's courtyard as if her feet wanted still the desert way and the skitter of sand beneath them. She clung to the promise that the caravan would stay only one night. Still, Uncle Abd ar-Rahman warned her that once they left Homs, the pilgrim's path would not return to the desert again for many days. Not until many days after they had joined the main hajj caravan in Damascus, not until after Jerusalem would they leave settled places again.

"The Rebel. Ah, yes."

Rayah fought off her distraction long enough to overhear the conversation her mother was having with Abd Allah.

"The Greeks, before their Christ, called that river Orontes, a God," Sejah mused on.

"Heathen ignorance," Abd Allah condemned the belief.

Rayah didn't know how her mother knew this. Perhaps the same way Rayah herself had known to call the river "he" in her own mind. She hoped this meant her husband of the spirit had not completely abandoned her, and that she might grow into her mother's discernment.

Sejah ignored the eunuch's condemnation. And he, with new softness, didn't press it against the mere story Sejah continued. "The God burned with desire for a dark-eyed nymph, the daughter of Oceanus. Orontes chased her across the valley in leaps and bounds. Here and there she ran and, leaping his banks, he pursued her. And when he came, panting, at last to the northern Mountains of the Bull, he roared in frustration at the rocks among the fountains of which she took refuge. He cut the girdle of the encircling hills, undid their stony bonds, then plunged off cliffs to drown his sorrows in the depths of the sea."

Rayah found herself panting. For a mere story. Tears started to her eyes. For what?

"I take refuge in God, we should not feel thus," she said, angry at herself. "For gods only ever were demons. First the Christians washed them away with their baptism, then Islam definitely vanquished them. Islam will not let them live."

Yet her mother knew the tale, among all her other lore, and how the images so closely described the Rebel as they had seen it—him—upon their approach from the desert. Had the Romans understood the myths of this land better, they might have handled this God with more skill than their failed dam slowly sinking into the putrid swamp. How was Islam to understand such tales in the new lands they conquered?

A sudden clamor of bells cleared the courtyard air, sheeting like a waterfall over its walls. In all her hearing of the Conqueror's Muslim tale, Rayah had never imagined such an unIslamic sound, pulsing off the walls like circles in a pond from a cast stone. Auntie Adilah, silent until then, now removed her veil and turned up a face transfixed with joy. Rayah remembered the same expression on the woman's face turned up to catch the rain at the end of the drought.

"There are Christians here."

These were Adilah's first words in Homs, although she waited for the echoes to die into silence before she said them. During the ringing itself, none of them had said a thing. Adilah alone performed the gesture, hand crossing face and heart, with which followers of the Nazarene bless themselves. Only Sejah didn't seem surprised by the action. Of course, the two women had spent three days curtained within a howdah together. A howdah, a sacred *qubbah* known to bring the best out in those who struggled, whatever their struggle. Their jihad, as Arabic called it.

"Of course there are Christians here," Abd Allah said. "Many more Christians than the thin lamina made by my master, his son and the few other Muslims. Mu'awiya ibn Abi Sufyan, the new governor in Damascus, has nothing but Christians in his counting rooms, for Christians alone understand the running of an empire. They see that the taxes are collected and sent south to al-Medinah with the hajj." Abd Allah spoke as a native of this place. "Your oasis of Tadmor is so much of the desert, your people belonged to Arab tribes and clans long before the Conqueror came. You adopted Islam easily, for Christianity only ever sat lightly upon you."

"That is not the case with all," Adilah murmured.

"Even now, the Muslim governors prefer to build themselves citadels out in the desert. They pitch tents within the thin walls and sally forth to hunt and ride, all the traditional pleasures of the homeland they have had to forgo for God. Why, I have seen my master, may God—"

"Is it possible to visit a church?" Adilah interrupted the eunuch's ongoing attempt to talk them all into feeling at home here, if only for one night.

"My master's son has ordered a fine mosque built over the tomb of his conquering father."

Making the women comfortable included urging on the caretaker's wife to provide cool pomegranate *sharbah,* made with the tart, refreshing skin and all, and parsley-wheat salad with fresh bread. It did not, at first, include answering Adilah's question.

"Lacking his father's sword—" Abd Allah stole a glance toward the bundle where he knew the blade still lay, packed but unsheathed. "—Abd ar-Rahman ibn Khalid has ordered miniature swords made of silver to dangle from every lamp in the mosque. At evening prayers of a Ramadhan, when all the lamps are lit, it is quite a sight. Even outside the holy month, it is worth seeing. Perhaps my ladies would care to visit?"

"Oh, yes—" Rayah heard her voice alone answering, and so she stopped it.

"But the church?" Adilah interrupted with unaccustomed impatience, having taken no more than a sip of her drink.

Abd Allah bowed, acknowledging her at last. "There are many more churches in Homs than mosques."

Adilah found a church with the help of the caretaker's wife. She found holy women who embraced her. Rayah wept when the message came, but she wasn't surprised.

"'Come with me.'" The young monk, sent with Adilah's farewell, reported her as saying. She would not come back to the house herself. "'We could enter the convent together, child. I intend to visit the monastery of St. Maron north of here and then the place where St. Simeon mortified his flesh for the next life by standing on a pillar for thirty-nine years. The view is magnificent, I understand, from his church.'"

"Is that why the saint climbed onto his pillar?" Rayah could tell she made the young man nervous. Hardly older than herself, he had made the same choice as St. Simeon, almost, to flee this life and live celibate. The young monk, she assumed, would know the saint's motives if anybody did.

The young monk bristled as an escape from his discomfort. "Such an impious suggestion to make of the saint, even if you are the Conqueror's granddaughter." Then he said something about the channel that had carried the saint's waste away and into the sanctified vials of those lucky enough to get some, who used to come to him for healing. "The channel is still visible in the marble floor of the church built around his pillar."

Rayah found such a man every bit as distasteful as Abd ar-Rahman, and Abd ar-Rahman gained favor in her eyes because he was governor of this town and let such alone in their belief.

That Auntie Adilah should ask Rayah to join her made the girl realize how little the woman who had raised her understood about life, at least life as Rayah herself had to live it. One could be a Christian well enough under the reign of Islam. Apostasy was a different matter, however.

If Rayah left the caravan, Abd ar-Rahman was bound to notice. He was not so likely to notice that Adilah was gone. A lone woman who had once submitted, confessing Muhammad and his one God for the sake of a beloved brother and the child she thought was his?

Adilah could now at last follow her own heart. She could easily fade into the mass of Christians in Homs. And if she failed in her bid for freedom, her martyrdom would be the perfect culmination of her belief, her clamber to the top of her own narrow pillar.

Rayah's absence, however, would not go unnoticed. A bridegroom awaited her in al-Medinah. And her death for apostasy, with generations before and after depending upon her choices in this marriage, would not have import in heaven alone.

Adilah's religion did not take this into account. And because of that, Rayah knew she could not sacrifice her life—the lives of all the women of the desert who had gone before her—for such a belief.

"Tell her I'm sorry," she informed the young monk. "I thank her for everything and commend her to God in this best way I know to thank her: by letting my life and hers part at this point."

The young man left suppressing scorn that weighted his black wool with sweat, releasing musty odors that might have done St. Simeon proud. But neither the powers of earth, fallen though they might be, nor the future such powers were busy creating, stood on his side.

27

Dung-stained ground
that tells the years passed
since human presence, months of peace
gone by, and months of war,

Replenished by rain stars
of spring, and struck
by thunderclap downpour, or steady,
fine-dripped, silken rains,

From every kind of cloud
passing at night.
Darkening the morning,
or rumbling in peals across the evening sky.
—The Mu'allaqat of Labid

That night, a wind blew rain in off the unseen sea to the Rebel's valley. It was the first night in her life that Rayah had slept under a different roof from her Auntie Adilah. Save the three spent under tent wool in the desert, it was the first night away from the roof under which she'd been born.

Gusts caught at the corners of warped and untended shutters, keeping her awake. Sejah, however, slept undisturbed beside her in the brazier-heated room, no doubt on the very cushions where the Conqueror had spent his final days. Caught under the eaves, the wind in this urban place sounded not like the jinni but like the moaning of a wounded man. More than once, the impression was so forceful that Rayah sat up, staring into the eerie dark, the words catching in her throat, "Who's there?"

When at last exhaustion drove her to sleep, it could not have been for long. A crash and an actual yank on her arm tore her awake once more. She thought it was the dark-haired jinni of her dreams. "Husband?" she asked the night. Why did he not take her in his arms then and quiet her heart with love?

No presence came to lie beside her on the unfamiliar cushions, however. The haunting was not her silent lover after all, but something from the realm. Definitely something from the realm.

Her husband had recited verses to her, but never verses from the Quran such as gurgled now from the rain-sheeted courtyard.

> "Spend all in the cause of God, but do not throw
> yourselves with your own hands into destruction.

"Spend all in the cause of God—" A verse from the longest surah, that of the Cow.

Rayah repeated the familiar words with the unknown reciter. Then, her bladder full, she rose from her sleeping mother's side and threw a blanket over her shoulders, slippers on her feet, to walk through the dark and empty courtyard to the privy. No reciter was there, but of course she had not expected him to be, nor to reveal himself until he himself desired it.

The marble flagging slipped with cold rain like serpent skin.

"But do not throw yourselves with your own hands—"

The recitation came from the fountain. A hollow, frothing sound. She found her steps pulled that way, sliding without her volition, even though it meant leaving the overhang. She drew the blanket up against the raindrops that slipped between her sleep-warmed skin and her gown.

The center of the coping, where the water bubbled out, was not the usual statue or pillar draped with figurative flowers. It was an unhewn stone, black, metallic. While circling pomegranate tree and flower bed upon their first arrival, she'd noticed its presence filling the entire yard with a strange heaviness. Or had that just been the approaching storm? The thing Auntie Adilah had gone to the Christians to escape?

Now the stone drew her to it across wet marble and wet air as if it were a deep, dark well into which she had fallen rather than the same shaft tall and solid.

"—Into destruction."

Leaning over the coping, Rayah reached out over the rain-dimpled water and touched the black stone. Sky stone, her fingers told her. As if a spark had jumped from her to it. Fallen from heaven. And as that spark jumped, it suddenly exploded to fill the courtyard with light.

The next instant, thunder followed, rolling off one wall, then off the next.

"Destruction!"

But the sound did not kick with fear half as much as the sight.

For, lying face up in the chill, lightning-lit water was a body. She'd never met him in her life, but she recognized him. From a previous jinn-vision. From the months of hearing his life's apology out of Abd Allah's parchments. From bits of her mother's face and her uncle's.

His throat cut ear to ear into an evil grin, the Conqueror of Iraq and Syria still held the Sword of God in his hand. Its tip lay propped up against the tall black sky stone as if the two metals from the same source had yearned to rejoin.

That one flash of light revealed the face, its pockmarks whitened by death to look like craters in a full moon. So much so that Rayah almost looked over her shoulder to see if it were a reflection, the nearly full moon breaking through a shroud of clouds. Except that she knew to do so would cause madness. And no moon broke through the heavy cloud cover.

Though at least three fingers' depth of water gently lapped over the features, the eyes remained open, staring up at her like the water snake after its prey. And the blue-white lips moved, reciting Quran, sending bubbles of scripture to the surface.

Rayah screamed, and then her mind went blank. As blank as her dead grandfather's must now be.

The gentle eunuch brought her around. Blessedly, the recitation had ceased. Rayah babbled two words of what she had seen, then could no more.

It didn't matter. Abd Allah knew what she had seen. "Even thus did I find him. When he died."

"He killed himself," she stated with a shudder. "The sword that could not be resheathed without tasting blood in his hand."

"I pulled him out before any of the other servants came. The pink in the water dispersed. I told no one but his son Abd ar-Rahman. And he made me swear to tell no other, for the shame to the family. A suicide, Muhammad taught, will spend eternity in hell dying the same way over and over again."

Rayah remembered the recitation ringing through the yard. "I know. Blessings on the Prophet and all Muslims."

"Yet you saw." Awe made the eunuch's voice jagged. "You and your mothers are always gifted when it comes to fountains."

Rayah didn't feel gifted. She felt cursed. The image–bubbled verse rising to the pinkish surface wouldn't leave her eyes, open or closed.

The eunuch had carried her away from the ill-omened fountain and out of the rain to a covered alcove beside the pomegranate tree. Plump cushions lined the three walls, but the weather brought out a muddy smell from the fabric larded with months of dust and neglect.

Rayah wondered, with that image of death in his mind from reality, how the scribe slept at night. Remembering he had been tortured since, in Tadmor and partly due to her, she knew he must not sleep well—ever. Yet his concern for her—

Abd Allah fingered the ragged ear where his emerald had been as if his thoughts ran alongside hers. "That stone in the fountain sat in the Christians' main basilica when your grandfather conquered this city."

Rayah saw that his regard had gone back to the center of the fountain. She shivered and could not let her gaze follow his there.

"A sacred stone, then?" she asked.

She heard rather than saw him nod, a rustle of his ragged ear against the stiff, high collar of his robe. "Which the Christians obviously took over from the pagan temple on which they planted their church. The age-old healings the stone brought could not cease."

"But the Conqueror did not merely take over the same stone when he turned the basilica into a mosque."

"Mecca and the Ka'ba already have Islam's sacred stone."

"Which I shall soon see, inshallah," Rayah mused, "when our pilgrimage ends in the twin holy cities."

"Rather than hack the stone to bits and bury them as he did with the pair in al-Hira, or accomplish what he did in Nakhlah, Khalid the Conqueror had it brought here, to the center of his own private courtyard."

"For safekeeping."

"He never told me that—but yes, perhaps that was his purpose."

"You haven't read this part in your parchments."

"Nor will I. He didn't dictate this to me. He said it only after we were finished, after we had sat all those months looking at the fountain. Or rather, he looking at the fountain, I at my parchment and ink. He told me, now that I remember, the day before—"

A gust of rain and wind blew into the silence Abd Allah left. Tiny waves rippled over the marble in another flash of lightning. The accompanying thunder resounded, but quieter, more distant now as it flew toward the eastern pass to the desert, to dissipate before it ever reached Tadmor. Home. But home no more.

"Like the stones at al-Hira, like that even of Mecca, it must once have taken the blood of sacrifices," Rayah said after the resonance had died, in a voice hushed and heavy. "In the Time of Ignorance."

She heard Abd Allah's nod again and tried to sink deeper into the extra blanket he'd given her.

"I had thought I'd recognized the stone before," he said, almost wistfully. "I remember my mother holding me up to kiss that stone in the basilica."

Rayah wanted to stop looking at the thing that demanded attention with the splash of water over it, its simple, weighty presence in the center of the courtyard. She wanted to stop talking about it, but Abd Allah seemed unable to tear his gaze away.

"You were born in Homs then?" Rayah had to ask the next silence that fell, filled only with rain and the splash of the fountain.

"I was. You are surprised?"

She was surprised. The man had never mentioned anything out of his past, only that of his master. It was as if the cutting of his flesh had scraped him clean as new parchment, just waiting for the Conqueror to speak and give his life meaning.

"So you have family here?"

"I suppose so."

"But you will not visit them? We leave tomorrow. Why didn't you take the time tonight? Or shall I see if I can beg my uncle to put off our leaving. A day at least, with family—"

"Little Blue Eyes, there is no need."

She had offended him, but she didn't know how. Because she had not thought he might be native to Homs? Was that an insult? Many from other parts of Syria, she understood, insisted the bad swamp air made the natives crazy.

"I only thought—" she apologized. "I mean—I thought men who had been cut— I mean—"

"Men who have been cut as I have."

She was grateful for his help. "Yes. I thought you were slaves, taken from your families. Brought to a place that wasn't your home."

"Sometimes it is our families who do this to us."

Rayah could find no words.

She knew what generosity on his part it took to speak his next sentence. The confession did not come easily to him, for he spoke it all in a breath.

"I was a third son. So although I was told to kiss the stone and pray to grow to be a man, a father of many sons to make my family proud, the time came, in a year of the Persians—"

"So the Persians did this to you?" Rayah still wasn't ready to accept what her ears had already told her. She hadn't been able to save him from the attacks to his person; if only she could save him from having to speak of them. "The Persians took you from your family and did this to you? I have always understood those people to be like that, indolent lovers of luxury and careless of how they got it. Well that my grandfather conquered them." But she couldn't add "God bless him" to the mention of the man in the fountain.

"No, not the Persians, Little One. Although that Firuz with whom we must travel to the Holy Cities beat me, tore my ear and broke my leg, I don't even blame him. He did only what his master ordered. Otherwise, I do not know if I could travel with him.

"No, not the Persians. With our farmland ravaged in that year, my family decided I would be worth more not as a man but as you see me now. If I did not have to provide for a family, I could be taught to read and write. I could find employment with high officials, either in the empire or with the church. The perfect servant because I would never have any family ties to interfere with devotion to whatever master fate threw in my path. From that high position, gained at the cost of my manhood, I might even reach out a hand to my cousins and nephews, help them to advancement.

"Of course, then the Muslims came, making 'the church,' the former empire, moot. And I was a ready convert, for here is a family, so I thought, to replace the one that had betrayed me. I remember, as they gave me opiate-laced wine, as they tied the leather thongs around my parts and as they cut—I felt the cut, for all the opium—I remembered the stone and my prayer for children—"

Rayah could tell the damp was affecting his just-healed leg, the leg broken by Firuz the Persian. The eunuch had to travel on it for the next month, a hard way into strange territory. She could feel the pain as it were her own, and she cursed her healing gift in its imperfection. But she did not have to ask now if Abd Allah would rather not stay behind in Homs, where he was known. Where he had family.

Gently, she touched the ragged scar of his ear where the emerald had once winked. "Islam desires men separate from their families, too."

"I see that now. I did not think so at first, when your grandfather the Conqueror originally brought me to this courtyard and began to share his family with me. And then I came to Tadmor and met you—and your mother. . . ."

"But it need not be so. It is the case when men battle for God, but with the women they leave behind the lines, other things can take priority."

Rayah shrugged aside the extra blanket and got to her feet, ignoring the jinn-pain, her leg throbbing in mirage of his. "I ask only that you will see me to this marriage," she said, "where I may use the gifts I have been given to make a nest within the stone of steel that is al-Medinah."

He reached up and touched a curl straying on her shoulder with a fatherly hand. "Little Blue Eyes, there is nothing I desire more."

28

Whatever is man's nature,
If he deems it hidden, shall be known.
This I know of today's or yesterday's
happenings, but of tomorrow's I'm blind.
—Labid ibn Rabiah

That dark night in Butah, I smiled apologetically to my milk brothers for Dharar ibn al-Azwar, my second's, rudeness over the matter of the fuel for fires. Malik met my stare steadily but without a flicker at his lips. Even Mutammim offered no blind smile in return.

"Well," I said, hoping now that we were alone the sons of Nuwaira might be more forthcoming. "How are things in your pastures, my milk brothers? What news? Mutammim, have you any new poetry?"

There. Let him answer that question. That must bring us to Sejah soon enough. If he did not have poetry, then it must be because he stood in her shadow.

Now, briefly, a smile did pass his lips. "Odd that you should ask that," he said. "Let me tell you a story."

A poem would have been better. A story seemed like more avoidance. But I said, "Please do."

"I was riding back to our Arabs one day six months ago or so."

That would have been about the time of the Prophet's death. This would be interesting. But I was also glad none of my men was by to hear this.

"I had no other guide to my sightless eyes," Mutammim continued, "than my young son, riding on the neck of my camel before me. Darkness came upon us, and the boy soon declared himself lost. I had almost given up hope and thought we must make the beast kneel where we were and wait for morning. That was when my son announced joyfully, 'Father, a light.'

"Now, I felt a shiver of apprehension at first." Mutammim raised a hand to indicate his milk eyes. "As one with direct experience of the jinn, to my lifelong sorrow, I knew they lit their fires in the night desert, too.

"'Is it a campfire?' I asked my son. 'Is it a fire made by men?'

"As we drew nearer, he assured me it was, fire like any other he had ever known. We made for it in all haste.

"To my surprise, in that area of ad-Dahna, it wasn't one of our tents. The man who welcomed us in was a stranger.

"He had, my son told me, a short, pointed beard of the purest white. 'And he is bright-eyed,' my son whispered, 'as if he had stolen your eyes, Father.'

"The man's guiding hand on my arm led me to believe he was sparse of flesh but active. Without my son's word for it, I wouldn't have credited the stranger with the age to support white hair, though I recognized that sort of wisdom immediately. His voice was deep and resonant, the sort of voice I have always longed for in my own reciting.

"'Welcome, welcome,' the stranger said.

"I craved to ask his name, but the one receiving hospitality in the desert at night must let his host volunteer that information, if he cares to. He may keep such things a secret, in case there is blood between the clans that might spoil the meeting. So I sat where the stranger told me within the warmth of the tent, and soon the flesh of a young camel and fresh curds spread before us. Almost as if they'd been waiting for us.

"'So we meet at last, O Mutammim ibn Nuwaira,' the man said presently.

"I promise you, Khalid, I nearly choked on the mouthful. For if I had not asked my host's name, neither had I given him mine.

"'I cannot tell you how long I've hoped for this meeting,' my host went on. 'I have heard of your fame throughout the desert. You are a great poet, I hear.'

"As soon as I could swallow, I muttered something about, 'Folk have been pleased to call me so.'

"'Defeated the poet of the sons of Taghlib in the street of al-Hira when you were hardly more than a boy, so I heard.'

"I muttered something.

"'Well, I hope to hear some of your verses. As soon as you've eaten, of course. Please, eat up, eat up.'

"I had lost some of my appetite by then, but I did my best to show our host honor, and I knew nothing could slow down my son.

"At last, when the platters were removed—by what invisible hands, I know not, and my son did not tell me who our host had as servants or younger kinsmen—he asked again for poetry. And so I recited. I'm sure you've heard this one of me, Khalid:

> "I stood here by the rocky spurs of Thahmadi,
> over the beloved hearth of Khawla,
> crying, crying till dawn. . .

"I had gone no further than this when my host stopped me.

"Anger rattled in his tone that I had heard no hint of before. I could not imagine what had caused it.

"'This is your poem?' he demanded. 'You composed it?'

"'Yes,' I said in confusion.

"'Then tell me where the hills of Thahmadi are.'

"'Oh, now that's just a name I made up, from my imagination.'

"'Well, let me tell you that you sought shelter tonight in the hills of Thahmadi. My herds grow fat on those hills, O son of Nuwaira.'

"I didn't know what to say. Surely I knew our dirah as well as any. Before I could overcome my confusion, my host asked again: 'And who is this Khawla you speak of?'

"'Just a woman's name,' I stammered. 'It means a deer. I just liked the name, and a poet must always invoke a woman, his ladylove, in his first stanzas.'

"Now my host called to those behind him, and immediately I heard the patter of small, bare feet upon his rugs.

"'Recite the qasidah I taught you,' my host ordered the new arrival, and a small, girl's voice began to do so.

"'She's not above five or six years old,' my son whispered.

"She recited the whole thing, the hundreds of lines, all the way to:

> "'Whatever is man's nature,
> If he deems it hidden, shall be known.
> This I know of today's or yesterday's
> happenings, but of tomorrow's I'm blind.'

"I tell you, I shivered when she said that word 'blind.' For a moment, it was as if I could see once more—and then had the light taken from me all over again and in one, sharp pain.

"'Thank you, my dear,' my host said, and I heard him take the child upon his lap. 'This,' he said, 'is my daughter—Khawla. Not your ladylove. My daughter.'

"I didn't know what to say and struggled only to hear something to help me understand in the black silence around me.

"'I,' he said presently, 'I composed those poems you claim as your own. I gave them to you.'

"'But—'

"'*I am the one who took your eyes as payment when your mother bartered them for the lost son of a herdsman. That was years ago for you, perhaps, but only a day or two for me. I would hope you might remember that, and give credit where credit is due. I, Mutammim ibn Nuwaira, am your* shaytan.'

"*And suddenly, for the first time since I was a child, I could see: the fire leaping against the walls of the tents, the fire on the old man's face—a face very like my own will be. I saw him eat with his left, as tradition tells us is common among the jinn, while men eat with their right. I saw his daughter's blue eyes. My own son's face wherein I tried to read the face of his mother. One brief glimpse with these old, milky eyes.*

"*I had time to say, 'My son, I see—' Time to realize my words were gone, never mind the poetry. Then the old man took the gift away again.*

"*And then I understood the full meaning of the word I had taken for granted so long. Shaytan. The adversary. Without my struggle against him, I'd never have any poetry at all. 'Satan' your master turns the word to, Khalid. And would remove him from the lives of his followers altogether.*"

I, the Sword of God, had nothing to say. But my milk brother's story wasn't done.

"'*Now, as for that milk brother of yours,' the old jinni said.*

My heart leaped, I tell you, into my bartered right arm.

Mutammim went on, oblivious of me although my name was on his lips. "'*Milk brother?' I stammered. 'You mean Khalid the Qurayshi?'*"

"*You mentioned me to the jinni?" The night grew cold. In my milk brothers' tent, my heart grew colder still, settling in my elbow.*

Mutammim went on as if my words had been an unwelcome interruption to what he had seen, what he saw now behind the milky film of his eyes. "He is all mixed up with this new religion preached by Muhammad of Mecca,' I said.

"*The* shaytan *spat. 'That does not matter. Islam does not matter. Khalid ibn al-Walid still owes me. You gave your eyes, O Mutammim, for which I gave you poetry in return, because of your goodwill. Khalid stole the scrap of cloth that represented his arm in our trade. I want that arm, and the day is coming when you may help me to get it. And for this cheater, I will give nothing in return.*'"

I could not meet my milk brother's blind eyes. My arm felt as if it had been spread with honey and set upon an ant hill. My heart cramped with terror.

Out beyond the tent, I heard an infant cry, cold even in his mother's arms. And the wind on the sand dunes was a far-off moan.

29

Who even out of the green tree hath given you fire, and lo! ye kindle flame from it.
—The Holy Quran, Surah 36

It had grown even colder that night in Butah, a deathly chill creeping up my right arm from the scar my daughter had sliced—and then repaired with the spell of her own hair. Where was Dharar and the fuel? Camel dung, thistle—I didn't care what it was so long as it burned.

Mutammim had stopped his story about meeting his shaytan in the desert and didn't appear inclined to tell any more. What I really wanted was an explanation as to whether he actually experienced this or whether he had merely made it up to press home a point. I wanted to believe the latter. As a good Muslim, I had to believe the latter, but if that were the case, I wished he'd make the fact—and the moral—plainer.

But Mutammim said nothing more.

Finally, I spoke: "Don't call him my master."

"Whom do you mean?" Malik asked.

"Our brother Mutammim said 'my master' turned the word shaytan into his great evil Satan," I replied. "I suppose he referred to Muhammad, blessed be he."

"So I did," Mutammim said. "And so, God knows, did Muhammad. Change the meaning, change the world."

"Just don't call him 'my master.' Not here, not now. Not surrounded by seven hundred Muslims, as you are."

"Your Muslims, Khalid," Malik said. "Your master."

"He is yours as well. You paid the taxes. You answered the call to prayer." I found myself pleading now, pleading to their hard reticence to speak. "My brothers, he must be. For your lives."

"You shared our mother's milk," Mutammim said. "Does that not mean more than any master?"

"That doesn't mean we must share your master," Malik added. "In fact, if our *mother's milk taught you anything, it should have been that a man of the desert should submit to none as his master."*

"A man determines his life, not by his friends but by whom he chooses as an adversary. As shaytan. *As a poet, I know." The empty whites of Mutammim's eyes consumed me.*

"And this I learned," said Malik, "although I am no poet. This I learned—from her."

"Her? From whom?" I demanded. But I could already guess.

"Sejah bint al-Harith," my milk brother, the sharif of the Banu Yarbu replied. "The Poetess. The Prophetess."

"One greater, Khalid, than I," Mutammim said. "Because she has known her shaytan *from the beginning. And embraced him."*

"No master," I repeated. "No master but God."

"And the jinn beyond the laws of man and of nature, whom you owe."

I shifted in my cloak, pulled the red turban down closer over my head, seeking warmth. As I did so, I found I could hardly move my right arm to perform the task. I had to use the left. Years of stolen power had caught up with me.

"Very well," I said in a rush of panic. "The jinni you met, your shaytan, *was right." Gasping, I got the words out. "I did. I did take back the scrap of my sleeve I offered to his people with the witch Umm Taghlib's magic. The scrap—my arm—I offered in exchange for our lost playmate—who is dead now, anyway."*

"In exchange for my eyes," said Mutammim, edges carefully rubbed from the prickle of his bitterness.

"Your eyes? I had to give al-Harith my jinn-granted love. I had to give our daughter, born of a night whistling with Fire Spirits. Is that not price enough?"

Malik stared at me. Mutammim would have done so had the jinn left him eyes with which to stare.

They didn't know. They could not have guessed. I saw that God—or the jinn—did not even gift them with comprehension at that moment.

I did not want their comprehension. I did not want—nor did I deserve—their pity. I wanted the lashes of their camel goads.

My gaze fell upon the branding iron hung from the tent pole. Leaping up, I tried to reach it down. My arm refused to obey.

No. I could not lose the use of my right arm. I would cease to be a Muslim if that happened. I would cease to be the Sword of God, leader of men. I would cease to be Khalid ibn al-Walid.

I reached instead for the sword, closer, at my side. I finally drew it out awkwardly with my left hand.

"Here." I handed it to Malik.

I remembered the proof I had given my milk brothers' tribe on the occasion of the death of their kinsman Hala at the Ka'ba by the hand of my cousin Omar. Omar who now sat at the right hand of the khalifah, to whom all the taxes plodded their way. I remembered the Bushra sword, white hot. Leaning my tongue toward it, touching and feeling—nothing.

I wanted to feel nothing again, for what I did feel was too great.

"Hold it in the fire," I instructed Malik. *My captive. Holding my sword.*

Without fresh fuel, very little of the fire lingered, only winking red streaks when Malik lifted the camel dung aside.

My milk brother did as I asked him, watching my face more closely than he watched the process, however. He must find me unfathomable. Mad, perhaps.

"You know how it is when the strength of a man's right arm begins to fail," I said, "when the jinn take it in palsy or tremor. Or when, even as a child, his left arm, by some trick of the jinn, carries more life than his right. That will not do for the battlefield where sword meets shield and shield, sword. Branding the flesh can make the Fire Ones abandon the limb, returning the strength. I want you to do that for me."

Undo what my daughter had done with this same blade, caused the weakness to enter in a gash.

Malik nodded, his mouth set it its usual firm, brave line.

"Go ahead," I urged him, crouching beside him, extending my arm, thrusting it forward. "I know your skill as a brander of camels—"

The blade flashed, glowing, to touch at the top of my daughter's gash. I cried out, with surprise more than pain, surprise that he would actually do the deed. The fire had not been that high.

Before Malik could touch at the other end of the gash, I breathed deeply and, beyond the fire—nothing but ash now—I noticed two figures. Dharar, certainly, and maybe Bilal. Come with fuel? No.

How long they'd been there, how much they'd heard, I didn't know. But they ran forward, shouting, "Traitor!" at Malik. Such lunacy.

I was suddenly sick to my stomach. I couldn't sit here any longer, take the other burn. I snapped up the sword and told the Muslims, "Relax. It isn't what you think."

They took some convincing. I had to get to my feet.

To Malik and Mutammim, I made some sort of cursory farewell.

"I said, build up the fire," *I ordered my men as I pushed by them out of the tent and into the night. My teeth chattered with sitting in the cold tent, with the shock of my blistering flesh and with the cold.*

A wind had risen like whiplashes. It worked its way between every fiber in even the closest and heaviest weave.

Few of my men, I noticed as I went by the tents the Muslims had pitched en-circling the Tamim, had proper clothing or shelter. I had driven them hard, with that cursed right arm of mine. Some wrapped themselves in raw and still-warm skins as they sat about the weak fires. So perhaps Dharar was right: The fuel had been evenly divided.

I did not cause trouble by demanding to know what herdsman's flocks they had pilfered the skins from. "More taxes," they would tell me. The herdsman could count it up to the wolves, and my men, having smelled and seen the flow of fresh blood, would be renewed in spirit.

The more honest of my followers, some without cloaks, in nothing but their izars, praised God and huddled against one another to keep warm. That's the dif-ference between those of faith and those of deeds.

The red leather of my own tent, though well anchored, snapped and cracked in the wind like heavy breathing. I turned uneasily before entering and looked back over the small, wind-whipped fires. Was it possible that I had marched my men into an ambush?

"Your master." Both of my milk brothers had said it. Neither of them had claimed Muhammad as his own. A man defines his life by the adversary he chooses. Had they apostatized? God forbid. By all that was holy—

If so, if this was an ambush, then it was on a scale that had never been dreamed of before: Every single clan of Tamim had welcomed us in without flinching or any tremor of deceit. By doing so, had they enticed us into their very center? That seemed the most plausible explanation for what I felt. And yet, it was impossible. It would serve me right, coming as I did in force against my own milk brothers, to have them turn treacherously back onto me. They would be perfectly justified in doing so—before the coming of all-consuming Islam. Somehow I knew that that was not what was amiss.

And yet, I had given Malik my sword, and he had given it back. I had sat in their tent, vulnerable, my right arm refusing to rise, and he had not attacked, only burned me when I asked him to.

Shivers sparked my restlessness, partly from the weather, partly from the antici-pation of I knew not what. I wandered back out of my tent to check on the guard. I exchanged a few words with them, assured myself with my own eyes that they were catching every movement it was humanly possible to catch in so dark a night.

The moaning of the wind on the sand dunes would cover many noises. It almost sounded like whispers. The sound of jinn, people said.

"Increase the watch," I ordered. It would mean more men would have to leave their fires, but so be it.

Mutammim's strange, impossible story about the shaytan *came back to haunt me. With yet another violent shiver, I supposed I could not hold the guard responsible for the movements of jinn and afreets.*

By God, something new and unfamiliar had sat in my milk brothers' faces, Sharif Malik especially. My men had not known him since childhood. They could not tell. I found it impossible to say what made up the change I sensed in him.

With a fierce spit into the night, I dismissed the idea of ambush. But when I did that, I received the clear impression that my milk brother was in love. In love, it's true—however preposterous that might sound of a hard and fearless sharif of the desert—and, in spite of his many, many wives, for the first time ever in his life. Love was perhaps too specific a term, a term too loaded with prejudices. But it did seem to me, who knew him well, that something had happened to Malik ibn Nuwaira between this evening at Butah and the last time I'd seen him. Something like Mutammim's visit to his inspiring shaytan. *Something for which the impossible tale might be merely an image—*

This something had opened, it seemed, a deep and flowing well within Malik ibn Nuwaira. As if in a dry season, he was jealous of this newly discovered source. He was trying to keep it hidden with brush or piles of stones. He even tried to sweep away the tracks of his animals after they had used it. Though I did not know exactly where or what it was, I knew it was there. And whereas, before I had been a welcomed guest at any well of Tamim, this was one now, for whatever Malik's subtle reasons, to which I would be denied access. What had come between us that I was no longer a perfectly trusted milk brother? Milk brother and milk son, for I hadn't even been allowed to see Umm Mutammim.

But of course I knew the answer. Malik had told me. "My master," Islam. At least in part.

Islam had come, ripped like a flash flood through the wadi between us, since the last time we'd met. Would I spend the long, cold night in wakefulness trying to deny it?

I turned back to my tent. My half-cauterized arm burned fiercely. On toward midnight, the first change of the watch was about to occur. It was the middle of the month, and the moon was nearly full, giving all the desert a jinn-haunted look. Deneb, the white star that makes the tail of the swan, had already dropped below the edge of the great sand dunes, creeping along the northern horizon. The later constellations appeared very bright in the wind-scoured sky, barren and offering no more rain. Raising my face from the hunch of a cloak to study this, however, stung my eyes to tears.

As I pulled back the corner to enter the warmer, stiller air glowing with the light of a single lamp against red leather, my thoughts had at last reached some sort

*of calm. Maybe I sensed only the calm of cold, benumbed exhaustion, but I thought
I could sleep and puzzle it all out in the morning.*

*Then there, in the sanctuary of my own tent, an apparition loomed black, out
of nowhere. My arm burned.*

*The phantom waited for some few moments for me to give it recognition, but as
I was too startled to do so, it finally took the initiative. "O brother of my lord and
master?" it spoke hesitatingly.*

*The swathed figure sorted itself into the form of Layla bint al-Minhal, with all
the history between us. By God, this woman would never let me forget that when
Malik had married her, she had been an unwilling captive. And that I had rejected
her, though we had all but been betrothed.*

*Still, feeling relief that this was no jinni, I greeted her warmly. "Peace to you,
O my brother's wife." She offered some life on that cold, dead night.*

30

A bundle of myrrh is my beloved to me
He shall lie all night between my breasts.
—Song of Songs 1:13

Within the *qubbah* curtains where she had taken Auntie Adilah's place, as the growing caravan headed south through settled fields planted to winter wheat, young Rayah heard more of her mother's tale.

Khalid ibn al-Walīd's story has run so far ahead of mine on this journey of ours. Let me backtrack in words, if we cannot do so with the camel swaying beneath us.

Having cut Khalid ibn al-Walīd with his own sword, I left first my native tribe of the Tamim and then the Valley of Nakhlah, asylum there also cut off. After ten days of yellow grit and sand with only the shimmer of the jinn's mirages—ever-shifting and unattainable in the distance—I came out of the hills of Mawan to the Valley of Yamamah. At least six wadis descended the hills in the same direction, more on the other flanks. The sharp scent of growing things cut through the dust clogging my nose. Twin pools glinted like blue eyes in the center of the valley, filling the air with their fragrance. They and carefully constructed dams and canals supported a large oasis. Yes, even stands of wheat bent in the breezes that followed me down the wadis. Not strange here, in this foreign country, daughter, but there, in the desert— And ancient tombs as high as a man and five times as long bespoke the reverend age of the place.

A mud-brick wall centered the valley, squeezing the lush green of palms and every kind of fruitful plant over its rim as if it couldn't contain the billowing bounty. Yamamah looked, daughter mine, very like that Tadmor we have only just left. This convinced me, when Yaqub the young turpentine seller first brought me here, that this is where you should be born. You were conceived in Yamamah, Tadmor is where you should grow, in a similar place, although so many of the plants were unknown to the desert-born such as I.

I did recognize white-bearded Musaylimah of the Banu Hanifa, called Rahman "the Merciful" after his God, the same name the Jews and Christians gave theirs. Musaylimah stood with a number of other elders of his tribe before the single narrow wooden doorway into the garden-shaded compound.

I told my camel to kneel and, adjusting my young woman's veil and gown, covered with dust from my journey, I swung myself out of the *qubbah*.

"There, gentlemen, you see?" I heard Musaylimah say. "My bride. And all these years you have tried to replace my dearly departed Warad with one of your daughters, was I not right to refuse?"

Musaylimah left them then and stepped toward me, his arms outstretched. "Welcome, my daughter, my bride, my heart."

Later, I'd taken it all in, but I'd yet to remove the veil, so that still only my eyes were revealed to the Banu Hanifa. That's when Musaylimah told me, "Our Yamamah was named for our ancestress, also such as you: blue-eyed, a Poetess, a Prophetess who could see caravans coming from a hundred Roman miles away, just as I saw that you were coming and told my people to expect you. Welcome. You are like our family, like our founding mother, so make yourself at ease with us.

"And now, shall we join our two prophetic powers into one to stand against this monolith from Mecca?"

He was an old man, your father—

Musaylimah, whom the Muslims call "the Liar," Rayah thought, sickened. My mother is, indeed, Sejah bint al-Harith. This woman whose very travel sweat slicks my own skin beneath these curtains.

—Old, yes, skin wrinkling on his knees and elbows like an elephant's and suntanned like leather. The hands with which he touched me were calloused, popping with veins, age-spotted. His beard was white, but he was kind and gentle. I did not have to hide who I was from him. We consummated the marriage, in fact, in tenting made of bits of my *qubbah*, the frame itself in a place of honor beside the pavilion.

And Musaylimah mixed my virgin blood with yellow wax, which we formed into the figure of a man. There is a reason Muslims despise figurines, especially of their Prophet.

Musaylimah scratched symbols he called "writing" on the figure's back. He said it made up the name of Muhammad ibn Abd Allah.

Within the garden was a bush I'd never seen before. It grew beautiful blood-red, many-petaled flowers but stabbed my finger when I reached to claim that beauty. My new husband tenderly sucked the bead of blood. Then he broke five of the thorns off, stuck one flat-side down on my nose like that animal said to live in Africa whose horns make hilts for rich men's daggers.

As we laughed at this gentle play, he broke off one more thorn and then asked me to come up with some verses as he pierced the figure at the level of the eyes, the ears and the forehead. With his rhinoceros-horned knife, Musaylimah made a gash at the figure's throat, then broke off its arms and left leg. Attaching a black cord to the remaining right leg, he wrapped the figure in black cloth and set it within a black ceramic pot. (I had also never seen ceramic pots, for who would try to carry such fragile things in a camel pack? But there were such in Yamamah.)

Musaylimah threaded the black cord out of the lid, added a bit of fabric singed in our lamp, a bit of onion skin and the tears it had brought from my eyes. A lump of our wedding bread as large as his thumb and the pits from two dates we had eaten finished the ingredients. A slab of wood was laid over the mouth of the pot and then the whole buried but for the very tail of the thread, which rose like a blade of grass to let the magic escape to the air.

I thought of my friend Saffiyah, three years or so Muhammad's wife. Would this grieve her? Or reinforce the magic of the red cinnabar she had taken with her to her bridal bed?

The tree Musaylimah chose to bury the pot beneath among all the trees in his gardens was one plant I knew. A few grew scattered in the dirah of the tribe of Tamim, although most are in Yemen and in the Hadramawt, the Court of Death: the myrrh tree, scraped for bitter tomb perfume like the terebinth for turpentine.

"Now go!" my husband and I said together. "Go and free the world of Muhammad ibn Abd Allah."

Under the *qubbah* curtains to the swing of the camel she shared with her mother, Rayah fumbled for the heaven-forged sword, still unsheathed and thirsty for blood. The same sword she had seen in a flash of lightning in the fountain of Homs, the cause of death of her grandfather, Muhammad's most famous general. One night during the pitching of the pilgrims' tents, she'd taken it in with her, thinking this would be safer.

With one quick swing, she ended that obscene blasphemous tale of Sejah bint al-Harith. She lunged for her mother's throat that had dared such blasphemy.

31

And every man's fate have We fastened about his neck:
and on the day of resurrection will We bring forth to
him a book which shall be proffered to him wide open:
"Read your Book: there needs none but yourself to make out an
account against you this day."
—The Holy Quran, Surah 17

A change had come over Layla, too, since I'd last seen her, though not in quite the same way as that affecting Malik. She now wore the full face veil, more severe, even, than Muhammad, blessed be he, had insisted upon for his women. This seemed to me certain proof, if nothing else was, that Malik's submission was not a ploy.

Her veil was not quite the plain and austere thing a Meccan Muslim would have his wives wear. It sported some embroidery and the adornment of a few shells. But I thought nothing of this. If Islam was going to make women respectable, it would still have to meet their vanities of fashion from the beaked burka of Bahrain to the clattering shells of Tamim, both of which predated the revelation.

That she might be the dark of the night in Butah embodied, that jinn might move her behind that veil, did not occur to me at all. I welcomed her presence like a warm enwrapping cloak. The veil allowed me to see her as just that—or not to see her, you might say. I could accept her as one does the presence of one's cloak against the night—without considering its feelings. When I could not see the stone-hard features of her face, I did not have to be reminded that here was a creature who loved, however unreasonably, and who had been firmly put aside. Even after so many years, were she not veiled, the reflection might have pursued me like a dust demon, a jinni's swift mount. It might have swept me back to her native tent, enjoying her father's hospitality as he planned to give her to me. . . .

No. I would not go there.

"I saw you pacing all this night, disturbed in your mind, and I was concerned," the voice from behind the veil said. "What ails my master's brother?"

That she had the power of speech did little to add depth to her presence in my mind. I might say fire dances when I know perfectly well it has no feet wherewith to dance. Likewise, she behind the veil did not have the wherewithal to feel concern.

"Nothing," I replied, at which she fell silent and demanded no more.

The luxury of her veil kept me ignorant of the stirring, twitching, heaving battle she fought against that silence. At length her well-feigned serenity convinced me that I could speak my thoughts aloud as if only stars and my horse were there. A horse can understand language, I've always liked to think, my own particular voice. It nods and makes soft noises of comfort when I can trust no other.

So at length I revised that "nothing" to say, "Some strange thing has come over my milk brother since last I saw him. I cannot think what it could be nor why he will not share this trouble with me as he has done every other thing since we shared the breast together."

Again my words were met by silence. I had almost convinced myself that I had not spoken aloud but only bandied the thought from one side of my mind to the other when at last she spoke to dispel my imaginings. "Then my master's brother is ignorant of. . .of all that has happened in the pastures of Tamim in these last months."

"Since the Prophet—blessed be he—entered Paradise?" *I asked.*

"That is not an event we count time from, as you do," *she replied.* "But it seems to me the times coincided closely enough—what happened here with the death of Muhammad."

I remembered Mutammim had dated his visit to the shaytan's *tent to that same time in early summer, too.* "What has happened here?"

I received only silence again as struggles I did not understand went on beneath that veil. I had given her anonymity, the character of a cloak, then a fire, then a horse. But now I saw that she had information for me. She was not, behind that veil, merely a senseless wall of desert stone against which I could continually throw my own words to see how they sounded in echo. That veil, which not only concealed, but also opened up possibilities of identity, allowed me to think of her now as a letter or a book. The new-burned blister on my arm throbbed.

As my scribe might, I folded her up quickly and took her where there was light so I could better read what she had to disclose. I invited her to sit and be comfortable by the fire—for I, at least, of all the encampment at Butah, had fuel. Here she unfolded herself, spread out the volumes of her enveloping covers and, with some little encouragement on my part, began to disclose her story.

"The Poetess led a great army out of Iraq into our desert in the last six months."

That was her first statement, and with it a sudden clarity came to my mind. In that one flash I could see, could feel by means of an all-too-familiar power, exactly what had happened here in the pastures of Tamim. And yet I could be asking for details and explanations for the rest of that night, for the rest of my life, indeed.

"Poetess?" I asked, my voice cracking on the words as if I had not used it for decades.

"The Prophetess, the Poetess, Sejah bint al-Harith. You remember her, the herdsman's daughter. That night in al-Ashtat when she, a little thing of eleven years, defeated all comers, including az-Zibrikan himself, in the poetry competition. She taught you her power with the edge of a sword, as I recall. The scar upon your arm is still there."

From the burn down, jinn fire shot along my arm. I drew in my breath as if to speak, but it was more from pain. I let Layla go on.

"I claim the honor of having been her understudy. And of having exposed her glory to the tribe."

"Yes, indeed you do," I admitted.

"I have been like a mother to her," Layla continued.

She seemed to desire some particular response to this statement. But veiled as she was behind shells and embroidery, I could pass over her desires and concentrate on my own.

"What was the army she led?" I asked. I would not have been surprised to hear that her followers were all jinn on rain-cloud war mares.

"The Banu Taghlib," Layla replied.

"Her mother's tribe."

"Yes. How curious you should remember that. There are few who remember her mother at all."

"It is not so curious. I was present at the battle when Bint Zura was taken."

"Yes," Layla said with moment to remind me that she, likewise, had been taken in that battle.

I refused to think in that direction.

Layla did what she could to keep the conversation directed upon me, which was closer to herself, it seemed, than talk of her companion captive. "You were the hero of the day," she said.

"That no longer matters," I persisted.

None of my victories, I see now, really mattered.

"Tell me," I plied her, "how Bint al-Harith came to be with her mother's people. The sons of Tamim and the sons of Taghlib have ancient enmity one with another," I protested.

"We are treated together against Islam."

Fire leaped through my arm. "I see."

She spoke in the present tense, as if the treaty still held. There, in the presence

of me, one of the leaders of Islam who had spent six bloody months fighting any
such treaty.

Oblivious, Layla went on. "She rode to us from Yamamah in the shabby old,
battle-worn litter al-Harith had cut loose of the dead white camel. It turned out
to be the sacred qubbah of the sons of Taghlib in which the Poetess's mother had
ridden at the battle of Dhu Qar. Do you remember it?"

I did, very well. Too well. I no longer felt cold. In fact, hot blood raced in my
arm, in my neck, at my temples, at my wrists.

"When Sejah rode east toward Yamamah in the restored qubbah, the Taghlib
recognized it approaching from afar and hailed it as the return of their sacred spirit
to the tribe. Its rider, too, they hailed, as their salvation."

"'The coming salvation of the Arabs,'" I murmured to myself.

"Exactly. The very words they sang, the entire tribe, as the maids greeted her
with timbrel and dances and all the great sharifs made sacrifices for her coming.
Her maternal uncle, the son of Zura, now a very great sharif, he felt it a privilege
to mourn al-Harith as 'brother' and accept his daughter his own. And to this horde
were joined the Banu Hanifa from Yamamah under their prophet Musaylimah."

"The Liar!" I exclaimed, although he suddenly seemed more honest than many
I knew, too many.

"By the Poetess and by her divine words," Layla swore, warming to her subject,
"I wonder that you did not hear of her great army there in Mecca. They heard of
Muhammad's death and marched from al-Hira and from all the northern pastures
south into the desert. By the Poetess, I wonder that you did not see, even so far away
as Mecca, the dust they raised or hear the sound of their many hundred thousand
footfalls as they marched. The army covered the land as far as the eye could see, all
the sons of Taghlib and their many allies, following a single pure white camel on
which perched the renovated qubbah. The tribes they passed did not have to be
fought and beaten or even coaxed into submission. They flocked to join her ranks as
thirsty camels to drink at the single well after a five-nights' ride.

"But perhaps because her conquests were so easy and caused no destruction,
perhaps that is the reason you heard nothing in Mecca. From bloody battles always
some few survivors run to spread the news and call for vengeance in other tribes.
Some young sons are always left alive after a slaughter to remember the wrongs done
to their fathers and to grow with no other thought than to claim blood for blood.
Even as your Muhammad's influence spreads, always some dissenters prefer exile to
Islam."

I knew what conclusion I had to reach. I said it. "But the way she advanced
was completely different."

32

**O you who believe! Choose not your fathers not your brethren
for friends if they take pleasure in disbelief rather than faith.
Whoso of you takes them for friends, such are wrong-doers.
—The Holy Quran 9:23**

For one moment, the urge to seek comfort on Layla bint al-Minhal's bosom nearly drove me to do so. The leather of my tent was growing stiff in the cold, but still it pulled against the guy ropes, whipped like the quirt of a man beating his camel in fear of his life. Outside, on the unseen, besieging rim of Butah, a pack of wolves howled to the full moon, hunting for fresh blood to warm them. And the warmth of a woman against the cold and violence—

I understood that al-Minhal's daughter spoke the truth: There would always be those who opposed Islam even as the pain in my arm made me doubt I was up to the task of countering them. What could mere flesh do against the Fire Spirits whom Muhammad claimed to have tamed but clearly had not?

A movement of force calls up a counterforce in return, I thought. The rise of Islam had taught me that.

"But Sejah creates no opposition," Layla bint al-Minhal went on as if she read my thoughts. "Without compunction, she gathers the tribes to her as the wild grouse hen her chicks. How much stronger is this bond than that forged with strife! With tenderness and meekness she herds us. And how much more willing is the flock to follow the shepherd who sings to them the evening song than he who would beat them to follow a dogmatic and narrow trail. None can deny her power, but none wishes to, either, for it is the power of poetry, single words with many, many meanings, a meaning for each different heart. Sejah does not move as the sword does, spraying bits and pieces in all directions. Rather her army (call it army, only take all sense of war away from that word) spreads rapidly forward. But it spreads even as night comes over the sun-stricken countryside, from east moving gently, coaxingly west."

And is this the woman who would not see me in the turpentine sellers' house in Tadmor, who refused to leave her harem? Did I drive her there? Who can stop the night, or keep the sun from rising? The incongruency makes me see even this courtyard in black and white.

"So did she lead the way here to the pastures of Tamim?" I asked, jinn-possessed by the mere telling of the story.

"Even so," Layla replied, "and even so did she win us, every one, to march beneath her banner."

I noticed that her words were suddenly in the past, but I avoided any remark.

"Because we were her kin, she favored us with positions of honor. My master, your brother, became her general. And I—Poetess be praised for her generosity—I received again the post I had when she was but a child and she would whisper the verses she snatched from heaven into my waiting ears. The verses I know would make your Quran seem like lumps of lead next to fine-wrought filigree gold. This veil I wear is a symbol of that office. It is similar to hers—the veil of a virgin about to become a bride. I wear it in imitation of her, that I may more closely partake of her spirit, which is of the dark and hidden things of the desert, not of the mind-scorching and garish day."

I shivered now to look at that sheet of black that faced me, shivered as the cowrie shells shivered in the half-light of the fire. I wondered how I had ever thought Layla looked Muslim. Here was a pagan thing, a thing at which Muhammad (blessed be he) would spit and say charms if ever he saw it. By God, the evil eye! As Muhammad used to say, "that narrow eye that puts the camel into the cooking pot and mankind into the grave." This pagan thing had put a spell on me before I was even aware it had eyes at all, hidden under that fabric.

I longed to hear more of the Poetess's words. I intended to keep Layla in my tent reciting all night and all the next day so I could declare, ere another evening had come, that "I, too, submit to the power of these words without a struggle."

But first I had to have the answer to one more question. "How is it that Sejah is not with you now?" I would much rather swear fealty to her than only to her second.

"My master and the father of my son—he was chosen to be her general. He wanted to be a good general."

"So?"

"But he never stopped to think in his haste to be victorious that she was the Prophetess, the Seer, that her will must be obeyed before his own."

Her voice, for some reason I could not ascertain through the veil, burdened the following silence with a heavy despair. This I could not endure, being so full of hope and new direction myself. I spoke sharply, "What happened?"

My tone did not frighten Layla. The personal despair she felt put her beyond all fear, even of any harm I might do her in my anger. "You know my master," she said. "He is very like you. How should this not be so, seeing you sucked the same milk as infants? Yet I have always thought you had somewhat more compassion, a heart more able to be humbled than his. For this reason, I have continued to. . .to love you all these years, though you loved me not and gave me to him instead."

"By God, what does that have to do with anything, your sorry pining?" I shouted.

"I care not for Muhammad's god," Layla shook her head, and the shells on her veil waved slowly like mourners singing at a funeral. "Only for you. But if it is your will, O master of my heart, I shall forsake both he who is the master of my body, and she, the Poetess. . . ."

I stopped her with a sharp oath, for she was obviously unable to control her drivel, her blasphemy, of her own accord. She had committed herself to a side in battle and might as well die a martyr now, as there was no going back once the lines were drawn. She had spoken her battle cry. But the cause she espoused was not my own. Indeed, we were not even on the same battlefield any longer.

"By the Poetess, the Salvation of the Arabs, tell me what has become of her."

The voice from behind the veil was quiet and emotionless as she suffered this change in topic, then as she rehearsed the tale. "Sejah's inspiration told her that we should encamp here at Butah until a further sign was given. But my master, trusting his own understanding of the ways of war more than that of a girl who is barely a bride, said it would be better not to wait. 'We should use the weapon of surprise,' he said, 'and attack al-Medinah all at once while the Quraysh are yet grieving and confused over the death of their prophet.'"

I admitted that, had I been Malik, my reason would have directed me likewise.

"But Sejah awaited a sign."

"What sign?"

"The jinn alone know. Still, her words to me indicate that she was ever opposed to conquering men to side with her, to beating them into submission. She was waiting for a sign that you of Quraysh were confused enough, brokenhearted enough, frightened of your own bloody hands enough to come out seeking her to heal your self-inflicted wounds upon her bosom. But you would have to be very humble to admit to your need."

"Humility is not a manly trait, and the Quraysh are the most manly of men," I said.

"I know," she said and sighed.

I remembered then all the indecision and anguish I had suffered at the Prophet's death, but of my own weakness I said nothing. I waited to hear that of others.

Layla continued, "At last the Prophetess gave in somewhat to my master's in-

sistence and allowed him to lead a small band of men to the Qurayshi borders to flaunt his unpaid taxes and to worry you with raids.”

“Of this part of the story I am aware,” I said, remembering how Omar had brought me the details. And assigned me to take care of the trouble.

“It is something a man would notice,” Layla agreed. “But Sejah made my master swear he would make no full-scale attack without her, nor would he refuse to return at once if ever she gave that order.”

“Then what happened?”

“Sejah ordered him to return. Malik had prepared one final raid, and he delayed his obedience just one day to complete his plan.”

A pause followed her words during which I had no need to tell her to continue. I could sense the outcome of the raid perfectly.

“The raid was a disaster. Ten men killed. Ten, on just a petty raid. And more animals lost than they had managed to carry off in all their months of raiding. My master and the few survivors straggled back here to Butah, only to discover that the Poetess and her army had moved on without them. We are abandoned to our fates.”

“Where is she gone?”

“My master does not know.”

“Surely he can follow the tracks.”

“An army led by the jinn leaves no more track than the passing of a cloud over-head. Malik has no choice but to wait here in Butah until she sends for him—if she sends for him. Most of the Tamim see your arrival as a permanent punishment, an eternal condemnation which, as you have seen, they are willing to accept as justice given at her hands.”

Now I understood. I nodded to the veil. Then I gave myself over to conversation within my own mind in which I matched all the segments together with her emo-tion removed to see if they did indeed fit together. They did without difficulty, and so I accepted her story as true. Only one thing remained that did not quite fit in. “And where were you, Bint al-Minhal, while your master led his raids?”

“I stayed here in Butah with the Poetess, hearing her words, treasuring them in my heart.”

“Yet you did not continue on with her to—to wherever it is she has gone?”

“I asked—she told me to stay here and wait for my master's coming.”

No veil could hide the hint of panic in her voice. It made my thoughts leap to the next question, though I did my best to keep her unstartled by a quiet approach. “Malik does not know where Sejah has gone?”

“No.”

“But do you?”

Dead silence. That answered my question. I asked the next one, “Why didn't you tell Malik? Did Sejah tell you not to?"

"No."

"Why didn't you tell him?"

"He is my master, the cause of my servitude and lifelong grief. He is the father of my son, but I hate him. I will not tell him. And I will not even tell you if you are going to tell him."

"Layla, I am the cause of your captivity. I am the one who gave you to him. I am the one who killed your father. Didn't you see that? Split his head open—so, like a ripe melon."

By causing this pain, I meant to awaken her from her foolish dreams to the earnestness of the situation. I little guessed that she had power to do likewise to me.

"I would rather die with the secret in my throat than to see them united again."

"See who united?"

"My master and the Poetess."

"Why?"

"Because he loves her."

"Malik loves Sejah?"

"By my life, yes. More love than believer has for prophet. He burns for her as the parched sand for water."

There. . .there was the well my milk brother had sought to hide from me. I had guessed, but believed a man's dissemblance.

My daughter and my milk brother? Malik was a sharif, a worthy man. He didn't know she was my daughter, that the kinship was too close, blood curdling the milk, as the saying was. I was a Muslim. I couldn't confess to the demon night that made her, made the sword with which I won the admiration of my fellow Believers.

Yet I wanted a father's prerogative to make the match. Now that Muhammad was gone, the other option might be my cousin Omar, powerful on the khalifah's cushions. Much as I disliked the man, that match would prove me a careful father. It could best assure her future, not this riding around in a qubbah after poetry.

Jealousy silenced me as only one who is at once a father, a devotee and, yes, a lover can be silenced. My throat went dry with the emotion; it scratched as if I'd swallowed a handful of sand. I forced a calm and these words from it: "Has he made an offer of marriage?"

Layla nodded. "But she told him she was already married."

"Married?"

"That she had promised herself when she had had no other protector and that now they were married."

"Married?" I repeated again stupidly. "To whom?"

"Musaylimah of Yamamah. It is, in part, his army she leads, of course."

"Musaylimah? The Liar?" Then I remembered what my daughter had said just before she rode out of Nakhlah. When I had been too feverish to think clearly. "By God—"

"That is what you call him. Sejah says that with any other, her wifely duties would interfere with her due toward the shaytan. None is more jealous, as the saying goes, than one made of fire when he has taken for himself a paramour of the daughters of the earth. I remember how Sejah's mother forswore all men, how she wanted to enter a convent. . . ."

These words gave me some hope of avoiding a total loss of sense to the possession of a jealous jinni.

But then Layla said: "My master is not so easily put off in affairs of the heart. I know full well what use he made of those private meetings with her, general with Poetess. I know as only a wife can know when her husband no longer requires her for his release."

I have since thought that men as well as women may find continence of the body restful when something of the spirit stimulates them. I think Layla, in her jealousy, lied, the one stretched truth in all the perfect honesty. But at the time I was not ready to think like that.

My mind went blank with madness.

A clap of hands outside my tent announced someone desiring admittance. That brought me back.

"Come," I called, pacing from tent pole to tent pole with a wild impatience.

My second, Dharar, shadowed the peeled-back leather in the doorway of the tent, come to see if I had any final orders before he retired for the night. What had he done about the fuel? I had no time to ask. He raised his brows to see me alone with a woman.

"My milk brother's wife," I explained.

Dharar said nothing, but a prurient twist to the corners of his mouth around those camel teeth told me what he thought. He had lusted after the wife of one of our defeated enemies himself. I had not carried out Omar's order to stone him. He imagined a way to pay me back.

Fool, I thought. He thinks I covet Malik's wife. I didn't think to disabuse him. I never guessed what spin his presumption would put on my next words.

"Have you seen that the prisoners are covered? It's cold. Be sure you cover them and then, yes, you may go to bed." I was thinking of Malik's small fire, his cold tent. I meant cover them, see that they had extra blankets or rugs, if there were any.

"Cover them," Layla demanded, her eyes strangely wild. "Did you say 'cover'?"

But wolves and wind and jinn howled from the dunes of ad-Dahna then. And I did say "prisoners," didn't I? I truly do think I said that. Somehow, they had sud-

denly become "prisoners" instead of fellow Muslims.

But they weren't Muslims, were they? Layla had just betrayed them. The taxes and prayers—the ploy of wily apostates.

33

For us a female prophet has arisen.
Her laws we follow; for the rest of mankind,
The prophets that appeared were always men.
**   —An anonymous poet, contemporary with**
**   Sejah, quoted in *The Perfumed Garden***

Everything Rayah knew about Musaylimah the Liar was hate and fear. Flee. Slash. Kill.

◆

Teacher Sitt Umm Ali's voice was still hard and keen in Rayah's head. "Musaylimah the Liar, may his name ever be blackened and his soul burn in hell. Likewise his demon whore wife Sejah bint al-Harith." The Quran teacher's hennaed hair flamed around her scarf as she told the tale as part of their lessons.

All the girls sitting in the circle around Sitt Umm Ali had seconded the older woman, "*Amin*, amen." Trembling with zeal, with fear, with anger, Rayah had "*Amined*" among them.

"When Musaylimah dared to come to treaty with the Apostle of God, eternal blessings on his name—"

"*Amin.*"

"—the people of al-Medinah feared the Liar's evil. They wanted the Apostle to order his death."

Now Rayah could hear her mother's voice justifying the man, telling the tale in her words and his. "'I am no Liar. I come only to speak on behalf of the young woman to whom I have been betrothed since she was a child.' He spoke of me, Sejah, of course. 'Pray—by your God and mine, the Compassionate, the Merciful—do not send the forces of Islam to Yamamah against us, either now or in days to come. Just allow her the poetry of her own inspiration, as you allow the Christians their book and the Jews theirs.'"

Sitt Umm Ali's voice rang clearer with her version. "Two wives of Muhammad, blessed be he—the favorite Ayesha and Hafsa the Playful—teased a third wife, Sawdah, the serious, diligent one. 'The false Messiah is coming,' they told her. 'He the Christians call the Antichrist. Musaylimah's coming is a sign of the end of times when the righteous dead shall rise and God will burn the wicked with an eternal fire.'

"The two wives went on, 'You burned our husband's meat yesterday. Last week, you hurried your prayers so you could tend to the hides you were tanning. You tattled to him, bothering the Apostle of God with trivial things. Think of your sins, Sawdah bint Zamaa. Think of the fire the false messiah Musayimah brings with him. Hellfire for evildoers.'"

"*Amin.*" Rayah had felt the girl next to her tremble and trembled, too. Trembled until tears came. "*Amin.*"

Sitt Umm Ali had tugged with passion at her hair and pressed her story on. "For the fear of God, Sawdah, blessings on her, ran shrieking to the far end of the storeroom to hide herself from the just wrath of God. 'Let a mountain fall on me rather than this.'"

Sitt Umm Ali's gaze had circled her students, trying to get each one of them to think over her own sins and then to pray she might never commit another.

"But isn't God merciful?" Rayah had asked, then recited the first verse whispered into any child's ear when she was born, murmured over any food before she took a bite. "*Bismillah ar-Rahman, ar-Rahim.*"

Had those words—Rayah stopped now to wonder—been whispered in her own ear? Or had her mother, Sejah the false Prophetess, wife of Musaylimah the Liar, refused to let it be done, though still exhausted from the labor and pushing out the afterbirth? Had this allowed a jinni's words to fill Rayah's little shell-like ear first?

Sitt Umm Ali had scowled at the student, her only student who could not take the lesson and let it be. Still, Sitt Umm Ali could never resist a chance to prove herself a font of sacred knowledge.

"'What are you two up to?' asked the Prophet of God, blessings on him, of Ayesha and Hafsa when he came running at the sound of Sawdah's screams.

"Then, with gentle words about the compassion of God, the Prophet, blessings on him, told Sawdah not to fear. He coaxed her plump, jar-shaped body out from behind the storage jars. He told how he had sent the false Messiah packing back to far Yamamah. She was a good and dutiful wife, he couldn't ask God for better. He would pray for her and, if she fasted and prayed, she would not burn in hell.

"May all generations praise him, the Prophet called Sawdah out of the storeroom. She came out sniffling, wiping her nose and her eyes. Then another wild shriek as she fought off the tissues of spiders clinging to her ample bosom, the sticky, wriggling white egg sacks from her white hair."

"Alas, God shield me," the young students had groaned instead of "*Amin.*" Their flesh had crept with earthly horrors of spiderwebs far more than for the thought of flesh blistering with the first licking tongues of hell.

There was always more to the story, any story.

Sitt Umm Ali hadn't said, but Rayah had seen only too well, with the help of a jinn-dazzled vision, Ayesha and Hafsa, Mothers of Believers, giggling in spite of their husband's sharp glances, in spite of hellfire.

Now, many, many stories later, Rayah moved to end the blasphemy of Sejah the Prophetess's tale. Sejah the Prophetess had admitted to invoking evil spirits against the Prophet of God, eternal blessings on him, along with Musaylimah the Liar whom, in her wicked stubbornness, she had married.

Allowed him to father her child. Her daughter, Rayah.

Had she been the daughter of rape as the Muslim army moved north, had she even been the product of incest, Rayah thought, she could have borne it better.

But she was not.

So when, within the *qubbah*, all this fiery bitterness rose in her, Rayah had lunged for her mother's throat with her grandfather's sword.

The air between sword point and brown, corded neck suddenly floated with spiderwebs sequined with shimmering egg sacks. Each sack tinkled like a tiny bell as the wind of the sword passed. The webbing clung to the heaven-flashed blade, slowing it, slowing lightning so it hung in the air, visible, blinding, burning the back of the eye, for what seemed like half the hour of a prayer. The tinkles gathered themselves together into the giggle of the curly-haired jinni boy.

The blade cut. But mirage and magic slowed it. Sejah had time to shift her position within the *qubbah*. The shells decorating her desert dress, like so many spider sacks themselves, acted as armor. The blade cut a kneeling leg instead.

"Don't, O wife, don't," whispered the jinni.

"She is your mother," Rayah thought he was going to say, for somehow she had some sense of what he would say before he actually said it.

Instead, his words were, "She is life. *Rahman*. Merciful." A name of God. From the word for "womb."

"Your father made the pilgrimage to Mecca a second time, after Muhammad's death—" Sejah spoke without pause, as if nothing had happened.

"Blessings on him," murmured her daughter. On the Prophet? Or on her father?

"After the tribes of the desert had revolted and the Muslims began their Riddah War to put down that rebellion."

Only then did Sejah lift up the bloody hem of her dress to reveal the gash, knee and thigh meat opened to white sinews. Like a camel hamstrung.

I do not want to heal her.

Rayah struggled in her mind.

All Muslims will praise me for what I have done, ridding the world of such blasphemy.

"But you must heal her," said the tinkle of the jinn. "We have given you the gift. You must use it or we will withdraw it back to our world again."

As if they moved of their own volition, against her will, Rayah's hands stretched out. One settled itself on the whole flesh to each side of the wound she herself had caused. Blood glued her to her mother, just as it had at the first moments of her birth.

The camel continued to plod beneath them, but Rayah's mother had thrown open the curtains on one side of the *qubbah* the better to view the damage the Sword of God had done. Rayah saw that Abd Allah struggled to keep up with them on that open side, his face wrinkled with concern, favoring his just-healed leg with a hobble and a walking stick. He said nothing in judgment, however. Mother and daughter had to work this out themselves.

The land through which they passed on their way south to Damascus was greener than any Rayah had seen in her life, the fields recently planted to winter wheat. But from one of those fields, over Abd Allah's head, Rayah watched a spin of dust take shape.

Like smoke twisting out of the lamp, like the carded wool had twisted through Sejah's fingers and onto the spindle all the years of Rayah's growing up, the dust grew and began to move. Faster than a man can run, it twisted down upon them, catching up the hem of the eunuch's robe, making him throw his arm up over his face, drop his stick and stumble out of sight. The camel bellowed with annoyance.

"*Ar-Rahman, ar-Rahman.*" The prayer came to Rayah's lips as the force twitched through her fingers and centered on the Name of God. Energy pulsed through one of the girl's hands, then through the other, twisting one half of sundered muscle with the other.

Rayah trembled from head to foot and wanted to pull away but could not. Her teeth chattered; she repeated the prayer with them clenched tightly together. Her eyes, her eyes were the worst. She squeezed them closed against needles of pain.

Then she opened them, met her mother's blue gaze. The sorrow there, the anguish eased the prick of Rayah's own.

At last, the arcs of energy released her. She washed the still-pulsing wound with wine, then washed her own hands before plucking a hair from her own head and threading a needle.

Rayah hesitated, the needle over the sundered flesh.

Her mother saw this and said to the scribe who had managed to catch up again, "We will have to halt the camel for a moment."

Abd Allah nodded and did so. The caravan would go on, but slow enough that they could easily overtake them. Men like Abd ar-Rahman would not investigate the business of women too closely.

"As I did for your grandfather." Sejah hissed through clenched teeth. This stilled the tremor of weakness in Rayah's hand that had threatened to render her unable to hold the needle.

As the stitching proceeded, Sejah continued to speak. A catch of breath interrupted her now and then, but she never stopped completely.

"When my husband Musaylimah returned from Mecca, he said, 'I undertook the pilgrimage before announcing who I was and setting all the Muslim ladies in a dither. Things are very changed there. The Gods are gone, the rites a stark linen garment compared to the gaudy embroidered brocade that was once upon a time. I did manage to kiss the Goddess's stone, however. In fact, I was encouraged to jostle with the crowds to do so. Having kissed her private parts, her source of life, I now kiss yours, my love. From her to you by my lips, so. Let us see if that does not grant us a child, a blessing denied because, I am sure, I am grown so old.'

"But because the rest of the rites of fertility were gone from Mecca, we made our own there in Yamamah. When he returned. After the death of Muhammad—"

"Blessings on him," Rayah elaborated to cover the little gasp of pain her mother gave as the needle went in.

"As we discussed our preparations, my husband told me, 'In Medinah I did see your friend Saffiyah—'"

Rayah held the needle poised in the air. "The Jewess who married God's Messenger in your stead?"

Sejah nodded until she could let her pain-halted breath out again. "'Or,' he went on, 'I did not see her exactly, since she, as one of the widowed Mothers of the Believers now, must stay in her room and speak to the world through a curtain. But she told me to tell you she used your formula so she would never conceive a child by the man who had killed her family and married her all but on the field of battle—'"

"Colocynth pulp, tamarisk dew, the inner skin of a pomegranate set inside, before the womb." Rayah recited the list to reassure her mother with this, at least: that Rayah, too, still valued the advice concerning these methods before she went to her own marriage.

"And then Musaylimah told me Saffiyah had added one more word, not for the prevention of birth, a word the context of which he did not understand. And that word was—"

Rayah pulled the hair over-tight and wanted to stab the needle like a sword. She knew what the word must be and what both her mother and Saffiyah meant to convey by it.

"Peace," murmured the jinni. "*Ar-Rahman, ar-Rahim.*"

"Cinnabar." The poison.

Sejah gave a brief, satisfied nod, although even to move so much must be agony. At least she had taught her daughter the way out of the marriage toward which they rode, although how to avoid not getting into it in the first place eluded her. Silence was the instruction between them for the next two or three stitches.

Presently, Sejah went on. "In cooking the ritual meal for our rite, there in Yamamah, I used what I had learned from my mother at my conception, though she died with my birth: arugula."

"Ayesha's plant," Rayah covered the next gasp of pain her mother gave. "Hair of a fox's tail—"

"For that beast's cunning."

"Sparrow's brains, the bones of a toad eaten by ants, her own menstrual blood, her urine, the lamb's testicles, musk—"

"For the odor of that small deer in rut. Those were for him. For me, licorice, *samh* seeds, honey and sesame—"

"Cooked into a halwah."

"In the garden we entitled the Garden of Love, my husband erected a tent of red leather, red the color of holy Hubal. Within, he set gold braziers burning with green aloes, musk, with ambergris and sandalwood. I arrived in the litter on a pale camel led by the virgins of Yamamah. I wore my complete veils as had the priestesses of old who served the Goddess of Life beneath red banners. When strong men carried me on a tray into the tent, the flap dropped quickly behind me and then behind the men as they left once more. For the perfumes had to be trapped within the leather to such an intensity that the vapor could penetrate water. Grain and rose petals carpeted the floor. There I entered my husband's arms. There he entered me. There we were to linger three days. There you were conceived, dear child—"

The stitching was done. Rayah smoothed on an ointment of aloe, frankincense and myrrh, and wrapped the leg in clean linen. She avoided staring at the tears, the first she had ever seen her mother shed from those steely eyes. Nonetheless, tears of her own dampened the cloth, so Rayah worked quickly.

"'The Garden of Love,' my husband Musaylimah repeated as he lay back, satisfied." Sejah bint al-Harith lay back in the *qubbah*. Surely not satisfied.

"'Soon to be renamed the Garden of Death.' My voice trembled with dread as I said it, but I couldn't keep the thought in.

"'The Merciful One forbids such a thing.' Musaylimah rose on one elbow with concern to hear my prophecy. 'It cannot be true.'

"'And yet it will be. For even as I entered this tent, I saw the dust rising from the Muslim army on the march on the horizon.'

"He scrambled for his clothes now. 'Why did my men give no warning?'

"'Lie still, Husband. I saw at a greater distance than the eyes of ordinary men may reach. And my father Khalid the Conqueror rides at their head.'

"My husband did lie back, but pulled me to his arms as if he could protect me. Or as if I could protect him. Though he lay still and spoke calming words, I could hear the hastening beat of his heart through the graying hairs on his chest.

"'False prophets, they say, tell people only the news they want to hear, foretell only victory and success,' he said. 'There speaks our Prophetess. She alone knows the way to truth.'

"The tears in his beard dampened my shoulder."

Sejah fell silent, partly from pain it seemed, but more because they had rejoined the caravan. And the caravan had begun to overtake others on the road; the great ancient city of Damascus neared. Abd Allah, dusty but seeming stronger on his feet, came and closed the curtain for his ladies against the world.

And they were mother and daughter alone. A mother who had just told her daughter the magic of how to conceive aside from praying and awaiting the will of God.

And the daughter who had tried to cut such information from the world but then had relented. She wiped the unearthly blade clean and finally, finally slid it home to its sheath.

34

بسم الله الرحمن الرحيم

One tear after another I urge back, yet they come ever
     again. It storms tears, yea, a torrent.
It overflows like a bucket riding from the well to
     water the graves and seeds in the open fields.
Then I think of a beloved brother in the middle of
     the night—I must think of him—gone—when the late-
     rising stars have appeared.
                    —A lament of Mutammim ibn Nuwaira for
                    his brother

The next thing I remember from the chill of Butah is the wild scream of women's grief.

The wind, I thought, but knew it was not. The pain started on my tongue, which had touched glowing iron for my milk brothers' sake, then went choking down my arm.

"You said 'cover.' You told your men to cover them," Layla repeated, trembling.

"Cover," which in soldiers' slang can mean "kill."

I bolted from my tent, leaving the woman a discarded black heap behind. By the time I reached my milk brothers' tent, it was too late. Sharif Malik already lay dead, his life sundered by Dharar's sword. The blood pooling on the carpets left little in the ghastly white face for me to remember him by.

My second-in-command had not thought Mutammim worth the trouble of murder. He was a blind man and sat moaning in the corner of his tent, holding his dead brother's hand, as if he were witless as well.

I didn't know what to say. What could I say? I hoped he didn't know I was there. But how could he not?

Then—then I saw my milk mother. Umm Mutammim came shrieking from the woman's quarters. Her hair was uncovered, her face unveiled in grief. She had torn away great fistfuls of her already-thinning hair, loaded it with sand and ash. Her dress was open to the waist. The flesh I remembered as firm and round sagged loose and wrinkled now. With her own nails, she clawed that flesh, crosshatched it with red-running sores. She fell to her knees before her dead son, the one she had suckled on the other side at the same time she had suckled me, and shrieked all sorts of incoherent things. Mutammim took her in his arms and together they rocked one another, searching desperately for comfort.

Did they find it eventually, blind son and stricken mother? I don't know. All I do know is that they seemed to find more than I could, either within my heart or without. I wanted what they had within each other's arms.

I stepped toward them. "Mother—" I begged.

And suddenly, she was on her feet. A fury, she came at me, those blood-streaked hands she had used on herself raised like talons at my eyes.

"You," she said. "You. Khalid ibn al-Walid." She spat against the evil she'd just allowed to pass her teeth—my name. "I nursed you. I nursed you like my own son, and this is how you reward me?"

"Mother, I'm sorry. Mother, I never meant— He was like a brother to me. Closer than any blood brother I have."

"By all three hundred sixty gods at once, may every drop I ever gave you from my own breast curdle to poison inside you."

A fire in my chest convinced me her curse had taken hold. She stepped closer. Dharar, standing by, drew his sword to protect me.

"Whore's son," I yelled at him. "Leave her be."

"But Abu Sulayman, you said—"

"How could you have misunderstood me so? A thousand infected boils upon your religion, man. Anything she does to me, I deserve. And so do you. By God, let her kill me so my pain may end."

And Dharar, armed though he was, stepped back, pale with fear.

Umm Mutammim threw her fists at my chest. The wrinkled, old hands felt no harder than the drop of moths. I caught the left one, caressed it, murmured, "Mother." I stared into wrinkled-rimmed eyes that seemed no longer to know me.

Her right hand dropped and fumbled at my side. She reached for my heaven-created sword and drew it from my scabbard. I heard the scuffle of Dharar's feet toward me again, and again I waved him back.

Please, let her kill me.

But such release was not to be. My sword in her hand, Umm Mutammim took a step or two away from me.

Very quiet, very still, she said: "A curse upon these dugs that fed you."

She lifted the one of them, gone flat and loose as a slab of wrinkled leather in her old age. With a flash of my blade, she cut it right from her then threw the bleeding mass at me.

I fell helpless to my knees as the sticky wet hit my face. "Mother—" I whimpered.

She cut off the other and tried to throw it, too, although she collapsed as she did and it only dropped, quivering, halfway between us.

Shrieking women came and helped my milk mother away. Later, I heard, she died from shock and loss of blood, and come morning she and her son were buried together on the cold hills of Butah.

Mutammim and his infernal poetry will not let that night die. He goes among the tribes, living off their charity, reciting:

> *"One tear after another I urge back, yet they come*
> *ever again. It storms tears, yea, a torrent.*
> *It overflows like a bucket riding from the well to water*
> *the graves and seeds in the open fields.*
> *Then I think of a beloved brother in the middle of*
> *the night—I must think of him—gone—when the*
> *late-rising stars have appeared."*

And, by God, his blindness spared him the sight of any of it.

Is it the power of the poet or of my own mind? I see the scene as clearly as if it were happening this very moment: Bint al-Minhal, heavily veiled so she is little more than a shadow, stooping down to wrap Malik's lifeless body in her cloak, to lean her veiled cheek upon his blood-drenched chest. His head with the thick hair to fondle, the lips to kiss—it is elsewhere, severed from that chest with a single blow.

I stood to answer for my deed before the highest court in the world. I stood before Abu Bakr with my red turban stuck with arrows, trophies of the times my life had escaped Paradise by only fabric's thickness. Times the One God had favored me. I showed the khalifah my naked blade, shiny with heaven's metal. He exonerated me. He understood.

"Who am I to put up the blade that heaven has unsheathed?" Abu Bakr asked.

My cousin Omar envied the attention I got for the deed. He wanted me dead—"For executing innocent Muslims," he said.

By God, Malik was more than that, I wanted to scream. He was my milk brother, closer than a brother of blood. And his mother was mine, the swinging of her butter skin the beat of the life in my veins. . . .

But sitting back and weighing the justice of things that happen on the battle-field is the luxury of those who sit at home and watch from afar.

Omar calls me bloodthirsty. If you send men out to spread doctrine by the sword, when is such a name a compliment and when a curse?

Yes, I'll admit I made a mistake. I'll admit to confusion, to the creeping black madness of the open desert, such a madness as creates mirage. But I'll not admit that Omar can so self-righteously condemn me to death, he who sat at home in peace. I reserve that right for myself.

By God, if I were a poet, I'd write verses of my own to make Mutammim's sound like children's singsong.

> *"Therefore my eyes, come! Weep for Malik when the wind*
>   *(in winter, time of want) topples the herdsman from his post.*
> *Mourn Malik for the sake of carousing, good-hearted youth.*
> *Mourn for the sake of a hostage who must remain in chains*
>   *until he is bent to their shape.*
> *And for the sake of a widow who has a child clinging*
>   *to her side and he, unkempt and ill-fed, like the*
>   *young of wild goats. . ."*

I would add a verse of my own to this but the reasons I have to mourn Malik's death defy all meter and rhyme.

And then Layla stood before me, her skirt stiff with blood and ripped all the way up to her thigh in mourning. She said nothing. What could she say? Malik, rumor reported, had called out her name as he knelt to die, and his last words (before a confession of faith in Sejah the Poetess, which made Dharar give the final sign) had been: "You, woman, are the death of me."

Malik's other widows (there were four of them), his daughters and all his sisters shunned this daughter of al-Minhal like death itself and would not even let her join their mourning circles. I had given her to him, him to her, and I had taken him away. Now she came to me again as the source of all that was both good and evil in her life. She knew not where else to turn.

"Malik is dead," I said. It hardly needed saying. I said it aloud merely as a change from its constant pounding in my brain. "Tell me now, since you can't tell him, where Sejah the Poetess is."

Layla remained motionless, dumb before me.

"Where is she? Layla, where's the Poetess? By God and by my life, tell me where she is."

I had nothing left to base my self-esteem on but then, neither did she. Hence the ferocity of our deadlock. I would draw something from her, even if it were only her life. Or die myself in the attempt.

I flung the palm of my hand across the unmoving veil. Shells on her veil broke

with the impact of my slap. She fell backwards and down, but just so might a cur-
tain fall when knocked from its rod. Not so much as a gasp of breath-sensitive life
sat beneath this curtain. I stood nursing my shell-wounded hand for a moment,
then I jumped at her again and dragged her to her feet by the wrist.

In answer to my hoarse yells, four men appeared within my tent. "Witness!" I
shouted at their amazed stares. "Witness that I, Khalid ibn al-Walīd Abu Sulay-
man, take this woman, Layla bint al-Minhal, widow of Malik ibn Nuwaira (on
whose grave may soft rain fall) here and now, of this moment, to be my lawfully
wedded wife. Before God the Merciful and the Almighty. Amin."

No sound answered me.

"Here. Here is bride-price for her. All the goods I took from Malik's tent. Bride-
price. Now witness."

Still no sound.

"Witness!" I ordered my men with a voice that doubled even my loudest battle
cry.

"I witness, I witness," the four repeated one after another. They sounded like
spies confessing under torture.

"Now leave me to my bride," I ordered. They did.

Alone with her, I realized my right arm was giving me trouble. It was not
just the dull ache I'd been suffering for a couple of days and had attributed to the
cold. That long white scar from elbow to wrist, crosshatched still by the marks of
the stitches, burned by the tip of heaven's sword, now jabbed with pain as if the
stitches were being renewed. I was using that hand to hold onto Layla's wrist. The
pain perverted my senses. I kept having the impression that the wrist in my hand
was shrinking, and I had to clench tighter and tighter to prevent her from slipping
through my fingers.

I flipped Layla down among my cushions and bedding like one more quilt;
the force of it sent clouds of dust into the air. Our marriage was consummated as
quickly and with as little pretense as it had been legalized. As I had ordered Malik
and the others killed. Indeed, all these events seemed part of the same single sense-
less action. They were deeds full of anger, but an anger that came and activated me
from somewhere outside myself.

It horrifies my scribe to think of such deeds in this calm, cool garden. I can tell it
by the dimming of the emerald in his ear. But he's stopped trying to rewrite me.

So how do I rewrite myself? Rewrite my life now all behind me? Say that something
beyond me, something no more substantial than smoke, caused the pain that caused
my helpless anger that caused the deeds? How can I, the Sword of God, admit to such
weakness?

Pain and anger ejaculated from me. The beneficence of a prayer, a quick "God willing" aspirated into the eternal and patient void. Such a word opens the soul, unclogs it of the filth of a lifetime, even if some doubt exists as to whether God is even there to hear you.

I lay back spent and savored the fresh, cold air entering my lungs as I felt it had been unable to do for quite some time. After the air followed thoughts. They, like the air, were fresh, clean, invigorating. They were also so condemning that I preferred my stupor and tried to return to it. But I could not. And so, at length, I submitted fully to my thoughts, as merciless as they were healthful, like the amputation of a gangrenous hand. The arm throbbing below my right shoulder. But pray God, the remedy did not come too late!

Layla—my wife—had not moved a muscle since I'd thrown her down. I reached out a hand—gently, gently—for I hardly dared to touch her. As a man sifts the mute and barren sand beneath him for a clue of the route of a raiding party, even so did I finger the fabric of her veil. I had taken her, you see, without removing even so much as her veil. Even now she lay, hidden as a landscape on a moonless night, beneath her voluminous robes and beads and bangles.

By God, what was I to say? It would be just if God decreed I should never have power of speech again, only the torment of thoughts with no place to spit their poison out. One part of me felt that. Another part, the prideful part, wanted to say: "There. You wanted me. All these years, so you said, you wanted me. Silly woman. Am I still what you wanted?" But I was long past all such pride.

"Layla," was the total great oratory I could come up with after all that thought. "Layla," again, the pleading of a prayer.

Still no sound, no movement. At length I rose upon an elbow and dared to lift the veil gently from her face.

Layla clenched her eyes as if against very bright light. A fat tear swelled at each crow's-footed corner. I saw then that she did have wrinkles after all. Time had affected her as it had affected me. A thin web of wrinkles hung before the poet-beautiful features of her girlhood. Between them was yet another veil, that of her tattooing, which, at the time when she had been neither a girl nor yet quite a woman, had been imprinted upon her. A delicate pattern of lines and dots declared protection sought from the various gods. Years of Islam would not erase them.

And then I saw something I had never suspected, something that the black veil sewn with shells had allowed me to remain blind to. Layla bint al-Minhal was neither young girl nor old woman, nor was she mindless stone nor a mare to follow only instinct. Nor was she like any of those other dogmatic and one-sided images I had set upon her person to make dealing with her a simpler process. She was all of these things and every thought and emotion that had passed over her since her first twinge of childish consciousness as well. A man presents you with all his hates and *loves at once when he gives you his name and that of his father. They are heritable. But for a woman, like this woman, like any woman, torn from her hereditary devotion by marriage (capture and force makes little difference), time exists to think. Layla had had time to create her own new, original devotion between a lost father, a new-found son, a strange husband, and myself. All these thoughts and drives and beings and emotions lay layer upon layer like so many veils.*

Those tears in the corners of her eyes—they were the first personal expression she had allowed herself since the disastrous consequences of our first talk. Even these she tried to call back, but they slipped away from her and down her cheeks. One cheek wore a pattern of dried and brittle beads of blood—the mark of my slap and of the broken shells that had been forced through both fabric and flesh. Perhaps the salt in the tears made the wounds sting afresh as it careened over them.

I bent softly over her, drawn to her face as one is to a delicate bird's egg in the harsh and lifeless desert. I hesitated a moment, then I dared to plant a kiss upon the sound cheek. It was the first kiss I had given her.

All the sweetness of both first and last kiss was in it, for our future was as yet but heaven's will. We knew it not, and Layla stirred as if that kiss were the very breath of life to her. She opened eyes swimming with tears and met mine. Then she braved a little smile.

Then I think I laughed. Either that, or my sound was a cry, as close to crying as long training would let me loosen before a wife. I buried my face in her breast, among the multitude of amulets she wore there.

A vision of Umm Mutammim cutting her breast, throwing it. I tamped down the thought.

How many of Layla's talismans, I thought, were for me? Magic stones and coins, blessed to such and such a goddess ostensibly to keep Malik true. But with the quiet undercurrent of prayer, had her heart whispered my name with every one? Also around her neck, my senses found out a string of cloves stimulated to sweetness by her sweat in spite of the cold that night. I closed my eyes thinking of the verse the common poets say to their loves, "You are the slumber of my eyes. . . ."

I would wake come morning to find this all foolishness.

I would be overwhelmed by greater powers of body and spirit. But that night I found this power—a simple, straightforward power rather like a mother's love—to be quite sufficient for my needs. I slept upon that breast as if she'd suckled me to oblivion and forgiveness of all the past irreparable and chaotic night.

I did not wake until midday. Even in winter when the heat is not intense, the oppressive silence of that time of day seems equally so.

In that silence, there was singing. Layla was singing. The sound seemed to come more from her breast beneath my ear than from her mouth; she was barely whispering it aloud.

"Onward to Yamamah!" were the words, like a lullaby.

> *"Onward to Yamamah*
> *With the flight of soaring pigeons;*
> *Where the fighting is the fiercest;*
> *And no blame shall fall upon you.*
> *Onward to Yamamah!"*

I knew from the instant she spoke them whence she had these words. I was on my feet in a moment. I found her veil and tossed it to her. I must ignore the veil-upon-veil face I had discovered beneath it while there were more pressing things to be done.

"'Onward to Yamamah,' then," I shouted. "The Poetess has spoken it!"

35

In the Name of God, the Beneficent, the Merciful.
This is given by Khalid ibn al-Walīd to the people of Damascus.
When the Muslims enter, the Damascenes shall have safety
for themselves, their property, their temples and the walls
of their city, of which nothing shall be destroyed. They have
this guarantee on behalf of God, the Messenger of God, on
whom be the blessings of God and peace, the khalifahs and the
Faithful from whom they shall receive nothing but good so long
as they pay the poll tax.

—The treaty drawn up and signed by Khalid
ibn al-Walīd upon his conquest of Damascus

Before the gates of Homs, Khalid the Conqueror broke his sword—not the divine one—over the helmet of a giant Roman general. Instead of falling back to rearm, Khalid moved in and took the enemy in a lover's embrace. Khalid cracked the giant's ribs through a boiled leather breastplate, sending the splinters into vital organs, leaving the foeman dead and the way to the city open.

Pilgrims who joined the caravan in that spot pointed the place out to Rayah, whom they knew as the Conqueror's granddaughter, soon to be married to the Conqueror's grandson. And because this image of the man was such an improvement over the moon-pocked face she'd seen in the fountain—his throat cut by his own hand still able to make her shudder—she devoured the stories.

They pointed out the baths near the citadel in the center of town where Omar's spies had discovered Khalid. Omar's men had discovered the Sword of God drinking the local mixed wine and listening to poets, squandering tribute money meant to go to the Muslim poor.

"On poets? The Prophet, blessed be he, had poets killed," Omar was reported to have said. "He did not feast them. God do so much and more to me if I do not do the same to that heathen son of al-Walīd."

"'A poet who recites the words of Sejah bint al-Harith might know where she has taken cover.'" Abd Allah, the scribe of Khalid ibn al-Walīd, retold the Conqueror's words from that time.

Fellow pilgrims, ignoring this conversation, pointed out other history as they passed. Here spread the Meadow of Brocade, here Khalid had caught up with the thousands fleeing fallen Damascus. As part of the capitulation treaty, the refugees were allowed to carry off all their goods within a three-day truce.

But God had willed it to rain. The wealth had weighed the fleeing people down. They had been obliged to abandon their worldly goods. Bolt after bolt of costly brocade unwound in the swampy meadow, their gold fibers and jewel-like tones catching the sun when it finally broke through the clouds. And the Muslims descended, triumphant.

Khalid the Conqueror had given the fugitives their three days, but not a moment longer. By shortcuts and hard riding, his well-mounted troops soon made up the head start they'd given a vast company burdened by treasure, women and children.

Khalid the Conqueror had taken the daughter of the emperor Heraclius that day, newly widowed as her commander-husband fell to Muslim swords. Khalid had tried to give her as a prize to the young man named Jonah who had converted to Islam and betrayed Damascus to the Muslims' siege ladders. A woman had motivated Jonah, but that woman had turned a dagger into her own breast at his treachery there among the unraveled fabrics. After that, Jonah had had no interest even in an emperor's daughter.

"Neither had the Conqueror." Abd Allah mused at the embellishments given the tale by travelers as they passed on. "He had searched the captives taken in the meadow growing flowers more costly than lilies or anemones. He had searched them for one woman, one woman alone, and not found her."

The eunuch looked up at Sejah and their eyes met. To them, the story of the meadow as they passed held more than what the other pilgrims saw in cropped grasses and placidly grazing goats.

"Yaqub the turpentine seller, Adilah's lost brother, he abandoned his goods earlier than the rest." Sejah spoke quietly. She had to keep her sword-cut leg still to help the healing, and it was hard to find the comfortable position on the back of a moving camel after years on a rooftop. "He spirited me away before the Muslims encircled the hapless refugees. Rather than heading north after the retreating imperial army as the rest attempted, he took me east, into the desert and toward his oasis home of Tadmor."

"Then the Conqueror was not far wrong when he guessed you were in that company."

"Indeed, he was right. He had me running once again, heavy with child as I was."

"So Khalid, too, had no interest in the emperor's daughter, only his own. When Heraclius offered ransom for his child, Khalid let her go without a single dinar payment."

"And that was counted charity."

Abd Allah smiled, inexplicably loving the sharp edge to Sejah's tongue, which only ever made Rayah cringe. "After that, the towns of Syria welcomed his arrival with music."

Such landmarks and their tales were how the caravan judged its daily progress.

Rayah had the feeling of history unwinding as she followed its course backwards. It was as if the wool her mother had spent all these years spinning so tightly were untwisting back to staple with every step the camel took. Was this a freedom? Or a tighter web? What sort of life would Rayah herself have at the end of this undoing? She would have to do her own twisting.

And so the caravan came to the walls, as high as six warriors, where, shortly before Rayah's own birth, Jonah the Lover had betrayed his native Damascus to the ropes and ladders of Khalid's men. The Muslims had gone over by night just here, where the triple-arched Eastern Gate opened into the famous street called Straight. The Sword of God had proceeded by torchlight to line the straight street with straight lines of defender corpses until he came to the city center, before the Church of St. Mary.

There he met his second-in-command Abu Ubayda coming from Jabiyeh Gate, the Gate of the Tax Collectors, at the other end of the straight street. Abu Ubayda had made his progress unarmed, unbloodied, and stood now flanked by the city's Roman leaders.

"I have sworn by God and by His Prophet that we will take the city known as the Queen of Syria peacefully and allow all who wish to leave Damascus safely and with all their goods." Abu Ubayda spoke quietly.

Muhammad, peace be upon him, had named this man, one of his original ten Companions, "The Trustworthy of the Nation." When, at the Battle of Uhud, rings of mail had been driven into the Prophet's cheek by blows from Khalid's still-pagan men, Abu Ubayda had been the one trusted to pull them out. He had pulled them out with his teeth, breaking the shark-like incisors. Every time Abu Ubayda grinned now, any Muslim remembered the Apostle of God with a prayer for his peace.

Khalid did not respond quietly, there in the straight street. "And I have purchased the Queen of Syria with precious Muslim blood. By God, don't you see, you peace-blinded sop, that these men surrendered to you only when they knew I had already climbed the wall? They were afraid of my heavenly sword. These wily Romans sought to cheat us out of our fair plunder when they knew they were defeated. As God is my witness, I will not let my brave soldiers—who scrabbled up the walls of Damascus with their bare hands—be cheated of what is rightfully theirs."

"The Conqueror knew you had taken temporary shelter in the shop the turpentine sellers rented not twenty paces west of the Church of St. Mary, Lady," Abd Allah suggested.

Sejah shifted her leg on her cushions and said nothing, remembering that torch-lit night, the screams, the clanging arms, the church bells rung in alarm, the words she had chanted to the sky. And then the ringing peace.

For the Queen of Heaven, by whatever name, had heard the prayers of Damascus that night. There, in the shadow of her basilica, the sack of Damascus ended. The peace of the Companion with his simple, broken-tooth grin carried the day. Churches on Khalid's, the sunrise, side of Her dome were converted to Muslim worship along with the revered head of John the Baptist preserved by a miracle. Churches on the sunset side remained intact.

And Sejah the Prophetess escaped to Tadmor with her turpentine seller.

Even as he stood peacefully grinning beneath the Church of Saint Mary, Abu Ubayda had known what Khalid had not known. Afraid the news would bring the siege to a halt with Muslim grief, the Companion of the Prophet had not let the contents of a message to him personally from al-Medinah be known until the surrender.

The Prophet's first successor, Abu Bakr, never heard of the victory. He was dead and buried at his Prophet's side. Omar ibn al-Khattab, Khalid's bane since childhood, had been acclaimed khalifah in the dead man's stead. And his very first act of office was to remove that godless, bloodthirsty cousin of his from command of the Muslim army in Syria.

"Iraqi forces are also being recalled to that other side of the desert," Abu Ubayda was reported to have said to pacify the irate deposed man whom the Companion knew was a better commander than he would ever be. But who could go against orders from al-Medinah, although Abu Bakr had mostly been content to let the generals have their heads?

"You might go with your Iraqis, O Sword of God."

"I'll stay in Syria," had come Khalid's terse reply.

"But why, brother, if you cannot command here?"

Who would want to try to keep such a man in line along with the burden of all his other new-ordered duties? Abu Ubayda was wise enough to know he didn't want that job.

"I have my reasons," was Khalid's alleged reply.

The numbers of people gathering for the hajj in Damascus had grown so large in recent years that the inns within the city walls Khalid had scaled could no longer contain them. Most had to be content to camp outside the walls on the northwest side, blessed by winds from the distant ocean and near where Abu Ubayda, the Trustworthy One, had camped during the siege. This was far from the monastery near the Eastern Gate the Conqueror had held; the monastery's inhabitants no longer provided for the

Muslims as they had when they thought any new regime would be better than Roman tyranny. But Khalid had left his mark on this field of pebbles, too, for once the hajj moved off, Damascus's garrison trained the descendants of his horses here.

By day, the pilgrims rushed around to purchase their animals—donkeys with their eyes, ears and noses daubed with festival henna—and food—the sacks of dates seeping their honey through their seams onto camel fur. The merchants of Damascus bearing their wares out to the pebbled field had their prosperity assured for the rest of the year.

Once these necessities had been taken care of, however, the gathered pilgrims had little more to do. They had to wait for the caravan leader—as once Khalid's father al-Walid had been, marching the other direction—to announce the departure. With fresh hopes and fresh feet, the journey would begin with a joyful circuit of the city—banners flying, drums beating—ironically tracing the sites made holy by the Christians' Saint Paul. In place of the tales of the misbeliever Paul, tales of the Conqueror gained more favor. Pilgrims gathered to hear the tales and to add their own versions, sending faith to their feet, stories peppered with prayer.

The pilgrims camped in the order they would follow all the way to Mecca, the men from this city next to those of their neighbors on the map. This order would prove especially important on the night marches, when the caravan avoided hot days in waterless stretches by traveling in the dark. Neighbor would look out for neighbor.

Now Rayah heard her grandfather praised in territorial waves, like voyaged hills with valleys in between. And rather than the tight-twisted tale of her mother's spindle, the tales rose in a heavy, all-saturating cloud of dust. The disk of the setting sun turned it roseate. The heavy air smelled of camel dung turned to powder by a million footsteps, of men washed with dust when they had no water. At night, however, with the tales, the smell was of cumin in hot oil overall, olive oil here rather than the butter of the herds of the desert. Cumin flavored the raw meat of her grandfather's life.

Of course, these days, not everyone undertook the hajj as mere religious duty. Omar ibn al-Khattab sat as khalifah in al-Medinah. His network of spies, spies in every battalion, in every conquered town, upon every road, spies upon spies, gave plenty of reasons to make the trip to plead for the mercy of God the Compassionate. A march of more than eight hundred Roman miles, nearly a million paces, was sometimes the only way to keep life's uncomfortable secrets.

Rayah considered the way of the world as she watched and listened to the menfolk from behind her curtains. She watched them lay out their wares—more, the details of their lives as they made up their wills, "being of sound mind"—about to set off upon what might well be their last journey. Her own? First and last, surely, once she was married and trapped within a stranger's harem.

And she watched as Firuz, the slit-nosed Persian slave, returned triumphant from a foray into the markets. He returned leading a white camel. "For the *qubbah*."

His master Abd ar-Rahman scowled. "You paid too much."

"Not so." The slave talked back. "I merely mentioned what it was for, and the breeder whom God so blessed allowed honor to make up half the price."

"But we cannot give such an honor to women."

"What is in Islam like unto the *qubbah*? Where the soul of the tribe once resided?"

"Nothing, *al-hamdulillah*. Only God Almighty in His heaven. Surely you would not have us go back to the Time of Ignorance, heathens that you Persians are."

Rayah, listening, did wonder at the Persian's interest in the ways of the Arabs. But Firuz had converted after his enslavement, and this Islam that stretched over empires, peoples and lands then came to the fore.

"The Quran, Master." Firuz stroked the place where the beard had been torn from him when he was shamed, as a prisoner.

"What do you mean?"

"I mean, the Word of God, created before even the world came into being. That deserves a place in a curtained litter, riding before the faithful upon their religious duty."

"Yes," Abd ar-Rahman agreed, stroking his beard still honored and intact.

"Next year," Firuz declared before his master could decide otherwise. "You will be coming back to Syria." Odd, Rayah thought, that the slave did not say "we." "You can see to it that a special camel is found, hung with gold and rich curtains, to carry the Quran at the head of the pilgrims then. There is no time to do it justice this year. But rather than waste a strong camel back, we will let it carry the *qubbah*."

"Yes." Her uncle like the idea. "Still, such a woman? We cannot honor Sejah."

"You are thinking of her as the Poetess, Master."

"Of course, I'm thinking of that spawn of *shayatan*, the Poetess."

"The Days of Ignorance, of poetry and misbelief are past. Think, Master. She is also your sister. And her daughter is your son's bride. Think of the honor that will be reflected upon you when you ride into al-Medinah thus honoring your son."

So when the caravan leader gave the sign, the white camel took up the burden of Rayah and her mother within their closed litter.

But Damascus was still in the future of the tale Abd Allah read.

36

Gentle now,
doves of the thornberry and *moringa* thicket,
don't add to my heart-ache
your sighs.

Gentle now,
or your sad cooing
will reveal the love I hide,
the sorrow I hide away.
           —Ibn Arabi (1165–1240 AD)

From the horrors of Butah, the ruins of my milk family, I made forced march across the broad tablelands and pastures of the Nejd to Yamamah. The remnants of two previous Muslim armies lay scattered in ruins over the fields of the oasis. The army of Ikrama ibn Abi Hakam and that of Shurabil ibn Hasana had shattered themselves to bits here. They'd thrown themselves to no effect against the powerful wall of faith and temporal might that Musaylimah ibn Habib the prophet (we call him now "the Liar") held over the Banu Hanifa and this, their homeland. Defeat was something the Muslims had not had much experience at, and they could not accept it graciously (if ever any man could).

About Yamamah with the air of fouling corpses of our slain also hung a mystique that made men flock to join me to take revenge and to be part of so great a victory. It also made them shiver inexplicably as they looked Yamamah-ward, as if the long cold finger of a jinni ran up their spines.

Joining us were boys who had just turned fourteen and were carrying their dead fathers' swords for the first time. Survivors of Shurabil's and Ikrama's vast, defeated armies came out of the shadows of the stones where they had taken refuge like rainwater from the sun. The capitulated tribes of Tamim and Asad came, too: Action and fresh glory would help them forget their shameful defeats.

Abu Bakr, though he would rather have initiated the move himself, sent us his *blessing and his flag—the black dress of Ayesha, his own daughter and the Prophet's favorite wife. This is the banner beneath which the major force of Islam is always honored to march.*

But whatever bellicose motives stirred half of Arabia to march in the dust at my heels, I cannot claim responsibility for them. I—and I suppose I was alone in this—did not march to Yamamah to fight. If I could, I would have shaken the army from me as a dog does fever-infected water. But how can one shake an army of thirteen thousand?

A day's march from Aqraba at the pass of Saniyat al-Yamamah, one of my forward detachments encountered and captured a similar group of spies sent out by Musaylimah. To prove to any doubters on either side that my business was in earnest, I had the men beheaded on the spot when they were brought to me. Only their leader did I spare. Bound in chains, I had him kept in my tent until both he and I could have time to compose our thoughts and speak together as man to man, not dogma to dogma. Meanwhile, I had Layla give him the best of our food as if he were an honored guest.

My captive turned out to be Mudja'a ibn Marara, one of Musaylimah's ablest generals. When this news flashed through it, the Muslim camp rejoiced. This joy soured to anxiety within me, and that anxiety wound about my insides like double-twisted thread around a finger until I feared atrophy. I feared that the jubilation of thirteen thousand men might carry them quickly beyond my control. I returned to my tent and sent Layla into her harem. The interrogation began more abruptly and on a sharper note than I had meant it to.

Yet Mudja'a seemed congenial enough. Something in the food, perhaps, had calmed him. Or perhaps the blood moved more slowly than he was used to through the manacles on his ankles and wrists. He spoke openly of the numbers Musaylimah commanded, their positions and their strengths, the things that must sometimes be dragged from a captured spy with horses. He gave the information so willingly and with such good nature. Perhaps he thought that the news that Musaylimah awaited me with more than three times my force would frighten me into a submission. At any rate, Mudja'a was able to end his recitation with a small bit of humor. Such is the usage of old and well-worn soldiers when they have seen so much of both victory and defeat that it's all pretty much the same to them.

I joined him in his chuckle and let it lighten my next question, the question that was of most moment to me. "And has Musaylimah no other tribes with him? Some of the Tamim? And the Taghlib, perhaps? Is there not in your ranks a poetess named Sejah?"

Muja'a ended his laugh. His mouth and his eyes clamped down hard. Had I just suggested that the Banu Hanifa had in their possession the secret to the Greek's sea fire? Some other deadly weapon, impossible to combat, with which they hoped to surprise us?

"Very well." *I announced myself satisfied with that answer for the time being. His silence had told me at least that she was there. I could wait for more, and meanwhile all the army of Islam could wait, too, right where they were in the pass of Saniyat al-Yamamah.*

Layla took the prisoner a quaff of milk in the morning and stayed with him hardly longer than was necessary for that duty alone. But when she passed by me on her return, she said under her breath, "The prisoner will talk now."

Another man might have killed his wife then and there, thinking that the only attributes she might have to turn a man's head were worthy of her death if misused. I might have suspected her and done the same had she been any other wife but this one. Perhaps I should have mistrusted her more—what happened later tells me I should have—but that day I benefited her with the doubt. She had, after all, brought me this far on my quest.

She passed by me, carrying her sloshing milk skin, swathed in her veil, which sometimes makes women seem to float above the world. Now it made her shuffle— at least when she was near me—as if the weight of the world were all too much upon her.

She whispered that I should go interrogate him now. By just such whispers in passing do women tell their men the most vital of the world's communications.

So I left my men, went in to Mudja'a and heard his tale. I tell it now as time and my own fancy have colored his words.

"She came alone from the desert on a single camel.

"In times such as these, with the Muslims a sandstorm in the desert, a leader needs more consideration in his matches. He should marry only one who will bring camels and warriors with her.

"Against our advice, the advice of all his council, Musaylimah married her. He is an old man; she seemed to give him new vitality. But how could the bed of a young virgin be enough?"

I hated to ask him, but I did. "Was it enough?"

"It was enough to send our prophet to al-Medinah to sue once more for peace. When the answer was no good, when Abu Bakr, Muhammad's successor, insisted on the same taxes as his predecessor, Sejah the Prophetess met her husband by a desert well. Foreseeing how the bargaining would go, she had already gathered an army from her grandfather's tribe and from her dead father's. See how women have broader connections than men because their lives carry them from people to people?"

"Now was your council convinced?"

"God forgive our misbelief, no, not yet."

Sejah and her army reached the borders of Yamamah with a success both swift and terrible. To the men of the place, the sons of Hanifa—who had had no trouble defeating two great armies of Muslims—this change in their fortunes was alarming and breathtaking. She had captured their Prophet's heart with spells. And now, at the borders, she captured the sacred camels of Yamamah, including some said to be descendants of the flying camels of Antar himself.

When they had had time to catch their breath, Yamamah's council sent a band of spies out to investigate and bring word as to what this strange new power might be. Mudja'a had been one among the number on this mission as well.

"By the Rahman of Yamamah," was his testimony, "we came upon them by night—campfires like stars, from horizon to horizon. They were encamped on the gravel plain beneath Jabal Mujazzal near a place that is sacred to us for the sweetness of its wells and its trees.

"As my companions and I drew closer, we were amazed to discover that the multitude of fires was actually dying down, untended and deserted. This mystery did not keep several of my companions from the temptation to loot. Because many of the enemy army's goods had been left behind, it was an easy thing for my men to fill their pouches and to strap the saddlebags across their shoulders.

"But I felt a need for more caution: It was all too unnatural. I was soon justified, for as we turned to leave, a great white cloud rose up from the ground and filled the sky. Those laden with goods sank to their knees right where they were and could not rise to make any escape. Moaning and wailing, they waited for death while a few of us managed to flee to the shelter of several large boulders. From this safety, we adjusted our eyes to reality and saw the cloud to be a mass of white turtledoves startled by our presence. They rose as if roused by the jinn."

I remember I chuckled at this point in Mudja'a's tale and made some comment about the quality of the guard on the place and the similar quality of the spies.

But my captive was sober and said, "Know you not what the turtledove means to us? The name of our country, al-Yamamah, signifies our devotion to this bird. The traditions of our fathers tell us that once our land was a rich nesting place for the turtledove. These creatures were so tame and numerous in ancient days that every child had one or two perched upon his shoulder to coo him to sleep with divine and prophetic notes. But the sacrilegious ways of many generations put those birds in too many soup pots. Now there are but ten or twenty birds left that live about the sanctuary in Aqraba. They are most sternly guarded by our prophet, and he is known to have them whisper heaven's secrets in his ears.

"Well I knew that among the prophecies the birds had brought him was one difficult of interpretation, but it is generally assumed to mean that 'when the turtledove returns to Jabal Mujazzal, then should we look for the coming salvation of

Yamamah and of all the Arabs.'"

A shiver slithered across my shoulders at the captured spy's words. The feeling turned to a parched burning in my heart as he proceeded with his tale. He told how, having recovered from their shock, he and his companions decided to follow where the flight of those birds took them. Up the rugged face of Jabal Mujazzal they went, a scrambling, stumbling way through the dead of night. And there, upon the peak, they came face-to-face with a wonder of which Mudja'a found it hardly possible to speak.

"It was all too much like a dream, and in this dream, the distinction between the spies and the spied upon faded into one great, seething mass. A white and pure heart stood in the center of this mass.

"Even in the blackness of the night, we sons of Hanifa could see how pale the camels were. Three of them, spoils of the sacred herd, gleamed pure white, like the inner thigh of a girl in the moonlight. That was, after all, what the camels symbolize, all bedecked with garlands of flowers—young girls in their holiday finery.

"Great woolen tassels like earrings continued the disdainful droop of the animals' muzzles. Woven, multicolored bands like necklaces draped their shoulders and necks. On their heads were crowns of ostrich feathers and on their jowls, painted in brilliant henna, the tribal signs of Taghlib, Tamim and Hanifa. The signs on the camels were alive, as live and ongoing as the people themselves.

"The camels had brought up their cud and were chewing, scorning the crowd making such a fuss about them, daring them to do their worst. They had a mouthful and were therefore beyond all hurt.

"It was a wonder to see. A wonder to see a camel sleek and jiggling with fat in the hump in the season when it was ten strides between dry, stubby clumps of grass. These holy ones had been hand-fed on dates and curd, human food. It was a wonder to see flowers in bleakest winter.

"Closer inspection betrayed that the tufts of acacia bloom on the mountainside were dry and brittle—about to turn to dust. But they were nonetheless astonishing. And it was a wonder to see the army as numerous as stars. In pilgrim's simple garb or in pure nakedness, they circled round about the creatures.

"Some forced the camels to their feet and drove and led them upon a large, flat stone where they were made to stand. Their drivers stifled their usual herding cries and whistles. Only the animals made deep-throated sounds at being disturbed.

"All grew quiet, deathly still. Attention strained toward the eastern horizon, against the slopes of Jabal Mujazzal. The air was thin, damp and cold. We shivered. We were acutely aware of breathing. It was too dark, too quiet to be distracted by anything else. The cold air entering, so full of dew, unlike any other air we'd ever breathed. The air seemed to have been conceived and birthed only moments before *it touched our faces. Life clung, tenuously, quaveringly, to that thin stream of what one normally takes no notice of.*

"*Then the girl, the Poetess still in the veil of one on the verge of marriage, descended from the stone where she had stood somewhat apart. For all the cover of transient being she wore, she made an eternal, ever-present figure as she came down amongst us and began to lead the company, without a word, to the right, around the camels three times. I tell you, O son of Sulayman, I forgot breathing and listened with suppressed awe only to the march of a thousand thousand feet, stone crushed against stone. I forgot the lights of the sky to behold that single burning, leaping coal that inflamed all the rest.*

"*Three times around, the company halted. Now when we looked to the eastern sky, we could see her.*"

"*The Poetess?*" *I asked.*

"*The morning star, like that hole left in the roof of a black tent by the pierce of a pin. A few fibers broken unevenly through which the vibrant sun of noonday dances to the darkness within. The folk gave a single cry of praise to that star, calling her 'Mother' and 'Worshiped One.' Then everyone drew a knife. Men lifted their lances, sons their father's swords, women their cooking knives and children the bits of flint they used to hack herbage for their animals.*

"*The camels were taken so much by surprise that they barely gave a murmur. Yet such swift work was made of it that when we reached their hearts, they were still throbbing. Both the serenity of the beasts and the swiftness of the act boded well for the army's fortunes. We divided the sacred life of the camels among the tribes. We ate it raw while it still quivered and stayed warm and sticky, the fat like hanks of spun silk hanging, making the tent poles bend.*

"*By the time the sun rose, a hot and envious glare in her eyes, killing the holy star of sacrifice, all that was left on the broad, flat stone was a blood-soaked scrap of bridle and tassels. All three camels, from their white hair to the marrow of their bones, had been absorbed by their people: pressed on the tongues of their sleeping infants and gummed by their toothless old ones. As it was happening, the whole world seemed the flash of knives, the drip of blood, the curl of the throat as it time and time again had to accept this grisly food.*"

"*Then what happened?*" *I asked.*

"*When it was over, the people stood about a little dazed at what they had done. Stunned, we needed time to return to normalcy. But as the sun climbed higher, the people remembered their tents, their fires, their belongings and that the enemy might soon be upon them. They turned from the mountain and in silence descended into the valley. A gulp of cool water would be good for the heavy burning in the stomach, a pillow welcome for a dizzy, blood-drunken head.*

"We spies, too, came down from the mountain, moved and dizzy from what we had seen. Some of my men turned traitor on the spot. They went to throw themselves at the feet of the one who had led that weird and otherworldly ritual. The others, myself among them, did not hinder our companions. But we felt constrained by duty to put off doing what we longed to do until we should return to our counsel. We needed to tell them all that we had seen of turtledoves and of the sacrifice on Jabal Mujazzal. Heaven cannot be thwarted by man."

37

Ibn al-Mubarak said while with his companions during a battle,
"Do you know of anything better than what we are doing?"
They said, "We know of none."
He answered, "I do."
They asked, "What is it?"
He said, "A virtuous man rose during the night and beheld his
sleeping children uncovered, and so he covered them with his
garment. His deed is more virtuous than what we are doing."
—A hadith of the Prophet, blessed be he

Musaylimah *the prophet of Yamamah had great skill at reading signs and portents. He saw clearly that it would be death from him and all his people and yet—*

"How can you say that, Master?"

My scribe refuses to pick up his pen. He leans back against his cushions and folds his arms across his sunken chest. As if he stood in judgment of me. Because he had all manly feeling cut from him, he thinks he knows better.

He has more to say. "I mean, knowing what you know. No prophet may come after Muhammad, the Seal of the Prophets, blessings on him. And surely the history you tell must prove this out."

"Yet Musaylimah the Liar knew the truth. I'll rephrase, but you will write."

Although Musaylimah saw clearly that it would be death for him and all his people, he and his forty thousand men came out to meet me and my thirteen thousand Muslims. They perched along the ridge of Wadi Hanifa with all the broad plain of Aqraba behind them to free their powerful maneuvers. They also stood before a small walled garden outside the walls of the city of Yamamah proper. That garden, not the larger town, appeared to be the center of their defense.

Any attack of ours would have to come at them from below. I would think twice about fighting any army at such a disadvantage, never mind this one, with all I knew about its otherworldly support. So I pitched camp on the opposite side of the wadi and sent envoys over to speak with the prophet to find out what they could about the condition and continued safety of the Prophetess. Mostly, I hoped to give myself time to think.

But the sight of the enemy made my men restive. By God, it made them mad! They were in no mood for talk. I, to whom they looked for fatalistic encouragement, could not very well speak to them of the virtues of restraint. In fact, no such virtue existed.

They were within earshot of the sons of Hanifa. I could not keep them from exchanging insults across the no-man's-land. Those Muslim generals fighting strangers of foreign tongues today—Persians, Africans, Greeks, whomever—can have no idea of how we fought in those early days.

By God, we shared the same poetry.

I did what I could to keep control by dividing all the commands up across the grain of ancient tribal lines. I have received praise for this first attempt to bring reality to Muhammad's vision of one Arabia united behind reciters of the Holy Quran. The old ties of blood should count as nothing before the new ties of faith. I did this from no foolish idealism, however, but hoping against hope that Tamimi camped with Asadi and Meccan with Yathribi would have enough to do arguing with each other. I hope they would therefore keep peace with the Banu Hanifa.

But asking men, fired by Islam, to sit on their weapons there, within spitting distance of the enemy, was like giving a child a kerchief full of sweetmeats and asking him not to eat for a week.

I had only just begun composing a second message in which I stated my position more clearly. "These are the terms under which I would be willing to join forces with yours—with those of the Prophetess." I had just given those words to my scribe, just started to fight with him over getting them down on the palm frond he had draped over his knees.

Then old Bilal's call to prayer rolled up through his round, black chest like sound through a great water jug: "Prayer is better than sleep." And fighting better than either. As the prayers ended, the cry went up, the glinting ring of iron in the morning gray: "Allah akhbar, God is great." I knew there was no time left to place bets.

That early-winter morning we turned from Mecca toward the rising sun was cold. The breath billowing from the cavalry—the men, the camels, the horses—as they hastened to answer the call made them seem like fantastic fire-breathing monsters. Those on foot, too poor to own a mount—and they were numerous—welcomed the activity. At last they could chisel their limbs out of the stance with arms and legs crossed tightly across their bodies—as herdsmen stand on watch—a vain attempt to keep in the warmth.

I had just finished leading prayers when a couple of men from al-Medinah went, fired with faith anew after their prostrations, to taunt the sons of Hanifa out of bed. This little recreation soon came to blows. And after this first blood had fallen, blood feud grew as only it can in the desert where everything else, every green leaf, must struggle to survive. There was no stopping it then. At least a hundred men had died before I reached the forefront.

The way the Arabs fight, each man his own hero, makes it very hard for a leader ever to feel like one. Each single little general who leapt forward to claim martyrdom for himself made a hell for the rest of us. Each one lay with his individuality, his once-tightly-bound collection of blood and intestines, spilled over the ground and seeping into the skin of those yet alive. In that blood-hot bath, I could no longer trust that the drive to fight and to live was my own.

"God is great! Hail Muhammad!"

"Hail Musaylimah!"

Somehow out of the utter chaos I managed to spot the driving figure of the enemy prophet. I beat my way through friend and foe alike to reach him. Seeing that man face-to-face was the most devastating blow I received that day, a day full of dreadful blows.

Musaylimah ibn Habib, prophet and Rahman of Yamamah, was an old man. Other men may be more generous in their descriptions of him. These men did not have to see him face to face as their son-in-law, to think of him husbanding the world's most glorious and most tender bit of female flesh. By God, there can be no doubt, whatever else you think of him, that he was over seventy. He had none of the charm such an age might give a man. He was short, and his skin was yellow. His eyes, yes, were prophetic blue, but they were small and closely set on either side of a flat nose. His teeth were bad and his belly, a distended pot, was rather like a hunchback, only upside down and back to front. One could see it holding his robes up away from his body—even fine armor could not disguise it. It made me wonder about the organ that hung beneath it, being so misshapen itself.

And yet, I had thought to give her to Muhammad, had I not? While he still lived. She would have been a widow now. . . .

I shouted my battle cry at him as I approached:

"I am the son of many sharifs.
My sword is sharp and terrible.
It is the mightiest of things
When the pot of war boils fiercely."

"What do you want, O desecrator of holy ground?" Musaylimah shouted back at me.

"What terms will you accept, O Liar?"

He had lied, about his ability to husband Sejah the Prophetess most of all. Some struggling men of mine jostled me from behind.

"None but your head," came the old man's fierce reply. His shaytan—*and here I will call it by Muhammad's variation of the word, his Satan—flitted constantly by his side. You could see the old man cock his shriveled, yellow head to one side to hear the inspiration.*

"By God, where is the Poetess?" I demanded. "What have you done with her, you fiend?"

Musaylimah shook his head rather sadly and solemnly and began to recite:

> *"Verily we have given you jewels:*
> *so take them to yourself and hasten;*
> *yet beware lest you be too greedy*
> *or desire too much. . ."*

Before I could begin to make sense of his holy gibberish, some of my men saw what I was about. They thought I meant to hold the prophet as a steady target for their lances. If they had been able to cut him down then, several hundred Muslim lives and many hours of battle might have been spared. But I did not intend that. Nor did God intend it either. For with his second sight, Musaylimah saw them coming. He slipped back behind the safety of his bodyguard.

Then I felt myself powerless. I milled about here and there watching as the army of God battered itself to pieces against the Banu Hanifa, which held like a wall of stone. And when that wall took the breath of life and began to march down the wadi sides on top of us, Muslims scattered like grains of sand before the wind into the safety of the desert. For all my vows, I went with them.

Slowly, painfully they regrouped about me, the beaten Muslims, their little flickers of individual pride blown out with one puff of wind. They sat around me, dumb with exhaustion and surprise, but I had no time for them. In my mind, a battle of even greater intensity was being fought, and the outcome there would determine the final victor on the plain of Aqraba.

Some last few stragglers brought me the word:

"The Banu Hanifa have entered our camp. They're sacking it. Some have already claimed your tent as their own, O Sword of God."

"They have found those behind me, then." I spoke of Layla.

"They found her cowering among the bedding."

"And have they slain her?"

"They determined to at first. But Mudja'a was also found there, still in the chains of a captive. He spoke for your wife, said she was under his protection."

Then the announcement: "Take her at once to my harem within the city walls,"
Mudja'a said.

My men watched my reaction to this news carefully but with shielded eyes,
when they thought I could not see them. What was I thinking of? they wondered.
My wife of less than a month, the woman it was already being rumored that I had
killed my own milk brother for—had she given me reason to mistrust her? Had she
entertained my captive with more than food and water? They had noticed—had
I?—how Mudja'a had agreed to speak all he knew after only a word from her.

The captivity of my wife, the disgrace of my army, the vow of so many years ago
that I would die rather than face defeat—these things might have moved another
man to the revenge I planned. But what moved me was none of these. They were
the words of Musaylimah himself. They were senseless jargon, what I could make of
them, but they made me begin to think that, wherever she was, Sejah the Poetess
was no longer there with him in Yamamah. She should have been there in the thick
of the battle, leading the charge of her men from her sacred litter. I could not have
missed her. Even in that dusty, bloody, hellish mess, I would have felt her presence
if vision had been obscured. She simply was not there in battle. I need not hesitate
to fight the Liar, then, for fear of any harm to her.

Perhaps she was even. . .

No, heaven forbid that I should even glimmer on the thought. But it brought
me to my feet from my seat in the shade of my horse. It cleared the haze of mirage,
the ring of battle from my head.

By God, would I punish him!

38

O my daughter.
The bridegroom is my foe.
He cannot pay me enough.
—Traditional Arabic poem

With tightly pursed lips, I turned to the stumbling, swearing scuffle of men about me and called a regrouped order out of that chaos. This time I was in earnest. I ranked them differently: Meccan with Meccan, Tamimi with Tamimi, son of Asad with his father's cousins, and so on. A united front of all Believers equal and the same had failed. As God is my witness, I swear it will always fail, for such is the very nature of the men I led.

I passed from group to group in review saying quietly to each, "What are you, men of al-Medinah? You who first gave shelter to the Prophet. Do you flee in battle like the coward Meccans beside you who spat on him when he was among them?"

To the Meccans I said, "Muhammad, blessed be his name, was of your blood. Many of you are kin to him or played with him when you were small. Does such blood grow cold in a fight?"

So I passed from group to group, coaxing blind hatred from them and turning it against a common object. Genealogies began to be chanted in their driving "the son of. . .the son of. . .the son of. . ." rhythm. I then reeled my horse and sounded the second charge, grinning with pleasure at the prospect.

In the first drive we regained our lost camp. Layla was gone, but I had no time for her anyway. The charge carried us on across the wadi. In the mass of struggling men, I hacked away almost without looking at whom I brought down. Always I strained my eyes to try and see a qubbah fluttering above all the rest, to hear the shrill voice I knew only too well.

A few women fought among the Muslims: Umm Umara, who had stood beside the Prophet at Uhud, others. But they were the sort with hardened masculine faces and forms that one could look straight in the eye. And they were moving with me, not against me. I could ignore them.

All I could hear and see among the enemy was the short and yellow-gray but strongly knotted form of the Liar. He was calling on his god and driving his men with the cry that this was their own land they were defending, their children, their wives. In this he had advantage over what I could call up to my soldiers' remembrance.

The Muslims staggered with the first solid impact of this force.

And then it seemed that even the hand of God turned against us. For an unprecedented wind arose from the desert and came south, bringing with it all the sand and dust raised by a million agitated feet right into the faces of the Faithful. The sons of Hanifa praised their god with shouts of jubilation.

Enemy swords came out of the blur of sand and struck without bodies to strike back at. The screams of men and animals came out as throttled chokes. Eyes gouged out and left hanging on the cheek—like that of Katada, the son of al-Nu'man at Uhud—had no miracle wrought by the Prophet, blessed be he, to heal them. Those without such wounds wished for them, so stinging was the sand. Those who had time, room and vision enough to move backward did. Hundreds of others fell. Gullies ran with blood down into the wadi as if with water from a cloud burst.

Yet I refused to turn.

I have been blamed for this by those back in al-Medinah. "Any man with sense," they say, "with any love of the Merciful God, would have called a retreat and not thrown three hundred lives away like so much dung in continuing that single charge."

But I would be blamed for not continuing if I'd taken that strategy instead. My motives are always suspect, not without reason, by those pure and dogmatic monotheists.

I prayed as the sand stung my face through the wrap of my red headdress, and I am one usually content with form five times a day, if that. I prayed to Muhammad's God because those were words I knew how to address. But I also prayed to another because I recognized her power in the sandstorm and could not bear to have her against me.

"I am come to help you, by my life," I prayed. "So please—help me." And I cared not who heard this and called it blasphemy. Therefore am I suspect in al-Medinah. . . .

And then, from the devastation and total loss, Muhammad's God (or Sejah's) brought victory. So much blood flowed that the sand and dust were turned to a red mud. Though Fate continued to blow the winds southward, they no longer carried sand with them. I found the head of my army again and went there, working my way along the front, appealing to this miracle and to the glories of martyrdom.

The mud sucked at my horse's hooves and stained them to the fetlocks. The foot soldiers slipped about in it, but their slipping started to be forward instead of back. Slowly, slowly, the forward movement gathered momentum. I urged my horse until she reached a gallop between the men I cut down.

I fairly sang with exhilaration as I flew:

> "I am the son of many sharifs.
> My sword is sharp and terrible.
> It is the mightiest of things
> When the pot of war boils fiercely."

"O sons of Hanifa! To the Garden! The Garden of Compassion where He will surely save you!" With those words Musaylimah croaked the full retreat.

I reined in my mare. She and I stood, just out of spear's throw from the walls, blowing hard. No amount of clannish rivalry, no amount of blood, no amount of help from God could scale the walls of the Garden that now stood between the Muslims and the Liar.

Thank God, I thought. What were the chances that Sejah was alive? That she was within those walls along with all the fled army?

Pulling farther back to a hillock more than arrow's shot away, I found I could look over their walls. From that vantage, I surveyed the Banu Hanifa regrouping about their commander. I could see also, in a place apart, the bright red and gold curtains of a sacred marriage tent. So was my daughter there after all?

The garden walls would give me time and my half-victory some leverage with which to bargain for the contents of that tent. I knew siege warfare, though most of my men did not. Let them yell at the enemy all they wanted before the walls. I would have at least the time it takes hunger and thirst to work upon an army before they could possibly self-ignite again.

It was midday. The Muslims, for the most part, were quite content to sit right down after their prayers and catch their breath. The heat came down and the flies came up from the field of the dead and dying. The most ambitious of my men went about here and there, picking up plunder and remembrances. They dispatched non-believers still struggling with life and gave last water or recited the Holy Quran to those who called upon Muhammad and his God. But mostly they sought out shade and, from a safe distance, exchanged idle taunts with those upon the walls. Or they simply slept.

That is good, I thought. Now we can bargain peace. Now can be time for daughters.

But I should have known: There are always some with little patience. The heat and smell of victory were too much on them, like the effects of wine. And a heady wine Muhammad had given them to replace that of the grape he had forbidden.

They never dismounted, nor even reined in their horses, but kept milling around, a handful of them, circling round and round. The blank walls offered not so much as a fingerhold to an army that had not thought to equip itself with a length of rope for scaling operations.

I had to keep a clear eye on these few restless men. But I was too exhausted, too distracted—never mind what excuses I can offer.

One of the Twelve, as they were called, those men from al-Medinah who had sworn allegiance to the Prophet when he had had few friends, approached two of his comrades. This man's name was Baraa. He was old and revered, not only for his early faith, but for the wisdom of his years. "If you two on horseback," he said, "will lift me up, I could grasp the top of the wall and climb over it."

"That will not do, O father of many sons." One of the comrades answered me later that he had at first refused. "You would be in twenty pieces before you touched the ground."

"Then that is God's will. Nevertheless, I would try. And should I gain martyrdom in the attempt, praised be God."

The other comrade began to reiterate the first's refusal, but he saw the spark of possibility and of faith stirring like a fish in the dark water of the old man's eyes. "Paradise will be your reward," he answered instead.

The commotion his appearance caused on the other side of that wall first roused my attention to the plot: the curses, the slashing of swords, the groans. But the turmoil did not diminish at once into enemy cheers. Instead, it began to make its way toward the gate in the mad rush of a stone bouncing down a mountainside. Then, incredibly, I saw the gate open a crack; the bolt must have been thrown. A single old hand thrust around the edge of the heavy wooden panel.

Immediately, the old fingers were slammed between door and jamb with such force that I expected a severed hand to go flying. But by then, the hero had help from the outside. Soon a stack of bodies propped open the door, Baraa's invisible beneath them all. It would be many hours before any power on earth could close that gate again.

The screams and clangs drowned my one thought. "My daughter."

The apostates now were trapped. Room did not exist between them to use their weapons properly. The Muslims pressed forward, hacking swinging room, like mowers in the abundant fields of Egypt's delta.

Every Muslim of the mass wanted to be known to history as the slayer of Musaylimah the Liar. As commander, I couldn't let myself be left behind outside the walls. But because of my men's great yearning toward his creeping figure, I found my way relatively clear to the false prophet's red and gold tent at the opposite side of the garden. I picked my way past trampled flowers and hacked palm trunks. Over-

turned braziers spilled precious incense smoking into the grass. Cracked bowls and jugs sloshed potent beverages, forbidden to Muslims, like the blood of the infidels. Here and there were the chopped bits of those great abominations: idols. A hand here, a male member, a breast—

Umm Mutammim, I remembered. Her breast—

Closing my eyes, I pushed on, slowed not by enemy swords but by my own misgivings.

I pressed on through the ruins of an orgy that had had as its center my daughter, my daughter around which satanic influence whirled. God would punish such evil. Even now, announced the screams and death rattles behind me, He did so with a vengeance.

Never mind God. I would punish.

I found myself in the deserted calm of the courtyard apart. This holy of holies was so revered that even in their last moments, no son of Hanifa sought a hiding place there. Here stood only the great red tent and, within that, the most holy of holy things.

Bent wings of acacia bearing flimsy curtains. The qubbah *of the Taghlib.*

I called her name. Only silence and the faraway ring of battle replied.

A pair of blood-spattered Muslims burst in, ready to strip the red leather of its gold trappings with such violence that the tent would come down on my head, on the qubbah *with its precious cargo.*

"Very well," I told them. "Take your plunder, won by God's grace, giving His share to the khalifah. The qubbah *and its contents, however, are mine."*

Over me, the leather quickly disappeared, pieces going for sandals, for bridles, for belts and sheaths.

Shadows fell and I didn't notice. My senses came to me only when shouts told me the Liar was no more.

Musaylimah had been killed by the great black freed slave who, though he had other names, was sometimes called "Father of Blackness" but most commonly, simply "the Savage." Everyone knew which Savage was meant. No other man could make a lance conform to his will as this one could. In days of unbelief at the Battle of Uhud, that same lance had sent Hamza, the Prophet's uncle, on to Paradise. Since that day the Savage had been seeking a way to make good that awesome debt to Islam. He had now found it with the selfsame lance.

"Sejah bint al-Harith," I spoke at last to the qubbah, *silent all this while. "You are a widow now."*

No answer.

"You are my prisoner. I am Khalid ibn al-Walid." No, that's not how I meant to phrase it.

There was no answer.

"Do not fear slavery with me, however. All these years, I've wanted to let it be known, and now it can be. I loved your mother. I told you. At the sacred site of Nakhlah. You are the product of that love. You are my daughter, not the daughter of some dead, pathetic herdsman's son. I will treat you as such. The rewards due a daughter of the Conqueror of empires shall be yours—"

The evening star had come out and stared down at the day's shadowed slaughter, hard and unblinking.

"Jewels and fine clothes—"

Suddenly, however, I knew that what I promised could not tempt the Poetess. To her, such things were but air compared to the spirits of the night to whom she belonged.

Worse, I knew I spoke only to such air.

I tore open the qubbah*'s curtains and saw it was so. The litter yawned empty.*

In the Garden of Compassion become the Garden of Death, the exhausted conquerors dropped to sleep right where they were, using their last victims as pillows. Come morning, the task of counting and burying both sides would occupy another draining day.

Old Baraa was only one of the close Companions who fell that day. Three hundred who could recite the Holy Words in their entirety were lost. This prompted Abu Bakr to command that they be written down, lest another such disaster take the revelation permanently from the earth. Umm Umara lost her stone-like head just three steps before her eager sword reached Musaylimah. Her death opened a narrow gap for the Savage's spear to fly. And Omar's brother Zaid likewise fell, and for thus losing him I shall never be forgiven by those in power in al-Medinah.

I made my men go over every enemy body carefully, undressing them even if the clothes were not worth claiming as loot. I had to be certain we had not killed a woman.

But I was satisfied long before the last tally was in that we had not. Sejah was not the sort of woman to betray her sex by pretending to be mine. By some power not of mortal man, she had slipped through both Musaylimah's grasping yellow hands and my own powerful ones. I had an image of her as a kite, a buzzard, hordes of which blackened the sky over the Garden of Death. A man shooed them from this corpse only to watch them move on to the next and perch there, cawing as if with laughter.

"By my life." I wept. My men thought I wept to see so many Muslims dead. Soldiers die, enter Paradise. But for no reason I could say, I lived. I lived, lived a soldier and a Muslim—for what? "By my life, where is my daughter? Why was she not in the Garden?"

"The desert and the tomb, these three. . ." Those words came to me as if in answer.

Three? Something was missing from the old proverb. Oh, yes.

> *"The desert, the tomb and a woman's lust,*
> *These three cannot be satisfied."*

Sejah, wherever on God's earth she was, was now a widow. Widows are notoriously the freest of women.

39

Goddess is ever gracious to the pregnant woman;
She brings forth from her a living being
That moves from her very midst,
From between the belly and the intestines.
She created woman a receptacle
And man to be contained by her
From the cradle to the grave,
To enter her and leave her
With but the fleeting pleasure of a single generation.
But the woman remains permanent
As the earth the herdsman wanders over,
And then a little lamb is brought forth.
—A revelation of Sejah bint al-Harith as
recorded in the history of at-Tabari

"You vanished from the Garden of Love become the Garden of Death? The jinn took you?" Rayah asked her mother.

"Nothing so magical," her mother replied. "Musaylimah—may the rain fall soft upon his unmarked grave—when he left me to stand with the Sons of Hanifa at Aqraba, he saw to it that the *qubbah* rested over a culvert that ran from the garden under the wall. The heavens sent the sandstorm, the sack of the Muslim camp by my husband's forces. I crept away then.

"Had that rash Conqueror who calls me his daughter but bothered to shift the cushions I pulled over the culvert when the nightmare sounds of battle and death told me I must flee, carrying my mother's, my grandmother's goddesses with me. Carrying you as yet no more than a clot of blood—

"But the Conqueror was not that sort of man. To forgive. To let go. Ever.

"So even with his death, my husband performed a magic trick as he had done when he purchased my freedom so long ago from the slavers. And I fled through the night on foot until I found a camel escaped from the slaughter and pillaging. The beast was as frightened as I was. Together we headed north and east to al-Hira, to the edge of Iraq, where my mother once met my father and sealed their fates."

"You hoped the place would make his heart tender?" Rayah asked.

"Something along those lines. Yes, those were my thoughts. But in truth, I knew not what else to do."

The pilgrim's caravan, Rayah's wedding train, was two days out of Damascus. Remembering the deprivations of the first Muslims to come this way, in the other direction, the hajj preferred to take the desert track. They skirted the Mountain of the Shaykh, where snow dusted the peak like salt. Then ahead rose the easy, flat volcanic plain before the dark heaving rocks of the Golan Heights. To the west, the plateau fell steeply to a clear, harp-shaped lake. The caravan passed a body of water called Ram Pool and arrived in time to pitch their tents amid willows and poplars where a river ran. The sides of the stream fell rampant down and had carved out light-colored limestone and marl beneath the volcanic rock.

"The place looks as if it had had the smallpox," Sejah said, and set herself to describe to her daughter how that disease was to be cured.

Before she could complete that, however, Abd ar-Rahman rode up to check on them and announced, "The Yarmuk." When they didn't seem impressed enough by that, he elaborated, "The site of my father's most important victory. Here the might of Rome, Syria, fell."

Veterans in the caravan happily led tours of the site in the lowering sun. "Here we fought for five brutal days because our commander—may God favor him and grant him peace in the next world, for he never knew it here—did not know the meaning of the word 'retreat.' Here, early on the second day, the enemy caught us at morning prayers. Many a martyr found paradise in this defile."

One of the pilgrims, sniffing the air, announced, "Ah, I smell the perfume of their sacrifice."

Soon all the group had feasted their nostrils on the blessed fragrance. Rayah smelled only dust and hot desert plants through the folds of her veil but nodded in agreement.

"Service to God is never a failing," the veteran went on. "Here spread our archers, mostly Yemenis; here theirs. Ah, that second day became known as 'The Day of Lost Eyes.'"

The veteran smoothed the edge of his turban over his own empty socket. A kick in the dust revealed arrowheads: iron tips heading this way, from the Romans, mostly chipped stone coming the other, from the desert. Spear shafts, fire charred. Bone amid the spoor of hyenas. Evening wind rustled the tufts of grass. Overhead, a kite screamed like the echo, distant in time if not space, from the men who had died in this place.

"Here, at the end of the fourth day, we took that bridge over the wadi. And here, here the Sword of God, Khalid ibn al-Walid, may God reward him, engaged his famous flanking maneuver against which no might can stand. After that, as he said—I heard him with my own ears, even if my eye was gone—'Syria couches quietly like a hobbled camel.'"

"And there?" Sejah asked, sensing something beyond Rayah's own ken.

The veteran spat. "There we left the enemy dead unburied for the beasts, after we stripped them of weapons, jewels and clothes."

Once prayers were over, Rayah saw her mother wander over to that place where the bones were hard to avoid. She was honoring Yaqub, the son of the turpentine sellers, who had taken pregnant Sejah to the haven of his family's home and then come to this empty field to die. And Rayah did not follow, nor did she betray her mother to Abd ar-Rahman.

Rayah would have found no bad thing in her mother's private mourning, nothing worth any comment at all, had it not left Rayah to return to their tent across the graying landscape alone. She wasn't afraid; the dead were dead. Even the day's victor, her grandfather, was dead, in the well in Homs. She was far from the dangers of the city, too.

She strode, the jinni dancing around her in the dust and sparse grasses, singing and promising to come and pleasure her again in the night.

In all his teasing, he should have given her earlier warning.

They were flesh-and-blood men, not jinn, some standing, some sitting, between her and her tent, the rest of the caravan, their cooking fires.

At first she thought they must be local herdsmen. Every valley of their journey had been home to at least one such and his bleating charges.

Her steps slowed as she realized this hollow, out of sight of the caravan, offered no pasturage. Caravan animals had been driven onto places east and south that did. No bellwether's wooden clapper clanged the rest of the flock to the best food. No ewe called for her young. And what herd needed more than a boy or two to mind them? Never the eight or ten grown men clustered in the hollow before her.

Rayah turned sharply left to go around the group. Alone, she had never before faced a strange land where no one knew her.

When those seated got to their feet and moved with the rest to cut her off, she began to run. It was no use. Heavy skirts did not encumber her pursuers' legs. Although panic blurred her mind, she registered clearly enough that a number of them did not even wear Arab robes. Persian trousers liberated their legs.

Her eyes came level with a tangle of camel thorn as her bare feet slipped in the loose soil half a step back for each she took forward. Strong hands caught her just before she reached the top of the thorn that marked the rise, where she might have seen the rest of the caravan, called to them for help. Her arm caught in the gray plant's spines, gashed deep. Though she twisted and kicked, the men easily brought her back to the bottom of the hollow where they had been huddled when she first saw them. Out of all sight, out of all sound but her own desperate cry.

Rayah realized that although the men talked over her writhing head, she understood no word. Added to the Persian trousers, this made her realize now who they were. Some Persian pilgrims, being settled people, preferred the longer but not so strenuous arc up the Euphrates and so to Damascus. Here they had met up with travelers on the hajj from her corner of the world in order to move south together, always the direction of their prayers.

Rayah's prayers now went any direction: to heaven, to the depths of the earth.

These men, then, were members of the caravan. But they were not Persian converts, taking this chance merely to gossip among themselves in their native tongue. Converts tended to mimic the Arab natives to their new religion in dress: the flowing izars—the costume of victory, now of hajj—or at least robes. When they could, they mimicked language, too. Arabic was the language of revelation, was it not?

Khalid ibn al-Walīd's victories had crackled like lightning there in the Persian east. This success had been over an ancient, worn-out empire led first by a woman and then a mere boy who had spent most of his life in hiding from his bloodthirsty kinsmen. Because of such gains, any Muslim who wanted to could fill his entourage with Persian slaves to fetch and carry, his harem with the prettiest Persian women.

Indeed, veterans remembered the Battle of the Chains. Khalid the Sword of God had begun this confrontation by writing taunting notes from the Garden of Death in Yamamah, over the fly-riddled body of Musaylimah the Liar. Rayah's father.

Then the Conqueror's invasion of Mesopotamia had worked to wear the Persian commander ragged. Khalid promised to meet his opponent on this field, then the next, fields far distances from each other across barren desert. At field after field, Khalid would appear then vanish again like a mirage into his native wasteland. March-weary Persian eyes could only blink, weeping together with sweat under cover of chain mail.

When the sides did meet, the common Persian soldier fell into Muslim hands already shackled to his neighbor: At the final stand, the enemy commander had had to keep his subordinates in irons to form a firm line. Otherwise they would have fled the field or turned to side with the whirlwind twisting into their green and fertile land from the trackless desert.

When she saw the sliced nose of her uncle Abd ar-Rahman's Persian slave Firuz push its way to the front of the dirty, scarred faces glaring down at her, Rayah knew she had it right. This man, she recalled, had grinned as he tortured her friend the eunuch scribe. That easy ability read now in his same tortured features.

The message of her veil—that she was a Muslim woman of virtue, that she had menfolk concerned about her honor—this made no more impression here than her Arabic words. In fact, the veil seemed to anger her captors all the more. It presented a challenge to their manhood on top of their slavery: their God-given right to ogle, to make every woman theirs with their eyes if nothing else.

One fold of her covering had tangled about her neck and threatened to choke her. Other folds bunched over her nose and right eye, making breathing nearly impossible. With her left eye, she tried to plead with them not to harm her. The eye's alien color and the threat she couldn't possibly carry through merely stoked the fire of their fury.

Firuz had not touched her; still, he did nothing to help her, either. He did not even meet her eye. But he did seem to be arguing with the big man who filled the air with a puff of garlic at each shout of words. The big man had given her right arm to another while he stuffed the folds of her veil into her mouth to finish her hope of any call for help.

Only her ears worked now and, with the foreign words, they carried fear to her heart more than anything. She did, however, begin to hear the name "Abd ar-Rahman ibn Khalid" repeated over and over, first on Firuz's tongue and then on the garlic breath. This kindled a distant mirage of hope. Overweening bully that her uncle was himself, it was good to be known as under such a man's protection to similar bullies.

"Is it true?" said the garlic breath.

Rayah took a moment to realize that she understood these words through the thick, somewhat prissy accent. Her captor had begun to speak Arabic.

Choking on dry cloth, she couldn't answer him, even had she understood what truth he meant. The truth she knew was the truth of the Quran—

"You are sister's daughter to that commander Abd ar-Rahman ibn Khalid, grand-daughter to the Conqueror?"

Rayah gave a grunt, the only sound she could make.

"Oh, no. The cloth stays put. You nod for me, yes or no."

She nodded.

Firuz said something, probably "I told you so," to the gathered men.

"That son of two cursed parents who has destroyed my homeland, blessed of Ahura Mazda, destroyed the temples of the sacred flame, killed my sons and brothers and made my wife and daughters whores?"

When he put it like that, Rayah knew her answer had been a mistake. She couldn't deny it now however, not without a long explanation that she had never even heard of Abd ar-Rahman ibn Khalid until some few months before.

A general clamor among the men let her know that each one had similar injuries seeking revenge. One or two of them even leered in, spat at her and expressed them-selves in Arabic: "Her blood, then, will do well as a beginning."

"We rape her first, then have her blood," said one gravelly voice like a wadi flood beneath all the others.

With her one uncovered eye, Rayah saw grasses tangling around her captors' feet, but they easily shook themselves free, the men's mild annoyance only making things worse for her. This was all the better her jinni could do for her? Oh, why had she trusted a spirit over the harsh reality of flesh and blood? Why had she trusted this husband of smoke enough to leave her home and throw herself thus among hostile strangers? Not halfway to her destination, and these strangers would be the end of her. Her ancestress, Queen Zaynab, paraded in golden chains through Rome before death in the coliseum—that end had been preferable to this.

Not the Battle of Yarmuk, then, but a recast of the Battle of the Chains.

40

For his own good only shall the guided yield to guidance, and
to his own loss only shall the erring err; and the heavy laden
shall not be laden with another's load.
—The Holy Quran, Surah 17

I had taken care to have Mudja'a recaptured alive after the Battle of the Garden of Love. With him, more like two old friends now than like two old enemies, I faced the walls of Yamamah proper, the walled city that had always been the main defense of the region. Had Musaylimah been able to reach those walls in his flight instead of just the garden, it would have taken a little more than old Baraa to force an entry.

"Are those yet other sons of Hanifa ready to do us battle upon the walls?" I asked Mudja'a. We could see them, their superb Yamami arms blinding in the sun, keeping a disciplined and regular watch upon the walls. The thought of so much more endless bloodshed put a weariness in my voice I could not conceal.

"That was the plan as I understood it, yes," Mudja'a replied. "The major portion of the forces was to stay here to supply reinforcement and also to assure that under no circumstance of Fate might the entire tribe be lost."

I thought of Abu Bakr's order—kill every soul of them—but quickly brushed it aside. "Go parley with them," I said, "and see what terms they will accept, now that their prophet is dead."

Mudja'a nodded and rose to comply with my order. When I made a sign to hold him back yet a moment, he smiled and said, "Do not worry, my master. I swear by our Rahman and by yours that I will not enter my harem where your Layla is."

But that was not what I was thinking at all. I touched his elbow. "Find out," I told him, "if Sejah is there. If she is not, see if you can find out where she is. If she is. . .well, bring me word if she is."

"Yes, my master," Mudja'a replied with a look of secret communication deeper than the one he had sent me at the mention of Layla.

"They will surrender both the fortress and their souls to Islam," was the reply Mudja'a brought back.

"On what terms?"

"*That none of them be either killed or enslaved.*"

"*None?*"

"*Those are the only terms they will accept. You may have all their weapons and gold, their horses and precious ornaments. They forswear all these vanities that lead to contentious life. But they will have their freedom and your word that they are protected. Layla, of course, will be returned to you.*"

I ignored his last statement and the little smile that went with it. "*What are their numbers?*" I asked.

"*As many again as you have already slaughtered here on the fields of Aqraba. Perhaps more.*"

"*More, by God?*" I shook my head weakly. We usually don't count them on the battlefield. But when one considered taking a town, he had to take the women and children into account, too. At least I had to be aware of them, aware that men always fight harder with their little sons at their heels. The help of women is not to be scoffed at, either. The harems, even if they do not actually fight like our Umm Umara, run for water, reload quivers, sing their songs—plenty of things to make their numbers felt.

"*Sejah? Is Sejah in there?*" I asked.

"*No, Master.*"

"*Liar! You lie like Musaylimah himself. She is, or they would not dare to ask such terms of the Sword of God.*"

The truth was that I had sensed her for myself. Weakly, it is true, but definitely in the march of soldiers around the parapet, as if she animated them. I strained for familiar features, the impression was so strong—a veil, anything—on every lance-carrying figure I saw. I did not think I actually saw her, but then, I could not be certain how the past week or so had changed her. She had become a bride and then a widow since I'd seen her last. Both events can change a woman's aspect severely, though perhaps not this woman's, who had so much strength in and of herself.

"*They offer you three days in which to decide, but after that they will take no terms at all but the death of every Muslim.*"

"*You're lying, Mudja'a. She is in there.*"

"*By God, my master, I didn't see her. All I could learn was that she had been there but that she is now gone.*"

"*Where?*"

"*I don't think they know. On my life, I would tell you if I knew.*"

I believed him, but I also believed my own feelings on the matter, as I had believed my lack of them before I attacked Musaylimah. Abu Bakr would have to be disappointed this time, for I would not attack a town that gave me that feeling. I would have to satisfy his lust for blood elsewhere.

"Very well," I said. "They have my oath, by God. Submit to Islam and there will be neither life nor prisoners taken."

The gates of Yamamah opened to us. I rode through their narrow streets in triumph. None came out to witness our triumph with the sullen, futureless faces of the conquered I knew so well, however, but women, very old men, cripples and young children.

"Where are all the fighting men I saw upon the walls?" I demanded. "Where are those whose great numbers you told me of?"

"Here you see them," Mudja'a replied, "these women and old men. It was their numbers I gave you. There are no fighting men of Hanifa left."

"You mean to say that I, the Sword of God, succumbed to a trick? There are no men left in Yamamah, and I was beaten by an army of women with swords in one hand and their babes in the other? By God, Mudja'a, I'll have your liver for this."

"Don't blame me, Master," Mudja'a said with a steady tone. "It was not I who taught them this ruse."

"It was Sejah," a restored Layla told me. Then she explained how the Poetess had taught the daughters of Hanifa to wear armor. "She promised us with a word of prophecy. If we did as she instructed, held out and refused to fear before any threats, she promised that the trick would work. 'None of you will taste slavery,' she said, 'and your sons will grow to replace their fathers as proud, free men of the tribe.'

"They have believed," my sometime wife concluded, "and you have unwittingly fulfilled her prophecy."

"The Poetess was here, then?" I suppressed an explosion of prideful anger with that question.

"Yes, she was," Layla replied.

I said nothing more of the matter, stopping my tongue.

Instead I looked about the room where we sat with Mudja'a in his home. It was pleasantly cool there, the floor of tamped earth a step below and darker than the level of the painfully bright and fly-infested street without. The walls around us felt as natural as a cave. Though they met at corners and had general tendencies toward the parallel, no span's width could be said to be truly straight. Great rough masses bulged out from the walls; some of these could have served fairly as divans or shelves they were so large. The imprints of hands covered the walls. Generations of hands, women's and children's hands, pressed there in cool blue paint when more protection against evil was needed. Or simply on rainy winter days when the children were restless and could not play outdoors.

What had Layla picked up from these walls? I tried to determine. Something, that was certain. She had come in as a slave, but for some reason and for the first *time in her life, this seemed to have given her a desire to be her own mistress. Not only was the desire there, but the will and the self-confidence as well.*

Looking about the room, I had been above listening to the conversation that continued between my wife and my captive. They were personable and individual—intimate, I thought. And I was not included.

I put a stop to them at once as I, by God, had power to do.

"Well, Mudja'a," I said, "there remains but one more problem to be dealt with."

"What is that, my master?" The chuckle some word of Layla's had induced in him died half-formed upon his lips, delivered stillborn by the tone of my words as if by the hands of an evil-eyed midwife.

"You."

"Master?"

"I have twice made you my prisoner. You have spied and fought for the enemy. You presumed to take my wife as your own. All these are crimes deserving of death. By the word of the khalifah of Islam and by that of the Poetess as well, you are condemned to death. Even were my wife to plead for you, I could justly ignore it. What is to prevent me from marching you to Yamamah's marketplace and beheading you on the spot?"

"Nothing, Master."

Layla's reaction demanded my notice as much as his. She was absolutely silent.

"Mudja'a," I said, "give me your eldest daughter to wife."

"Master?"

"For bride-price I offer you your life. Give me your hand on the bargain, my friend."

Laughter burst full-grown from Mudja'a's lips as he made a leap for my hand and called me sometimes "master," sometimes "son," sometimes "friend." I joined his laughter with no hesitation that might give the blackness of my thoughts away.

Sacks of gold, bundles of costly fabric, jars of grain and baskets of dates, flocks of sheep and goats, horses, camels, arms and weapons without number. Like gas belched up after the great feast of carnage in the Garden of Death, I sent the plunder of Yamamah back to al-Medinah. And among that loot, too, went Layla bint al-Minhal, to join my other wives in the harem I will never visit again. A man is a fool if he bothers with more than one wife while he is soldiering. Then I had Mudja'a's young daughter, and now I do not care.

But Layla never reached her new home, at least, not the home I'd designated for her. Somewhere on the journey—in the middle of the red and shifting sands of

Nefud I like to think, but I was never given certain details—she wandered away from camp. A sharp wind erased her tracks; men never found her. The jinn, they said, led her off. That is a polite way of saying it was suicide. As her lifelong love for me vaporized, the mirage of her life drifted away with it.

I have pretended not to care and have done fairly well. But, by God, that woman has destroyed the desert for me. That open space, once like open arms to me, is now filled with dread. I never feared the wolves or thirst or heat out there. Sometimes at night I did fear the jinn, but by day I could always pretend they did not exist, that their mirages were nothing more substantial than my own fading image in a mirror. But now those spirits have a name. It is Layla—the night itself embodied.

What, by God, might I find left of her? I often ask myself, and call myself a coward. Somewhere in the Great Nefud, I reply, a woman's forearm bones, stripped of all their flesh, jutting from a blood-red sand dune, dangling even yet a bracelet. She had that bracelet of Malik, who had it in turn from his mother. I cut my teeth on that bauble. Perhaps a shell or two of the veil Layla had copied from Sejah, Sejah with whom she had no more in common than that. As different as cool night and blazing day. Identical veils, however, made them as alike as two sisters, as two grains of sand.

That would be enough to undo me.

41

O men! If you doubt the resurrection, think, of a truth
We created you of dust, then of the moist sperm of life, then of
clots of blood, then of pieces of flesh shaped and unshaped, that
We might give
you proofs of Our power!
And you have seen the earth dried up and barren: but when We
send down the rain upon it, it
stirs and swells, and brings forth every kind
of luxuriant herb.
—The Holy Quran, Surah 22

After this, the death of Layla, the fall of Yamamah, the disappearance as if from the very face of the earth of the Prophetess, I went mad, truly mad. What else can be said of the consuming passion for conquering, violence and death that sat on my shoulder? It drove me like a whip laced with bits of iron over the next four or five years until I was oblivious to anything else. Even the change of seasons was lost on me.

I suppose it is for this madness that the world will remember me when I am gone, but, by God, it is something I long to forget. The adventure-hungry youth, the old soldier in retirement, the eunuch who can never bear arms—all those who long for the fabled thrills of war that have eluded them will come to my history looking for that. Just so the lover hears love poetry when his lady is denied him. I am sorry to disappoint them, men to whom I might have had much entertaining to say if we had met around a military campfire during those days. I liked to brag as much as the next man, and I knew I could always silence anybody's "next man" with my tales.

Now I want only to forget. I have grown tired of reciting my deeds—not only tired, but sickly. They are like bad water, having sat too long and festered. Were they to pass over the back of my tongue again, they would bring vomit up after them. What I have been telling here is what has come to be more and more important to me.

When Muhammad's God Himself calls me to give account of my life, this is what I shall say. I shall avoid all mention of those conquests I carried out in His name—unless, of course, He asks me straight out. In that case, I shall not be able to deny it before his All-Knowing Eye.

But as long as I am yet master over my history, I will brush across only the face of the events of those years. My recitation from now on will be like the last rays of the setting sun highlighting the peaks of this red-black lava landscape tortured into mountains that I call "memory." They are immovable from my brain.

I ride at the head, the very needle-like point, of a long, dark line of horsemen. We ride out of the desert like the blade of a sword. I bellow my battle cry:

> *"I am the noble warrior,*
> *I am the Sword of God,*
> *Khalid ibn al-Walid!"*

Whole armies surrender at the mere sound of my name, accepting Islam along with their lives.

For those who do not know my name or do not believe all that they've heard, my instruction is swift and demonic. Beside me ride other similar demons. There is Zarrar ibn al-Azwar, a young man who scorns the protection of armor, for it weighs him down and encumbers his lighting-like movements. He fights, stripped naked to the waist, against the worst Roman artillery can throw at him. He dances simply, lightly out of any harm's way before treating them to a taste of the Naked Champion's deadly sword.

There is Zarrar's sister, Khula, too, beside him. She has taken over his shed clothes and dresses, rides, fights like a man. She muffles her face so the enemy cannot see. She wounds a few of them. Then she unveils so that the shock of seeing a soft and tender female face beneath that turban will bring home death, which her female arm has not quite the strength to endow on its own. For Muhammad's God she has made the supreme sacrifice—greater even than those who attain martyrdom. She has denied her sex for Him.

My friends Amr, Ikrama, Abu Ubayda, Shurabil, my brother Hisham, my sons Sulayman, Abd ar-Rahman, Muhajir—they all ride beside me, follow my lead. Between us we leave nothing standing of the two greatest empires this world has ever known—the Persians and the Romans. The greatest, that is, before the world learned of us.

Once, seeing the floor of the mosque at al-Medinah covered knee-deep with rich plunder I had taken, more coming in, and realizing that it was only the khalifah's one-fifth he saw there, Abu Bakr said, "By God, women can no longer bear sons like

Khalid!" I was told this in hopes I would be flattered.

By God, what woman would want to bear such a son? Women must live on to taste the aftereffects of war. I, too, am suffering through those effects now, though I was a man and a soldier and thought thereby to avoid them. Now I can answer Abu Bakr (though he is dead), "By God, what woman wants a madman for a son?

"And so you never saw her, Sejah, your jinn-gotten daughter, nor anyone connected with her again?" my scribe asks with ripe pomegranates reflecting from the tree into the emerald in his ear.

"Have I given that impression?"

He spreads his ink-stained hands in an open, inviting gesture.

"Very well. That is almost true, and yet not quite."

"Master, explain."

Sejah's maternal uncle, Ibn Zura, I met at the Battle of the Chains, where he fought against us on the side of the doomed Persians. He shouted a verse at me from the ranks. He challenged me to a duel to avenge the blood of his many kinsmen at my hands, my stealing of his sister all those years before, my many crimes against him. The wounds I had inflicted on him had not healed in all those years.

I might have thrown down my sword when I came face-to-face with him. The spirit moved me to do so—it would have been the brave and honorable thing to do, and it would have made the course of history follow a more generous path. But brave as my spirit was, my flesh was an unwilling coward. I dispatched him with two swift blows and that was that.

Then, at the conquest of al-Hira, five months, maybe six after Yamamah—

This is what happened at al-Hira, that wonderful string of wells where first I met her mother. "The coming salvation of the Arabs— Coming salvation—"

"Master? Master? Do you sleep?"

"Dream. Dream of a well. Dream only of what might have been. Where was I?"

"At al-Hira."

"Indeed. So I was."

And after I'd torn down the ancient standing stones, had them pulverized and buried, Abd al-Masih and the other elders of the Encampment came to sue for terms. Abd al-Masih said he had seen two hundred winters and summers pass; he was, in any case, too old to be called a liar. History will say it was Abd al-Masih's great and reverend age that softened my heart at this place when it never softened elsewhere.

The old dotard greeted me. "O Commander of the Muslims, the earth destroys its fool. But the intelligent cannot be stopped from destroying the earth."

A man can't kill another whom God has allowed to live two hundred years, no matter what rot he says.

And Fate was not content to taunt me merely with the old man's words. I actually saw her herself one more time. At least I think it was she. It was hard to tell. No, I am certain of it.

It was still at al-Hira. I was taking the oaths of allegiance from all the populace, the men first and then, on the next day, when their modesty would not be interfered with, the women. According to the example set by Muhammad, blessed be he, I took the female oaths not hand to hand, as I did from the men, but in a bowl of water. She dipped her fingers in one side and I in the other with the water acting as a purifying buffer between us. On the day of the women, I might well have had my second, Zarrar ibn al-Azwar, take over this duty from me. I had done so before and would do so again.

But some sense of impending culmination moved me to stand up that day with my hand in the bowl of water. Somehow, I did not think this duty beneath me towards the women of al-Hira. Al-Hira was, after all, the place I had first become aware of women as something more than wives and mothers. It was where I had first been stirred by a desire I could not name, much less satisfy. It was where I had thought to raid the sanctuary of a convent and been taken captive myself. It was where I had first met her who was to be my destiny equally with Muhammad, the son of Abd Allah.

So I stood beneath the shade of an awning and the women of the Encampment filed past one by one. One by one, they presented me with their work-knotted and Christian-cross-tattooed hands. One by one I heard them murmur "I swear" as they passed. I saw them pull their sleeves down as far as they would go, to spare even their wrists from my gaze that ravished, they thought, their very fingertips. I noticed circlets of white flesh about their brown knuckles: they had removed all rings that were not grown a part of them. They didn't want me to crave this one more than another for her family's wealth.

As for their faces, they were all well and uniformly veiled—Christians with their nuns and enjoined modesty were Muhammad's first example of what he wanted his women to be. I chuckled at their precautions as one may chuckle at the harmless, fanciful antics of children. I craved no one of them. Besides, Abd al-Masih had won, with his simple wisdom, the freedom of every woman of al-Hira.

Abd al-Masih's daughter Kiramah alone did I claim as plunder and that was an affair out of my hands. Muhammad, blessed be he, had foreseen our conquest of al-Hira before his death. During this prophecy, he promised this woman of fabled beauty to a faithful (meaning in this case credulous and silly) soldier of the ranks named Shuwail. Shuwail got her, but found beneath her veil that she was over eighty years old—so long do legends endure unchanged. Hoping to save some face before his companions, he gave her her freedom again for a ransom of one thousand dirhams. It did not occur to his simplicity that he might have asked for ten times that and received it without a moan. One thousand was the highest number he knew.

So even Kiramah bint Abd al-Masih passed me as a free and veiled woman, and I looked on neither her nor any other with any particular notice. They might even have kept their rings on.

One, however, on towards the noontime prayer. . . I could hardly believe it was she. In veils and loose-fitting robes, she must be very far gone before one can tell a woman is with child, but in this case I had no doubt. I might doubt my sweat and the stir of the earth I felt in her presence. No, I knew the feel of that power all too well. Besides, the water in the bowl made waves and even splashed a little on the ground as if being worked upon by the cool, dark force of the moon.

Whose child was it? Musaylimah's? I quickly counted. It had taken my army but six months to whirlwind from Yamamah to al-Hira. But surely my star-gotten daughter would not submit to such a one?

Then the power that waved about me took my mind back to the Valley of Nakhlah, and I remembered. Such women submit to no man. They only cause submission.

Malik's child, I thought again. That was possible. The time was right.

But then, there were always the jinn.

Two, no, three women had already passed by after her while cursed spirits of smokeless fire held my mind enthralled. By God, to be confounded so beyond all action by nothing more than pregnancy? But then, by God, is there anything more wondrous, more mysterious, more like the divine in all this world? Muhammad himself was told to recite:

> *"O men! If you doubt the resurrection, think, of a truth*
> *We created you of dust, then of the moist sperm of life, then of clots of blood,*
> *   then of pieces of flesh shaped and unshaped, that We might give you*
> *   proofs of Our power!*
> *And we cause one sex or the other, at Our pleasure to abide in the womb*
> *   until the appointed time, then We bring you forth infants, then permit*
> *   you to reach your age of strength. . .*
> *And you have seen the earth dried up and barren: but when We send down*
> *   the rain upon it, it stirs and swells, and brings forth every kind*
> *   of luxuriant herb. "*

It is a wonder in a world of wonders.

Five women, six, and I lost sight of her altogether. Even pregnancy could not make her stand out in the crowd. I made some sound of protest, I called out. The woman with her hand in the bowl at that moment thought I meant her and froze, then began to weep in terror.

Zarrar was at my side in a moment. "Nothing. It's nothing," I assured him.

"Pass on," he bellowed, and they did, their pace much more rapid: ten, twelve past her until I lost count.

Yet she did not leave me this last time completely without word. A message was impressed most firmly upon my mind and, though I got the sense of it at once, I only now will try to place the fetters of language upon it.

"You," she seemed to say, accusing me yet not without the note of mercy, of pity, of understanding by which I will always know her. "You, Khalid the son of al-Walid, my uncle, my master and—yes, I know it, too—my father. You are out to conquer the world, to empty the teeming cities, to sweep away the clutter, faith upon faith, society upon society, law upon law, built up over centuries. You seek to replace it all with the clean, neat phrase: 'There is no God but God.'

"Such simplicity is well for a battle cry. But it will never serve when the dust settles. It will not do when the merchants unpack their bags again, scholars pull out their books to tease their minds, poets begin to compose. It will not do when mothers, rocking their children, find themselves in need of some little ditty to soothe and keep time. Let those 'intelligent ones' forge blindly on ahead, destroying like locusts. It will be my task, like Mother of Rain, to coax the battered stubble into green again. I bring life above the obliterating sand and from hidden, buried roots after four, five or more years of drought."

"Come not to destroy the law but to fulfill it," the Christian proverb says. My daughter had returned to the holy retreat from which I first dared to startle her mother.

"My first task, then," Sejah continued to say, "is to voluntarily join myself to this company of women, Muslim women, humble, everyday women of little or no ambition. Moving here and there among them, serving them as I may, I always encourage them to call to mind the ways their mothers taught them. They must remember to serve Mother of Rain and call upon the attendant female spirits when they suffer in childbirth. Those who know magic and can cast spells to make a husband grow fonder, to protect ailing infants or to fill a barren womb must do so and bring comfort to the rest. Those who can foretell oracles with piles of salt or bits of bone and feathers must keep up the practice and teach it to their daughters or nieces. If a sacred tree or stone is passed by the wayside, due reverences must be shown to it—scraps of cloth donated or a measure of grain poured in offering. Places where Goddesses and Gods are known to have lived must be indicated and given deference. If the puritans about us will not allow them the name of divinity, then we may call them the haunts of certain jinn or the tombs of saints. But for the *welfare of future generations who might pass those places of power, they must not go unmarked.*

"Your battle-cry dogma, O my uncle, will not do in days to come. It will not do when daughters become mothers, when slaves are freed for having borne their masters sons, when a strange land must be made a home. And so, to whomever will listen, I recite my poems and all I can remember of the shaytan *gifts of old. I have even taught some to repeat them after me and to compose verses of their own in the proper ancient fashion."*

I told myself—once the ceremony was over and I dried off my fingers, gone to prune flesh—that she would be easy to find. Al-Hira wasn't all that big. I had seen her. I knew she was there. Still, I couldn't very well go pounding on door after door, not after they'd all submitted. I thought it would be easy. . . .

"Here," her voice taunted my search, "hidden from your view beneath the anonymous veils, forbidden to your gross and violent actions in the sanctity of the harem, here my battle will go on apace. Think not that you have made me submit, O Sword of Heaven. By submitting, I defeat you, for I and all my kind are the very base on which you build your empires. You make our base too narrow, too confining and we shall never support you. I shall win in any case. For you but deal in death, which is the end. I deal in life, which is always a new beginning."

Ah, little daughter of mine, ah, Sejah, lady, mistress. Now I know. I know, how our own weapons turn against us.

42

**Three there be that try the soul of man—
money, power and misfortune.**
—Arab saying

The loose sleeve of the largest of her captors, the one who smelled of garlic, slipped up to his elbow. Rayah's own struggles in the arms of the Persian slaves caused it. That and a gust of wind from the desert beyond Golan.

The oozing yellow wound of a skin disease scabbing among and along the dark hairs turned her stomach. She thrashed even more to escape. It was hopeless.

But then, somehow through the choking folds of her veil pulled tight across her nose, another gust of wind managed to reach her nostrils. Her head cleared like a chip of broken glass.

Rather than revulsion, she moved closer. She made certain her burly captor saw her own arm, which he grasped at the elbow, before it moved. She moved toward him instead of away. This confused him into inaction for a moment.

Her palm pasted to the pus. She fought down the bile rising to her throat, wiped fear and escape from her mind, concentrated on healing.

The vision behind her eye was of the pus drying, hardening, turning to gold dust, sloughing off and filling her hand with its richness.

The Persian stared as if a spear had transfixed his heart.

One of the other Persians pushed forward, trying to knock her down so the rape could begin. Her hand came away, full of gold. The sick flesh beneath had not had time to completely heal, but the pus and redness had gone to healthy scabs.

The next wanton shove sent her hard to the ground, a Persian on top of her, yanking on the strings of his trousers.

"Stop, you damned fools," she heard the burly one say as if from a great distance, then only Persian as her head and arms were pinned against sharp pebbles on the ground. Ruched skirts exposed her legs, her chest crushed, her lungs smothered, her vision blinded.

And suddenly she felt lighter. Then lighter still, and the pebbles ceased to stab.

Rayah covered her legs and, when no one stopped her at that, she shifted her veil so she could breathe, finally see. The air entering her lungs unhampered, in short gasps, relieved her to the pit of her stomach.

The burly Persian had plucked his comrades off her, tossed them aside like rag dolls. Now he had his arm on display to those who had picked themselves up.

One of the others said something that must have had the sense of, "Indeed, it's true. I saw how bad it was. It even smelled bad."

The rest crowded around and exclaimed. They looked down at her, crossing themselves or spitting behind them in wonder.

All but one fellow. He kept insisting on something—Rayah didn't like to think what—slapping at the burly man who kept stepping between her and the insistent man. Finally the burly man tried out his healed arm and laid the other flat on the ground with a single blow.

"I tried to tell them you could heal." Firuz alone dared to approach her. He offered a hand and then thought better of it, whether safeguarding her virtue or from manifest fear.

Rayah got to her feet on her own and turned to leave the place.

"I beg—I beg you will not mention this to my master." Firuz hastened to catch up with her.

Had she been going to do so? Her first reaction to his words was, yes, that was exactly what she ought to do. Abd ar-Rahman would see justice done. She realized, however, that only Firuz's words had set the idea in her head. And she remembered the danger a woman put herself in to confess compromise without a witness. Especially a bride on her way to her groom.

Rayah licked her fabric-dried lips beneath her veil, grateful for the divine distance the covering gave her.

"Please, Sitt, show compassion."

This was the first time Rayah had heard herself called the same honorific title as her mother: Sitt. And on Firuz's tongue.

"These are desperate men, men who have lost everything, everything." Firuz spoke from personal experience through a slit nose.

The rest of the Persians nodded in agreement, the depth of their losses written on their faces: this one had lost a father, this one a room full of dark-eyed children, this one a beloved wife. The men did not have the benefit of veiling.

"Then it will not do for them to lose their lives, all they have left, for revenge on me, a woman who must go where Abd ar-Rahman orders," Rayah murmured so they had to strain to hear. "Who is as much a slave as they are."

"But I must have revenge or die," countered the burly man, cradling his healing arm as if it were the child that had died there.

"By edict of Omar the khalifah, Persians are not even allowed into the holy cities of pilgrimage," Firuz added.

"Nowhere near the seats of power," said a third.

"Except as slaves." Rayah met his eyes with her blue ones. "Trusted slaves, as close as brides."

"Except as slaves," Firuz agreed slowly.

"I know Abd ar-Rahman ibn Khalid is my mother's brother. I also know the deeds of his father, and I know my uncle is not what his father was. He had his governorship handed to him, barely lifting a finger for himself. His son I go to marry, in him the energy of the ancestor must be even more diffused. They do not know how to build their own campfires, erect their own tents. Now they want palaces and luxuries, there in the middle of the desert. Their trust expands to fit their desires. It is not the same with the generations of women."

Rayah bit her tongue to keep from saying more. She had already said enough. She could tell by how the men looked from one another, nodding. They had the message.

"I will prepare a salve for that arm, brother." Rayah swept the corner of her veil in the direction of the big man. "If you can find me some garlic." She knew he would have no trouble with that. "The Prophet Muhammad, blessed be he, recommended garlic for such wounds, as well as for scorpion stings and viper bites."

Had Muhammad done so? How would Rayah know, who had not been born until after the Prophet's death? But if not him, then his wife or daughter. They would be fools if they didn't know such recipes. And one thing none of her grandfather's generation had been was fools.

"Lady, I have this rotten tooth—" One man stepped forward. Yes, she had smelled that rot as he'd lain on top of her.

Then another. "And I have a growth upon my tongue. For God's mercy, Lady."

"Come to my tent," she told them as she turned to go. "After a while and one by one, so as not to raise suspicion in the son of the Conqueror. And when my mother and the eunuch are there. Come to my tent."

And she even bent to touch the man who sat in the dust still holding his bleeding head.

As she walked out of the gully and up to where the caravan camped, her veil nodded in satisfaction as the jinni toyed with it. That had gone well. Anyone going where they were powerless needed friends among the other powerless; with the powerful, not so much. Power would wax and wane to no reason a single woman could control.

She thought the same thing as she watched her mother returning to their tent from the fields of the dead. With her was the eunuch. Rayah saw him put his arm around the older woman as she stumbled, weak with grief.

43

By the heaven, and by the nightly visitant!
Would that you knew what the nightly visitant is!
It is the star of piercing brightness.
For every soul there is a guardian watching it.
—The Holy Quran, Surah 86

The neighborhood of al-Hira, renamed Basra, is now resettled with Muslims granted the land as a reward for military service. All up the Euphrates from that spot, I fought Persians. I killed them and took their submission. In the overwhelming smell of blood and death, I lost the scent of my child.

The orders came from al-Medinah, from the Prophet's successor, Abu Bakr.

How could such a doddering old man have known where to send me to best bend my purposes to Islam?

I didn't know myself at the time. Only that the orders annoyed me, when they came to set me on what I thought to be a path away from my daughter.

"This is Omar's doing," I bellowed at the messenger. Poor fellow. It wasn't his fault. "Omar sits on his behind on his cushions in al-Medinah and tells old Abu Bakr what to do to me. He wants me to leave all these victories and go to help the Muslim forces fighting in Syria?"

"Abu Ubayda ibn al-Jarra, Commander of the Faithful in Syria, finds himself, by the will of God, hard-pressed."

"He would. Such an incompetent, without a leader's bone in his body. His bite on the battlefield is as hampered as his bite of bread by his broken teeth."

"But remember how he lost those teeth, sir. Tending to the wounds of the Prophet, blessed be he, at Uhud."

My daughter was here. Somewhere in Iraq. She had to be. To cross wasteland in her condition?

"It was a mistake to try to take on the world's two great empires at once," I shouted at the road-weary man, "and Abu Bakr was too much of a fool to see that. Why doesn't he send Abu Ubayda here so we can mop up one side of the desert before *taking on the other? Indeed, prophecy dried up when Muhammad, the son of Abd Allah, died."*

"Precious blessings on him."

"Precious blessings on him," murmurs my scribe as his pen scratches.

"Precious blessings on him," I say, last of all, as if I've never said the phrase before.

Precious blessings indeed when a man's heart is not conflicted. When his mind no longer doubts.

I peel a pomegranate, just to study the seeds.

As if I'd never done that before.

The messenger from al-Medinah stood shifting from foot to foot. He was no doubt wondering what of my rant he would report when he returned south. I so little cared that I went on.

"Abu Bakr should leave these decisions to those who actually know something about fighting, who see the infidels' ground as it lies, whose blood is at risk if he makes a faithful but bad choice."

"He makes you, Abu Sulayman, commander of all the Muslim armies in the world."

Did he indeed? Now, that was more like it. Commander of the Faithful was the least I deserved. But where was Omar's untrustworthy hand in all of this? I would have to hear more.

"The rightly led khalifah, may God bless him and all Muslims, did point out that there are two paths westward around the desert." The messenger would get all his words out, intimidate him as I might try. "He gives you, as the commander of your eight thousand Believers, the choice between the routes."

"Oh?" So much for the title of commander. "What are my two choices?"

"The conventional caravan route runs through Dumat al-Jandal, which town you have already conquered, destroying their idol of the god Wadd."

"I thought you said Abu Bakr wants me in Syria as quickly as possible." I dismissed the idea with a wave of my hand. "That route would take weeks."

"Weeks are better than to dismiss the khalifah's orders altogether," the messenger warned, adding carefully, "May God guide him aright."

"Yes, may God guide him, indeed. The Merciful One hasn't done much of that up to this point."

The messenger blanched at what he must find to be blasphemy. He pressed on calmly, however. "Then, O Sword of God, the other option open to you is to follow the two rivers of this land north, through what is called the Island, al-Jazirah. If you do so, you may swing wide of the desert in a crescent, then to come down into Syria and grab the Romans there between Commander Abu Ubayda and yourself as if with pincers. That way is better watered than going through Dumat al-Jandal."

"Now Abu Bakr tells me where the water is and where it isn't? Well, why don't you take word back to him that if we went to Syria through the northern crescent, we would run into strong Roman garrisons sitting by those wells and at those river fords?"

"Garrisons that, with God's will, you would defeat."

"With God's will," I repeated. I could not be half so sanguine about the Most Merciful's will being on our side. "And which we would send scurrying before us to strengthen their comrades against Abu Ubayda. He would fall before them in the months it would take us to beat our way through to aid him."

The messenger looked at me miserably. He had ridden himself ragged with this news, only to have me dismiss his pains and his haste altogether. "Then, sir, take the southern route through Dumat al-Jandal as quickly as God may give you strength to march. You should break camp and set off now. The khalifah, may God guide him aright, would not give this order if it were not in accord with the help and hand of the Merciful One."

I cuffed the fellow none too gently on the shoulder so that, in his travel-weakened state, he almost went reeling. "What if I don't break camp except to engage the Persians over the next hill there? What if I forget all about the deluded old man in al-Medinah? He says I am commander; staying in Persian seems the obvious plan to me."

I relented a bit and added to the fellow, "Go get you some food and rest. With the Most Merciful's will, tomorrow you'll feel better."

That night, however, the wind came up. I don't know how the messenger slept, but gusts blasted through my red leather commander's tent with sharp, insistent slaps. Sand lay in a layer on top of my blankets when I awoke. Grinding my teeth on more sand and brushing out my beard, I repeated the few words I'd heard on that wind.

"She did not go east from al-Hira, but west."

My daughter—with the child she carried—was in Syria. All this time.

I left my tent to be cleaned up by my slaves while I went out, as was my custom, particularly after such a night as we'd seen, to inspect my precious horses. Under careful guard, they fed happily on Persian grass, growing strong and sleek for the next ride at the Persians.

How well the cavalry, under my training, had done against this eastern empire! What a bad signal it would give to those followers of women if I took the pressure of my horses away. Yet how useful swift-mounted men would be to Abu Ubayda's campaign in Syria. However, any march westward would be disastrous to my beauties. Half of them would be in no shape to bear warriors even if we didn't ride but led them every step of the way at a careful pace. Even on the shorter route Abu Bakr suggested through Dumat al-Jandal—?

One of the herdsmen called me over to look at the worst injury from that night: a stone caught in a hoof. Expertly, I flicked it out and told the man to wrap the hoof in herbs and sacking for a day or two.

"But tell me," I asked the fellow then. "Among all the believing Arabs with us now, is there any who knows the wastes of the Syrian desert well?"

"You mean south of Dumat al-Jandal?"

"Yes."

"I don't think so," the man replied. "Such empty land, with terrible grazing. No tribes ever venture there. It would be suicide. It is land God, all praises to him, created when He wanted to be alone."

Crows squabbling in a nearby fig tree gave me my next words.

"Yet, if a crow flew over that land, he would find it the straightest path to Syria from here."

"No crow would fly that way, sir. No bush to rest in. No water."

"Still, ask around, would you? See if you can find such a man."

By evening, as I sat eating a mutton stew these Persians make at that season with the tang of tiny unripe plums on rice, the horseman still had not come back to me. I sent for him instead.

"You did not return with word as I asked," I chided him, wondering if more discipline was necessary.

"Indeed, sir. It is as I told you. No men know that desolate place. Only God and—"

"And?"

"Well, there is one man who traveled the route with his father as a child—and lived to tell the tale."

"And you did not bring him to me?" In my fury, I tossed the rice platter against the tent pole, where it shattered satisfactorily.

"Please, sir. May God still your anger. The trip they made was thirty years ago. He was but a lad and—"

I was on my feet now. I had the herdsman by the front of his Persian-style shirt.

"Please, sir. Rafi suffers from a serious inflammation of the eyes. He is almost blind."

I let the herdsman go. He dropped like a rag. I stepped gingerly over the rice and pottery shards. I sat and picked up one of the tiny green plums, served uncooked in a small metal dish by the side, which the Persians eat with salt. Then I found I had no appetite.

"She isn't here," the voice of the wind had said, "but westward."

I tossed the plum back in the dish. "Bring this man to me."

We stepped out beneath the Persian sky, stars he couldn't see. Myself, I saw plainly how that towering constellation which the Greeks see as twins had risen with the red planet of war in their midst, rendering them asunder like a spear wound between them. From a desert point of view, I knew their rising meant that the season had turned from early summer to the height; we could expect high clouds, but no drop of rain anywhere until Canopus, that bright star toward which the southeastern corner of the Holy Ka'ba points, rose again.

The man, named Rafi ibn Umayra, was indeed blind. A milky film from too much sand, too much sun, coated his eyes.

"Sometimes I can see the form of a camel up close," he assured me, but, "God has ordained that I will never see the stars again."

So not quite as blind as my jinn-struck brother Mutammim, who now wandered the desert reciting curses of me.

Then I stumbled over a guy rope in the dark. The night camp held no such terrors for him, this Rafi, who stepped gingerly aside. He was set guard of the camels by night because he could hear the enemy approach before another man would see them.

"Tell me about the Syrian desert," I ordered.

"There is nothing there," he said.

"They tell me you crossed it."

"Thirty years ago, as a boy, with my father."

"So it can be crossed."

"A man, a boy and four camels, two of which died."

"An army?"

"No. Impossible. And for my father and me, it was spring, not the edge of summer."

The night sky tells a man of the desert all he needs to know of the route before him, and I studied the constellations over our heads. "Tell me more."

"More than that it is impossible?"

"Go on."

"The route from here?"

"Yes. Imagine God were to will I go myself."

"Well, you would go through al-Hira—"

Al-Hira. Yes. That is where I last saw her. Yes. I thought this, but let the man continue.

"By way of the wells of Tamr Muzayyh, you would come, God willing, to Quraqir."

"Then?"

"Then—nothing. For five days, nothing."

"Suwa. You reach Suwa on the Syrian side, and there is plenty of water at Suwa."

"My father showed me a spring a day before Suwa, but we still rode five days to that spring, and another day on to Suwa, with always the danger of getting lost along that way."

"Five days," I repeated. "Tell me more about the spring."

The man shrugged helplessly. "Nameless. A shallow pond. Just to the south of two mountains like a woman's breasts. Closer to Suwa than to Quraqir. O Sword of God, forgive me. It has been a long time."

"Would you come with me?"

"Master, by the will of God, I am blind."

I nodded, and held my breath as a shooting star fell.

"But God never gives Believers a challenge He doesn't make possible through faith."

Ah, but Believers in what? And what happens to all those hearts when the faith of a whole army fails them?

44

God bless the eyes of Rafi, how did he succeed
In finding the way from Quraqir to Nawa?
Five days it had marched when the army wept;
No human ever made such a march before.

> —A soldier who was on the march with
> Khalid

"**I** said keep those camels away from the wells." I went after the disobedient lot, new converts from Persia, with my camel goad.

"But Quraqir is another day away." One of them, a half-healed wound from some recent skirmish across his left cheek, had the nerve to talk back.

"Keep those animals dry." I spoke low but clear, threat in my voice. "At Quraqir then, God willing, they will drink twice as much."

Before Quraqir even came into sight the next day, the thirsty beasts could smell the place. They picked up their feet eagerly. I'd already kept them the five days out of al-Hira without water, allowing only men to drink. At every source since, the men refilled the large camel-skin water bags; a pair balanced each pack animal that could be spared from carrying armor and weapons. And the food: none at all for the camels, dates and hard meal balls alone for the men.

At Quraqir, I stood pondside and watched each watering. If the camels didn't seem to me to sink their muzzles deep enough, eagerly enough, I sent them back into the open desert to lope around under the blazing sun for a while. Coming at the end of the line helped them center their attention to drink as much as possible.

The pool bubbling from the spring had already shrunk in the heat. I could tell by the acacias that formed a ragged ring around the hole. After rains, the trees must stand up to their fringe of leaves in water. Their naked trunks now seemed obscene. The water tasted vaguely of bitumen.

From time to time, as infrequently as possible, I looked up from the watering, over the trees, toward the lowering sun, the direction we must go. The unknown land rose in sandy dunes there, pale sand streaking hard, empty, darker gravel.

Mirages floated over that horizon. Sometimes the visions looked like rain clouds. Sometimes they took on the appearance of pools of water, the very one we stood at, in fact. Sometimes like cities complete with shimmering domes and palaces.

These illusions were the jinn at work, luring us on. To our deaths? Or to glory, and the glory of the Almighty?

All I could think of was eyes, blue eyes, which saw the jinn and heard them every day and could discern truth from falsehood.

The watering, the sweating backs of slaves, went on all night, leaving only a pool a man could jump over and the mud churned by thousands of feet. At last we set off to the slosh of water in every camel's belly. We started at first light, hoping to make as much progress as possible while the air remained cool. We could not take the relief of night marches, not even, as sometimes worked with caravans, with torches. The land we had to cross was too unknown, trackless. We could not afford to wind up a hill only to find there was no way down. We could not backtrack. We had to face heat-numbed plodding, hour after hour, instead.

I had between eight and nine thousand men. They could not move as quickly as one man and his son. Or as a woman alone. We took no horses, no donkeys, just camels, those bred for the worst of the desert. Horses I sent by Dumat al-Jandal. Women and children had been sent the long, watered way to al-Medinah to wait until the day, God willing, when they could be brought to Syria to rejoin their men. Personally, I'd given up keeping any females with me long ago. Only the one who floated ahead like the mirage.

The sun pounded like drums on our heads. My rules for rationing water filled mouths and nostrils with sand, and shuffling feet raised the dust. Halts for urination grew less and less frequent. We washed for prayer in sand, which dried and cracked the skin.

Most discouraging of all was to look at the man who rode at my side: Rafi ibn Umayra, his face completely swathed, for his eyes were of no use and the glare stabbed them like knives. To the men who followed, gasping "Allahu akbar" at every step, Ibn Umayra already looked like a man in a shroud. And how must that have worked on my soldiers, to see themselves led into a trackless wilderness by a jinn-like man, a man in a shroud?

At least he would have that shroud, their red-rimmed eyes told me their jealous thoughts. The rest of us will drop unburied.

If we ever stopped moving one leaden foot in front of the other.

Kahinahs were known to melt lead in small spoons over fire, pour it into water, and tell fortunes by the shape into which the metal hardened. Islam had forbidden such dark arts. And yet, molten lead seemed to form around every lonely step each man in the army took.

And every step was harder than the last.

Did my daughter melt the whole army of Islam in her crucible? The thought of dropping into cool water to take on a new shape made me see white, turned my head with madness for long stretches.

On the third day, the sun rose behind us like a smith's furnace. My mind wandered back to the forge of Rudainah, how she had welded sky to earth. The same force pressed the soul out of every man, every beast on that track, and flattened it in long shadows before us. We will never, I felt, catch up to our blade-thin souls again.

Thinking thus, several minutes of numb staring passed before what I saw before me sank in. I saw a man draining the last of the water from the skin on the near side of his camel.

I cannot say that fury sprang me to life, for even righteous fury felt jinn-heavy. I urged my camel forward to lord down at the miscreant from my height, but height alone intimidated. Any energy I had, even so early in the morning, lay in a sheen of grime-smeared sweat along my skin.

"What sort of fool did God create here?" I demanded. "Do you know no better than to take all your water from one side, leaving the camel to march unbalanced? Every step becomes twice as hard for him then."

Cowering lay beyond the soldier's sapped strength. As did speech. He simply pointed to the other side: just as flaccid.

"How could you have been so careless, man?" I demanded next. "You know the water has to last us five days."

I don't think I had the vigor to more than mumble these words into my beard. And when I managed to lift my head against the press of the sun on my red turban, to lift my hand to shield my eyes, looking down the column, I saw that nearly every water skin hung loose from the swaying humps. Some empty skins had broken free and blew around the desert as the jinn's playthings. Not all these desperate men could have been so disobedient. I must have miscalculated.

The jinn must have turned my head, that was more like it.

I stole a glance at Rafi. The swaddling kept me from seeing either pity or scorn in his features. The cloth about his mouth moved. I heard him reciting the Quran: "Surely my prayer and my sacrifice and my life and my death are all for God." The more he recited, the more blessed moisture got trapped in the folds of cloth, helping to keep his lips from cracking, his nose from bleeding. When he had traveled this route before, his father must have done the same, to poetry.

I readjusted the tail of my own turban similarly across the lower half of my face, as high to my eyes as I could against the glare. Like a woman protects herself against harsh realities, I thought. I saw how the red had bleached to pink.

By the time the sun was at its zenith that third day, no water skins re-

mained. *The camels, freed of their loads, kept plodding along. I watched the swing of their humps enviously, although they'd markedly shrunk since we left Quraqir.*

At the very heat of the day, we found shade at the skirt of a mountain. Those who did not fit in that cover lay behind their camels or under a cloth stretched between two low poles. That was when I gave the order. "Every fifth camel that once carried water and food—sacrifice them."

But I showed them how. "Careful of the stomach, the first of their three."

"In the Name of God—" whispered like wind over sword blades.

Sand-colored stomachs streaked with blood slid out onto more sand like fetuses. Those men not from the desert I showed how to harvest the parallel water cells from the stomach side: one cell allowed per man, the result of the forced watering at Quraqir. The water was blood-warm, curdling with its hint of acid, rennet and hair. But it quenched the thirst like vinegar and left a man fingering the hilt of his sword, ready to kill for more. It served.

Flies and meat suddenly surrounded us. We ate the livers raw, without salt or sauce. Small fires struck on dung—even drier than usual—cooked the tender muscles from near the kidneys on sword blades. The rest of the meat we abandoned, our mouths too dry to salivate more.

Buzzards came sailing over the mountaintop and darkened the sky behind us as we pressed on toward the sunset.

Every fourth camel gave each man a cell of water after evening prayer, every third at dawn when the thought of more raw liver threatened to bring up the precious liquid.

As I rode sunward on the afternoon of the fourth day, she appeared to me. My daughter. Or, veiled, her mother, my love. Dancing on the heat waves. Bracelets and anklets glinted so brightly, I had to look away. I could hear the tinkling of the ornaments, completely muffling the spell-casting shuffle of the camel pads.

I took a breath, but the oven-heat did little to clear my head. Did this mean the daughter, too, was dead?

Or did it mean the jinn had her now, heart and soul, that she was one of them?

On the fifth morning, I saw an empty camel wandering at the side of the column that moved at a snail's pace.

"How can this be?" I demanded. "Every camel not carrying anything has been killed now for the water in its stomach."

"God willed that the rider dropped from its back with exhaustion," I was told.

I could not bring myself to order the saddle cloth removed from such a beast and its throat cut for the water cells.

After that, we could not leave the buzzards behind. They began to keep pace with us.

"Ya Rafi," I said to the living corpse beside me. "Today is the fifth day. Where is the well you found with your father? The entire army of Islam is on the point of death."

"The breasts of a woman," the blind man croaked.

Indeed, looking up into the glare ahead, I saw that my daughter had undressed. A wanton for the world. I shook my head, waited until it stopped reeling, and saw the pair of mountains.

But what mountain does not look like the breast of some woman or other?

Nonetheless, I pulled my camel in that direction. Those men who managed to follow me scouted around.

No well.

"Look for a thorn tree that hunches like an old man," said Rafi ibn Umayra.

The plain held no tree, not one shrub or blade of grass to point to moisture.

"Look again," Rafi said, then began to recite scripture again, "Lo, we belong to God and indeed to Him we shall return."

"Well, here—yes—here's an old root," called one man off to the left. "We might cook the last camel liver on it, if we want to add to the heat. But it hasn't been a tree since my father's time."

"Blessed be God. There. Dig there," spoke Rafi hoarsely, then spoke no more.

Along with others, I ran and sank my camel goad into the sandy soil. It came back damp, the soil revealed dark with blessed damp.

Without thought, I'd planted my feet on the downward slope. Two more stabs with my goad added to the staves and bare hands of others forced me to leap out of the way as a spring shot out. Then we were all on soaked knees, drinking, laughing, splashing.

I took an overflowing skin to Rafi and handed it to him with ceremony. He removed the shroud from his lips to drink but not from his eyes.

"God bless your eyes," I told him.

"Do you think," he said once his tongue was moist enough to do so, "that someone chopped down that tree? Do you think someone filled in the well?"

"I saw no footprints. It must have happened by the hand of God," I replied. I didn't want to have the thought that the last person to cross this way must have been my daughter.

I sent men with full water skins out to find the stragglers—and they were many—who had fallen behind. In the end, by the grace of God, not one man died in that crossing, not even the one whose empty saddle I had seen. Having drained the Well of Two Breasts dry and then passed on to Suwa where we rested and drank more, we were able to enter Syria with a triumphant push. We took Abu Ubayda ibn al-Jarra completely by surprise, not to mention the dozing Romans.

So we entered Syria to conquer it for the glory of God.

45

**Glory to God Who did take His servant for a journey by night
from the sacred mosque to the farthest mosque, whose precincts
We did bless in order that We might show him some of Our
signs: for he is one who heareth and seeth all things.
—The Holy Quran, Surah 17**

"Y ou were the last one to pass that way, those five trackless days without water, weren't you?" Rayah stared at her mother. "Did you fill in the well? Did you cut down the thorn?"

"Women must conceal certain things they know, things taught them by the jinn," Sejah replied. "We enter a harem and conceal them."

That was not a definite answer, but close enough. Rayah's stomach lurched, sick with the hatred of blasphemy.

"But I wasn't alone," Sejah added. "You rode all that way, in my belly. Sometimes at night, you'd waken me with your strong, thirsty kicks."

Rayah stared. One sort of sickness had changed to another that pressed out of her eyes as tears her mother must, at one point, have been too dried to shed. What dreadful love was this?

"God keep me from motherhood—" Rayah began, then bit her tongue at the sharp look her mother gave her.

"No. Never."

They were four days beyond Yarmuk and the Golan. Rather than staying to the east of the river called Jordan, sacred to Christians because their prophet Isa had bathed himself there, Abd ar-Rahman had separated his small party from the rest of the caravan.

"The pilgrims will hunt the wild boars on that eastern side," he said. "Even though God has forbidden swine's flesh to Believers and this is meant to be a holy caravan. Violent altercations will occur over this that the hunters—because they are armed—will win. A man with political ambitions such as mine cannot get involved in such a fracas.

"And there are leaders of the community of Believers in Jerusalem with whom it would be more profitable to counsel."

So they had forded the descending stream and found themselves in Jerusalem. The place called, in Arabic, simply al-Quds, "the Holy."

"If God is willing, you ladies will be very comfortable here before you begin your arduous pilgrimage."

The innkeeper's bird-like wife paused at the door to see if she could say anything else. Was there any way she could get more gossip out of the mother and daughter pair who, up to that point, had remained taciturn? All she knew was that they were kinswomen of the powerful man who had her husband cowering downstairs.

Rayah sensed all this. For this inspiration she was grateful, since her mother hadn't said a word, had made no attempt to communicate in this Syriac with the strange accent.

"We had a wife of the Arabian prophet as a guest here," came the hostess's next foray. "The woman arrived here out of the desert on pilgrimage, going the other way from you. Even one such as she had no complaints, and I'm giving you her room."

Sejah turned suddenly from her silent contemplation of the fountain bubbling in the yard below. "A wife of Muhammad?"

Her unexpected speech and its keen tone took their hostess by surprise. "Yes, if it please my lady."

"Which wife? What was her name?"

"Saffiyah, if it please you. She was, so they said, a Jewess in former times, in the times of ignorance."

"Saffiyah." A sigh like a desert wind came from behind Rayah's mother's veil.

And Rayah remembered her mother telling her Saffiyah's story: How they had been friends as girls. How two husbands and a father had died at Muslim hands. How her second husband had died with the secret of the Jews' treasure still buried in his seared breast. A secret he kept from Muslims but perhaps not from his wife, become his widow.

And how Saffiyah had become Muhammad's bride on ground with their blood barely cold. She had done it to spare her friend Sejah.

And then how Saffiyah had taken the cinnabar poison to al-Medinah with her, to hold in her hand the power to add slowly, over time, to her enemy's food. And how Muhammad had died. . .

Sejah took two quick steps across the carpeted floor toward their hostess before she limited herself to speech. "Is she—? Did Saffiyah bint Huyyay return to al-Medinah then, after her pilgrimage here to the holy city of her ancestors?"

A pilgrimage that would have taken her past the ruins of Khaybar, where treasure might be hidden.

"No, she left our inn to find permanent lodging in town, I recall," said the inn-keeper's wife.

"But still in Jerusalem?"

"Yes. To wait out the widowhood, which must last the rest of her life."

"Saffiyah—here? Where?"

"I'll discover for you, Lady," said the hostess, bowing out.

The woman did discover. Saffiyah the Jewess was in Jerusalem, having chosen to live out the rest of her days in the holy city of her ancestors rather than that of her dead third husband. Muslim soldiers guarded her as was only right since the community of Believers was paying for her small home on the Mount of Olives. These pensioners, however, saw nothing wrong with the sister and niece of the son of the Conqueror coming to call with their guardian eunuch while Abd ar-Rahman made his calls to men of power.

"A sacred rock?" Sejah commented to her friend and daughter. "That is like the standing stones of al-Hira, which my father destroyed."

"He conquered Jerusalem in the name of Islam, too," said Saffiyah.

"And did not destroy the stone?"

"By the grace of God, he did not."

"Then perhaps he was not such a fearsome father after all. Near the end."

Visits to the *beytl*, the sacred rock, the site of the ancient temple, were allowed only on Mondays and Thursdays, "Days my ancestors reserved for reading the Torah," Saffiyah said.

When Thursday arrived, she took her guests there. The guardians of the holy place greeted her by name and with honor. They wore white linen and curious bejeweled breastplates. She came every Monday and Thursday.

A mosque had been built on the south end of plateau. It was little more than pillared sides with a roof of thatch, however. And a *qiblah* that turned its back on any sacred stone apart from the Goddess's ancient one as black as night that rested in Mecca's Ka'ba. Rayah and her companions offered the noon prayer there, behind the women's screen so no man could see the aberrations Sejah and Saffiyah introduced into the rite. But afterward they went to the stone, which proved the center of most of the guardians' attention.

Thatch shielded the stone, too, and a railing of teakwood from far India surrounded it; the fragrance came off on Rayah's hands. A lot of treasure lay behind such attentions. The guardians cleaned the area, lit lamps made of glass filled with perfumed oil. They burnt incense, then laved the stone with an oil made of musk, ambergris melted in rosewater and saffron.

"You can tell in the city when it is Monday or Thursday," Saffiyah told her guests. "The fragrance of worship enters every alley."

It had certainly entered Rayah's clothes, and would cling to their folds until far into the desert.

"When first I came here," Saffiyah told them further, "the Christians would not let the Jews come up to this place. We–they, I mean–had to pray at a wall below. But I went around the Holy City, telling the powerful men tales of my husband Muhammad. I told how one night, after he had eaten alone with me, he disappeared. When we discovered him, he revealed the seventeenth surah of the Quran. He told me he had ridden on a black horse up here, to 'the furthest mosque,' then from here to heaven. He told me he prayed at the north side of this rock.

"I told them, too, of the Day of the Two Qiblahs. How Muslims in al-Medinah prayed facing northward, toward Jerusalem until my husband began to fall out with my people, the Jews. One day at prayer, he faced north to begin with then suddenly, in the middle, he turned around and faced the Ka'ba and its sacred stone instead. Just as if God had changed the direction of those magic needles sailors sometimes use to tell direction.

"At the same time, when I first came to Jerusalem, I consulted with the local learned Jews. They looked in their books and discovered what rites were appropriate for the stone here where the temple once stood. With Muslims to arbitrate between us—I mean between the Jews and the Christians—and in soil I had fertilized with my tales, I got these new guardians installed as they had not been for more than six hundred years."

This lady, may God be pleased with her, and her people had not been allowed here for almost six hundred years, Rayah thought. Now they are.

And the next time Rayah prayed toward Mecca, it was with more devotion than she had since her pilgrimage began.

Rayah and her mother embraced the widowed Mother of Believers fondly. Alas, they could not linger in the Holy more, for Uncle Abd ar-Rahman had finished his meetings and now they had to hastened to catch up with the main caravan as it turned to enter Arabia.

46

**Verily, on the friends of God no fear shall fall, nor
shall they grieve.**
—The Holy Quran 10:63

Medinat an-Nebi, the City of the Prophet. Here, too, Rayah could look for remnants from the past of her grandfather and all her mothers.

Was that tree on the outskirts of town where Asma bint Maysa had been told by her *shaytan* to wait to welcome a child poetess who would take up her calling?

And which might be her house? Would blood-spattered walls show the room where Asma died? With all the new building in town, it seemed unlikely that a single wall from that time still stood.

The stone blocks of the diverse fortresses that had dotted the oasis in the tales when the old town's citizens fought among themselves had been torn down; none expected attacks any more as Muslim armies had chased the battle lines months away to the edge of the known world. Everywhere, new elegant homes were under construction, mimicking Persian or Roman palaces depending upon which empire had yielded their owners more plunder. Attempts at growing new plants carried across the desert could be seen, although the dismal stumps of failure were more common. Their new caregivers had never been farmers and did not really care now to try the impossible.

The slave market alone still stood, although much expanded. Rayah knew she could not hope to see the place where her parents, neither of whose names she dared to say, had first met, her mother one of two or three others on display under a scrap of tent. Not among the armies of slaves, mostly females, offered now to Medinan harems from all over the world.

Only scenes from the winners' lives were being set now in stone. A new elegant main mosque with mosaic, flowing fountain and the ostentation of a minaret was taking shape where once the Prophet, blessed be he, had sat under palm fronds.

Only here did Rayah's heart begin to pound with fear driven by recognition from the stories she'd been told. Her heart knew that Omar ibn al-Khattab must be sitting in state here under a new pillared portico, claiming modesty and austerity while dispensing justice to the world.

Things grew worse, infinitely worse, when their camel with its *qubbah* was forced to kneel around the eastern, backside of the new structure. Only here did simple walls and roofs still remain. These were the huts of the Prophet's widows, the childless Mothers of the Believers, where God's Messenger, blessed be he, was known to have laid his head with each in turn. Here, in beloved Ayesha's arms, he had died and lay buried beneath her floor. The bereaved women still lived under these palm fronds. Here opened the Gate of Mercy, the Bab Rahmah, through which the Mothers of the Believers' believing daughters entered to pray and would as long as heaven and earth stood.

And here Abd ar-Rahman tore open the *qubbah*'s curtain. He looked at Sejah, only Sejah, and told her, with a toss of his head, to dismount. Rayah moved to join her mother.

"Not you," Abd ar-Rahman said.

Rayah gave a cry of grief and threw herself into her mother's arms, the mother she had tried to murder not so long before.

"Hush, child. It must be," Sejah said. "But do not fear. I will see you again."

"Inshallah, say 'if God wills,'" Rayah begged.

"If it pleases you, 'inshallah.' But I know I will."

And Rayah wondered if that was blasphemous presumption, here in the very shadow of the Prophet's Mosque. Or was it true prophecy?

Her mother didn't stay to answer, but disappeared into veils behind her stepbrother.

Rayah reached a hand out to Abd Allah for support, but without a second thought, he chose the most dangerous, perhaps the shortest route. He chose to follow Sejah. When Abd ar-Rahman offered him, "You can stay here, too, eunuch," the scribe stood there beside the mosque on his bad leg, with his ragged ear. Arms crossed over his chest, he refused to move except forward through the women's gate with his mistress.

Abd ar-Rahman shrugged. "Take that one home," were his orders, pointing to Rayah in the *qubbah*, which the camel drivers hastened to obey.

After that, Rayah wept and didn't bother to peek between the curtains, where she huddled alone with a sword and a manuscript. She wept until the camel knelt again in the courtyard of a fine new house smelling of wet plaster. Then she knew she had to dry her eyes. She could do nothing now for her mother—she felt she never had been able to. She could do nothing for Sejah bint al-Harith except to look out for her own future.

Around Rayah swirled a confusion of female faces: her new harem. If she chose.

But what other choice did she have? If she married, it would be so. Even if she did not, her uncle Abd ar-Rahman would see her in the same place, his niece in his house in al-Medinah. His second family resided in Homs, but here, somewhere, was the mother of his oldest son, a woman of an old Meccan family, kept carefully near the center of the world's power.

The home itself might be comfortable when—if—it ever got finished. But the physical surroundings had very little to do with whether Rayah herself could live comfortably there. Her mother—oh, what was happening to her mother now in the great mosque?—had taught her that a strip of tenting could be comfortable in the desert and nothing comfortable in a room on the third floor.

Rayah didn't know a soul among the—seven? eight?—women who came out to circle around her. They moved too fast for her to count. Some wore somber black, some affected brilliant Persian dress, some took a Roman touch to their garb in jeweled fibulae, in earrings. Some combined everything—which, of course, they might change tomorrow—so she mustn't depend on outward show. Even though show was obviously very important to a large majority of them. This did not promote comfort.

They all seemed plumper than she was expecting, from a pampered life, so the food was good. But that wasn't her main concern here, either.

Who in all this swirl was the mother-in-law, the sister-in-law, the auntie? Who was the pretty one, the lively one? The kind one? Was that one shelter in a storm? No, see how her eyes snapped at the girl beside her, then back at Rayah. Could she trust that one? What was that one's name? Sarah? No, she'd misheard. That name belonged to that one, and seemed to be a pet name.

And the lively little one like dear Bushra? Where—?

No. There could be no one like Bushra.

Their scrutiny of her was all the more keen since so many of them had but a single object—Rayah herself.

"Those eyes—"

Yes, always the eyes first. Get past that. Rayah opened her eyes wide and stared at the speaker. She tried to back it by a smile, but knew that came out only more shy and awkward.

A sign against evil formed half consciously in a set of long fingers. "'I seek refuge in my Lord—'"

"But I remember the Prophet, blessed be he, as you do not. He had eyes of that color, too." That one with age and authority had tales to tell— Mother-in-law?

"She looks strong enough."

"She could mother fine sons."

"For *my* son, did the camel driver say?"

No, Rayah had failed again to see which of a trio of older women said that. Besides—

"Never!"

"Calm, sister. What does a camel driver know?"

"And the father of my son, gone over a year, doesn't have the care to come home first before he must be off to the mosque?"

"Before dumping this on us."

"She's shabby, ragged."

Rayah fought her exhaustion to stand tall, fought her thirst and hunger to moisten her lips at least.

"She did just come off the pilgrims' way, give her that."

"She looks like the family. Doesn't she? There must be some truth in her. That chin—"

"Except for those eyes. Not those eyes."

"And didn't they say she's an orphan? That shows very little sense and greater ill fortune."

No, Rayah could not think her mother dead or dying at this moment. She shifted and tried to stand taller. They still hadn't invited her to sit or even to come out of the sun's glare in the courtyard.

"Hush, sister, really. It is all in God's hands."

"And didn't our Lord through Muhammad, peace be upon him, command us to have compassion on the orphan?"

"Compassion, yes, but not to lose sense altogether and marry our sons to them."

"But those eyes. . ."

"Can she see anything with them?"

"Maybe she's blind."

"She doesn't speak. Dumb as well."

"Jinn-possessed, certainly."

"She doesn't even understand God's Arabic."

"None of these women who come from the battlefields do."

This particular pair of young women who looked as alike as twins actually seemed to be ganging up on her, Rayah thought. In truth, the accent made Rayah shy to attempt speech, but she understood every word. And they were speaking about her as if she couldn't.

"We could just kill her. A kitchen accident. No one would ever know."

"Auntie! How with the fear of God can you even suggest it?"

"She probably comes to us as spoiled goods."

Rayah felt herself shrink again. She knew they would consider her so, after what the jinni had done that night, that wonderful night. Several other nights on the pilgrimage road, when fear overcame her, he offered comfort. Panic thudded in her sweaty temples.

"Those eyes. Surely jinn-possessed."

"And with such a mother. What did the slaves say about her?"

"Vile gossip that doesn't deserve repeating."

"Surely Abd ar-Rahman brought her to us to make her disappear. How can we hold our heads up in al-Medinah with a *jinniyah* in our midst?"

"My son doesn't want such a bride. A mother knows. I'm looking out for my son."

"You are certainly correct, Umm Khalid."

That was the first moment Rayah heard her bridegroom's name—Khalid, named for their communal illustrious grandfather, no doubt. She closed her eyes with the prayer that he'd inherited very little else of the old man. But the name also told her who the mother-in-law was, Umm Khalid, Khalid's Mother, the title of respect.

When Rayah opened her eyes again, she stopped turning from speaker to speaker in confusion and centered her attention on the one called Umm Khalid.

"But not all jinn are wicked," Rayah heard her own voice speak up, cracking with nerves, disuse and the thirst of the way; she still hadn't been offered a drink.

Silence dropped upon all the women like many lengths of a veil. They stared at her as if the camel she'd just ridden in on had spoken instead of her.

Rayah took advantage of the unnatural muteness. "Did not God's Messenger, peace be upon him, reveal, 'I have not created jinn and men except that they worship me'"?

"She speaks," said the bitter one.

"She speaks God's Arabic," said the kinder one.

"She recites the Holy Quran," said Umm Khalid, and that was what mattered.

"Can you recite all the holy words?" said one of the two who looked like twins. The one with the tiny scar on her brow.

Rayah nodded. "I have more than half of the surahs by heart, by the grace of God, and work to learn more, inshallah."

"So not all," the bitter one triumphed.

"But in Syria?" said the kinder one. "You learned that in Syria?"

"With God's help, yes."

Another brief silence fell. The women exchanged glances. Rayah watched where all the glances ended up, watched how the power of silence flowed.

"Wouldn't that be nice, not to have to listen through the grilles when the men recite?" said the kinder one.

Even the bitter one was ready to concede, "We would certainly hold our place then against Umm Muthanna."

"Everything does not have to be a contest against Umm Muthanna," Rayah suggested. "She is our Muslim sister, after all." She had no idea who Umm Muthanna was, but she would certainly be Muslim.

Half of the women nodded at this calming wisdom. The other half were willing to overlook the platitude for a chance to beat Umm Muthanna at her own game.

"I could certainly help any of you to learn as well," Rayah suggested. "If the gracious lady who has memory of our Prophet, peace be upon him, will help me."

And no one was willing to admit she had no interest in memorizing the Holy Quran.

"I wonder how my son will take this," Umm Khalid mused.

"He should take it very well," said the scarred twin, sulking.

"Too well," her sister elbowed her, teasing. "You wanted Khalid ibn Abd ar-Rahman for yourself."

"So did you." And the scarred twin burst into tears and fled the courtyard.

"Oh, leave her," said the other twin when some tried to call after her. The other twin added a Quranic reference to her qualifications at this point: "My twin would cut her hands while eating meat over our cousin Khalid."

Rayah caught the relationship—mother's nieces, no doubt—and the Quranic reference. "As did the women of Pharoah," she said, "when they caught a sight of the prophet Yusuf, peace be upon him."

She was still unhappy with how that particular exchange had gone and vowed to heap extra kindness on that hurt young woman whenever she got the chance, whatever the outcome of the proposed marriage.

"He should take it very well, inshallah," the bitter woman repeated to Umm Khalid. "He who has just become a *hafez*, able to recite the holy book word for word, himself and has no time for the arts of war."

"Nothing like his grandfather," Umm Khalid confessed.

"You should have sent him out to the desert to nurse, as is the custom."

"The custom of pagan times of ignorance. We cannot stay far enough from the desert tribes these days. Many of them are still in secret rebellion, those who have not been shipped off to fight Islam's battles at the edges of the world."

"So you have only yourself to blame that you have a bookish son."

Rayah thought she might like to send her own son to the desert, should God will she have one. Or go into the desert herself, some part of the year. But she would fight that out with her mother-in-law when—if—the time actually ever came. If the woman actually ever accepted her.

"Bookish, yes, thank God," Umm Khalid countered. "Well on the way to becoming a judge among Muslims, if God so wills. Yes, by the grace of God, my son is a *hafez*. But it does not necessarily follow that he wants a wife who might correct him if, God forbid, he makes a mistake. He, after the example of our present khalifah—may God lead Omar ibn al-Khattab and all Muslims aright—likes women in their place."

Rayah had to take in her breath at this, steel herself for more to come. She wondered how much was actually her intended Khalid's opinion and how much was Umm Khalid herself wishing women "in their place," a calm, comfortable, untaxing place. Far from jihad.

But this was the person, Rayah reminded herself, who had to be won over, much more than the son. This woman standing with both hands on the small of her back as if in discomfort.

"Auntie," Rayah dared to try the title for the first time in this harem. "Perhaps if we went inside and got comfortable out of the sun, you would like me to rub your back. I know that can help the pain sometimes."

Later, after food and a rest, Rayah caught her first glimpse of her intended through the harem grille.

To the racing of her heart, she saw he looked uncannily like her jinni: same curly hair, same dark eyes. Only the skin was pallid, the limbs weak and thin.

And his reaction to the few hints his mother dropped, all praise, of the bride his father had brought back from Syria for him, was an unattractive whining fury. "What do I want with the product of such unbelieving parents? And jinn-blue eyes. They tell me she has blue eyes." This before storming out into the safe world of men again.

"Never mind," Umm Khalid said when she returned, taking the cushion closest to Rayah among the women with a grateful stretch of her improved back. "The hajj is almost upon us, to which my husband insists you and your mother go. There can be no marriage until the hajj is past. Inshallah, his father and I will bring him around, for he is willful and young."

Rayah swallowed nervously over that news. But also in the statement was word that her mother still lived. She had stood before Omar and not died. God was indeed Compassionate, Merciful.

47

How many a noonday heat,
far from Mai,
the pace of my thick-humped mare unbroken,
the black-white locusts twitching

In pathless wastelands
whose stillness
in the mirage of forenoon and midday
almost blots out the gaze,

As if the flat hill summits
were entwined in pure silk
parting at times to reveal them,
then sewn back,

When the chameleon
struck by the heat
begins to twist his head
and reel—

How many a rider
drunk on sleeplessness
as if swaying from the two ropes
of a concave well

Have I shaken from his stupor
as he nodded his head
like a staggering drinker
after his last drop of wine.

When he expires in the saddle
I bring him back to life
with your memory. . .
           —Poem of Dhu ar-Rumma

"Here I am at your service, O Lord, here I come."

The caravan had arrived on the barren hillside that marked the edge of Mecca's sacred precinct. Nothing much must have changed in this place since the Prophet Muhammad, blessed be he, made his own pilgrimage here from al-Medinah in the tenth year of his exile. Rayah imagined nothing much of the gritty reddish-brown dust would change in a thousand years.

And nothing had changed much, either, from the time when, in this same place, Rayah's great grandmother had screamed in birth pangs. "In a *qubbah* formed of this same bend of acacia wood." Sejah touched the curve over their heads as she retold the event. "Don't forget, my daughter. And here your grandmother screamed her first cry at the shock of breathing fiery, dust-filled air."

Outside the *qubbah*, as if in a different world, Abd ar-Rahman ibn Khalid brushed aside a Qurayshi in a ragged izar who came begging for a chance to be their guide to the holy sites.

"Off with you," Rayah heard her uncle Abd ar-Rahman say. "You think I, the son of Khalid ibn al-Walid, do not know the town where I was born? Off with you, I say, before I run you through with my father's divine sword. I have inherited it, you know."

In fact, Rayah still had the sword, she and her mother, riding in the *qubbah* between them. Sword and *qubbah* and the Conqueror's parchments and the red headdress dangling from the white camel's headstall. Until Rayah married, they remained theirs.

And her mother remained hers, as well.

For when Abd ar-Rahman had led his captive before Omar ibn al-Khattab in the Prophet's Mosque, hoping—for what? For a stoning? At least for recognition that he was his father's equal—his hopes had been dashed. His entrance coincided with a report received in al-Medinah that twenty ships full of grain had arrived as taxes from newly conquered Egypt and were unloading at the Red Sea ports. How could a lone, poor woman, defeated enemy of more than a decade ago, deserve more attention than the wealth of empires?

"Remove your sister from the business of pious Muslim men," Omar had ordered, "if you have any honor at all."

This left Abd ar-Rahman annoyed and short tempered. He had yet to recover from that.

But the begging Meccan guide didn't know this. Abd ar-Rahman's sharp words sent him bowing off to look for other quarry. A once proud and free man of the desert now become a slave.

Then, with words like honey poured on thorns, as if his voice could never be so harsh, Abd ar-Rahman turned to the women under his protection. "Look, look, Mecca *al-harem*," he told Rayah. "Look, look, Mecca the forbidden. We dismount here to purify ourselves for the approach."

Rayah thought of the gatekeeper Zabbai back at home in Tadmor. Tears started to her eyes as she wondered how the dear old man was doing. He had stood all his years at just such a boundary, although on a smaller scale. He determined which guests might be invited into the men's majlis and which could go on under the guardian silver hand centered with the lapis lazuli eye. He had kept the conquering Sword of God himself from penetrating for years. Until Zabbai had let in dear Abd Allah, who carried the world with him in a bundle of parchment under his arm.

Uncle Abd ar-Rahman used the same word to describe the precinct around Mecca, centered on the stone fallen from heaven: "harem."

The *qubbah* lurched steeply forward then back as the camel sank to his knees with a groan. Rayah parted the curtains and descended, stretching her back and legs.

Abd ar-Rahman grew awkward when he no longer had just a camel and curtains to face. "It is time to purify ourselves for the pilgrimage," he repeated, distracted. "I should not see women too much from now on, so you—you purify yourselves."

For him, purifying himself meant leaving her quickly. But what did it mean for her, a woman, to purify herself? All she knew was how Sitt Umm Ali back in Tadmor had taught her to prepare for prayer.

How was the old woman doing? A new rinse of henna on her hair, bright color contrasting with the wrinkles more and more each time.

Rayah turned to help her mother descend from the *qubbah*, but the eunuch was already there.

"He's gone now," she heard Abd Allah say and assumed he meant her mother's brother. "The men and their rites will keep him busy."

"Mecca the forbidden," Sejah repeated Abd ar-Rahman's earlier statement. "Mecca *al-harem*." The emotion with which she then faced her daughter took Rayah by surprise. "I have had enough of harem, those twelve, thirteen years it took to raise you."

Rayah had just been following her thoughts forward to the last harem she had stayed in: that of Umm Khalid in al-Medinah. Abd ar-Rahman had not wanted to be hampered by any of his other women on this pilgrimage. More than once on the eleven days' travel south, however, Rayah had found herself thinking of the new women who had welcomed her, especially her aunt and prospective mother-in-law. They would be a challenge, but Rayah found herself looking forward to it.

Getting her own mother accepted as an aunt in the household held out particular troubles, troubles of which Rayah had seen only the first sparks that one night Sejah had joined her under the new roof.

But the hugs and tears with which Umm Khalid had let her go, promising "to speak your name to that son of mine every day," made Rayah anxious to begin her new life. "I even know a love spell I will set for him."

Rayah had tried to dissuade Umm Khalid from that promised activity. But she had to admit she wouldn't mind learning such a spell. And wondered if Omar would consider it Muslim or not. She decided she didn't care what the khalifah thought about what went on in Umm Khalid's harem.

She realized that the woman with her, her own mother, was talking to her now. "To see you become a woman, Little Blue Eyes. To see you come to your power, to make me proud."

Had prophetic vision read Rayah's thoughts? Thoughts she didn't even know she had.

"To become the woman I imagined when I named you Rayah when you were tiny and helpless."

"Rayah?" Rayah repeated.

"Rayah. It means 'banner,' you know."

Rayah did know. But she'd never thought of this word from the desert language in the context of the name that had always meant simply "me" to her.

"To boldly lead the way where none dared." Was her mother seeing visions?

"Or to keep rolled up safe and sound in cedar wood?" Rayah met her mother's gaze, blue eye to blue eye.

Sejah smiled. "To unfurl when the time is right. To let me know that, in spite of stoning and whips, in spite of new religions and all new verses, that the power of my mother and of my mother's mother will not, cannot, be extinguished although I myself had to flee."

Sejah turned and looked at the way ahead before adding, "Mecca the forbidden? It is forbidden to me."

Rayah was afraid to ask. She had to ask. "What do you mean, Mother?"

"I mean that I am returning to the desert from whence I came. To the desert that the Goddess, praises to Her, created when She wanted to be alone."

Terror churned in Rayah's heart—like a butter skin from a tent's center pole. "Alone?" But of which life was she more afraid, that which her mother chose? Or that she would live on her own without the lean, hard woman behind her?

But Sejah wouldn't be alone, would she?

"The jinn," Rayah said.

And the young woman's own demon lover gave her a nudge to say, "You have it right."

"The jinn, yes," said her mother. "The jinn and Abd Allah."

"Abd Allah?" Rayah turned to stare at the eunuch scribe.

"I think I must," he said. "Even though I have no experience of the desert except during this last month of our pilgrimage travels."

"Never mind," Sejah said to assure him. "I have forgotten nothing, spun it from my heart to my thread all these years."

"It wouldn't matter anyway." Abd Allah took the hand Sejah laid on his arm. "We hadn't been reading my master's tale—may the rain fall gently upon his troubled soul—too many days before I knew I would go anywhere she went for the rest of my life. Even if it meant to the heart of the howling desert. No, I think I knew it even before I laid eyes on her, even as I sat drinking sherbet with your old gatekeeper, and she refused to see me. Ah, what a woman is this, I told myself. I, who could never hope to have the love of a woman—"

"But who are more deserving than many another I have known. . . ."

Rayah stared first at her mother, who, she noticed, had changed into the old decorated dress, a *kahinah's* dress. Rayah stared at the scribe, then back again. She had never seen such a look in her mother's steely eyes. They had gone to water.

Rayah considered: How welcoming, how safe the outcast desert was for two spurned souls who had found each other. Since the Conqueror's old companion Amr ibn al-Asi had recently conquered the rich, fertile land of Egypt, no one would spare time for them or the desert any more.

"But what about me, the life I must begin shortly with that cousin of mine? What about me?"

"You, my banner?" Sejah looked at her daughter as if she had forgotten she ever existed. "It is a choice you have made, daughter, and I cannot say that, given the future of the world, it may not be best for you. You do not need me now to live that life, and I certainly wouldn't enjoy it. In fact, I can only make it more dangerous for you, because of the banner I carried when it was my time. If my name and my past become known, as they surely must with your uncle Abd ar-Rahman anxious to shout his triumph, angry now that he didn't get the notice he wanted for me. I, too, have seen Omar ibn al-Khattab, who always hated my father, and I have seen what he is."

"But—" Rayah said again.

"Do you want to come with us? Fold up your banner and retreat?" Sejah asked.

"It wouldn't—" Rayah began.

"No, you don't," Rayah heard her jinni say.

"Yes, for me, it would be retreat." Rayah didn't believe him or herself when she answered this way. "But—"

"Come with us now if you like," her mother said. "You see that Abd Allah has purchased three camels for us from other pilgrims in need. All are shes, one in milk and two with calf, due to deliver as winter comes. We understand the first rains have brought green to the land beyond at-Taif and the Valley of Nakhlah. . . ."

Sejah's voice trailed off, perhaps lost in visions of her new life with its desert cycles. Or of where once her mother had touched the herds of al-Harith and the crippled man himself with fertility. Or perhaps she thought of what had happened between her parents in Nakhlah, her origin, the origin of the Conqueror's Sword of God.

A dust devil twisted across the barren landscape behind her mother, the Poet-ess and healer. Rayah knew it was her *shaytan*, her demon love, making his presence known. Rejoicing.

"I will stay with the caravan," the younger woman said. "I must be a Muslimah in this new world. I must enter Mecca the forbidden. It is my fate."

Sejah nodded. "If you change your mind, just speak it to the wind, to the jinn. Word will fly to me on the desert breeze."

"Thank you, Mother. The kahinah in the wilderness, I know, like your grand-mother in the stories. But you have taught me well. Inshallah, I can face this on my own. Just as you faced the lonely seclusion in Tadmor for my sake."

"My Rayah, my banner." The two women embraced. Rayah's tears released the dust in the fabric of her mother's dress with the smell of mud in winter rains. And she saw that the same had happened on her shoulder. For, she realized with a shock, she was now a finger or two higher than the coin- and shell-veiled head of the older woman.

"Come now, Lady," the eunuch said. "My dead master's son is occupied with his rites. We can get around that hillock before he notices us gone. If the girl is in the *qubbah* when the caravan is ready to move on, he will not notice we are gone until the desert has erased our prints, and he can no longer follow."

They were gone.

Through tear-blurred eyes, Rayah stood staring at the last bare footprints her mother had left in the sand before leaving. Then she went to the *qubbah* and got one of the three stoneware pots she had begged Umm Khalid for in al-Medinah. She scooped up the sand where the prints rested and sealed the jar, what she would keep of her mother.

But no. Here was the *qubbah*, the red silk, the manuscript, the sword. A plethora of things. Blue eyes. The twist of a jinni in the sand, a verse of poetry in the head. Rayah felt herself richly endowed indeed.

Then, having no other tutor, Rayah performed purifying rites that suited her and taught them to a trio of women nearby. When four of them did it together, confusion vanished like her mother, the eunuch and the three camels had done.

It was the seventh day of the month of pilgrimage in the twenty-third year of the Hijra.

Hijra, flight. The same word as the name of Hajar, that ancient Mother of Believers who was abandoned in the wilderness by her believing husband. A woman at a well, who created her own well by the help of God, to whom belongs all praise, for it was her desperate hands that clawed at the barren desert floor for water for her child. Thus was created the holy source of Zamzam that flows beside the Ka'ba and its sacred stone.

When she got to Zamzam on her pilgrimage, Rayah filled the second of her jars with water from the sacred well. Umm Khalid had asked for it, praising its curative powers.

The Ka'ba provided the third of the jars' contents as well. Flocks of pigeons filled the sky above the pilgrims, making their own circumambulations. Goddess birds. Three of them came to her hands behind a pillar where she made her prayers with other women. She cut their throats as sacrifice and collected the blood for later.

48

I fought so many battles seeking martyrdom that there is no
place in my body that does not have a stabbing mark by a spear,
a sword or a dagger. And yet, here I am, dying on my bed like
an old camel dies. The eyes of a coward cannot close in sleep.
        —The last words of Khalid ibn al-Walīd as
        reported by ibn Qutaybah

Evening prayers are past. It has grown too dark for my scribe to see; his earring
has winked out, his pen stilled.

"Master, would you work late tonight?" he asks. "Shall I ask the servant to
bring lamps?"

"You are not too tired to continue?"

"I? Master, it is your will."

"My will." I cannot stifle a bitter laugh.

"I worry, Master, about you."

Says such a one whose every hope for a future, in Islam or out of it, was cut from
him years ago. He worries about—? But I stop mid-retort.

A nightingale has settled in the pomegranate tree. Ah, what poets have not done
with nightingales! The tones that break your heart, the peace of a man in his own
courtyard. The messages between parted lovers. Cool descends, memory blurs. A breeze
sighs through the pomegranate tree, knocking overripe fruits to the flagstones, where
they burst in blood under night's cloak.

The fountain purls. I see again a woman at the well, beckoning. . . .

My scribe clears his throat, testing to see I have not nodded asleep. Again.

I cough on the tears clogging my throat, and after the fellow has fetched me a
drink, I start over.

"So the day came just after I conquered the Syrian cities of Qinsirin and Awasim,
sparing the lives of the self-righteous monks of the place for the sake—for the sake of
Muhammad's plea for mercy. Although in truth they deserved the sword. More than
the lone guardian of Nakhlah. . ."

"Master, let me send for light."

"No, lamps will only attract moths to their deaths. Like my sword attracted the monks, desiring martyrdom."

"But I should write these new words of yours."

"Some things are better left unwritten, as some things are better left unsaid. And some deeds, I've come to know, are better left undone, although it is in our power, even our right, to do it. Like the murder of the monks, I suppose, no matter how much they deserved death, if only for persisting to believe God favors them in spite of proof to the contrary. Proof riding on the tip of my sword."

"You will retell all this to me when I come tomorrow?"

"Tomorrow." I repeat it like a foreign word with no meaning to my ears.

"Yes, so I can write it then. For your heirs."

"Inshallah, if God wills."

He takes that as an affirmative, and I don't disabuse him.

The woman beckoning at the well. . .

I continue my tale. After the half-man on his cushions bestirs me once again.

"The summer fighting season was not so much advanced that we couldn't still push on deeper, ever deeper into Roman territory, up into the heights of Anatolia. To, in the end, Marash, where the people make a sort of flour from the roots of orchids— But what of that?

"As a reward for Qinsirin and Awasim, to prepare for the unknown we might find in Anatolia, I took a few hundred of my men, the mobile corps, for recreation in Haleb. The rest of the army stood set to march up with us later. For recreation and—yes—because I knew that city was a great center for poets. No poet would fail to come and try his fortune with a man called the Conqueror. Many poets might have heard of the one poet I sought and could not find.

"So one sweltering afternoon, I betook myself to that luxury of Roman decadence I've recently become very used to: the bath. It's just Mecca-ward of the new mosque we had elbowed into the old church built by Saint Helen, the mother of some misbelieving emperor or another.

"The people of Haleb make a very interesting product called 'soap' to go with their baths. They make it of olive oil, in soft creamy greens and golds like the oil itself. Even without being impregnated with the innumerable fragrances bathers can choose from, it makes a man cease to smell like a man, and his skin comes away as soft as an infant's. I can hardly recommend it to a soldier preparing for jihad. Nonetheless, as I've said, the steam of the bath has its allure.

"No wonder people say fire spirits tend to haunt such places, that baths are of dubious morality.

"No wonder my upright cousin mistrusts them from as far away as al-Medinah. That among my trusted companions drifting through the steam, relaxing to the sounds of poets, Omar had placed his spies. As they are now everywhere, around the campfires of the armies of God, no less. At the doors to our harems.

"Very well, in that steam, too, was a concoction based on wine—boiled, mind you, so even drinking could have no effect. It makes the skin glow after the final massage. Ah, what a balm! My battle-jarred joints long even now for the touch of it. Or maybe it was the massage by one such as yourself of which my cousin disapproved. Or of the aches I had earned while he sat at home— Who can say? The bastard eaten with jealousy, finally in a position to take his vengeance—"

The fountain purls. I remember drinking wine all those years ago in al-Hira and going drunk to the convent.

And the woman—

My throat is spoiled for wine ever since.

The eunuch prods me gently. "But Omar condemned you for this use of intoxicating liquids, even though the Holy Quran speaks only of the evil of drinking and you enjoyed it only in the massage."

I realize I have let my mind wander on without the dark figure hunched on his cushions across from me again. I realize it only after his unnatural voice enters the world of memories written in scars on this skin of mine.

"That is so." I resist temptation and manage to go on. "But more than the use of wine or the indulgence in warm water and massage, I think he hated the poets."

"The poets, Master?"

"Is it not the purpose of a poet to consult with his *shaytan*, his Satan, his adversary? Under such inspiration, to speak against the power of this world. And what does Omar hate more than Satan if it be not verses that compete with the holy revelation of the Quran?

"In the baths in Haleb I met one poet Omar hates in particular. Ashas. Because Ashas is the most famous. Save for she who, for all any of us knew then, might be dead."

"Yes, even I have heard of Ashas, heard his verses recited." So the fellow confesses to listening to poetry. A dangerous admission, with Omar's spies all around.

"And of the verses he composed for you." He ventures on.

"Verses praising me, yes. What man does not love to hear his deeds praised? Especially when it's not clear how many more he might live to accomplish. For which I gave him ten thousand dirhams."

"Heard of the verses, but not the verses themselves. Would you, Master, recite them? Now, as the first stars come out?"

I regard the stars and remember—

"Not tonight." Even as I say this, I know that my denial—in a world where every mind struggles to memorize the Quran, if only the first surah—means these verses of Ashas' will be completely wiped from the mind of man.

"Suffice it to say," I go on quickly now, for the pain is almost gone from this old wound, "that when word of this payment reached al-Medinah, Omar—for whom nobody will ever rhyme two words together, trust me—said his famous words."

I don't have to poison my tongue with Omar's words. My scribe knows them, too. "'O Khalid, you have done; And no man has done as you have done. But it is not people who do. It is God Who does.'"

"And when we came back with plunder from Marash—far more than ten thousand dirham's worth, believe me—news of my dismissal greeted me.

"'Fie,' I said to the face of the pious, whore's-son messenger who gave me the news, battle dust still in every link of my armor. 'I care nothing for your dismissals. This one is the last one. It was you who called me back, remember? You are authorized to take away my rightful share of the plunder so I don't bathe any more? I still have my sword, though you take away the field on which to use it. And don't I have a lock of the Prophet's hair wrapped in the red turban on my head?'

"Well, I will pass the lock of hair and its benefits on to those who can appreciate it, who will use it for the good of mankind, of womenkind. If it is the will of God.

"This I thought, but even more I said. I didn't care because I had the red turban itself. And what no man present at my shaming understood was the more important message the poet Ashas had imparted to me in that bath. My scarred skin growing taut and youthful with wine, I heard a more important message than what a fine commander I was.

"Ashas versified about traveling through Tadmor. He had learned of a healer there, a healer and a poetess. 'One greater than I,' were his self-effacing words. Words I paid ten thousand dirhams for. Had I been dismissed before taking Marash, the city would never have been taken. And now I had more important work to do than one more conquest."

With a sigh, I conclude to my scribe, "As I do now, my friend."

I hear the fellow shift uncomfortably at this appellation. I have never allowed it to him before.

After a moment, he realizes I have nothing more to say. I leave it to the nightingale now, and the wind.

"Good night then, Master. Until tomorrow."

"It will be as God wills."

"*Amin.*"

He leaves silently. I regard the stars to which he called my attention. They smile quietly, those spots of light that once led my milk family through their night wanderings. That once fell from heaven burning upon my love.

I pick up my sword—our sword—and unsheathe it. A snake-like hiss in the dark. It cannot be resheathed until it has drawn blood.

I die even as an old camel dies. I die in bed, in shame. The eyes of a coward cannot close in sleep.

No, God forbid.

The purl of the fountain calls me.

49

**. . .demanding blood
as if they were desert jinn,
feet anchored in stone**
—The Mu'allaqat of Labid

After the duty of pilgrimage was over, Abd ar-Rahman took his niece with the returning caravan as far as al-Medinah in order to marry her to his son. After losing his half sister in the desert—something he didn't want to talk about—at least he would have control over part of the embarrassment he'd brought with him from Syria.

Rayah married her cousin Khalid, with a sacrifice of fourteen sheep and a camel, in the house smelling of new plaster. In wedding finery, she danced with her new kinswomen at the wedding, music kept sedate so Omar's spies wouldn't hear. Circling her hips to cradle a child, she opened and closed her hands to reveal the beautiful henna painted there. Crowned with a wreath of jasmine, she carried the fragrance to every corner of the new, strange house, and gave it a more permanent air.

And carefully she dripped the blood of the Ka'ba's pigeons on the blankets of their first night together to make up for that her jinni had already taken from her.

"In the name of God, the Compassionate, the Merciful," was the only thing young Khalid said to her before he consummated the marriage. While she opened the vial.

She helped him feel like a conqueror. Her jinni taught her how, and young Khalid, clearly, had no jinniyah.

Afterwards, in the dark, before the world should be told and the public ululation begin over his victory, young Khalid asked her, "You are a Muslimah?"

"Of course."

He made her prove it by saying the confession of faith. If she hadn't been before, she was now.

"But you're from Syria."

"I was born in an oasis there." Could she say it without tears? "Tadmor."

No. But perhaps in time.

She felt him shift on their communal cushions before he said, "My grandfather, may God find favor with him, was the conqueror of Syria."

"Indeed. He died there."

Young Khalid's interest heightened. "Did you know him?"

She felt she knew him. As well as any. And she had heard his voice, yelling outside the gate. "Yes. He was my grandfather, too."

More silence followed. Young Khalid struggled with a wounded pride. "I was named for him." He tried to up his bet, but Rayah heard the uncertainty.

She smiled in the dark and thought of the manuscript she had hidden under the covers on which they lay. Perhaps she'd burn it, to put her grandfather's version on the same level as her mother's—a tale told by lamplight.

And the sword? For our son, she told herself. If God wills we have one.

"I know many tales of that Companion of the Prophet, may God grant him peace," she said aloud. "If you'd like, I can tell them to you."

"Yes, yes, I would," young Khalid said, rising to throw on his robe and go to announce his own success to the waiting party.

The moment he was gone, Rayah sat beside the streaks of his triumph.

"Are you there?" she whispered.

Her jinni twirled in the smoke of the single lamp light. "I'm here."

She had seen his smoke-curly hair instead of her cousin's. "You're not jealous?"

"In the world I come from—"

"The Time of Ignorance?"

"Some call it thus. But they have not been able to rid the world of us, as we have not rid the world of them. We gave our word to the All-Merciful we would not attempt to do so when first the world was made."

"In your world—?" she urged him to finish saying what he had begun.

"A son takes his name from his mother. A woman takes more than one man. No, not all gone."

"Stay with me. I know I will need you."

The smoky curls bobbed. "Of course. I only need the invitation."

Rayah set a mirror behind the lamp. The smoke slipped into her empty jug.

A jinni jar is like a harem, she told herself. Keeping power until it is needed.

And then all her new relatives came to give their approval to the blood on the sheets.

She would tell any young woman who came to her in tears to touch the red turban with the lock of the Prophet's hair tied within it. And then to do the same thing with the pigeon's blood.

❧

And they did come to consult her: young women, Persian slaves, mothers, old women preparing for paradise. More and more they would come as her reputation spread. Already in that first week, she had noticed that most of her patients were women. Men seemed to prefer the cures that involved writing a verse of the Quran, no more, soaking it in water and drinking the ink or wearing it on a cord around their necks. Rayah could write such amulets, but then she would insist on herbs or some other remedy, which some of the men called outright witchcraft.

Rayah met her husband young Khalid mostly in the dark. She told him tales to relax his mind after its day with the law. Once, during the day, when her mother-in-law pointed him out to her through a grille, Rayah did not recognize him.

Rayah did like her mother-in-law very much, a merry, motherly woman such as Sejah, her own mother, had never been. The woman had already seen certain herbs and drugs brought in to welcome her daughter-in-law to her new home. A good, helpful grandmother for the blue-eyed daughter Rayah had every reason to believe God in His mercy would soon send her.

Besides having the love of her jinni, Rayah was too busy in this lively household of women, getting to know them and her patients. She hardly noticed the lack of a husband. He was good for all she needed him for.

She remembered the date precisely: the twenty-sixth day of the last month of the twenty-third year of the Hijra. She had been married less than a week. She was summoned to someone rather than having the patient come to her.

"It is the Mother of the Believers herself," said the round-faced, full-lipped African slave who came with the request. "Ayesha the Beloved."

Muhammad's favorite wife, the youngest.

"What is her illness?" Rayah asked. "I need to know what medicaments to bring."

She considered a tisane of anise and chamomile, perhaps, or soaking the lady's feet in basil water. What else but stress and nerves could ail a woman widowed so young, childless, and confined to her best behavior?

"Bring nothing, Lady. Just come."

Rayah hurried to comply. She hadn't been long in al-Medinah, but long enough to know that no one said "No" to Ayesha the Beloved.

In the alley outside her new home, however, a lurking figure leaped out of the shadows at her and the little maid. The slave tried to scream for help, but Rayah saw who it was and stilled the girl: Firuz the Persian, now a slave of her house.

Sawdust sprinkled his hair and tunic from the work he did: The household rented him out to carpenter the former mud-brick dwellings into palaces, the wealth of two empires funneling into the city where wood had always been an incomprehensible mystery. Imported grain needed new mills to grind it.

"What is it, sir?" Rayah asked him.

"I have seen them."

"Who?" She feared he might be speaking madness.

"Children, Persian children. Enslaved, enslaved so young and here so far from home."

What to say to such anguish? What to say with the little maid all wide eyes and open ears? She was not Persian, rather African, but the rest of the description fit her.

"Alas, my good man—"

Rayah began her soothing a beat too late. Firuz got into his own matter first.

"A vial of poppy juice, Lady. For the love of God, poppy juice."

Poppy juice for suffering children? Rayah studied him. This man had tortured harmless Abd Allah, relishing the pain he inflicted. Now he wanted drugs to ease pain?

A broken man who could break others in his viciousness.

For the first time since they'd parted, Rayah craved her mother's counsel. Whatever could the slave want with poppy juice? He stood there straight enough, undoubled with pain. Poppy juice was powerful stuff. She wanted to ask the man more questions, judge the state of his mind. But Ayesha waited.

Should she or shouldn't she? Rayah wanted to beg the wind.

The answer settled firmly in her mind without further debate. "Just a minute."

"But—" protested Ayesha's maid.

Rayah ran to her room. A moment later, she pressed the drug in the carpenter's calloused hand and didn't look back as she led the girl on.

50

O Ayesha, Arabs who have professed Islam are no longer Arab,
but people of our desert, while we are the people from the
center of their desert. If we call them they respond to us, and if
they call us we respond to them.
　　　　—A tradition in which the Prophet rebuked
　　　　Ayesha for refusing to accept a present from a
　　　　Bedouin woman

Upon arrival at Ayesha the Beloved's room, Rayah paid her respects to the
fallen leaders first, as was only right. She kissed the very stones of the tombs
of Muhammad and Abu Bakr as the men on the other side of the grille could
not.

"Omar would not approve." Still veiled, her hostess spoke. "'If any of you worship
Muhammad, know that Muhammad is dead.'"

"'But those of us who worship God, know that God is alive and cannot die.'"
Rayah completed the saying of Abu Bakr as she arose. "And Omar, may God lead him
and all Muslims aright, does allow a new minaret to be built, does he not?"

The widows of the Prophet, may God rain precious blessings upon him, lived just
beside the great mosque of al-Medinah, along the eastern side, as Rayah had already
been told. Except for Saffiyah, of course, who had quietly taken herself off to Jerusalem
(some even thought she was still in seclusion in her little room in al-Medinah) and the
second Zaynab, who had more recently died. That left four of them, each in her own
room, living out the rest of their lives. During his lifetime, Muhammad had been able
to pass through the door of his house directly into the holy space to lead prayers.

The Prophet, blessings on him, had taken ill with his poison fever while in Ayesha's
rooms. The other wives had given up their rights then to the favorite wife until he died
in her arms, and the Believers buried him right where he lay. When God willed that
Ayesha the Beloved's father Abu Bakr, the first successor, also took ill with what he
knew would be his final fever, he told his daughter, "Let me lie beside the Messenger of
God, who was always the center of my life."

So Ayesha, now a woman still in her thirties with only half her life lived, spent her days within the same room as the bodies of these two men, her father and her husband. At night, she lay down on the pounded dirt floor under which they lay.

She had sewn her cushions, according to the famous hadith, from a plundered tapestry portraying Coptic saints. At first, she had delighted in the pictures and hung the cloth whole on her wall. Until her husband the Prophet, blessed be he, came to call. He had demanded she take the blasphemous images down before he came in. And work them into cushions for the backside.

Day and night, worshippers came to the small grille between her room and the mosque to pay their respects to the tombs. Ayesha had a screen and a hanging rug to preserve her modesty, but she always had an ear open to the prayers and thus learned the secrets of the people's hearts.

At Rayah's words, Ayesha the Beloved drew aside her veil.

Rayah moved from the tombs and kissed Ayesha's living feet. "Lady, may God bless you and give you long life."

Ayesha sighed, a wry twist on her lips, which may have once been beautiful with innocence but had been wry now once too often. "I am well enough, *al-hamdulillah*. But I hope He will not keep me bored as I am for too long."

At that moment, some worshipper tossed a coin in through the grille. Like a cat, Ayesha leapt up and snatched the coin, stowing it in her bosom.

Rayah could not hold her tongue. "Should a gift of the faithful not go into the common treasury?" Part of Omar's criticism of her grandfather had been his personal use of such funds for poets and baths.

Rayah knew she had not spoken the khalifah's name aloud, but Ayesha understood some things she did not say.

"And yet that Omar, may God lead him aright," the Mother of Believers carefully added, "keeps such a tight fist on that treasury. He never gives anything even to us, the Mothers of Believers. I only take what my husband, may God bless him, would want me to have." Tears beaded the long-lashed lids of the doe eyes.

Rayah was sorry she'd judged, or at least that she'd let her judgment pass her lips. Hoping to drive the indelicacy from her hostess's mind, she quickly spoke what she hoped would change the subject. "I thank you, Lady, for the honor of letting me call upon you. I confess, I never thought I would have the chance to see Muhammad's best beloved, to be at her service."

Ayesha waved as if at an annoying fly. "And yet I have seen you."

"My lady?"

"Yes, when first you entered al-Medinah. With your mother, they told me."

"My mother is—is no longer with me."

"The both of you riding in that litter."

"Ah, the *qubbah*." Thank God for this safer subject.

"*Qubbah*? Is that what you call it?"

Rayah thought for the second time that day that she wanted her mother's assistance.

"I hope, Lady, your health is well." Rayah attempted another diversion. "Is there some healing I can enact for you? That is my gift from the Almighty."

"I'm interested in the *qubbah*, as you call it."

"It—it is nothing, Lady."

"Nothing, you say?"

"Just an old tradition of my family. From the Time of Ignorance."

"Would that I could have such tradition, such ignorance. Oh, I can imagine an army taking its last stand around such an emblem. With me inside."

Not bare breasted, I hope. Rayah blushed at the idea. "Indeed, Lady. Such was the tradition of the women of my family."

"I have thought of little else since I saw you pass."

"But why do you think of battles and fights to the death here? Here, where you are so well cared for—?"

"Muhammad, may God reward him—" Truly the woman must always be careful to say that blessing, living in this tight space with his corpse. "—never loved me because I was content to sit around like these other cows." Ayesha waved her hand toward the cells of her sister wives with a jangle of bracelets.

"I do believe that, Lady, and never meant to suggest—"

"And do you think all is well in the community of Believers? Do you, child that you are?"

Rayah considered her words carefully, remembering for some reason the touch of the calluses on the Persian slave's hands as he took the vial of poppy juice from her. "I would hope that a community founded by one God would continue forever in the path God set for them."

"Then you are very young. And naive."

Rayah had to bite her tongue to keep from saying, "Thank you, Lady."

"Take my stepson-in-law Ali, for example. My husband, God reward him, would never want the moping piety that boy espouses." She called him "boy" although the man was surely older than she. "And this is not to mention Omar, whom we have over us now. What is to be done with that whip-wielding pincher of dirhams, I do not know."

Rayah looked anxiously around, certain that if Ayesha could hear prayers at the grille, those praying could hear her. Rayah remembered the khalifah's spies that had been the undoing even of such a man as her grandfather.

"Oh, Omar won't do anything to me," Ayesha assured her. "He doesn't dare anything but trying to starve me to death on a diet of curds and cheese and praying the dust settling on me crushes me soon. Well, I won't have it, and that's where the *qubbah* comes in. I want it."

Again, Rayah longed for her mother at her side. She moved her mouth a little as a wind curled the curtain hanging in Ayesha's doorway.

"Well, then, you shall have it. I will have it"—or one like it, Rayah thought—"brought here as soon as I return home." She thought of Firuz the Persian and knew if he had made one, he could make another.

"And a camel to carry it. I will need a camel, a well-bred camel."

"The tradition among my mothers was a white camel."

"Yes, a white camel." Light shone in Ayesha's dark eyes.

"But they are very hard to come by. I regret that I have not such an animal to offer my lady." For her mother had taken her white one out into the desert.

Ayesha patted the embroidered bodice of her gown where sat the coin and no doubt many others. "I shall put out the word to all the tribes of the inner desert for such a beast."

Satisfied, Muhammad's beloved called for soured milk to be brought for her guest and a basket of dates. In the Days of Ignorance of her mother's history and her grandfather's, this hospitality would have happened first, before compliance was ever agreed upon.

"Have you heard another tale of mine?" Ayesha obviously loved a fresh pair of listening ears.

Even had she heard the tale, Rayah would not deny her hostess the pleasure. No more than she would, in the end, have denied her mother's tales. "May God bless your tongue in the telling."

"Well, you might have heard the gossip. It wasn't like they say at all."

"Indeed, by the grace of God, I heard no gossip."

"A tale of me and another, more common, camel litter and a verse of the Holy Quran revealed just for me?"

Rayah would not thereafter ever be surprised when more than a quarter of the traditions she heard all sourced back to this bored woman and the cell she occupied. The cell so like a deep well. Forever after, Rayah herself would bring up the words of Ayesha as refreshment to the world whenever she could.

"My husband," Ayesha patted the soil beneath her. "He always liked me best, may God favor him. He brought me along on the journey to punish the apostate Banu Mustaliq. When we halted, I discovered I had lost my necklace—the Prophet's wedding gift—somewhere along the route. I left the close curtains of my howdah and went in weeping desperation to look for it. The fool driver thought I was still within and got the camel to its feet before I returned."

Overhead, Bilal, the black muezzin with the accent like rich date syrup, gave the call to prayer. Rayah prayed with her hostess over the tombs. Because there were only two of them, they got the task finished sooner than the men in the crowded mosque outside.

"So where was I?" Ayesha went on, hardly lowering her voice as the men continued to pray. "Oh, yes. There I was, all alone in the desert, and the caravan had moved on."

But some noise from the mosque disturbed her.

51

Halt. . .
by the rim of the twisted sands between ad-Dakhool and
    Haumal,
then Toodih and al-Mikrat, whose trace is not yet effaced
    for all the spinning of the south winds and northern
    blasts.
        —The Mu'allaqat of Imru 'l-Qais

Inside the mosque, a single voice had begun to speak, booming and cracking like a whip and fire rolled into one. She couldn't hear the words, but Rayah knew it must be Omar ibn al-Khattab, khalifah of all the Faithful, preaching. Her curiosity bubbled. He was kin to her, after all. She would like to see this cousin of her grandfather's, the bane of his life, risen to such power while her grandfather, the younger man, lay disgraced, dead by his own hand, back in Syria.

Instead, she disciplined herself to murmur "Uh-hmm" to Ayesha's tale, and the older woman went on.

"I must admit, he was as beautiful as a jinni and young, almost my own age, this Safwan ibn Muattal who found me after I had found the necklace. Who stayed with me during the desert night. Who brought me safely home."

Rayah wondered if Ayesha actually knew how lovely jinn could be. Did the Mother of Believers court with demons? No, Rayah decided. The phrase was just an expression. But perhaps the woman did consort with handsome humans. That was not at all ruled out by her tone.

"And my husband, may the precious blessings of God be his, received a revelation that I was innocent. How that rankled Omar, who wanted me stoned to death. Or he at least wanted me thrashed, as an example to all men of how they must watch their women."

The drone in the mosque burst. A sudden commotion thrust its way into the room through the grille. Shouts, screams. Running feet.

Ayesha scrambled off her cushions and took the practiced route to her curtained window. Rayah followed in time to see the flash of a running man. His arm dripped blood to the elbow. His hand gripped the gore of a double dagger by its center hilt. The twin blades flared forward like bull's horns. She saw his face flush with a dark grin. Beneath a slave-sliced nose. She recognized him, even in this unnatural expression, for she had imagined such an expression as he did his demon's work upon the scribe Abd Allah: Firuz the Persian slave.

Sight of her, even through the grille, must have slowed him. Someone in the crowd got close enough to throw a cloak over that face and stop the escape.

Her poppy juice deadening the pain so he could plunge deep, Firuz the Persian turned that same wicked knife on himself. He died at the grille to the Prophet's tomb, leaving a smear of blood on the stone.

"The jinn told me to give it—" Rayah whispered in horror.

"The khalifah!" came numerous cries from the mosque. "The infidel has murdered Omar. Death to all Persians! Death to all slaves."

"May God reward him in paradise," Ayesha murmured as she sank back down amid her cushions.

Did she mean Omar? Surely not the murderer.

Rayah joined her, equally loathe to see more, even through the protection of the grille.

In the courtyard of the dead Prophet's house, a wailing set up.

"Hafsa," Ayesha croaked, looking down. "Omar is—was her father. Always such a jovial sister to me. I should go to her."

But she didn't. Not yet. Out in the narrow streets, they could hear the riot beginning as every Persian, every suspect slave was tracked down for revenge.

And then the pretty little slave came and clapped outside the Mother of Believer's curtain.

"Yes? What is it?" the mistress asked.

The girl's dark eyes darted here and there. "Lady, forgive me, but men are asking for the blue-eyed healer."

The sick turmoil in Rayah's belly solidified into a rod of burning terror. They knew her connection to the murderer, knew that her drugs had eased his final moments. As they hunted the street for the little Persian slave children Firuz foolishly thought his action might save, they wanted someone to torture in his stead.

Ayesha sensed something. "Tell them she is under my cloak; she has my protection."

The girl hesitated, clearly unwilling to carry that message back to men who wanted the blood of slaves, even of little female slaves not from Persian but from Africa.

"Not that my cloak means much anymore," Ayesha muttered. "Not in these days of a single law, a single justice overruling any will of women."

"Oh, Mother." Rayah tried to set those words onto a breath of wind to carry out to the desert for aid.

Then she saw the little slave trembling, tears oozing like tar down her motherless face.

I was the one who wanted to come here, to leaven that one-man lump of dough with womanhood, Rayah told herself.

"Never fear," she said, whether to Ayesha, the child, or to herself. "I will go. But lend me your cloak anyway, Lady. I'll be grateful for the extra covering."

"May the Merciful One be with you," Ayesha said as they parted. "I want the *qubbah* more than ever now."

"We want you to come to the khalifah's house," the men outside told her.

Safely bundled in veils, Rayah allowed only one blue eye to meet theirs full of horror.

"If it is God's will, we want you to heal his wounds."

"Omar still lives then?" she asked. Her dread for her own life lifted, but new dread took its place.

"By the grace of God. Please, Lady, hurry."

How was it possible? Firuz, if anyone, knew his business. But as they walked through the streets of al-Medinah, echoing as keening and revenge raced side by side, dust demons twisted around her ankles, stirred by the many rioting feet. Stirred by the Beings of this Place, the jinn. Even within the safety of her clutched veils, the smoky spirits inhabiting that dust began to spiral through her right hand. She knew she could cure. If—if God were willing.

When she entered the austere room, Rayah saw that the khalifah certainly didn't claim anything for himself he denied to Muhammad's widows. Then she saw the man himself laid out on his narrow bed. She had to wonder at his continued existence outside paradise. Six deep blade cuts had occurred with but three slashes of that double-bladed dagger. The deepest scored right through the navel—although the crowding men were careful not to expose this naked male flesh to her eyes.

She would have to touch if her hands were to heal. They wouldn't like that.

They couldn't keep the smell from her, however. The bowel had been pierced and was already pressing its own contents into the open air.

The tingling in her hands had grown painful, yearning for its release in cure. Impossible as the wound seemed, she knew she could mend it. She envisioned the edges of blood-slick bowel closing beneath her touch, as the pieces of her little cousin Bushra's skull had shifted back together that first day by the fountain. Rayah envisioned the poison flushing away from this man—

"A woman?" groaned the man suffering on his pallet. "How is it that a woman pollutes my room?"

Rayah reeled back from the hatred in his words.

Some man among the many packed into the breathless, fly-filled space began to recite the Holy Quran.

The dying man's lips moved along with the recitation. "There," he murmured in sudden comfort. "There is the power that will cure me, make me fit for the life to come, where I shall be rejoined with my beloved Prophet. Depending on the fickle jinn or—" He gave a groan as his bowel moved, although he tried to suppress it. "—Or women. That will not—not do."

Rayah had almost reached the escape of the door and was grateful. One of the men who had brought her from Ayesha's stopped her, however.

"Forgive him, Lady. He is delirious. If I and my brother here hold him down, we will see that you can work your magic."

Rayah considered the man's earnest face. She liked what she saw there. In a flash, she considered it all: Her grandfather and his ongoing feud with his cousin Omar, which, in the end, had driven him from his command. Driven Khalid ibn al-Walid, the Sword of God, to die "like a camel" in his own fountain on his own divine blade.

What she had known of the Conqueror—pounding impotently on her mother's harem door—even what she had learned of him through his own tale, made her only fear him, not love him. And yet, when she bled her woman's blood, it was his blood. This was a family. This was a feud dating back into the Time of Ignorance. Family Muhammad had sought to do away with beneath one God.

She considered Firuz. He had tortured her dear Abd Allah. Had taken his own life rather than accept the same punishment himself. Yet he had saved her from violence in the wadi of Yarmuk, then done this deed and died with her painkiller in his veins.

Women might be safer if they threw their lots in with the single-minded, violent men around them. But the world was made of mothers as well as fathers. God may be one, but He had made the world of many minds. It was better to follow His will and keep it that way.

"Please, Lady. Come," the man insisted and almost tried to take her arm, although the thought of pollution stopped him.

"What? Is that woman still here?" came the moan from the sickbed. "Her presence will kill me. O Believers, hang your whips where your wives can see them, remember and obey. O Believers—"

"You see that the khalifah prepares himself to die," Rayah told the man who tried to keep her. "The will of the khalifah is the will of God. I am sorry. It is God's will that Omar ibn al-Khattab die of these wounds. It will take a few painful days for the poison to work its way through him. That, too, is God's will. I can do nothing for him."

As she left the room, she heard the dying man naming a council to choose his successor. No such council could be of a single mind. His successor would doubtless die assassinated, too.

And then Rayah bint Sejah bint Khalid ibn al-Walīd left the khalifah's house. Where the vicious blade had ripped at Omar's entrails, there Rayah knew she was already carrying a blue-eyed daughter she must keep intact.

In the meantime, her jinni danced and giggled at the side her own form cast in shadow. He urged her to get one Mother of Believers, Ayesha bint Abu Bakr, a *qubbah* of her own. Before Omar's body joined the two she cared for more beneath the dirt of her floor.

The community of Believers would be of multiple minds in the days, months and years to come.

That was God's will.

In His name, Who is Compassionate, *ar-Rahman*. An infinite well of mercy.

THE END

SUGGESTIONS FOR FURTHER READING

I can't begin to list all the sources I have consulted for this work during the thirty years it was my passion. I content myself with listing those the reader may find the most useful—and only those in English.

Let's begin with the Quran. I consulted three different English translations: the Arberry, which many consider to give best the flavor of the original; the Everyman-Rodwell and the Abdullah Yusuf Ali. In some cases, when quoting, I made choices of my own.

For biographies of the Prophet, you may consider:

Muhammad: A Biography of the Prophet by Karen Armstrong

Muhammad: The Messenger of God by Betty Kelen

Muhammad: His Life Based on the Earliest Sources by Martin Lings

Muhammad and the Origins of Islam by F.E. Peters

Muhammad by Maxine Rodinson

Muhammad at Mecca; *Muhammad at Medina* and *Muhammad, Prophet and States-man* by W. Montgomery Watt

Then there are biographies of Khalid ibn al-Walid himself. The best of these, *The Sword of God: Khalid bin Waleed*, by the Pakistani general Syed Ameer Ahmed, is now available online, complete with sketches of the battles. Two others are *Khalid bin Walid: The General of Islam* by Major S. K. Malik and *Khalid bin Walid: The Sword of Allah* by Fazl Ahmad.

Among the myriad of losses of the present Syrian civil war is the loss of Khalid's mausoleum and mosque in Homs refered to in this novel. I read the account just as I was making the final edits, July 22, 2013. May the story not be equally susceptible to such destruction.

Of the great number of Arabic historians who've dealt with these matters, one of the ninth Christian century, al-Tabari, is available in a multivolume set in readable English translation from the State University of New York.

More than anything else, my love for pre-Islamic poetry spurred this work. There simply isn't enough of it to satisfy me, but there are translations and discussions by Christopher Nouryeh and Charles James Lyall. A.J. Arberry, as with his interpretation of the Quran, provided *The Seven Odes* and his *Arabic Poetry*. The beautiful translation at the head of chapter 27 was done by Michael Anthony Sell in his *Desert Tracings*. A slim but very interesting tome is *Religious Trends in Pre-Islamic Arabic Poetry* by Hafiz Ghulam Mustafa. Please note that I have given the proper poets' names with the verses that begin each chapter, but when I have used them in the body of the story, the credit went where the plot demanded.

The unseen world of the Fire Spirits, the jinn, can be explored in *Islam, Arabs and the Intelligent World of the Jinn* by Amira El-Zein.

Besides the time I spent living on the edge of the Arabian desert, which I consider the most formative of my life, modern anthropological studies and earlier travelers to these places helped me to create the world. They make wonderful reading, too, including:

A Pilgrimage to Nejd by Lady Anne Blunt

Personal Narrative of a Pilgrimage to al-Medinah and Meccah by Sir Richard F. Burton

The Arab of the Desert by H.R.P. Dickson

The Manners and Customs of the Rwala Bedouin and *Arabia Deserta* by Alois Musil

Drinkers of the Wind by Carl R. Raswan

I constantly consulted the articles in the *Encyclopedia of Islam* including those on Khalid bin al-Walīd, Sadjah bint al-Harith, Tamim, Taghlib, Banu Bakr, Malik and Mutammim bin Nuwayra, Dhu Kar, Kuraish, Lakhmids. . . . Well, the list goes on and on.

Descriptions of Jerusalem, al-Quds, just after the Islamic conquest are difficult to find, but F.E. Peters' *Jerusalem and Mecca* I found excellent.

J. Spencer Trimingham's *Christianity among the Arabs in Pre-Islamic Times* might also be of interest. And among all the recent scholarship questioning the received versions of early Islam, I found that *The Idea of Idolatry and Emergence of Islam from Polemic to History* by G.R. Hawting explains a whole lot. But if I'd followed his version, this would have been a very different novel.